THE STON

1 – 6

SPECIAL LIMITED EDITION

THE CURIOUS DISPATCH OF DANIEL COSTELLO

DEAD IN THE WATER

MEAT IS MURDER

THE CASE OF THE MISSING FIREFLY

MISTLETOE AND CRIME

ALL AT SEA

Published by RED DOG PRESS 2022

Limited First Edition

Paperback ISBN 978-1-914480-89-8

www.reddogpress.co.uk

-1-

THE CURIOUS DISPATCH OF DANIEL COSTELLO

CHRIS MCDONALD

1

A NIGHT TO FORGET

THE POUNDING DANCE music and the pulsing lights were everything Sam had hoped for and more. He'd loved this type of music since his teens and had set his heart on coming to Ibiza for his stag do ever since he'd first heard the opening notes to Adagio for Strings more than a decade ago.

Now that he was here, everything seemed… amplified; bigger than he'd imagined it. The music was louder, the beer was cheaper, and the girls were even more scantily dressed than he'd ever dared to envisage.

Of course, he was here on his stag, but a man could window shop, couldn't he?

He waved his hands in the air as the beat dropped and, along with the mass of bodies around him, writhed in time with the thumping bass. He took a swig from his bottle of beer, spilling some down the front of his custom-made T-shirt – a pink monstrosity with a horned stag front and centre, Sam's smiling face photoshopped in the middle of it all. He'd been forced into it at the airport and the boys had made enough of them to make sure he wore nothing else all week.

He looked around the bustling club, scanning for any of his mates, but everyone seemed to have either scattered or called it a night completely. He didn't have a watch, and the windowless room gave no clue as to what time it might be. He thought about having one last drink, but the tiredness tugged at his eyelids, exacerbated by the unholy amount of alcohol he'd consumed. The only thing keeping him going was that pill he'd taken.

As he made to leave the dancefloor, a hand reached out, the fingers interlocking with his own, pulling him back.

A pretty brunette swam into view. Her features weren't unlike Emily's, his future wife's, though her eyes were slightly bigger. She leaned in close to him, affording Sam a sneaky peak at her cleavage as her top gaped.

'Leaving so soon?' she shouted in his ear, above the swell of the music.

She pulled back, and he stared at her with bleary eyes, trying to make sense of what she was saying. Once it had computed, he nodded.

'One more dance,' she mouthed, leading him back to the middle of the dancefloor. He followed her, taking in her short skirt and tanned, shapely legs. When she reached the desired spot, she turned, and they danced, getting progressively closer until their noses were almost touching.

'I'm getting married,' he slurred, as he looked into her dark eyes.

'Me too,' she replied, holding up her hand to show a diamond encrusted ring. 'Everyone gets a freebie on their hen do, though.'

She took one more step and brushed her lips against his. He thought about pulling away, but only for a moment. Instead, he moved closer and pressed his lips firmly onto hers. Images of Emily swam through his drunken thoughts and this time he did pull away, mumbling his apologies. She shrugged, turned, and having got what she wanted, disappeared into the crowd.

Tears formed in the corner of his eyes and his cheeks burned with the shame of what he'd just done.

Looking up, Sam locked eyes with Danny. He wondered how much his best man had seen. Aside from the flashing lights, the place was dark and full of revellers – surely, he couldn't have seen the whole show. As Sam left the dancefloor and approached him, the answer was clear. Danny was looking at him with raised eyebrows and a slight grin.

'You dirty dog,' he said, clapping him on the shoulder as they exited the club.

Sam looked at him with a plea in his eyes.

'It was a mistake. She kissed me,' he murmured. 'You can't tell anyone.'

Danny held up a placating hand and dragged a finger across his chest, sketching an X.

'Don't worry, big man. I'll take it to the grave.'

ONE MONTH LATER

2

AN UNFORTUNATE INSIGHT INTO THE LIFE OF ADAM WHYTE

ADAM WHYTE SLIPPED a hand into his pyjama bottoms and scratched his undercarriage for quite an extended period of time. When his hand emerged, he lifted it to his nose and gave it a sniff. Though the smell was not pleasant, his face didn't show any displeasure. On the contrary. He judged the smell to be just the right side of acceptable and decided to push back his probably much-needed shower until tomorrow. His mum had been watching all of this happen from behind a book, a look of disgust etched on her face.

Adam lifted a pint glass full of water from the ground and slurped from it, before grabbing the PlayStation controller and expertly navigating through the home page of Netflix. He tapped a few buttons and the theme song for Sherlock began.

'Oh, haven't you watched enough of this today?' his mum asked.

'You can never get enough of the Cumberbatch, can you?' Adam replied.

She sighed and thought about her son. From an early age, he'd pretended to be a 'sloof', solving make-believe crimes with his friends. A few years ago, he had travelled sixty miles up the road to Belfast, to study psychology at Queens University. Predictably, he hadn't lasted long. In true Adam Whyte fashion, he'd become the popular lad on campus, much to the detriment of his studies. And so, after less than a year, he'd returned home, to the north coast of Northern Ireland; to Stonebridge, and had been stuck in dead end jobs since. Until a few days ago, that was, when he'd been fired from the pub he was working in, due to being late one too many times. Gone were the dreams of joining the police; of becoming a detective. Now, here he was, unapologetically scratching his balls in the middle of the afternoon in front of his own mother.

She watched him cover his eyes as the detective on the screen surveyed a blood-soaked body. Adam had never been good with blood – another reason a career in the police was never going to happen.

'Are you looking forward to the wedding tomorrow?' she asked him.

'It'll be good to see friends, yeah,' he said. 'And it's tradition for the groomsman to snog a bridesmaid, so there's that.'

He raised his eyebrows suggestively before turning back to the TV.

I wouldn't hold out much hope, she thought to herself, turning her attention back to her book.

3

A MIX UP

ADAM'S BATTERED RENAULT Clio crawled along the wide gravel driveway that was framed by sprawling, manicured lawns. Tall oak trees and Victorian lampposts alternated alongside the path.

Adam thought that if the ancient trees could talk, they'd probably tell him that his car was the worst vehicle they'd ever seen and that it simply being on the property was enough to tarnish the land.

After cresting a small hill, the stately home loomed in front of them. Tamed ivy crept tastefully across the stone walls and beautifully crafted statues of lions kept guard on either side of a huge, wooden door. The clifftop property, framed by the endless ocean behind it, was a stunning place for a marriage.

'Hard to believe we're only thirty minutes from home,' Adam said. 'Feels like we're in the middle of nowhere.'

He entered the car park and found a space. Colin, Adam's best friend, got out of the car and looked around. He stretched his lanky frame and looked to the unbroken blue sky.

'What's hard to believe is that they booked their wedding on the Twelfth weekend, of all the weekends available,' he said. 'I'm supposed to be getting smashed and watching some marching bands.'

'Oh, Colin,' Adam said, clapping his friend on the shoulder and pushing him towards the door. 'So uncultured. This is going to be so much better. There's going to be no drama, for one, and everyone knows girls let their inhibitions go at weddings. You might even get lucky!'

They walked in the front door and set their bags down, taking in their surroundings. Original wooden floorboards were paired tastefully with dark stone walls upon which framed portraits hung. A wide chandelier dangled above their heads, the golden sunlight that flowed in through a large window catching in the crystal fixtures. They followed the strip of red carpet that led from the door to the unmanned reception desk. They rang the bell and a second later, a well-groomed, suited man greeted them with a wide smile and a warm hello.

'We've got two rooms, under Whyte and McLaughlin,' Adam told him.

The man, his nametag announcing him as Francis, manoeuvred the mouse and clicked a few buttons on the computer, though a frown spread across his face and he started to shake his head slowly.

'We've got *a* room for Whyte and McLaughlin.'

Adam looked up at Colin, who appeared suitably confused. Realisation dawned slowly on his face and he squeezed his eyes shut.

'You've messed the booking up, haven't you?' he said to his friend, shaking his head. It was like their trip to London all over again.

He turned back to Francis, not waiting for an answer.

'Do you have any other rooms available?'

'No, I'm sorry,' Francis replied, shaking his head. 'All the rooms have been booked months in advance, due to the wedding.'

'Great,' Adam said sarcastically, taking the proffered key for their shared room. Francis told them that if anyone cancelled, they'd be the first to know.

Adam lambasted Colin all the way up the stairs. They turned left at the top of the steps and began making their way towards room number 14, stopping by a bay window to take in the sea view. The sun shimmered on the water below and they watched the waves break on the cliffs, the white spray splashing high into the air. As a seagull swooped and rose high into the sky again, they tore themselves away from the view and found their room at the end of the corridor. Adam turned the key in the lock and pushed the door open, revealing a beautifully decorated room.

A desk sat alongside one wall, a notepad and a pen perched on top. Various framed pieces of art decorated the recently painted cream walls, and a bookcase in the corner of the room held a selection of weighty classics. As nice as it was, there was one big problem.

Pushed against one of the walls was one double bed.

'You've got to be kidding me,' Adam mumbled.

SLEEPING ARRANGEMENTS DECIDED, (top and tail – not ideal but a compromise all the same) Adam and Colin set about getting ready for the first night of drinking. Adam pulled on his favourite pair of chinos – navy – and a red and black flannel shirt. He spread wax through his dark hair, trying to achieve the *just out of bed* look. He briefly considered shaving his slightly patchy beard, but he'd been growing it for a couple of weeks now and couldn't bear to part with it.

He looked across at Colin, who had settled on casual jeans and a white T-shirt, and felt the jealousy rise as he considered his friend's fulsome facial hair. Some people have all the luck.

Since primary school, he and Colin had been inseparable. As puberty had struck, the changes had set in. Colin had grown to six foot and developed wide shoulders which were used to good effect on the school's rugby team. Adam stayed at just over five and a half feet, and his weedy appearance had caused him to be picked last for any sport. They were nicknamed Little and Large, for obvious reasons.

Once ready, Adam pulled a DVD player from his bag and set about connecting it to the small TV already in the room. Colin gave him a questioning look.

'I thought we'd have a bit of spare time this weekend. The wedding isn't until Sunday, that leaves us with a lot of free time tomorrow. I thought we'd work our way through this,' he said, holding up series one of Sherlock.

'Great shout,' Colin answered, as his friend slipped disk one into the tray.

The next hour and a half passed quickly, both of them lost in an episode they had watched countless times.

'I have to go to this rehearsal thing,' Adam said, checking his watch as the credits rolled. 'It shouldn't take too long and then I'll meet you in the bar?'

'No worries,' replied Colin, taking a book out of his bag and settling down on the bed. Before he could open the book, his attention was quickly drawn away as he watched Adam make some last-minute changes to his hair. He shook his head at his friend's vanity.

'I can't believe I'm having to spend the weekend with bloody Daniel Costello,' he said.

'I know,' Adam replied. 'Odd choice for Best Man. I assumed his twin would've been nailed on for that job, but then, Danny and Sam were always close. The speech is going to be a train wreck, I reckon.'

With that, he headed for the door.

'Are you not taking your phone?' Colin shouted after him, holding up the iPhone that had been lying on the bed next to him.

'No point, there's barely any reception.'

He bid Colin a swift goodbye and walked down the corridor to Sam's room – the bridal suite. The groom-to-be's face lit up when he opened the door and saw who was behind it. He ushered Adam into the huge room, complete with king sized four poster bed and a glorious sea view.

Adam looked Sam up and down. He'd lost quite a bit of weight in the couple of weeks since they'd last hung out – presumably the work of the personal trainer he'd paid handsomely. Adam made a mental note to ask for his name.

'Alright, mate,' said Danny, who was sprawled on the bed. His shirt was buttoned down to near his bellybutton and he carried with him that sense of arrogance he always had, though had done nothing to earn.

'I'm good thanks,' Adam replied. He'd never had much time for Danny. He turned to Ross, Sam's twin. 'How you doing, man?'

Ross stood up and shook his hand, a wide grin on his face. Like Sam, Ross had thick, dark hair and gangly features. It had been nigh on impossible to tell them apart through school, though was slightly easier now on account of Ross's mangled accent – Northern Irish with a hint of Lancashire – which he had acquired from having spent four years at university in Lancaster. He was probably the only person in the whole country who supported Preston North End, too.

'Where's Emily?' Adam asked Sam.

'She's at her parent's place. Her side of the family are coming tomorrow evening for the meal. Until then, it's just us.'

'A bit like Lord of the Flies. A load of reprobates let loose in a house,' sniggered Danny.

Adam was pretty sure that Danny had never read that particular book. Come to think of it, he wasn't sure if Danny could read at all. Again, he ignored Danny's comment and addressed Sam.

'Sorry I couldn't make the stag; money is a bit tight at the moment and mum had already offered to pay for this weekend so I couldn't scrounge any more off her. It looked like you all had a great time.'

'It was a lot of fun,' Danny laughed. 'Sam had a great time, didn't you?'

A flash of *something* passed over Sam's features. Anger? When he spoke, though, his tone was nonchalant.

'Yeah, it was great, thanks. I tried paella for the first time, and we hired jet skis and mucked about in the bay. The nights out were mad, too. I've not drank since!'

Danny looked like he was about to add something, but was cut off by Sam pulling out a box from under the bed. From it, he produced four silver hipflasks and handed one to Ross, Danny and Adam.

Adam inspected it. It felt heavy in his hand, and the engraved initials were a nice touch.

'It's filled with a ten-year-old Bushmills single malt, so cherish it,' Sam said. They each undid the tops, clinked the flasks together and took a hearty swig. It burned as it trickled down Adam's throat and he did the same as the others; tried not to let the discomfort show.

'Let's get this rehearsal over with,' Sam said. 'Then the fun can begin.'

4

THE REHEARSAL

ADAM, SAM, ROSS and Danny walked down the stairs and out of the front door, breathing in the salty seaside air. They trooped across the grass and rounded the corner of the attractive house. Danny let out a long, impressed whistle at what he saw.

A huge white marquee sat in the middle of a wide garden, framed by the cloudless blue sky and a garden of roses that overlooked the sea.

They walked in through the open doors and took in the opulence. Rows of chairs, draped in ivory material and backed with a purple bow, filled the space. A wide aisle bisected them; the red carpet so thick it looked like you could sink into it. Fairy lights had been threaded through the material in the ceiling and five-feet-tall letters, spelling LOVE, had been positioned beside the stand-in alter at the front.

'Mate, this wedding must be costing you a fortune!' Danny laughed. 'Oh no, wait, it's not costing you a thing because you're marrying into North Coast royalty.'

The Campbell family, that Sam was marrying into, were well known for being high rollers. Emily's father, Trevor, was a stern man, as the CEO of a company probably had to be. He had a huge face, barely any neck, and the body shape of a gorilla. Her mother worked in one of the big banks in Belfast, only coming home at the weekends to their mansion by the sea in Stonebridge.

Trevor doted on his only daughter – it was the only thing he was ever soft about - and had offered to pay for the whole thing. He'd pulled strings and called in many a favour to get the weekend booked out at Milton Manor; the most exclusive venue in the area.

He was not a man to be trifled with.

The boys walked around the interior of the marquee, taking in the finer details and the stunning view from the large window. Adam watched Sam cast an admiring glance around, noticing the emotion in his eyes. This probably made everything seem a bit more real now.

They were interrupted by the arrival of the vicar, who shouted a cheery hello to get the boys' attention.

Reverend Fred, as they called him, was a well-known figure in their hometown and one of the nicest men in the world. As well as his weekly sermons, which none of the boys attended anymore, he was always at the heart of the community. Every Christmas, he took part in a sponsored sleep out, with all the money going to charity. He was often to be found in the shadow of the town hall, wrapped up in warm clothes and smiling at the late-night shoppers.

He called them to the front and they dutifully assembled, shaking his extended hand one at a time.

'Sam,' he said, turning to the front and smiling at the soon-to-be married man. 'I cannot believe that little Sammy who used to cry when his mummy dropped him off to Sunday school all those years ago is getting married.'

Fred winked at the rest of the boys, who pushed and jostled Sam playfully.

'I won't keep you for long, boys,' said Fred. 'I know you've got other things to attend to.'

For a few minutes, they listened intently to what Fred had to say. As the male contingent of the wedding party, their job was fairly simple. They'd all be at the front already, awaiting the arrival of the bride. The only thing anyone really had to do was Danny, who would be in charge of handing over the rings at the right time.

Fred then positioned them into roughly where they'd be standing. Sam in the centre, flanked by Danny, then Ross, with Adam at the end. When walking out, they'd pair up with a bridesmaid, link arms and make their way down the aisle and outside for photographs.

'Can one of you assume the role of Emily?' Fred asked. 'Just so that we can go through the vows. Sometimes it helps to say them once so that you know what's coming on the day.'

Danny stepped forward into the spot that Emily would be occupying on the actual day.

'Now, it'll have to be a secret that I'm marrying you two tonight,' Fred laughed. 'Don't tell Emily.'

'I'll add it to my ever-growing list of secrets,' Danny said, winking at Sam.

Only Sam seemed to know what Danny was talking about, judging by the colour of his face as he fought to bite back the rage.

The vicar carried on with the practice vows. Sam's voice caught on certain lines, and even Adam felt a little lump in his throat as he imagined how his friend was feeling.

After the vows, Sam and Fred hugged, before the vicar bid them goodbye. They watched him walk across the grass towards the car park.

'Let's go get smashed,' Danny said, breaking the icy silence.

5

A RIGHT OLD KNEES UP

COLIN MADE HIS way down the curved staircase, holding on to the heavy wooden banister. Safety was paramount in his workplace – The Stonebridge Retirement Home – and he often found himself adhering to the same rules he imposed on the old folks that he cared for. He often got funny looks from the visiting relatives – he supposed it wasn't all that usual for a man in his mid-twenties to work in such a place – but he loved every second of it and hoped to work there for many years to come.

Before he'd started there, he'd often assumed that old folk's homes were a stepping stone away from heaven. He'd started working there at weekends, to earn a bit of money while he studied at university, but he soon fell in love with the place and the people. His perceptions of old people changed immediately. They were full of life and stories, and he couldn't get enough. Upon graduating, he had immediately applied for a full-time position and was lucky enough to be offered the job. He'd never looked back.

When he reached the bottom of the stairs, he made his way through the foyer towards the room where all the noise was coming from. He smoothed his hair and opened the door, the volume of the music immediately increasing.

The wood-panelled room was huge. Circular tables with plush, velvet chairs around them took up most of the floor space, though a section at the end of the room had been set up as a makeshift dancefloor. Colourful lights blinked and twirled in preparation for whoever was brave enough to take to the black and white tiled floor first.

Colin scanned the room and found Adam at the bar, waiting to be served. Colin's feet sunk into the thick, green carpet as he crossed the room and snuck up on his friend.

'Looks like I've arrived just in time,' he said as he reached Adam, making him jump. 'Pint of Harp, please, and I'll go find a seat.'

Colin strode across the room towards an empty table next to a wide, decorative fireplace with a coat of arms fixed to the wall above it. A few minutes later, Adam plonked two pints and a couple of packets of crisps onto the table, before settling into the spare seat. Colin thanked him and took a huge gulp of the lager, the fizz immediately getting him in the mood for a big night.

Adam, on the other hand, seemed subdued. He thought about his interactions with people he hadn't seen since school. Most had moved to Belfast and were part way into their career. Some had even climbed a few rungs on that ladder already. He felt embarrassed having to admit that he'd dropped out of university, been unable to hold down a job and that he was still living at home with his mum. At school, he'd achieved excellent results in his exams, but what the teachers had constantly told him had turned out to be correct so far – he wasn't good at applying himself.

He took a sip from his pint and vowed to make a change – this time next year he'd have a job and a place of his own. He just needed to figure out what his calling was, and sometimes that took time.

He remembered reading that Susan Boyle had been 47 when she auditioned on whatever talent show she'd gone on, and the guy who founded McDonald's didn't do it until he was 59. Some people simply came into their own a little later in life – like a fine wine.

After that comforting thought, he cheered up a bit.

They stayed at the table for a while, sipping from pints and watching the room fill up around them. They knew a lot of people from their school days, and Adam recognised some of the faces as university pals of Sam's.

Shortly after eight o'clock, platters of food arrived from the kitchen, carried by a team of smartly dressed waiters. They placed the silver trays on a long table covered in a tartan tablecloth. It didn't take long for the aromas to drift to Adam's side of the room, and only then did he realise how hungry he was. He and Colin joined the queue and before long they were eagerly scooping an assortment of food onto their plates.

As Adam squirted a generous helping of ketchup over the pile of chips on his plate, he caught sight of Sam and Danny, huddled in the corner of the room.

It looked like they were arguing.

Danny showed Sam something on his iPhone, causing Sam to push him on the shoulder. Someone asked Adam if he was finished with the tomato sauce, causing him to take his eyes off what was happening between the groom and his best man. When he looked back, Sam was sitting alone and there was no sign of Danny.

Adam quickly moved on from what he had seen as his thoughts turned towards the mountain of food on his plate. A plate which was almost sent flying as Mike, Emily's brother, stumbled into Adam's path.

'Sorry, man,' he mumbled, before moving out of Adam's way, towards the bar. Adam watched him stumble away and marvelled at how brave he was in his fashion choices – pale green skinny jeans and a cravat were not the usual fare for the twenty-something Northern Irishman. Adam secretly wished he had the balls to try it, though.

BY TEN O'CLOCK, the food had long since vanished and the serious matter of drinking was well under way.

The dancefloor was filled, mostly with women, their dresses illuminated by the rainbow lights, while the men sat around the perimeter of the room, nursing pints and discussing the soon-to-be-closed Premier League transfer window. Some of the braver menfolk were already making their moves on the dancefloor, trying and failing to impress their targets. It reminded Adam of a primary school disco. Or a David Attenborough documentary. He wasn't sure which was sadder.

He took Colin's drink order and walked to the bar. Whilst waiting to be served, he tried to strike up a conversation with a girl he recognised when he had visited Sam at his university across the water. She was polite, though declined his offer of a drink.

Typical, he thought, as he watched her carefully manoeuvre her way through the maze of tables and into the arms of a white shirted man. Adam turned his attention away from the couple and back to the bar. He ordered two pints and stood waiting while they were poured.

Suddenly, at a table nestled in an alcove to the rear of the bar, an altercation arose. One moment, Sam, Danny and Ross were chatting quietly, when all of a sudden Sam rose and shoved his best man in the chest.

Danny toppled over the back of his seat and banged his head on the carpeted floor. He rose gingerly and stood snarling, arms outstretched like a boxer. He shouted something that Adam couldn't hear over the music.

Sam attempted to push himself out of his seat, but his twin forced him back down. Instead, Ross formed a wall between the two. He said something to Danny who threw his arms in the arm, turned and stormed past the bar. Adam watched him march out of the room without so much as a backward glance. Ross went to follow him, but Sam grabbed his arm and shook his head.

It happened in the blink of an eye. Adam glanced around the bar to see if anyone else had been witness to it, but was pretty sure he had been the sole onlooker.

Had the best man position just become available?

He grabbed his order from the bar and walked back to the table. He relayed what he had just seen to Colin, who listened carefully and dismissed it as a silly argument fuelled by wedding nerves and alcohol.

The rest of the night passed in a haze as lager turned into spirits and spirits turned into shots. At just after midnight, Adam and Colin stumbled up the stairs and unlocked their room after a few bumbling attempts. They both mumbled expletives as their bleary eyes focussed on the singular bed.

Adam fell asleep thinking that Colin's feet smelled of brie.

6

NO SHOW AT BREAKFAST

ADAM WOKE UP in stages, head fuzzy with a monstrous hangover that was just getting going. Even without moving, he felt the contents of his stomach swirl, putting him in two minds – lie still and hope for the best, or run to the bathroom in preparation. The last thing he wanted was to throw up all over the bed and be handed a hefty cleaning bill.

His arm brushed against something in the bed – someone! With his eyes closed, he tried to piece together the night before. He remembered being shot down by an array of girls, but his memories trailed off shortly after that third shot…

Gingerly, he opened one eye. The light flowing in through the insubstantial fabric curtain caused him to wince in pain. The sight that greeted him wasn't much better.

Colin's hairy back and bum crack was not the first sight he'd have chosen for his eyes to settle on first thing in the morning. It did little to alleviate the sick feeling in his stomach.

Bathroom it was.

Ten minutes later, he emerged from the bathroom feeling slightly better, though the taste left in his mouth was unholy. He looked at himself in the mirror and chuckled.

He looked worse than he felt. If that was even possible.

He sat down on the edge of the bed, his head a cloud of pain. He unzipped his bag and fished in the front pocket, his hand clamping round its intended target. From the dimpled foil packet, he pushed out two tablets and guzzled them down with a glass of tap water.

A few minutes later, Colin joined him in the land of the living. He stretched his long limbs, yawned widely and jumped out of bed.

'Morning,' Adam croaked.

'Morning. You feeling rough?'

'I feel like I've been hit by a car.'

Colin chuckled. His friend had always been melodramatic. And terrible at holding his drink. He watched as Adam crawled into a foetal position on the bed, eyes closed.

'I'm going for a run before breakfast, to clear the cobwebs.'

Adam's reply was merely a look of disgust.

'It'd do you the world of good,' Colin laughed. 'What are you going to do instead?'

'Pray for mercy and try not to die.'

COLIN HAD ALWAYS found that life's problems could be sorted out with a quick run. Working where he did, he encountered death on a regular basis. He considered himself stoic, but each passing affected him. The relationships he had with each of the old folk were so much more than professional. He grew to love them and each death rocked him. One of the old hands who worked there told him that running was a great way to help the head process what the heart couldn't.

So, he did.

And he found that it worked a treat.

Today, though, he was running for a different reason. He liked to explore places he'd never been before, and running was a great way to do it.

He jogged at a leisurely pace down the country lane, watching the sheep doze lazily in vast fields while the wind buffeted him from behind, giving him an injection of pace.

Glancing to the other side, he took in the endless sea and the waves peacefully approaching the shore of the beach in the distance.

Sometimes, he took for granted how beautiful his part of the world was. Days like today reminded him that he shouldn't.

After fifteen minutes, he came to a corner and stopped to catch his breath. He wished he'd had the foresight to bring some water, but he hadn't banked on the sun being so hot so early in the morning.

Scanning the road, he saw a petrol station not far away; the only building to be seen amongst the rolling fields, aside from Milton Manor.

He picked up the pace and reached the petrol station in no time at all. The young man behind the desk watched Colin walk to the fridge and seemed surprised to have custom so early. Colin placed a bottle of ice-cold water on the counter and took out his card to pay.

'We only take cash,' the attendant apologised, pointing to a small handwritten note stuck to the counter. He looked at Colin's sweaty clothes and clocked his annoyance. 'But you can just have it. On me.'

Colin's mood immediately brightened, and he promised that he'd bring the money on the next visit. He left the shop and downed the water before putting the empty bottle in the bin. He looked up at the roof covering the forecourt, which only had two pumps. It was a family-owned business. The Cox family who owned it must've encountered trouble before, as they'd installed two CCTV cameras, one pointing at the pumps with the other aimed at the narrow road that passed by it.

Reinvigorated, Colin ran all the way back to the wedding venue, keen for a shower before breakfast.

THE LEMONY SCENT of Colin's shower gel mingled with the smell of greasy bacon, causing Adam problems. He pushed his breakfast around the plate, not trusting his stomach to deal with the soda bread and potato farls that he would have ordinarily devoured.

He wasn't the only one feeling the effects of last night.

Most were still in bed, unable to pull themselves from below their duvets, hoping that a few extra hours in bed would see them through the worst of the hangover.

Some who had braved breakfast were copying Adam, raising a forkful of food to their mouths before setting it back down on the plate, stomachs roiling.

A select few, like Colin, were wolfing their food down. Adam looked at their emptying plates with longing.

Sam, the groom, looked over from his table and caught Adam's eye, calling him over with a flick of his finger.

'Have you seen Danny this morning?' he asked when Adam was beside him.

Adam shook his head.

'No worries,' said Sam. 'We were supposed to be having breakfast together. I'll go and see where he is.'

'I'll go, you stay and finish your breakfast. I can't stomach mine.'

'If you see Ross, tell him to hurry up and all. He drove home last night to sort something with his new girlfriend and I've not seen him reappear yet.'

Adam left the stench of the breakfast behind and walked to Danny's room, which was on the ground floor at the far end of the building. He thought to himself that Danny probably hadn't set an alarm, or, if he had, he'd simply hit the snooze buttons one too many times. That, or he might still be pissed off with Sam over whatever they were arguing about last night.

He passed a marble bust of some old dude who used to own the house and approached Danny's door. When he knocked, the door slipped out of its lock and swung open.

Inside, the room was dark. The curtains were more heavy duty than in Adam's room and were doing a good job of keeping the sun out. As Adam's eyes adjusted, he could make out a mound on the bed, tucked in under the duvet.

Adam called out his name a few times, but got no response. He walked to the end of the bed and shook Danny by the ankles, again getting nothing. The guy wasn't even stirring.

He walked back to the curtains and opened them, letting light flood the room.

With the room illuminated, Adam noticed that the room was a mess. A lamp was lying on the floor, its shade left at an odd angle, the plug upturned. His case was lying open, the contents strewn across the floor.

Danny had always been messy, Adam thought. He remembered a school trip to France, ten years ago. Their dorm room had stank worse than the smelly cheeses they had been pressurised into trying by overzealous teachers, mostly on account of Danny's poor personal hygiene.

Rounding the corner of the bed, Adam noticed the vomit on the mattress and on the floor.

Ignoring the putrid stench and the uneasy bubbling feeling in his own stomach, he pulled the duvet back.

Danny lay on his back, his dark hair plastered to his forehead. His face was ghostly white, save for the drops of dried sick on his chin. He was wearing the clothes from the night before, the top button of his shirt torn off.

Adam checked for a pulse, already sure of the outcome. Sure enough, he couldn't feel anything.

Danny Costello was dead.

7

THE GAMECHANGER

ADAM SAT ON the steps of the hotel, gulping in the fresh air, having just thrown up in a bush to the side of the entrance, narrowly missing the stone mane of the proud lion.

He'd never been good with anything squeamish. Once, he'd driven an ex-girlfriend to hospital whose appendix was about to burst. He reluctantly went with her into the treatment room and noticed too late as they inserted a needle into a vein in her arm. A single drop of blood fell and spread onto the bedsheet, blossoming like red petals. To his shame, he'd made his excuses and ran to the bathroom, throwing up on the tiled floor as soon as he'd got through the door.

The relationship didn't last long after that.

A drop of blood was one thing. A dead body was something new altogether.

Adam would never forget the glassy eyes or the translucent skin or the smell that TV shows never managed to capture accurately. No one ever threw up after discovering a body either.

He thought back to his actions, and, despite shivering at the thought, was quietly proud of himself. He'd made sure that Danny was definitely dead and had managed to hold it together until he had phoned the police. He'd taken control of a pretty messed up situation, and that counted for something.

COLIN SAT BY his friend's side, trying to console him.

He couldn't imagine finding a dead body, let alone the body of someone you considered a friend.

An annoying friend.

A friend most people had had some sort of altercation with at some stage, but a friend all the same.

This kind of thing didn't happen to people like them.

In the distance, he heard sirens. If Adam hadn't been the one to find the body, they both would have been excited to be in the midst of a real-life investigation. As it was, there was nothing to look forward to.

What was supposed to be a celebratory weekend where two friends joined together in matrimony had quickly turned to a nightmare. As well as the horror of a dead friend, it also meant that the wedding was probably off, causing Sam and Emily to be out of pocket to the tune of thousands.

Well, the Campbell family, but potato potato.

Colin shook his head at how unfair life could be.

ADAM LOOKED UP as the sirens grew closer. He could see them beyond the hedgerow, turning slowly into the hotel's sweeping driveway.

A police car emerged from the tree lined approach, gravel spitting from under the tyres as the brakes were applied. An ambulance followed close behind. They stopped close to the elaborate water fountain, the blue lights stopped flashing and two police officers emerged from the car who looked like they'd rather be elsewhere got out. Two paramedics followed suit, busying themselves in the back of the ambulance, gathering the necessary equipment.

Gravel crunched underfoot as they made their way across the front of the building, surveying the impressive building with minimum appreciation. One wore a short sleeved shirt with aviator sunglasses perched on his nose. He clearly thought he was too cool for school.

The other was ginger and hunched and look like he'd been bullied at school so had taken the job solely for the power it would bestow upon him. Adam quickly formed a dislike for both of them.

'We believe there's been a bit of bother, lads,' Sunglasses said with a smirk.

'My friend has died,' Adam replied.

'Shame,' Ginger said, though clearly, he couldn't care less.

'Why is there only two of you?' Adam asked. 'Shouldn't there be CSIs and the coroner?'

Both of the police officers laughed at him.

'You watch too much TV, son,' Sunglasses scoffed, walking past them and up the steps towards the foyer of the hotel. Ginger followed, as did the paramedics.

As soon as they were out of sight, Adam and Colin got up and walked around the back of the hotel. Since Danny's room was on the ground floor, they figured they could watch the police go about their business through the window, as long as they did it covertly.

They carefully took their positions, one on either side of the window. They heard the heavy door creak open inside and listened to the man from reception tell the police and paramedics that they were short staffed. Ginger excused him with a grunt and he left the room, slamming the door closed.

Colin stole a glance inside.

The two police officers stood with their backs to the window, observing the body, while the paramedics performed a series of checks. After a few minutes, they spoke, though their deep voices didn't carry quite so well and Colin had trouble understanding them.

Adam watched as the paramedics repacked their things and left the room while the police officers performed a cursory glance around the room and then made for the door again. He looked at his watch. They hadn't even been in the room for ten minutes.

As Danny's door closed, Adam and Colin sprinted to the front of the building and retook their places on the steps just as the ambulance was pulling away. A few minutes later, the police officers reappeared.

'We've just spoken to the fella who is getting married and he told us that you were the one who discovered the body,' Ginger said to Adam, who confirmed the rumour with a nod of his head.

'Do I need to give a statement or anything?'

Again, the policemen laughed.

'No, son. Statements are only needed if the death is classed as suspicious. This one isn't. I'm afraid to say your pal had a bit too much to drink and sadly passed away by choking on his own vomit, according to the paramedics.'

'But, the state of the room…' Adam started.

'Aye, he was a messy boy, wasn't he?'

Adam stared at them, incredulous at what he was hearing.

'You're not even going to investigate it?'

'We just have. Haven't you been listening?'

'But…'

'Listen to us and listen well, young man. Believe it or not, we know what we're doing. Even though we owe you no explanation, here is one anyway. Last night, a bunch of young twenty-somethings were let off the leash at a swanky hotel with cheap booze. Your pal had too much and died as a result. Now, it's tragic, but, as you know, it's the Twelfth weekend and we have bigger fish to fry.'

Adam couldn't believe what he was hearing.

'Is that the reason why you two aren't doing your job properly?' he said, standing up. 'Are you annoyed that you're missing the marching bands and were sent to the countryside on a jolly?'

Sunglasses took a step closer.

'Now, listen here you, ye wee prick, that's enough. One more word and this will not end well for you.'

Ginger took a step forward too, as if to underline the point.

Colin smiled disarmingly at the policemen and led Adam up the steps.

'We've spoken to the lad at reception and we'll arrange for the body to be moved later today,' Ginger shouted after them. 'As you said, all our best men are busy with the nasty Orangemen today.'

The police officers strode to their car and gunned the engine, taking off down the driveway at pace, leaving nothing but a bad taste in Adam's mouth.

ADAM THREW HIMSELF onto the bed and fought back the tears. Tears of injustice. Tears for his friend who wasn't getting a fair hearing.

'There's no way Danny died from drinking too much,' Adam said, piquing Colin's attention.

'He could drink most of us under the table, that's for sure.'

'And, when I spoke to him not long before he stormed out, he seemed grand.'

Colin raised an eyebrow.

'Are you thinking there was foul play involved?'

Adam didn't know if he was being ridiculous. Surely no one here; his friends, anyone in this stately home, could be capable of *murder*, could they?

'It couldn't hurt to ask around, I guess,' Adam said. 'The police have made their minds up and we've got a day with nothing to do.'

'Are you saying what I think your saying?'

'That's right,' Adam nodded, standing up. 'Our Sherlock marathon is cancelled.'

8

WARDROBE CHOICES

EVERYONE GATHERED ON the spacious lawn at the front of the manor. Some sought the solace of shade that a smattering of ancient trees offered, their branches and foliage casting long shadows across the grass. Others basked in the mid-morning sun, content to confront the sun's rays head on in the hope of topping up a tan that would look good in the wedding photos.

If there even was a wedding.

Rumours had started to swirl at the first sighting of the police car. The sirens had barely stopped when ill-advised and ignorant whispers began.

Some concluded that Danny had been battered to death.

Some suggested that he'd died of a drug overdose – he had been known to dabble from time to time, after all.

Tragically, some of Danny's friends only found out about his untimely death by way of this gossip.

Sam and Emily – possible bride and groom-to-be – emerged from the entrance of the stately home, cutting Adam's thoughts on Danny short. Emily had arrived not long after the police had departed, and she and Sam had taken residence in the bridal suite, presumably discussing what to do next.

They weaved their way through the assembled groups on the lawn. Emily occasionally touched hands with one of her friends in way of hello while Sam stared straight ahead as he led his fiancée towards the decorative bandstand in the centre of the garden.

If this was on TV, Adam would've laughed at how overblown it seemed.

They walked up the steps and took their places in front of the crowd. Conversations hushed, and all eyes turned to the happy couple.

'Can everyone hear me?' Sam shouted, sounding like a headmaster at the front of an assembly hall.

Murmurs from all sides of the crowd suggested that yes, everyone could hear him.

'We're aware that people have been talking and we wanted to let you know exactly what has happened. I'm really sorry to say it, and it is heart-breaking, but Daniel Costello died in his sleep last night.'

Though most people already knew or had guessed, a gasp clouded Sam's next words. He paused to let everyone get it out of their systems.

'We've deliberated and, obviously what has happened is a terrible tragedy, but we've decided to press ahead with the wedding.'

Adam glanced around the crowd, wondering if this came as unwelcome news to anyone. All he saw was happiness.

He pulled on Colin's sleeve and signalled for his friend to follow him.

It was time to put a plan in place.

ADAM EMERGED FROM the bathroom with a flourish and a twirl.

Colin sat on the bed with a look of confusion etched on his face. He tried to focus on Adam but it was sensory overload.

His friend was wearing the clothes he'd been given for the wedding ceremony, given that he was part of the official wedding party - a navy three-piece suit combined with a plain white shirt and a red cravat. Pointed brown shoes completed his look.

'You're a day early,' Colin said.

'Wrong, old chap,' Adam replied. 'This is my detective outfit. Sherlock had a deerstalker and a pipe; I have a fashionable suit. You have to look official.'

'But what are you going to wear tomorrow? And, if we're actually going to do a bit of digging, we're going to be talking to our friends. Our friends who are all dressed super casually. You're going to get laughed at.'

Adam considered this.

'They won't if we are both wearing suits.'

Colin laughed.

'If you think I'm putting on a suit to go and talk to our friends, you've got another think coming. I'm dreading wearing one tomorrow, given the weather. I'm already sweating just thinking about it.'

'Fine,' Adam said, knowing that the matter was settled. 'Let's make a plan.'

WITH THE BEGINNINGS of a plan in place, Adam and Colin walked down the stairs and made their way up the lavish corridor towards Danny's room.

Step one, they had decided, was to take a good look at the body, just to confirm Adam's suspicions that foul play was indeed behind his passing. If Colin was unconvinced, they would abandon their folly and simply retire to their room to drown in episodes of Sherlock.

Colin made sure that no one was watching them while Adam pulled the handle, relieved to discover that the door had not been locked after the police's visit. Adam slinked into the room and Colin followed, easing the door closed with a gentle click.

Inside the room, the air was cloying and the heat held in by the heavy curtains that the police had redrawn before leaving felt oppressive. Adam wouldn't admit it, but he could feel the sweat gathering at his armpits under the woollen suit. He looks at his friend's casual get up – a T-shirt and shorts – with envy.

Colin flicked the light on and walked around the bed, getting his first glimpse of Danny's body. In his line of work, he had seen dead bodies before, but it never became any less shocking. This was different. This body belonged to someone he knew, someone who had their whole life ahead of him.

He scrunched up his nose to block out the smell of the vomit and tried to take in as many details from the body as he could.

'What do you think?' Adam asked.

'I agree with you, there's something fishy.'

Adam noticed details, as if for the first time. Details he must've taken in subconsciously when he discovered the body, enough to form initial suspicions.

A lump and a vivid purple bruise bloomed at the temple on the right side of Danny's face. A trickle of blood had escaped from a small cut in the same area, pooling on the pillow below his head.

Adam had to look away when he noticed this as he began to feel woozy. Colin pretended not to notice his friend recoil at the sight of the blood.

Another set of bruises, either side of the jaw, seemed to glow like beacons against the white of the face.

They look like finger marks, Colin thought. As if someone had grabbed him roughly.

Aside from that, and the tracks of vomit on his chin, there was nothing else to see.

Adam checked the windows, pleased to find that they were secured from the inside. That meant one thing. Whoever killed Danny came in through the door and left the same way. That meant that Danny had let them in.

'So, what do we do now?' Colin asked, taking one last look at the body and moving around the bed.

'We talk to the last person to see him alive. And thus, we begin our investigation.'

9

THE INVESTIGATION BEGINS

COLIN SAT ON a comfortable chair in the wide corridor outside his bedroom, looking out the huge bay window towards the sea.

Eternally pessimistic, he wondered how long it would be until the cliff receded far enough to drag the beautiful stately home towards the rocks and waves below it. A couple of hundred years, maybe?

He wondered if what they were about to do was worth the time and effort. Would their friends laugh in their faces as they played at being sleuths, trying to uncover something that wasn't there to be uncovered in the first place?

Surely, the police knew what they were talking about in matters of death. Though, the bruising on Danny's still face was troubling.

The door behind him creaked open and when he turned to the noise, he tried to hide his smirk as Adam emerged from their bedroom, dressed in shorts and a T-shirt, his suit discarded.

Adam gave his friend a look that told him he didn't want to hear any *I told you so's.*

'You were right,' he said simply. 'Now, time to start the case.'

'Do you know who the last person to see Danny alive was?' Colin asked, rising from his chair.

'I have my suspicions.'

Adam's mind drifted to hazy memories of the night before.

He'd watched from the bar as the argument in the shadows had played out, as Sam's push floored Danny. He'd watched Danny trudge out, stopping only to whisper in the ear of a girl on the dancefloor. Adam couldn't remember who.

Twenty minutes later, Sam had left the room. To Adam's eyes, it had seemed as if his best man had left a trail of breadcrumbs for him to follow. Sam hadn't deviated to the dancefloor though, instead marching straight through the heavy doors into the corridor outside.

'We start with Sam.'

'You don't think he could have killed Danny, do you?'

Adam looked his friend in the eye.

'Before this morning, I didn't think any of our friends could be capable of murder. But a dead body says otherwise.'

SAM WAS HOLED up in the bridal suite. When Adam knocked, Emily answered, a Cheshire cat smile plastered on her face, not managing to mask the worry behind it. Since their announcement at the bandstand, she'd changed into more casual attire.

'Sorry that things aren't going to plan,' Adam said. 'It must be a nightmare.'

'Something to tell the grand kids, eh?' she half laughed as she walked away from the door, back into the safety of the room. Adam didn't know if this was an invitation to follow her or not, but luckily Sam's appearance in the doorway meant he didn't make a fool of himself.

'Fancy a pint?' Adam asked.

Sam looked momentarily panicked, as if Adam had asked him to choose a drink with him over his wife-to-be. His alarm was short lived, as Emily reappeared and joked that taking Sam from under her feet would be brilliant, as she still had last minute bits and pieces to prepare for tomorrow.

He kissed her goodbye on the cheek and the three of them made their way down the stairs towards the bar, engaged in idle chit chat, skirting around the headline.

The barroom that the party had taken place in last night looked completely different in the cold light of day. The tables had been pushed back into place, covering over the sins committed on the dancefloor. The balloons and banners had all been taken down, returning the room to its original stately grace. A grandfather clock in the corner of the room served as a reminder that it wasn't quite the afternoon yet.

Oblivious to its warning, Adam ordered three pints while Colin and Sam chose a table. He watched them converse freely with a feeling of unease spreading in his stomach – were they really going to question their friend in relation to murder?

With pints dished out, talk naturally turned to Danny. Generalities were explored first, before Adam's gentle attempts at probing earned a raised eyebrow from the groom.

'Look,' Adam stated, baldly. 'We think that, maybe, there's something more to Danny's death.'

'Something more, how?'

'Something suspicious.'

Sam looked sceptical.

Adam took up the mantle.

'The police said Danny died from drinking too much. For one, he didn't seem that drunk before he left here, and two, I've seen Danny drink enough to put me in a coma and still bag a girl at the end of a night out.'

'So, you're investigating?'

Adam's cheek reddened at the formality, and he saw Colin's eyes dip to the floor.

'We're... asking some questions.'

'You can't think I've got anything to do with it,' Sam scoffed. 'He was my best friend – my best man.'

'No, of course not,' said Colin, disarmingly. 'We just wanted to piece last night together - who had contact with him and things like that.'

Sam took a sip from his pint and nodded while Adam searched for the best opening question.

'Do you think anyone here would've wanted to harm Danny?'

'Yes. You know him, how abrasive he can be. He rubs people up the wrong way constantly and is always having scraps with anyone fool enough to rise to his crap. But, I can't see anyone killing him. He is...' Sam faltered. 'Was... annoying, but not to that extreme.'

'I saw you two have a bit of an argument over there,' said Adam, pointing to the corner of the room beyond the bar. 'What was that about?'

Sam looked as if he was vying for time, swilling the answer through his head before letting it escape his lips.

'He was just being a dick,' he said, finally. 'He'd had a few pints in him, and a couple of shots – we all had – and he was just being his usual annoying self. He was slabbering on about the wedding, about how Emily was stealing me and how he'd probably never see me again after the vows. It was pissing me off, so I told him to shut his mouth and gave him a shove. He left in a huff.'

'Did you see him again?'

'Yeah. When he didn't come back, I went looking for him to apologise. I went to his room and hammered at the door, but he wouldn't let me in.'

'So, you didn't see him again?'

'I'm getting to that,' he replied, testily. 'When he wouldn't let me in, I went down to reception and asked for a key to his room. I explained the situation, and the guy gave me it. I went back, unlocked the door and he was lying on the bed, texting someone. I apologised and so did he, and I left again.'

'Do you know who he was texting?'

Sam shook his head.

'Did he seem drunk to you?' Colin asked.

'No,' Sam said, still shaking his head. 'I mean, a bit. Not so drunk that he would've passed out.'

'What did you do after you left?'

'I went back to the party and stayed there until they stopped serving. I don't remember getting back to my room.'

'And the key?'

'I gave it to Ross. When Danny didn't come back to the party after our talk, I was going to go and see him again, to convince him to come back. Ross said not to bother, that he would go. I gave him the key and put the whole thing out of my mind.'

Sam finished his pint and looked at his watch.

'I best be getting back, I think. Emily will have a list of jobs the length of her arm for me. If you need anything else, give me a shout.'

'One last question,' Adam said, as Sam rose from his seat. 'Do you know anyone who would want the wedding called off?'

Sam looked aghast.

'No,' he said with a tone of finality. 'We've only invited people who mean something to us and who we care for. No one here would wish us harm. At least, I hope they wouldn't.'

They watched him walk away, his shoulders slightly slumped.

'It's time we visit the twin with the key,' Adam said, draining his glass.

9

A KICK IN THE BALEARICS

COLIN SANK ONTO the bed while Adam remained standing, pacing to and fro in front of the window, the glorious sunshine filtering in, turning him into a silhouette.

'What are you thinking?' Colin asked.

Adam stopped pacing. He mulled things over for a while, before sitting down on the end of the bed.

'Well, for one, I think the story he told us about why he and Danny argued was nonsense. He was always so tolerant of Danny, always sticking up for him and calming others down when his mouth got him into trouble. For Sam to lose it with him, whatever he was saying to him must've been really bad.'

'He looked put on the spot with that one too,' Colin added, thinking back to the pause he took before answering that particular question.

'I agree. The rest of the answers flowed straight off his tongue, but this one he had to think about. We need to find out what the real reason was for his reaction to Danny.'

'What about this key business?'

'It checks out, I reckon,' Adam said, 'though it would be good to check with whoever was at reception, to confirm.'

'Doesn't that go against confidentiality? I don't like the thought of someone snooping through my stuff.'

'He probably only did it because it was the groom. I can't imagine he'd go handing out keys willy-nilly. More than his job is worth.'

Before Colin could reply, his attention was snatched by movement outside. He got up from the bed and crossed to the window, sitting on the seat built into the bay. It offered him a perfect view of the lawn.

Crossing the recently cut grass was a girl. Her blonde hair appeared golden in the sunlight. She was wearing a pair of denim cut-off shorts and a bright, strappy vest top. From behind, it was difficult to make out who it was.

Plotting her path, it wasn't difficult to see where she was going. In the shade of the trees at the far end of the gardens was a swing seat, so far away the details of it were nigh on impossible to make out.

One thing *was* easy to see, though.

The lanky frame of the person sitting on it, watching the blonde advance towards him, was none other than Ross McMullan.

The next person they needed to speak to.

'I think you should lead the next one,' Adam said, following Colin's gaze.

'Why?'

'Well, we are a team. I led the first one and now it's your turn.'

'But, I don't...'

'Don't know what you're doing?' Adam finished. 'And I do? We're leading a murder investigation from things we've learned from the television. None of this is normal.'

'But you seem so confident.'

'Confidence is a shroud that allows the bearer to wear many faces.'

Colin looked impressed.

'Who said that?'

'I did, just then. Made it up. But it sounded impressive and that's all we can do – say things that sound good and hope that it tricks people into telling us what we want to know.'

Colin stood up and moved towards the door, ready.

'You sure you don't want to wear a suit for this?' Adam joked. His laugh was cut short when he saw Colin's narrowed eyes.

THEY WALKED ACROSS the garden, kicking clumps of cut grass to each other like footballers warming up before a match. Colin realised that he was feeling nervous and tried to think of the main points of questioning that he and Adam had gone over as they'd made their way downstairs from their room.

He wished he had a notebook to write things down in, but then, what they were doing was ridiculous enough already. The thought of pulling a notebook from his trouser pockets was a step too far.

Upon seeing them progress towards him, Ross struggled out of the fabric seat and extended a hand which both men shook. Ross stood awkwardly, stuck between retaking his place in the swing seat and seeming childish, or standing like an adult should when a discussion was clearly on the horizon.

In the end, he stood.

He reached into the back pocket of his chino shorts and pulled out a packet of cigarettes, taking one out and flicking the box towards Adam and Ross like an invitation. Both declined.

'I forgot you both gave up,' mumbled Ross, through lips clamped tight against the stick of nicotine. 'I don't know how you do it.'

Colin was appreciative of the slight gusts of wind that were playing with Ross's lighter, causing it to flicker and extinguish just before fulfilling its purpose. It allowed him time to get his head right and size up his opponent.

'Must be a bit weird, seeing your brother marry a girl you went out with once,' Colin said, pleased with his opening gambit.

'Not really. It was so long ago and we only went on a few dates,' Sam countered, turning his attention back to his cigarette struggles.

'It's mad about Danny, isn't it?' Colin pressed on.

'Crazy. I can't believe it. Rumours are floating round that you two don't buy what the police have said. I hear you've questioned the groom. Is that why you're here talking to me? Am I under arrest?'

Before Colin or Adam could answer, Ross laughed at his own joke.

'Ask away. I think it's a silly way to spend a Saturday and a complete waste of time, but we all like different things.'

'We'd like to hear about the argument that you stopped last night between Danny and Sam. We've heard Sam's version of it, but we'd like to hear yours too.'

Ross arched an eyebrow.

'Sam told you?'

'Yeah,' Colin said, surprised at how easily the lie slipped off his tongue.

'Flip,' Ross said. 'I thought he was trying to keep that as secret as possible, but I guess you're his friends. He can trust you.'

He took one last puff on his cigarette before stubbing it out in the bucket of sand at the side of the swing. He sat down on the grass and motioned for Adam and Colin to follow suit. He cast a conspiratorial glance around the trees, as if they could be enemies eavesdropping in plain sight.

'It's true. Danny saw him cheat on Emily on his stag do. He'd been lording it over him since, threatening to tell people if Sam didn't buy him a pint or drive him wherever he needed to go. Stupid little things, really.'

He sighed deeply and took the packet of cigarettes out again, before reconsidering and throwing them onto the grass beside him instead, before continuing his story.

'I was supposed to be best man, but it got changed to Danny shortly after we all came back from Ibiza. Sam told me the reason; about the girl and how Danny was blackmailing him into making him best man. He apologised and begged me not to make a big deal about it otherwise people would start asking questions and the truth would come out.'

'And that's what the argument was about?' Colin asked.

'Yeah,' he said. 'Danny was mouthing off again, and it was the straw that broke the camel's back. Sam snapped and shoved him. Danny gave him a look as he was leaving that worried Sam, so he went after him not long after in a panic. He was worried that Danny was going to blab to anyone who would listen.'

'Do you know what happened when he went to see him?'

'He came back looking much calmer. He said he'd sorted it and that he'd go back later to check again. He put up a bit of fuss when I told him to enjoy his night and that I'd check in later instead.'

'And did you?'

He looked sheepish.

'I was going to. Sam gave me the spare key to his room. I put it in my jacket pocket and then we all went on the dancefloor – the Macarena, ya know? Hard to resist.'

They all nodded in agreement. The song seemed to possess some sort of gravitational pull towards the nearest dancefloor.

'Anyway, when we were finished, I put my jacket on and went to Danny's room. When I checked my pocket, the key wasn't there.'

'Someone had taken it?'

He nodded.

'And it's still missing?'

Another nod.

'Did Danny let you in?'

'No,' he said. 'I banged on the door, but he never answered. I could hear the TV was on, so I assumed he was in there, but I've just chatted to Vicky and apparently he paid her a visit last night.'

'Vicky?' Colin and Adam said in unison.

Of course, the blonde they had observed walking across the grass earlier. Danny's ex-girlfriend.

'It might be worth having a chat with her,' Ross said. 'Big news there.'

10

EX'S AND OH'S

HAVING DISCUSSED THE upcoming football season and listened to Ross's pessimistic views on Preston's promotion chances, they left him to it. When they looked back, he'd settled back into his swing seat with a fresh cigarette, sunglasses on and head tilted back. Presumably, once they were out of sight, he'd be texting around, warning people that a couple of amateur sleuths were in town.

'Did you believe him?' Colin asked.

Adam nodded.

'I think the fact that he told us the real reason behind the fight shows that we can trust him, even if it was taken by questionable means…'

Colin glanced over at him, pleased to see that his impressed expression negated his words.

'Very tricksy,' Adam said. 'Sadly, the chat raised more questions than answers.'

'How so?'

'Firstly, why did Sam lie about the reason behind the fight? Does he have something to hide? Secondly, Ross looked pretty miffed that he missed out on being his brother's best man. Might he have had something to do with bumping off his competitor who took the title by means of blackmail? Finally, who has the room key? Whoever has that surely is the person behind the murder.'

Colin looked jaded at how little they'd achieved so far. It felt like gardening – however many weeds you ripped from the ground, there were always more waiting to spring from the gaps you'd created.

'The method of murder also remains a mystery,' Adam added, piling more onto Colin's already full plate. 'He wasn't battered to death, which means that it wasn't a crime of passion – the police would've spotted any outward damage. Which means that whoever killed him had planned it, which very much rules Sam and Ross in.'

'Both had means,' Colin agreed. 'One was being blackmailed on threat of a secret being exposed and the other was seeing his twin suffer, having had his best man title taken from him.'

Frustration rose in the air between them.

'The only way is forward,' Adam said. 'Let's go see what Vicky's breaking news is.'

VICKY WATSON WAS surprised to see the two men outside her door, but stood aside to let them in anyway, at Adam's request. Having always had a slight crush on her, Colin kept his gaze low, focusing instead on the rough grain of the floorboards.

The door clicked behind her and she made her way to the corner of the room, throwing herself into a velvet chair next to a writing desk. From it, she took a bottle of water and guzzled thirstily from it.

Colin snuck a glance in her direction, pity panging in his chest. Judging from the mascara smudged below her bloodshot eyes, whatever news she had to impart was not good.

Adam took in the room. It was almost identical to theirs; similar abstract art on the walls and a large window with a view that matched theirs. The big difference was that her room had two single beds.

A light bulb illuminated in Adam's mind. But first, to business.

'Vicky, we've come to speak to you about Danny.'

She sniffed, trying to hold back a sob, but to no avail. The floodgates burst open and she let out a wail.

Both men's eyes widened in alarm as they looked at each other, both pleading silently with the other to be the one to do something about it. Eventually, Colin rolled his eyes and got up from the bed, tiptoeing towards her slowly as one might approach a wild animal that might lash out at any second.

He tore a tissue for a box that was sitting on the table and reached it to her. She accepted with a quiet thank you before blowing her nose and placing the used tissue in the bin at her feet. She took a minute to compose herself, apologised and fixed them with a sad smile.

'What do you want to talk about Danny for?' she asked.

'Well, obviously you heard about what happened to him…'

She confirmed that she had with a slight nod of her head.

'…Well, we don't think that it was accidental. We think someone meant to kill him, so we're asking around. Someone hinted that you might have some information.'

'Ross,' she said. A statement, rather than a question.

'Can you tell us what you know?'

'As you know, Danny and I went out for about a while, about three years ago. He broke up with me and we started seeing new people. My mum and dad hated him, so it was never going to last, and I was quite relieved when he ended it. About three weeks ago, he started texting me again, completely out of the blue. Maybe he thought that there was a chance of seeing each other at the wedding and he was getting his feelers out early.'

'Did you text back?'

'Yes, but only a few times. I told him I had a boyfriend and that it was inappropriate for him to be contacting me. It didn't stop him. In fact, not even my boyfriend ringing him put him off, even though Neil gave him a right old shouting at.'

'Where is Neil?'

'He was here last night, but had to leave after the party because he was working today. He's coming back tonight… I hope.'

With that, she burst into tears again. This time, they let her get it out of her system without interfering. She wiped at her eyes, smearing black across her cheeks like warpaint.

'Why wouldn't he come back?' Adam asked when he thought it was safe.

'Because… I slept with Danny once he'd left. He'd said sorry downstairs at the party for texting, and told me to pass his apologies onto Neil. He'd already gone by this point. At the end of the night, there was a knock on my door. It was Danny. I was drunk and I didn't know what I was doing, but I let him in. He seemed… pleased with himself.'

'What do you mean?'

'You know, the usual Danny Costello swagger – boasting about this and that, and he was walking with a spring in his step.'

This news was unexpected. According to Sam, Danny was pissed off and cooped up in his room, still feeling stung about their argument. Although, him being up here, propositioning his ex-girlfriend explained where he was when Ross went a-knocking.

'Did he say why?'

'We didn't say much at all, if you get my drift…'

Something permeated the room – an awkwardness that Adam felt he could almost decant from the air and bottle. It hung thick around them.

'Do you remember what time this was?'

Colin asked the question, his words acting as a welcome candle in the dark.

'He came up at just after one o'clock and left at about quarter past. He didn't hang around.'

'And that's why you're worried Neil might not come?' Colin said.

She nodded, fresh tears forming in the corners of her eyes.

'Is there anything else that happened?'

'Actually, yeah,' she said, straightening up in her chair. 'When he was putting on his jacket, after… you know… an envelope fell out. It was open at the top, but I couldn't see what was in it. Though, when it dropped on the floor, it sounded heavy.'

'Heavy?'

'Yeah, it was loud. It didn't bang, it sounded more like a slap. Like it was full of folded paper or something.'

A physical clue – interesting.

With nothing more to go on, they left Vicky's room and were half way down the corridor when Adam turned back, hammering on the door again. Vicky opened it, tears flowing like a river down her cheeks.

'I was just wondering if… well…'

He paused, wondering how to word it to keep the offence to a minimum.

'Spit it out,' she said.

'Well, our room has one double bed and you have two singles. I'm assuming that, after what happened last night, Neil won't be coming tonight, so was wondering if you fancied swapping rooms? It'd make our lives so much easier.'

The door slammed shut in Adam's face milliseconds after he finished asking the question. Colin dragged him away before Vicky returned with something sharp.

'Idiot,' his friend said, punching him on the arm.

11

ANOTHER SNOOP

'WELL, ONE THING is for certain,' Adam said, while unlocking the bedroom. 'If Danny was sober enough to, you know…'

He made a crude hand gesture which caused Colin shake his head.

'…for a bit of how's your mother,' he continued, noting his friend's displeasure. 'It meant he definitely couldn't have been drunk enough to choke on his vomit.'

It was an interesting idea, Colin thought as he followed Adam into the room. He threw himself onto the bed; the traipsing around the long corridors mingling with the stupefying heat caused a sudden wave of exhaustion.

'Do we have time for a rest?' Colin asked, stifling a yawn.

Adam checked the time and shook his head.

'I've got a theory. I think someone did this to stop the wedding.'

Colin was unconvinced, but waved his hand at Adam for elaboration.

'If whoever killed Danny did it for that reason, it didn't work. The wedding is happening tomorrow, which means whoever did the killing may do more. We're working under a time constraint here.'

He sat down on the bed too and threw his eyes towards the ceiling.

'What I've realised is just how amateur we've been so far,' he said. 'We looked a bit at Danny's face, which didn't help us work out how he'd been killed. I think what we need to do is search his room. We know he had an envelope, but we don't know what was in it. Perhaps, whoever killed him was after whatever was inside.'

He thought for a few more minutes.

'We're going to split up. You go and search the room while I do a bit of work elsewhere.'

'Why do I have to search the room?' Colin asked, the colour rising in his cheeks. The thought of spending another second in the room with Danny's corpse caused a shiver to run through his spine.

'Well, you're used to bodies, in your line of work and…'

'You're a wimp,' interrupted Colin.

Adam was in no position to argue. Colin accepted his mission with a small nod of the head.

'What am I looking for?' he asked, rising from the bed.

'The envelope and anything that seems out of the ordinary,' Adam said, unhelpfully. 'Check anywhere you think something might be hidden. Desk drawers or in the suitcase, that kind of thing.'

Colin left the room with a sense of unease. How were they supposed to solve a crime, if they didn't even know what they were looking for?

He trudged down the corridor, hoping that some sort of Spidey-sense would awaken within him, though he didn't hold out much hope. He made his way down the grand staircase and passed a few people sitting in groups around tables in the foyer, catching snippets of conversation, all about the stricken best man.

He made his way down the corridor towards Danny's room, turning back every few steps to make sure no one was following him. The last thing he needed was company, or even worse, someone mistaking his meddling as guilt. Visiting the room once was a risk, let alone venturing in again with no suitable explanation as to why if he were to be questioned.

Casting one last clandestine look around, he slipped in the door, a sense of déjà vu enveloping him. Everything was as they'd left it.

The lifeless body was still on the bed; the bruises unmoved, though slightly darker, and the vomit uncleaned. Perhaps the police had instructed the hotel staff to leave the room untouched until after the body was collected.

Colin scanned around. He ignored the light switch for fear of alerting someone to the room, instead letting his eyes adjust to the dusky hues. He made his way to the middle and turned a full circle, hoping for some little detail to leap out at him.

Nothing did.

Instead, he moved over to the body and rooted through the pockets of his jacket and trousers. Inside, there were a few card receipts from the bar last night, but nothing of great importance.

Something else caught his attention.

The smell.

At first, as on the previous times, the overriding smell was that left behind from the vomit. But underneath it was something else, something smoky, medicinal almost.

Whiskey.

A small grain of doubt fell into the cogs of Colin's thinking, causing them to shudder to a stop.

The whiskey, coupled with the vomit, was a very obvious sign that pointed to an accidental death. If it weren't for Adam's persistence that something was amiss in all of this, Colin would've downed tools there and then.

Instead, he pressed on.

For a while, he searched in drawers, pushing the contents this way and that, coming away empty each time. He moved from desk to bedside cabinet to wardrobe, but there was no sign of anything suspicious.

Frustration rose like a beast inside him.

Why had Adam sent him on a fool's errand?

The silence in the room was interrupted by voices in the hallway outside. Voices that were growing louder by the second. Panicking, Colin crossed the bedroom in three giant strides, rushing into the bathroom and closing the door as quietly as he could behind him.

He stepped into the bath and pulled the shower curtain, wincing as the metallic rings scraped against the curtail rail. Visions of Psycho plagued him as he waited with his breath held.

Outside the bathroom door, two men were talking. From what he could make out, they were here to collect the body. They quickly discussed how they were going to move it, before putting the plan into action. Colin heard grunting, the rustle of fabric and a quiet bang as something fell over.

'You've knocked the bin over,' said one of the voices.

'Ah, the cleaners will get it later,' replied the other.

The voices were muffled as the sound of the bedroom door slamming filled the room. After that, Colin heard no more, though he didn't move from his spot for a few minutes, just in case. When he was sure the coast was clear, he scurried out of the bath and splashed water over his sweating face at the sink.

He grabbed a handful of paper towels and dabbed them on his brow before looking around, dismayed to find nowhere to put the sopping material. He walked into the bedroom and saw the upturned bin, stopping short when he registered the contents strewn across the floor.

Next to the desk was a tattered brown envelope and the empty silver packaging of painkillers.

He lifted the envelope first, smoothing the creases and returning it to as near its original state as possible. There was nothing on the outside to mark it as different to the millions of other massed produced envelopes currently in circulation.

He turned it in his fingers before reaching inside. Whatever was in there to make it heavy was now gone. In its place was a single piece of paper, its thin blue lines scrawled over in black biro. The hand that wrote it appeared both rushed and angry to Colin's mind.

He took in the message, turning it around in his head in order to try to make some sense of it, before shoving the missive back inside the envelope and the envelope inside the pocket of his shorts.

Next, he lifted the silver packaging. It belonged to regular paracetamol, though all eight blisters were empty. There was also no sign of the box from which they'd been procured.

Which made sense.

Danny would have no reason to own a box of paracetamol, since he was allergic to them.

Colin rose from the floor, eager to get back to Adam to discuss the things he'd found. As he moved towards the door, a quiet beep emitted from somewhere nearby.

Colin tried to zone in on where it had come from.

Getting down on his knees, he groped around under the bed, his hand settling on only cobwebs and lumps of dust. He moved around to the other side of the bed and repeated the task.

This time, his fingers touched something small and rectangular. He pulled it out from under the bed and held it in the shaft of light coming through the curtains.

It was a phone.

But not the up-to-date iPhone Danny made sure to get on release day.

It was a thin Nokia, as nondescript as they come. A small black-and-white screen told him that the battery was low. He dismissed the message with the click of a button, pocketed it and left the room, aware more than ever that time may be slipping away from them.

12

TUBTHUMPING

ONCE COLIN HAD left, Adam had a quick lie down. He felt bad, leaving his friend to do the legwork in the room, but he really couldn't face seeing the body again.

He also felt bad, knowing that he'd sent his friend on what could be a wild goose chase. There might be nothing incriminating in the room, but if there was, he fully trusted his friend to find it.

As partners went, he'd pick Colin every day of the week. He was loyal, trusting, and had stuck up for Adam since their first day at primary school together. He had a big heart, as evidenced by the job he'd chosen – a job not many other twenty-something year old lads would be seen dead doing. He was clever too – cleverer than he thought he was. He just needed some confidence.

Pushing Colin out of his mind and letting Danny in, he considered what came next. The case (he still felt weird calling it that) was progressing nicely, though it was becoming hard to keep track of the comings and goings. He resolved to fix that.

Jumping up from the bed, he grabbed the key from the sideboard and marched towards the door.

ADAM LOOKED AROUND the library. It was a nice space, not anything grand like the rest of the house, but rather cosy. All four walls were lined with bookcases that stretched from floor to ceiling, an elaborate chandelier casting sprinkles of light across the dark wood.

A wide selection of books filled the shelves; the cracked spines hinting that they had been well thumbed by many a visitor. It was a nice touch, having this room readily available in a place so remote. The solitude of the house probably seemed perfect for a getaway, but after a few days, Adam could imagine the books acted as a welcome distraction.

He moved the mouse in order to bring the computer screen to life. He tapped a few buttons, logging in with the details he'd been given at reception, before navigating to Facebook. He was a reluctant social media user, but the website was all he needed right now.

For ten minutes, he searched for what he required and collected his printing from the machine in the corner of the room.

Pulling the door open, he left the room, colliding with a solid mass that caused him to fall to the floor, his papers dropping around him like snow.

'Sorry, man,' said Mike, offering a hand and pulling Adam to standing. 'Didn't see you there.'

Adam took him in as he bent down and began collecting the papers. Mike, the bride's brother, had been in the same year as Adam, but was never in his friendship group. He'd been a sort of loner, regularly eating his lunch in the toilets, making him easy fodder for the bullies who'd made his school life miserable. He'd used university as a chance for change, emerging with muscles Arnie would be proud and a new found sense of confidence, as evidenced by the clothes he chose to wear.

Mike handed Adam the pieces of paper he'd scooped up without comment.

'How are you feeling today?' Adam asked, folding the wad of paper and putting it in his pocket.

'Alright,' Mike said, curiosity clouding his features.

'You were pretty smashed last night,' Adam elaborated.

'Oh, that. Yeah,' Mike laughed. 'I had a blast, from what I can remember, anyway.'

'I didn't think Emily's side of the family were coming until tonight.'

'We had a family meal at the house, and then Emily and her bridesmaids went off to sort what colour their nails were going to be. It was either sit around on my own or come to the party.'

'Party wins every time,' Adam said.

'Indeed it does,' chuckled Mike, before turning serious. 'Pretty bad about Danny. I felt awful for Emily when I heard – she's been planning this day since she was a wee girl. I heard you are doing a bit of detective work.'

Adam confirmed he was with an embarrassed half nod.

'Good man, yourself,' he said. 'If you find out who did it, give him an extra slap from me. The last thing my family needed was more stress on the eve of the wedding.'

Adam was about to tell him that he hoped it would never come to blows, but Mike was already saying that he'd see him at the dinner tonight while wandering off towards the stairs.

ADAM RETURNED TO the room to find Colin slumped in the seat, swigging from the hipflask he'd been given by Sam. The red blotches on his cheeks against the pallor of his skin suggested he had a story to tell, which he dutifully launched into.

'Jesus,' exclaimed Adam, his eyes wide at the thought of Colin nearly being caught snooping around.

Just you wait, thought Colin. He hadn't even got around to telling his friend what he'd uncovered.

From his pocket, he took the envelope. He set it on the table, letting Adam examine it. He imagined this is how going on the Antiques Roadshow felt.

Adam picked the envelope up, casting his gaze over the outside. There was no name, address or stamp, which meant that the envelope must've been delivered by hand.

Next, he examined the opening at the top. To Adam's eye, it seemed to have been ripped in haste. The line was not cleanly torn, as it would've been if a letter opener had been used.

No, this was done with speed.

Out of fear?

Perhaps

Or excitement, as dirty deeds often are.

Fishing inside, his fingers settled on nothing but the scrap of paper. The same scrap of paper that had made Colin's heart gallop not twenty minutes previously.

Unfolding the paper, he read the scribbled words.

£200. And that's the last of it, as agreed.

'The last of it?' Adam said. 'That would suggest that whoever gave this to Danny has given him more in the past.'

'And that would suggest that whoever gave him the money also had cause to kill him,' Colin added. 'But, why would anyone be giving him money?'

'To shut him up,' Adam said. 'We know he blackmailed Sam into giving him the best man gig. What if he was blackmailing someone else too?'

'Or, what if he wasn't?'

'You think Sam did this?'

Colin shrugged.

'It makes sense. Danny has been threatening to expose Sam's secret kiss. What happened if Sam snapped and decided enough was enough after the argument?'

Adam considered it. It made sense, but the timeframe seemed too quick for Sam to have committed the murder. They knew that Danny paid Vicky a visit after he'd seen Sam, so he was definitely alive when the groom had left. Could Sam have snuck back later in the night? Had he been the one who had stolen the key from Ross's jacket? It certainly was a possibility – after all, no one else knew about the spare key.

When Adam made no reply, Colin took out the second thing he'd found.

The empty strip of tablets.

'Why would these be in his room? He's allergic,' Adam said, twirling the packet in his fingers, the light reflecting off the silver packaging.

'You think that's how he was killed? Someone made him take the tablets that they knew he'd have a reaction to?' Colin asked.

Adam gave no answer, keen not to jump to conclusions, though the reasoning seemed watertight.

Danny had been allergic to paracetamol his whole life. After many a night out, he'd lamented his allergy as a curse; the hangover inevitable, to be endured without treatment. It was a well-known ailment and something that could be easily used against him.

It didn't help narrow down the culprit.

Adam moved it to the side, leaving a space for the final piece of evidence. Colin dutifully set the antiquated phone between them.

Adam looked at it with curiosity, his eyes narrowing.

'A burner?' he said.

The prominence and use of burner phones – disposable devices that aided with anonymity when committing nefarious deeds – were a mainstay of nearly every Hollywood film that had a crime in it.

'That's what I guessed,' Colin nodded.

Adam picked it up, pleased to find that it didn't have a passcode. Danny probably thought that he and it would never be apart, and so saw no need for added security.

Adam navigated through the menus to the call list, unsurprised to find it empty. Next, he moved to the messages. The sent box was empty but there was a two-word message in the inbox, received at 12:51 a.m.

I'm here.

Adam held the screen towards Colin, watching his friend's eyes as he tried to make sense of the message.

'So, he arranged to meet someone? I assume that's when the money was handed over.'

Adam nodded.

'That would make sense. He took the envelope, checked the money was all there, then went straight to Vicky to flaunt his wad.'

'Adam!' scolded Colin.

'I'm talking about the money!' replied Adam.

'So, who sent the message?' Colin asked, getting back on track.

'That, Watson, is what we need to find out next.'

Colin closed his eyes and tried to plot out their next move. He also wondered why he was Watson and not Sherlock.

Adam spoke, tearing him from his thoughts.

'I've got something to do here,' he said, pointing to the pile of printed papers. 'Can you go and speak to whoever is on reception?

Colin nodded, realising exactly why he was Watson while Adam continued.

'Find out if the person who was on the desk last night at 12:51 a.m. is about. Ask them if they saw Danny.'

'Surely he would've done his deal in secret, in some hidden corner,' Colin interjected.

Adam nodded.

'I would agree if I thought whoever sent that text was already in the building.'

'You think someone travelled here to give Danny the money?'

Adam nodded again.

'I do. I think if it was someone who was already here, they wouldn't have bothered with phones and messages. Too much of a data trail. I think he had to have the phone to get in touch with whoever came here to hand him that envelope. I think, after seeing the phone, that we can conclude that he was blackmailing more than just Sam. We just need to find out who.'

13

A SIGHTING AND A MONSTROUS USE OF BLU TACK

COLIN LEFT THE bedroom and wandered down the expansive corridor once more. He felt like he'd walked the hallways so many times that, should they need a tour guide in the near future, he would be in pole position for that job.

Once more, he descended the staircase with burning hamstrings, eyeing who was on the front desk as he did so.

It was a dark-haired man. Not the same one who had greeted them with a single key on arrival. This man was a little shorter with a clean-shaven face. Colin watched him converse with one of Emily's friends, his movements fluid as he took a key out of a drawer and passed it to her at the same time as telling her the directions to her room.

Colin waited until she'd gathered up her suitcases.

Plural.

A lot of luggage for two night's stay, he thought to himself as she walked away, wheeling one case while hoisting a smaller bag onto her shoulder.

'How can I help you?' the man behind the desk said. His accent suggested he originally came from Belfast way.

Colin stepped forward.

'I'm wondering if you know who was working on the desk last night?' he said.

'That was me,' the man said, extending his hand across the desk. 'James Miller.'

Colin shook his hand.

'I was wondering if you saw my friend…'

James's gaze diverted from him and Colin realised that someone had joined the queue behind him. James smiled at Colin.

'I think I know what you want to talk about.' He checked his watch. 'I'm about to clock off. Why don't you meet me outside and I can answer some of your questions?'

Colin nodded and stood aside, letting an older lady pass by him. He turned and walked through the huge door, coming to rest on the steps outside. He squinted into the sunlight, wishing he'd had the foresight to bring his sunglasses with him.

WHILE COLIN WAS watching the few clouds in the sky drift lazily past, Adam was busy in the room. He moved from table to wall, picking up a piece of paper, pressing some Blu Tack onto the back of it before sticking it onto the wall. Police officers usually had a case board, one that they could wheel about easily and add to when needed, but this would do for now.

When he had exhausted his pile of paper, he stood back and took his creation in. It may not be pretty, but it was already helping him to piece together the case like a jigsaw. He just needed to voice his theory aloud.

For that, he needed his partner.

COLIN JUMPED AS James tapped his shoulder. He had been thinking about everything and nothing, lost in the haze and heat of the day. Thoughts worked their way back and forth through his head; stupidity and embarrassment that he'd agreed to undertake the task of detective at all. Every time he had to ask questions, he felt like a boy playing a game with grown-ups who were simply humouring him. On the other hand, he'd managed to uncover definite clues that suggested that Danny was murdered.

James sat down beside him on the step, pulling a cigarette out. He offered one to Colin, who declined, before lighting his own.

'So, it was you who was working last night?' Colin asked.

James nodded, exhaling a plume of acrid smoke.

'We're always short staffed around this time of year, on account of the parades, which I have no interest in,' he explained. 'It means working a late night and an early morning, but I'm alright with that for the overtime pay.'

'And you thought you might've seen my friend who died?'

'Sorry to hear he was your mate,' James said, nodding. 'I'm sure it was him, because I was the one who showed the police to his room this morning. I recognised him immediately.'

'Why?' Colin asked. Danny didn't really have any distinguishing features to speak off; nothing that made him stand out from the crowd.

'Because I remember thinking last night that he seemed like he was up to something. He was loitering in the reception and when I asked him if he needed anything, he shook his head. He seemed like this bag of directionless energy. Then, his phone rang and he ran outside.'

'And you didn't see what he was up to outside.'

'No,' he answered, shaking his head. 'Like I said, we're short staffed and I'm not meant to leave the desk. I assumed he had gone to meet a girl or something. I didn't think any more of it until he came in again a few minutes later.'

He stopped to take another puff of his cigarette, which was burning close to his fingers. Colin remained silent, afraid he'd interrupt the thread of the story.

'When he came back in, he seemed changed. The frenzy of before was gone, replaced with… swagger, maybe,' he said, shrugging his shoulders.

'What do you mean?'

'I mean, he came in with his shoulders rolling, like he thought he was the big man. He was holding an envelope and going through whatever was inside. I was about to ask, because I was worried it was drugs, but he was gone before I could say anything.'

'Did anything else happen with him?'

'No,' he said, throwing his cigarette on the step and stamping on it, before lifting it again. 'I shouldn't leave that there. More than my job's worth!'

Colin thanked him and stood to leave.

'Oh, one more thing, actually,' James said. 'After he put the envelope away, he walked upstairs. I heard him talking to someone, another lad, sounded like a bit of an argument. I couldn't hear what they were saying, only the tone of the conversation and it wasn't friendly.'

He stood and began walking towards a red Corsa.

'Now, if you'll excuse me, it's time I got some shut eye.'

COLIN'S FACE FELL when he took in what Adam had been up to in his absence.

The wall was covered in paper, pages and pages of it. Pictures of people and a bird's-eye view of the manor house were connected with pieces of red string.

'Please tell me you haven't used Blu Tack to stick that up?' Colin said.

'Why?'

'It stains the wall. I don't fancy paying some bill to have it cleaned.'

Adam waved his concerns away with a flick of his wrist. He stood slightly to the side of his masterpiece, and Colin saw the glint in his eye that preceded a show. He pulled the chair out from below the table and sat down in front of the mass of paper, feeling very much like a pupil in Adam's classroom.

Before Adam began, he asked his friend to give him the skinny on what he'd found out from the receptionist. As he relayed his story, Colin thought that the information he was giving was slotting nicely into whatever theory Adam had conjured up in his absence, judging from the look on his face.

'No CCTV?' Adam asked when Colin had finished.

His friend's face fell.

'I didn't check.'

'Luckily, I did. Yesterday. There aren't any cameras on the exterior and none that I can see in the inside either. Do you want to hear what I've come up with?'

Colin nodded.

'Now,' said Adam, assuming a theatrical air. 'I'm not saying this is what happened or anything, only what I've managed to piece together.'

He pointed first to the pictures of the people he'd stuck up – profile pictures from Facebook, judging by the varied poses and locations of the photos.

Colin took in the list of suspects.

Sam, the blackmailed groom.

Ross, the twin who lost out on being best man.

Vicky, the ex-girlfriend who Danny had sex with.

Neil, Vicky's boyfriend who may or may not have known about his girlfriend's infidelity.

'I printed these off before finding out about the phone, so my theory has changed slightly. I still think it could be any one of these, but I think they are working with someone.'

'Who?'

'Whoever came by car and gave Danny the cash. There's no way of telling who that is yet.'

Colin mulled it over. It would make sense that whoever handed the money over would be behind the murder. But he knew it couldn't physically be that person because the receptionist heard them drive away. Could they have teamed up with someone in the house to get their money back and take away any further blackmailing opportunities?

'Makes sense,' Colin said, eyes focussed on the wall again. 'Is there anyone we can rule out?'

Adam considered this.

'I think we should keep them all in mind at the minute, but Neil is probably the easiest to rule out. The rest were definitely in the house and aware of Danny wronging them in some way. Neil was probably on his way home, oblivious to his girlfriend cheating on him. If only we had CCTV, we could clarify a few things.'

'I know where we can go,' Colin said, his eyes widening. 'But first, get the Blu Tack off the walls.'

14

LIFE THROUGH A LENS

'WE COULD'VE WALKED,' Colin said, watching the blur of hedgerows and sheep out of the passenger side window. 'It's really not that far.'

Keeping his eyes on the narrow road, Adam tapped the digital clock in the middle of the dashboard.

'Time is of the essence, dear boy,' he said. 'If someone intends to cancel the wedding through another act of violence, I think they will do it tonight. That means we must act swiftly.'

It sounded impressive, but unconvincing. Adam could feel the withering look his friend was giving him.

'And it's hot and I'm lazy, alright. Give me a break.'

Instead of turning left out of the stately home's long driveway, they'd turned right. Colin had protested that the petrol station was the other way, but Adam had held up an annoying, placating hand without parting with further explanation.

For a few miles they travelled at a steady pace, passing nothing but farms and fields of animals. A dog had chased the car half-heartedly for less than twenty seconds, running out of steam at the bottom of a small incline.

Eventually, Adam indicated into a driveway and turned the car, travelling back in the direction they'd just come from.

'I just wanted to make sure that there were no main roads nearby that could've been used to access our hotel. When we look at the CCTV, if he lets us see it, we can be sure that coming past the petrol station was the only way to get to the hotel – and to Danny.'

They made their way down the road, past the hotel, and pulled into the empty forecourt of the petrol station, coming to a stop at one of the two pumps.

Adam got out, twisted the petrol cap and inserted the pump. He put some diesel in, mindful of his limited funds, and replaced the pump before walking across the oil-stained concrete and into the building.

A woman with grey, frizzy hair sat behind the counter, separated from the customers by a wall of glass. Her brown eyes were magnified by oversized glasses, lending her a rather comical appearance.

Adam walked up to her with a disarming smile plastered on his face. He slipped a note into the cut-out section and watched her check that it was real by gliding a pen across its surface. Happy, she rang the register and set the note in.

'Anything else, dear?' she asked with a smile.

He leaned conspiratorially towards her.

'I don't suppose you heard about what happened up at Milton Manor last night?'

Sorrow pulled her features into a sympathetic frown.

'Yes, dear,' she nodded gravely. 'There have been a few youngsters down from there today to buy cigarettes and cheaper alcohol than they serve up at that place. I heard a young boy died.'

Adam confirmed the story with a nod, trying to figure out how to get around to his request. It was Colin who broke the silence.

'Daniel was a good friend of ours. He was due to be best man at the wedding. The police think that his death was accidental, but we believe it might've been something more sinister than that.'

'Oh, God,' she gasped. 'How do you mean?'

Adam held back a smile. Colin knew that old people loved a bit of gossip. What he'd just done was plonk a metaphorical pile of gold on her counter, just out of reach. All they needed to do now was let her know that they'd nudge it her way if she gave them something in exchange.

'That's what we're trying to find out,' Colin continued. 'You see, we're following a few leads…'

'I thought you said the police had drawn their conclusion already,' she interrupted.

'We're not the police, we're…'

'…private investigators,' Adam finished. 'And we'd like to look at your CCTV cameras, if we could. We believe it could help us crack the case.'

SHE STUDIED THE lads through the glass. She'd watched a lot of detective dramas over the years and these two young fellas, in their shorts and T-shirts, didn't look much like real detectives. They usually wore suits. But then, nothing this exciting ever happened around these parts and they seemed like nice boys. If she could play a small part in solving a case, she'd do it.

She looked out of the window to make sure no one was on the forecourt before summoning them around the counter and into the back room.

THE ROOM WAS not very big and what little space there was, was taken up by excess stock. On a small desk, next to a door on the back wall, was a monitor. Black-and-white footage played on it in real time, judging by the date and time stamp in the bottom left-hand corner of the screen. A computer hummed steadily under the desk, the blue light around the power button casting some brightness into the otherwise gloomy room.

'My son set this up after someone filled their tank and did a runner. I have no idea how to use it, but I'm sure you will. Your generation are much better at these things than us old fogies.'

She left and reappeared a few minutes later, carrying two bottles of water.

'For the workers,' she said with a smile as she set the bottles on the table. She checked if they wanted anything else and when they declined, she left them to it.

Adam hunkered down in front of the monitor and navigated through the menu with the mouse. He quickly found the file that would show them the footage they would need and loaded it up. They waited patiently while the antiquated machine worked, the computer whining loudly with the effort. Eventually, the screen changed.

It was much darker than the footage they'd just seen on the screen, due to the action taking place at night and there being no streetlights in the vicinity.

The footage began at 10 p.m.

Adam checked his notes. The burner phone's battery had long since died but luckily Adam had written the details of the message on a piece of paper. The message informing Danny that his visitor had arrived had been received at 12:51 a.m., so Adam fast forwarded to 12:40 a.m.

They watched the unchanging blackness on the screen for a while, until, at 12:48 a.m., a pair of headlights passed by and headed up the road towards the hotel. It passed too quickly to get any details and even when Adam rewound the footage and paused it, the footage was too distorted to make out the make or model.

So far, so unhelpful. Adam felt his heart sink at the thought of getting so close to an answer, only for it to evaporate when it was within grabbing distance.

They waited with bated breath for the car's return.

At 12:55 a.m., it came.

This time, lady luck was on their side.

Rather than pass by at speed, it pulled into the forecourt, where it idled for a minute, thick smoke pouring out of its wide exhaust. Adam pressed pause.

The graininess of the footage meant that they could not see the driver and the make and model of the car still eluded them, though Adam was sure that that information would be discernible to a genuine petrolhead. Sadly, neither of them were that bothered by cars.

One detail that could be seen was very useful indeed.

The next little breadcrumb of the case was laid before them. Adam scribbled down the details of the number plate that was lit up for them like a neon sign.

Now, all they had to do was figure out who the car belonged to.

With some progress made, Adam unscrewed the top of his water and glugged half the bottle, not realising just how thirsty he was. He set the bottle down again and watched the screen.

They let the footage run for a few more minutes, just in case. While they watched the blackness on the screen, they discussed their next steps.

Pins and needles began to prickle in Adam's legs and as he attempted to change his position, he knocked the bottle of water over, tipping it onto the computer's keyboard.

'You dickhead,' whispered Colin, looking round the stockroom for anything they could use to mop up the spillage. He grabbed an old cloth from the sink and dabbed at the keys, hoping to soak up the moisture before it seeped into the circuitry.

Happy that no lasting damage had been done, they turned their attention back to the screen. In the watery mayhem, one of them had pressed a button that made the footage move in double time. When they looked back, the time stamp showed that the footage had moved forward by nearly an hour.

As Adam moved the mouse to close the footage, Colin grabbed his wrist. On the screen, moving slowly from the direction of the hotel, was another car without its lights on. It was easy to tell that this was not the same car, due to the shorter body.

'What a stroke of luck,' Adam said, staring with disbelief at the screen as the car crept down the road and out of sight.

'So, whoever was in the first car delivered the money to Danny and whoever was in the second car took it back by lethal force. Do you reckon that's our killer?' Colin asked.

'I'm certain of it.'

15

THE DINNER

THE STATELY HOME reminded Adam of a game of Cluedo. Whichever door you opened, there was some grandiose room behind it.

The dining room was no different.

A long table filled the middle of the large room, the antique oak so polished you could almost see yourself in it. Heavy silver cutlery flanked intricately designed plates that looked like they cost more than Adam's whole kitchen at home. An ornate chandelier bathed the room in light.

Most of the places were already taken, so Adam took a seat between Sam and Emily's father, Trevor. He nodded a greeting at the rest of the table, not wanting to interrupt conversations already in full flow.

Sam, Ross and their parents were discussing something wedding related while Emily and her bridesmaids talked about the songs they hoped the band would play tomorrow night. Emily's parents were running their fingers up and down a drinks menu, choosing which wines to buy for the impending meal.

Adam snuck a look at the prices and gulped. He sincerely hoped that the bill was on the Campbell family!

Sitting silently on the other side of the table was Mike, Emily's brother. His shirt was so fitted around his huge arms that Adam worried the blood would reach an impasse at his biceps and fail to flow to his fingers. His eyes were downcast towards the table, but his demeanour suggested he wasn't in the mood for family time. Perhaps the stress of the weekend was getting to him.

Adam wished Colin could have come, but he'd been told that the meal was strictly for the wedding party.

A waiter approached the besuited Trevor, who ordered enough bottles of wine to get an army drunk. The waiter nodded his head sagely, approving of the choices as a sommelier would, before backing slowly out of the room towards the kitchens.

Trevor adjusted his position in his seat, turning to look at Adam with all the grace of a ship's turning circle. His huge buttocks hung over the side of the seat and Adam could smell the perspiration seeping through his heavy suit jacket.

'How are you, son?' he asked.

Adam and Trevor engaged in idle chit-chat for a while, before the first course arrived. Silence fell as spoons were plucked from the table and soup was ladled into mouths. Adam took great care not to spill any on his white shirt.

When empty bowls had been collected, Emily's mother, Cynthia, got to her feet. She tapped the stem of her wine glass with a fork, bringing silence to the room once more.

'The Campbell and the McMullan families would just like to say thank you to you all for being here tonight. Weddings are stressful at the best of times, but when you consider what has happened this weekend… well…' she trailed off.

Trevor took over, hoisting his considerable frame from his seat with a loud grunt.

'What my wife is trying to say, is thank you to the young ones. You've looked after Sam and Emily under difficult circumstances, not just this weekend but in the lead up to the wedding too.'

He glanced at the empty chair at the head of the table.

'Daniel Costello was a good boy, and we were shocked and saddened by what has happened to him. I've known his father for many years. Sam, my future son-in-law, has lost his best man and a friend, as have many of you. Please, let's raise a glass in his memory.'

Everyone stood with arms extended towards the vacant chair and clinked their glasses.

The remainder of the meal passed without incident. Adam held a hand over his glass every time an offer of more wine was made. He was sure he'd never have another chance to sample a £50 bottle again, but he was determined to remain sober.

Whoever murdered Danny was going to be brought to justice tonight, he was sure of it, and for that he needed a clear head.

After the meal, the party made their way into the barroom, which was decorated in much the same manner as last night. Beige pop music was playing, though the dancefloor was empty. It felt like déjà vu to Adam, who, for a minute, had the ridiculous notion that he had been given an opportunity to intervene with fate; to stop Danny's life from ending in the way it had.

He shook his head, keen not to let his imagination run away from him. He checked his watch. Night was drawing in fast and they still had so much to do. He clocked Colin by the bar, ordering a drink.

'You best be keeping a clear head,' Adam said, sidling up to his friend.

A glass of water was passed across the bar at exactly that moment. Colin motioned to it much the same way as an assistant might highlight the star prize on a corny gameshow, before picking out the slice of lemon and throwing at Adam's face. He watched with satisfaction as it bounced off his forehead.

'We've got to leave it until people are slightly more drunk,' Adam said, moving to a table with two seats.

'What do we do until then?' Colin asked, placing his pint glass on a coaster.

'We watch.'

AN HOUR LATER, and the dancefloor was filled. Those who had arrived late to the party were well oiled, no doubt thanks to pre-drinks in bedrooms with the alcohol purchased earlier from the petrol station at the end of the road. The pop playlist had been replaced by a function band, who stormed through songs that would be repeated tomorrow night after the speeches – whipping the crowded dancefloor into a frenzy with genuine wedding classics.

The finishing notes of *Come On, Eileen* rang out as the band downed their instruments and concluded their first set of the night, to much cheering from the appreciative horde.

As the dancefloor emptied, Adam seized his chance. He walked up to the microphone and tapped it to make sure it was on. A couple of dull thuds sounded through the PA system. The singer looked over at what he assumed was a drunken karaoke singer, but Adam held up a pacifying finger.

'A car with the number plate HFZ 4531 is blocking a staff member's car. Who does it belong to?'

This moment was not lost on Adam. Whoever held their hand up was admitting to owning the car that had stopped at the petrol station last night. The car that had just visited Danny to hand over money.

Trevor's hand shot up.

Adam left the microphone behind and walked over to him as he was pushing himself out of his seat. His eyes were unfocused and his cheeks rosy – he was certainly in no condition to drive.

'After all that wine at dinner, I'm not sure you're fit to get behind the wheel,' Adam smiled. 'I'll move it for you, Mr Campbell.'

Trevor pushed the keys into Adam's sweaty palm and patted him on the back with enough force to knock him forward a few steps.

Shaking slightly, he made his way out of the bar. Colin was waiting at reception and the two of them walked outside into the crisp air, their eyes hovering over each number plate in search for the car they needed.

Adam pressed a button on the keys, causing orange lights to blink in the encroaching darkness. They made their way to the expensive car and got in. It started with a faint purr, not like the spluttering his own rusty Clio produced upon coming to life.

He moved the car from its current position to a spot around the corner, out of sight of the windows from the bar. Here, out of the way of prying eyes, they had time to search for what they suspected might be hidden.

Adam opened the glovebox, though it was neat and orderly. Definitely nothing hidden in there. He rifled through any compartment he could, coming up empty while Colin climbed into the back of the car. He ran his hand under the mats and between the seats, again coming away empty handed.

Frustrated, he slapped the material covering the back of the passenger seat. His hand hit something solid. From the pocket, he pulled a plastic lunchbox and held it up to Adam, who stopped searching in order to appraise the find with his own eyes.

'I assume it's not food in there?' he said.

Colin ripped the plastic lid off, exposing another piece of the puzzle.

Inside was a phone. A phone that looked almost identical to the one Danny had been using as a burner.

Colin pocketed it.

'Time to find out what role Mr Campbell had in this,' he said as they exited the car.

16

THE BREAKTHROUGH

ADAM DROPPED THE keys back to Trevor, keen to make everything appear as normal as possible. The father of the bride thanked him profusely and offered to buy him a drink several times before he managed to get away. The band were back on, tearing through a Bon Jovi mega mix, and Adam was able to slip out of the room undetected.

While Adam was busy in the bar, Colin took it upon himself to partake in a little side mission. Instead of going back to their bedroom when he bid his friend goodbye, he carried on walking down the corridor towards the room Danny had previously occupied.

His first visit to the room had been necessary. The second visit had been risky, and he'd almost been caught snooping around by the authorities. Going back for a third time was surely madness. But the beginnings of a plan had formed upon leaving Trevor's car, and the plan was dependent on retrieving something from the stricken best man's room.

If he got caught, he could just act drunk and plead ignorance. He'd simply opened the door to the wrong room. And if anything, it was the staff's fault for leaving the door unlocked in the first place.

He crept down the corridor slowly, praying that the door *had* indeed been left unlocked by the staff who had other things on their minds. When he reached his destination, he cast a glance around before trying the handle. It seemed someone had been listening to his hasty prayer…

Adam and Colin arrived back at the room at roughly the same time. Adam shot his friend a quizzical look, though Colin shook his head.

Not here.

Adam opened the door to their bedroom and they entered, keen to uncover whatever evidence was stored on the phone.

Colin could feel the surge of adrenaline as the phone came slowly to life; the dim screen displaying a welcome message. He could see his friend's hand was shaking.

Adam was nervous. If Trevor *was* involved in this, it would be a major scandal on the North Coast. His business was worth more money than Adam could imagine, and it would be Adam's name forever attached to bringing it down. Also, the guy was the size of a house and built like a brick…

'Shall we see what it says?' Colin asked, noticing Adam's sudden reticence.

Adam shook himself from the image of Trevor standing over him with the veins bulging in his slab of a forehead. The call list was empty, as expected. Presumably, this phone was the only means of communication between Danny and Trevor. Danny would never have had the balls to blackmail someone by talking on the phone to them. Instead, he'd have relied on text messages – it was so much easier to say cowardly things with written words.

The presumption turned out to be correct.

Trevor was not as technologically savvy as Danny and had not thought to delete any of the messages he'd received or sent. Adam and Colin spent ten minutes taking in every detail of the correspondence, looking on with disbelieving eyes.

'Jesus,' Adam said, setting the phone down and letting the information permeate. Colin sat back in his chair and did the same. Neither spoke for a few minutes.

'So,' Colin said, eventually. 'Danny saw Sam and some random girl kiss on the stag do. He then got in contact with Mr Campbell to tell him that unless he paid Danny to keep the information to himself, he might accidently let that information slip to Emily who would be devastated.'

'£50 to start with, which Trevor probably thought was a one-off payment and worth it to stop a load of hassle. No wonder Sam said things have been tense between Trevor and him – imagine your future father-in-law knew you'd been unfaithful and was paying to cover it up!'

'So, he paid the money but then got another text from Danny a week later saying that he was feeling loose lipped and that he'd need another £50 to guarantee that his lips remained sealed. Then, no further correspondence until yesterday when he received another message asking for more.'

'Which he paid just after midnight. Then, an hour or so later, Danny was dead.'

'So, who is his accomplice?'

'If there is an accomplice,' Adam said. 'For all we know, Trevor has had no part in this, aside from being the victim.'

This was all becoming too much of a mind wrecker. Colin wished they'd never got involved.

'We don't know who the killer is or how they managed to persuade Danny to take tablets he was allergic to. We're no closer to solving this, and unless you fancy marching up to Trevor and asking if he is our murderer, which would be utterly ridiculous, there's no way forward.' Colin let out a long sigh. 'I need a drink. Where's your hipflask?'

Those three words hit Adam like a ton of lead.

The hipflask.

'When you searched Danny's room, did you see a hipflask that looked identical to mine?'

Colin wracked his brain but couldn't remember seeing it. He shook his head.

'I think I know who did it,' Adam said, moving to the door.

COLIN FOLLOWED ADAM down the hallway. The low rumble of the bassline and the thump of the drums drifted through the closed doors, telling them that the band were still keeping people's attention in the confines of the bar. Adam hoped that the person whose room they were about to visit was either on the dancefloor or sitting happily at a table, tapping his foot and not waiting for them behind the door.

A boy Adam recognised from school – and a girl he did not – sauntered past them, hand in hand, presumably towards one of their rooms. Adam felt a pang of annoyance. He should be enjoying the party and attempting to reap the rewards of being on the wedding party by trying to crack on with one of the bridesmaids. Instead, here he was, putting himself in harm's way to try to solve the murder of someone he didn't even *really* like.

When they reached the door they needed, Adam tried the handle, but it didn't budge. Thankfully, the room was around a corner from the main hallway and afforded them some privacy. Colin kept lookout while Adam attempted to work his magic on the lock.

For several minutes, he waggled a paperclip in the lock and was thankful to both YouTube and the ancient, basic locking system within the door when he felt it give. The door creaked open slowly.

Adam's heart raced at the thought of walking into the lion's den, but everything that this tiring day had thrown at them had led them here. He was now so close to discovering if his hunch was correct or not, and that fuelled his steps across the threshold and into the room.

Colin continued to keep watch while Adam searched the room. Aside from an open case on the floor and a few ripples on the bedcovers, one might assume the room was unused. Certainly, the keeper of the keys hadn't spent much time in here aside from getting ready for the evening's festivities.

Adam took a quick look in the obvious places but came away empty handed. He cast an eye around the room and settled on the case. Surely, if you had something to hide, it'd be in there.

He poked at some clothes, moving them out of the way while trying to keep everything as it was. As the seconds ticked by, his searching became more erratic. He tipped everything out and patted items down before moving them to the side.

'Hurry up,' Colin hissed.

'I'm going as fast as I can,' Adam whispered back.

Suddenly, something caught his eye. A colour that tugged at a memory. He grabbed the trousers and thrust his hand in the pocket, pulling out a wad of cash. He had no time to count it now, but he'd bet it totalled £200.

Sure that the hipflask was not amongst the clothes, he began scooping trousers and T-shirts up and was about to pile them back in the case when his eyes happened upon something.

In the case, sewn into the lining, was a zip. It was the same colour as the fabric and could be easily missed.

Adam pulled it slowly. In the silence, the noise of the material sounded like bison charging across a desert plain, such was the volume of the material parting.

Colin's head appeared around the doorway.

'There are footsteps on the stairs,' he whispered. 'I think someone is coming.'

Quickly, Adam reached into the compartment, his fingers knocking against something cold and hard.

His heart leapt.

He pulled the hipflask out of its hiding place and showed it to Colin. The engraved initials, D.C., twinkled in the light of the room. He reached in again and grabbed the other item – a key.

'Great,' Colin said. 'Now, let's go.'

Adam stood and watched as his friend peeked around the corner of the wall. Whoever had been ascending the stairs had obviously gone into another room along the corridor as the hallway was empty.

'Ready?' Colin asked.

Adam nodded and they both sprinted along the corridor, not stopping until they reached their room.

'WE'RE SURE IT'S him?' Colin asked when the adrenaline had once again subsided.

Adam shrugged. He looked at the pile of money, which totalled just over £300.

'The money doesn't necessarily point the finger of guilt his way. It's more than Danny had asked for. But I reckon it, coupled with the hipflask, do. Why else would he have it?'

Colin agreed, though took another few minutes to cast a spotlight over the evidence they'd uncovered, just in case they'd missed anything. He couldn't see that they had.

'How do we go about confronting him though?' Adam said.

Colin smiled at him. To his mind, it had felt like Adam had been the leader all day. Now, he had an idea. He went to his jacket and from it pulled out the item he had taken from Danny's room less than an hour ago.

Adam shot him a confused look.

'It's the phone charger for Danny's burner. I thought rather than us storming in and pointing fingers, we'd let our accused do the admitting. It's how it's usually done on TV dramas – you trick them into spilling the beans.'

'And I assume you have a plan?' Adam asked.

'That I do,' Colin answered.

17

A MEETING IN THE MOONLIGHT

ADAM TYPED A message on Danny's now charged burner. He kept it short and sweet and when he was happy, pressed send. Instantly, an alert appeared on Trevor's phone, telling him that a message had been received.

Part one of the plan was in place.

As he set the phone down on the table, a strange longing took him. Sure, he loved his modern smartphone with the world at his fingertips, but there was something brilliant about a phone that you could still play *Snake* on and only needed to be charged once a week.

While Adam was taking care with that side of the plan, Colin dealt with the other. When he was finished, he nodded at his friend.

'Twenty minutes or so,' he said.

Adam let out a long sigh. He was jittery, and his foot was tapping a rhythm on the carpet with such ferocity that it sounded like a death metal blast beat. Colin knew how he felt. The plan was in place, the adrenaline was flowing and all they could do was wait.

Time ticked by slowly. After ten minutes that felt like a lifetime, Adam stood.

'I can't stand it anymore,' he said. 'By the time we put phase one into motion, phase two will be ready.'

'Five more minutes,' Colin answered. 'We don't want to rush in and be out of our depth.'

'Three minutes,' Adam countered, and Colin ceded defeat with a quick nod.

COLIN LOOKED AT the time on his watch. If this evenings' entertainment was following last night's timescale, the music would be stopping in about ten minutes and the bar would be emptying out. If they were to be successful, they needed to get in and out of the bar as if partaking in a military operation.

They walked down the stairs, noticing more people in the foyer than anticipated. Perhaps the band were finishing early. Adam swore under his breath and picked up the pace, crossing the wooden floor in double time.

To their relief, the function room was still crowded. The band were storming through a rousing rendition of Dancing Queen and everyone on the dancefloor was showing their appreciation by singing along loudly.

Colin spotted their target in the middle of a dance circle with his back to them. He felt Adam tap him on the arm. He looked at where his friend was pointing – at one of the tables near the back of the room. The lights from the band's rig lit up the table at random intervals, allowing Colin to see a fashionable jacket draped over the back of a chair.

'Is that his?' he asked.

Adam confirmed it was.

Colin took a deep breath. If he was seen by the owner of the jacket, the plan would burst into flames. Before his courage could desert him, he took a step in the direction of the jacket, picking up the pace as he crossed the carpeted floor.

When he reached the table, he thrust Trevor's mobile phone into a pocket of the velvety jacket and moved away from it as quickly as he could, as if it were about to blow up.

He retraced his steps back to the edge of the dancefloor, keeping out of the light as best he could. He cast covert glances at the owner of the jacket and was pretty sure he hadn't been spotted. As he and Adam slipped out of the door, the band announced that they only had one song left.

So far, things were going to plan.

ADAM CHECKED HIS watch again. Twenty minutes had passed and nothing had happened. He wondered if the ambitious plan had been thwarted.

'What do we do?' he said.

Colin shrugged.

'Nothing's changed,' he said. 'He'll be here.'

Though his words were firm, his tone was not. Adam could hear the doubt in his voice, but, having no plan B, they did all they could do – wait.

Colin looked out of the large window of the marquee. It framed the full moon that hung in the inky, cloudless sky, illuminating the sprawling lawn outside.

It was like something from a fairy tale and he would've normally savoured such a picturesque scene, were it not for the fact they were waiting for a killer to appear in their midst.

Suddenly, a shadow appeared on the grass outside, growing longer by the second. A minute later, the fabric doors at the rear of the marquee flapped open and there he stood, bathed in the warm light of the moon.

'You two?' he said, noticing Adam and Colin at the front of the domed tent. 'You're the blackmailers?'

'Not really,' said Adam. 'Sorry, Mike, but we needed to make you think that to get you to come here. You see, we've figured out that it was you who killed Danny.'

'Very clever,' said Mike, holding up his father's burner phone. 'You used dead Danny's phone to send another blackmailing message to my father and put it in my pocket, knowing I'd see it and rise to it. Well, A+ for creativity.'

Adam snorted. The shy, retiring Michael Campbell of a few years ago would never have used such a corny line. But it seemed it wasn't only his appearance that had undergone a makeover.

'How did you figure out it was me then?' he asked.

Adam wished that they weren't so far away from each other. It made sense to stay away, of course; he was a murderer after all, but Adam's throat was beginning to hurt from having spoken so much today. And now he was expected to communicate from such a distance. He considered ringing the burner in Mike's hand, but thought it a bit over the top. Colin would never let him live it down.

'Well,' he said. 'we don't know everything, so we're hoping you can help us fill in a few blanks.'

Mike said nothing, so Adam continued.

'We knew Danny was blackmailing somebody on account of him having met with someone who gave him an envelope full of cash. We just didn't know who had given it to him. Luckily, a kindly lady at the petrol station down the road let us look at her CCTV footage. We saw your dad's car park up not long after Danny took receipt of the money.'

He cleared his throat, longing for a soothing mouthful of Lemsip.

'We knew your dad couldn't have killed him because we saw him drive away, though we suspect he's involved in some way. But another car came past a while later. Your car, I assume.'

Mike nodded.

'You see, when I saw you at the party, you weren't drunk at all. You made a scene to make it *look* like you were drunk. How could someone who was falling over themself drive a car? It was clever, I'll give you that.'

'I was hoping to remain unseen,' Mike said. 'When you bumped into me, I had to come up with something on the spot.'

'It was convincing,' admitted Adam. 'And it definitely threw us off the scent.'

'So, what put you back on it?'

'Colin found the tablet package you left in Danny's bin. Everyone knows he is allergic, so would have had no reason to have them. That's when we knew it was definitely murder. Then, we broke into your room and found his room key that you stole from Ross's jacket and Danny's hipflask. We just don't know how you actually got him to take the tablets.'

'Very clever,' Mike said, taking a seat in the back row. 'Shall I tell you my side of things?'

He took a steadying breath.

'After I got back from the stag do, dad was miserable. I didn't know why, but he was angry with everyone, even Emily. That's when I knew things were bad. Then, one day, I saw him with this old Nokia. He left it lying about and I saw the messages, I knew what Danny was up to.'

'Does your dad know that you know?'

'No,' he said. 'He has no idea. He would've kept paying to keep Sam's disgusting secret from his darling daughter Emily forevermore.'

'So, you took matters into your own hands?'

'I was hoping to remain unseen last night. When you saw me, I was looking for Danny to have a chat to try to persuade him to ease off. I saw Sam and him have a fight and watched him storm off. I was going to follow him then, but I needed him in a more receptive mood, so I waited. Later, I saw Sam come back from Danny's room and give Ross a key. I assumed it was for his room so I stole it when Ross was dancing.'

'And you paid Danny a visit?'

'I did. I went to his room. He was on his way out and, when he saw me, started to brag about controlling dad like a puppet. He wouldn't listen to what I had to say, so I walked around the corner and waited for him to leave. When I knew he was gone, I went back and popped some dissolving tablets into the hipflask. And then I waited for him to come back. As soon as he came in, I punched him, got him on the bed and held his mouth open while I poured a cocktail of whiskey and paracetamol down his throat. He tried to resist, but it didn't take long for his airways to close up and he died pretty quickly.'

Colin was astonished at how casual Mike had told his story – like he was telling them about a nice bike ride he'd been on.

'How did you know he was allergic?' he asked.

Mike snorted.

'Because he wouldn't stop going on about it on the stag do. He made it seem as if suffering through a hangover without painkillers was the same as being crucified. So, I pocketed that information to be used at a later date.'

'But why?' Colin asked, rage seeping into his words.

'Why?' Mike asked as he pushed himself to standing. 'Because him and Sam were the reason school was hell for me. They were the reason everyone else thought it was OK to pick on me or throw my lunch on the roof or…'

He trails off for a minute, before composing himself.

'And then, to find out Sam McMullan is marrying into my family was the last straw. Everyone knew Danny was a dick, but no one knew how awful Sam could be. I knew I had to find a way to get the wedding cancelled.'

'Why not just tell your sister about Sam kissing the girl on his stag?'

'Because I didn't want to hurt her, directly. Yes, I know she's dad's favourite and all, but we're close. She didn't deserve such blunt honesty.'

'So, you killed a man instead, in the hope that that would force the wedding to be called off?'

'Honestly,' he said. 'I didn't mean to kill him. I thought maybe he'd have a massive reaction, and we'd call the ambulance, and he'd be fine but Sam wouldn't have been able to go through with the wedding or something. But, hearing him brag about taking money from my family and watching him swan around like he owned the place, well… it changed my mind. The world is a better place without Daniel Costello.'

With his spiel finished, silence filled the marquee.

'So, what next?' Mike asked.

'What's next is that you are under arrest for the murder of Daniel Costello,' said a gruff voice from the door.

Adam and Colin watched as the small team of police officers slid from their hiding places and swarmed Mike, taking him to the ground before slipping cuffs over his wrists. One of the officers read him his rights as he was dragged into a standing position by the others.

Mike cast a pleading glance back at Adam and Colin as he was led out of the marquee towards the waiting unmarked police car at the end of the gardens.

Adam and Colin collapsed into their seats; the fatigue of a long, punishing day washing over them. Adam took the hipflask from his pocket and unscrewed the lid before taking a huge slug. He passed it to his friend.

'I'll tell you what,' Colin said, between mouthfuls. 'The old folk at work are going to love hearing about this.'

18

A GROWING REPUTATION

THREE WEEKS LATER

ADAM FLICKED HIS hair to one side, before changing his mind and sweeping it to the other. He looked in the mirror on the underside of the sun visor to make sure he'd made the correct decision before turning to Colin, who was in the back seat.

'Ready for a big night out?' he asked.

Colin flashed him a smile. The local nightclub, Atmosphere, always promised fun. The only tragic thing was, they were being driven there by Adam's mum, who had insisted that paying over the odds for a taxi was stupid.

'It's a shame Sam and Emily decided to cancel the wedding,' she said. 'But, if there's infidelity at the start, it's not a good foundation to build a marriage on. Sam has a bit of growing up to do.'

She looked at her son, who was drumming along to some abrasive metal song. When she'd heard what he had gotten up to on the weekend of the wedding, he had gone up a notch in her estimations. She smiled as she pulled into a space a few hundred metres away from the club, knowing they'd be mortified if she dropped them right outside the door.

To her surprise, Adam leant across and planted a sloppy kiss on her cheek. She assumed it was because of the several beers he'd had in his room with Colin before they'd left, but she appreciated the sentiment, anyway.

'Be safe,' she said as he slipped out of the door. Colin waved at her as they crossed the road.

ADAM AND COLIN stood at the bar, neither of them quite drunk enough to dance yet. They were jostled side to side as they attempted to order a round of drinks, eventually managing to do so. Beers in hand, they walked through an archway into a quieter part of the club.

They took a seat and talked about anything and everything for a while. After a few more beers, Adam felt the alcohol start to take hold of him. He could feel his thoughts drift and his speech slur.

Colin watched his friend's eyes start to squint slightly as the volume of his words increased.

What a lightweight, he thought.

Their conversation was interrupted by a high-pitched squeal. They looked round to find Zoe, one of Emily's bridesmaids, on her hands and knees, having tripped over the leg of a chair. Her friends were laughing so much they weren't even bothering to help, instead filming her squirm helplessly on the floor on their smartphones.

Adam jumped out of his chair and extended a helping hand. Zoe looked up and beamed at him, recognition spreading across her face.

'Do you just go around rescuing everyone who is in need?' she asked, touching his chest.

Adam tried to ignore the light touch on his chest and attempted to say something witty, causing Colin to cringe at what actually came out. Zoe didn't seem to notice, and if she did, she didn't care.

'I thought what you did at the wedding was very brave,' she said, grabbing his hand. 'Do you want to dance with me?'

Adam looked at Colin with wide eyes.

Colin nodded at him, as if encouraging a child to take its first steps. He watched as Zoe led Adam away. Her friends, who had laughed at her misfortune, sat down at a nearby table. Colin vaguely recognised them from the wedding weekend. One of them glanced across.

'I recognise you from the papers,' she said. 'Didn't you help solve the murder too?'

Colin nodded, getting up from his seat and moving to their table.

'I was the brains behind the whole thing,' he said.

-2-

DEAD IN THE WATER

CHRIS MCDONALD

1

COLD IS THE WATER

MATTHEW HENDERSON WAS in a bad mood as he watched the lights from the houses on the other side of the river reflect and distort in the dark water.

Tonight's practice had been a disaster.

With the race so close, he had expected more effort and urgency from the team. As captain, it was his job to get them going, but seemingly no matter what he tried tonight, it wasn't getting through.

He'd started with a rousing team talk at the beginning of the evening, keen to get everyone in the mood. The others had sat on the wooden benches in the club house, nodding their heads, though Matthew could tell the vibe was off—they were simply going through the motions.

He'd shrugged it off, thinking perhaps that they just wanted to get out onto the water. But that hadn't been the case either. Once in the boat, there'd been the same level of lethargy. The strokes were not in time and the cox looked like he'd been on a massive bender the night before, his face green before they'd even pushed off from the bank.

Matthew had cut the practice short and insisted on a team meeting once back on dry land. Upon reaching the jetty, they'd tethered the nine-man rowing boat and the single seater canoe to the moorings and had all stomped back to the building.

He'd started gently—softly, softly, catchy monkey and all that—though, when he realised his words were barely making a ripple let alone the waves he wanted, Matthew had unleashed a storm. He'd given the team a collective bollocking and had then moved on to individual reprimands. By the time he was finished, his face was blotchy and his throat raw.

'Catch yourself on!' one of the team had shouted back.

'It's hardly the bloody Olympics, is it?' another had muttered, before storming out.

One or two followed but the rest had remained and a huge argument had followed. Hurtful words had been exchanged and the night might even have ended in violence, had a few of the lads not got between Simon, the vice-captain of the team, and Matthew.

Once things had calmed slightly, he'd dismissed them all with a warning—come back tomorrow with a better attitude or he'd find more suitable team mates who shared his drive.

And now, as he walked down the jetty towards the small canoe, his headtorch providing the only light, he thought about the accusations that had been levelled at him.

That he cared too much.

That he wasn't a good captain.

That he was only doing this for the prize money, anyway.

Screw them, he thought, pushing the thoughts from his mind as he bent down to pull the canoe from the water.

And then, he heard something.

A noise from near the building.

He let go of the canoe and straightened up, peering in the direction the noise had come from, though the headtorch's beam was no match for the night's inky blanket.

He couldn't see anything.

'Is somebody there?' he called into the black, but he received no reply.

We need to get that security light fixed, he thought, and dismissed the noise as nothing more than an animal scurrying across the gravel. He once again turned his attention to the canoe bobbing in the freezing cold water.

His fingers closed around the rope securing it to the post and as he pulled it towards him, he heard rapid footsteps behind him on the wooden jetty.

He turned from his task once more to be greeted by a familiar face.

'Back for another round, are you?' Matthew said, drawing himself to his full height, hoping to be as intimidating as possible.

'I just thought you might've… I don't know… reconsidered.'

'I thought I was pretty clear earlier when I told you to f…'

His sentence was cut short as the figure lunged at him, though he was too slow to defend himself.

A hefty whack was delivered to the front of his head, and as he struggled to make sense of what was happening, he felt the solid ground disappear from below him. Pain surged up his back as he collided heavily with the edge of the jetty, before tumbling into the river. His senses immediately became overloaded by the shock of how cold the water was.

His head bobbed below the waterline and, as he resurfaced, he fought hard to take in as much air as possible, though already his body was beginning to shut down.

The person on the jetty was on their knees, holding out a hand that Matthew couldn't reach, and yelling something, though the words were lost on the wind.

The river was playing with Matthew now; tossing him around like a ragdoll, away from the safety of the river bank and away from the helping hand.

The same hand that had just sentenced him to his death.

2

FORE!

THE SUN WAS shining and not a cloud was to be found in the sky above the Stonebridge Memorial Golf Club—a sprawling eighteen-hole links course on the north coast of Northern Ireland.

Many of the holes hugged the rugged coastline, though this was not something Harry Gallagher had had to concern himself with. Every shot he had hit during his round so far had travelled as straight as an arrow along the fairway.

His approach on the ninth hole was no different. There sat the little white, dimpled ball; dead centre. He strode along the short grass with a smile on his face and the warmth on his back, quietly plotting his next shot.

He reached his ball and looked up, calculating the distance to the pin. He was no expert, but he held a finger up to check the wind speed and direction. Really, he had no idea what he was doing, but it made him look professional and he knew it would be annoying the life out of his friend.

He pulled a pitching wedge from his bag and took a few practice swings, the air around him making a swooshing sound as his club cut through it. Happy with his movement, he approached the ball and mentally prepared himself, before bringing the club down and making perfect contact.

He watched as the ball sailed in a perfect arc before bouncing off the top of the mound at the front of the green and rolling to a stop a few feet from the flag. He put the club between his legs and paraded around as if he was riding a horse. He knew his friend was watching, so he yeehawed loudly and slapped his bottom for extra comedic effect.

He looked around to see if Gary was enjoying his enthusiastic celebrations and was met with a sullen face.

I suppose I'd be annoyed too if my scorecard looked like his, thought Harry.

He replaced the club in the bag, hoisted it onto his shoulder and carried it across to the long grass to help Gary search for his ball. The vegetation was thick and it took them both a few minutes of poking around to locate it.

'Ha, good luck with that shot,' Harry said.

Gary simply huffed and chose his club. With his mood growing worse by the second, he didn't bother with a practice swing. Instead, he swung wildly, smacking the top of the ball which simply served to drive it deeper into the rough.

'That counts as a shot,' laughed Harry.

'Can't I just move it?' Gary asked. 'I'm never getting it out of here.'

Harry considered this for a moment, holding his thumb out sideways like the emperor in Gladiator, before jerking it skywards.

'Normally I'd say no, but since you've got no chance of catching me, I'll be kind.'

'You're far too generous, Arseholius,' Gary replied.

His current ball was deep in prickly gorse, and it looked like he didn't want to add injury to insult. Those spikes would make mincemeat of his delicate hands.

Instead, he turned his back on that one and reached into the front pocket of his golf bag, his hand closing around another ball. He had almost run out, having lost an unholy amount already today. He chose a flat spot on the fairway and dropped his latest victim. He breathed deeply and took some time to consider which club to use.

'I chose a pitching wedge, but you'll probably need a bit more power,' Harry interrupted, unable to contain himself.

'It'll be your kneecaps getting hit rather than this ball if you don't shut it,' Gary replied, causing Harry to howl with laughter.

Gary approached the ball and swung. It followed a similar path to Harry's, though in an effort to get to the flag he'd put a bit too much into his backswing. Rather than bob onto the green, it had skidded across the slick surface and fallen off the back.

Towards the edge of the cliff.

Gary threw his club on the ground and mumbled obscenities as he marched off towards it. Harry grabbed the bags and followed him, trying not to laugh. He knew better than to make another jibe—his friend seemed close to the edge.

Literally and figuratively.

'Oh my God!' screamed Gary, leaping away from the clifftop.

'Don't worry, man. If you've lost your last ball, I'll lend you one. Has it gone in the sea?' Harry replied, reaching his friend. His brow furrowed as he noticed how pale Gary had become.

Harry carefully approached the edge and peeked over, immediately seeing the source of Gary's surprise.

On the rocks at the bottom of the cliff, where the mouth of the River Bann meets the sea, lay a body. The exposed arms and legs were a mottled grey and the navy vest and shorts were soaked against the skin. One shoe was missing and the face looked to be covered in blood.

From his vantage point, Harry couldn't make out who it was.

One thing was for sure, though. Whoever it was, was no longer in the land of the living.

'Call the police,' Harry managed, before throwing up in a nearby shrub.

3

MADE OF THE WHYTE STUFF

ADAM WHYTE STRODE across the grass pushing the lawnmower. He moved the cord out of his way and continued, smiling to himself as he imagined a football pitch with its intricate patterns.

Mrs Laverty's lawn wasn't *that* big, but large enough to keep him busy for another half an hour or so. He looked at the house and saw the corner of the curtain twitch. The lady of the house may be old, but she had high standards and the reactions of an owl. He laughed to himself before noticing clumps of grass starting to form, so he paused to empty the collected grass into one of his heavy-duty sacks.

Once the lawnmower's basket was reattached, he continued with his job. His thoughts turned to all that had happened in the past month, since he and his friend Colin had solved a murder case. They'd become local celebrities for a few weeks and been in the newspapers, much to the local police's annoyance who'd written the death off as accidental and had been made to look foolish by a couple of amateur sleuths.

In the weeks that had followed the case, his attitude to life had changed. Gone was the young man who was happy to waste his days on the sofa. In his place was the new and improved Adam Whyte. The Adam Whyte who had set up his own garden maintenance business and, for the past two weeks, had gone from house to house, weeding, mowing lawns and brushing the leaves that had begun to fall as Summer made way for Autumn.

Most of his customers were little old ladies who couldn't manage with the more demanding aspects of gardening any longer. He'd do the dirty work while they tended to the flower beds, which suited him down to the ground. He enjoyed their conversations and the chocolatey treats they'd often pass his way.

Mrs Laverty was the only one who made him feel like he was in a Diet Coke advert by spying on him as he went about his work. Still, she paid him well and never insisted on him being topless, which was a bonus for the whole street. No one needed to see what was under his T-shirt.

As he was hoisting the lawnmower into the boot of his car, his phone rang. Cursing, he set the lawnmower back on the driveway and reached into his pocket. He didn't recognise the number.

'Hello,' he answered.

'Hi, is this Adam?'

He confirmed that it was. The voice sounded younger than his usual clientele. There was a pause before she continued.

'This is Elena Henderson. I was wondering if we could meet? There is something I'd like to discuss with you.'

'All my services are on my website,' Adam said. 'Is it grass you want cutting or…'

'No, it's not that,' the voice interrupted. 'I'd like to talk about my husband's death.'

Henderson.

It only dawned on Adam once she'd repeated her surname.

Matthew Henderson was the name of the man whose body had been found by two golfers. Adam's mum had worked with his mum years ago and she'd spoken warmly of Matthew. She'd even babysat him on numerous occasions. The news had caused her to be extra clingy for a week, always checking where Adam was going when he was heading out.

'I was sorry to hear about Matthew,' Adam said. 'But, I'm not sure what help I could be to you.'

'I've read about you. How you helped your friend. I thought you might be able to do the same for me,' she said. 'Can we meet this afternoon? Say, three o'clock?'

Adam thought about his schedule. Mr McCullough would have his head if he didn't cut his grass. Today was the old man's turn to host his book group and the state of the garden was something of vast importance. The others couldn't arrive to find grass longer than two inches! Perish the thought!

'Better make it four o'clock,' Adam said, his interest suitably piqued.

ADAM CHECKED HIS watch and hurried up the main street of Stonebridge towards his favourite café, The Last Drop. He wasn't a massive fan of hot drinks, but the double chocolate muffins were to die for.

He joined the short queue and wondered if picking at a muffin during a conversation about a dead spouse was bad form. He picked up an ice-cold Coke and eyed the cake display, deciding against it.

He paid and made his way to a table by the window which looked out onto the bustling, cobbled streets of his hometown. He watched people scurry past, some clearly with somewhere to be and others happy to drift lazily from shop to shop, waiting for something to catch their eye.

The bell above the door shook him from his thoughts. A tall, attractive woman with dark hair and a red, woollen coat had just entered. She scanned the coffee shop before her eyes settled on Adam. She gave him a quick wave and pointed to the queue.

What am I doing here? Adam thought to himself, suddenly feeling out of his depth.

This poor woman had lost her husband a few short weeks ago and, for some reason, she wanted to meet him based on what she'd read about the Daniel Costello case.

He breathed deeply, trying, and failing, to settle his nerves.

A few minutes later, she sank into the seat opposite him and set her steaming mug of hot chocolate on the table. She looked him up and down and an uncertain expression drifted across her face.

She probably wasn't expecting a scrawny, short-arsed twenty something, he thought.

'Thanks for meeting me,' she said, as she unravelled the scarf from around her neck and set it on the unoccupied chair between them.

'No problem,' Adam replied.

She bit her lower lip, as if uncertain how to begin whatever it was she had to say.

'Okay,' she said, finally. 'Well… as I'm sure you know, my husband, Matthew, was found dead a few weeks ago. His body was washed up on some rocks by the golf course.'

'I read about it,' Adam said. 'I'm really sorry.'

She accepted his sympathies with a small nod of her head.

'I'm sure you also read that the police investigated it and decided it was an accidental drowning. That he simply fell into the river after training and got taken by the current.'

'Training?' Adam repeated.

'Matthew was the captain of the Stonebridge rowing team.'

The Stonebridge Regatta weekend was one of the biggest events in the town's calendar. Each year, Stonebridge took on neighbouring Meadowfield in a rowing race on the River Bann, from the Old Bridge to the Millennium Bridge—a distance of just over two miles.

The Oxford-Cambridge Boat Race paled in comparison to how seriously this race was taken by the respective teams. And how much it meant to the people of the bordering towns.

It was a rivalry for the ages and for many years it was simply for bragging rights, but a few years ago, a local business had upped the ante.

Whichever team won got to share five thousand pounds.

'And you don't agree with the police?' Adam said.

'No. Matthew was always so careful around the water. As captain, he set the example. He never shut up about water safety. I just can't believe that he'd slip and fall into the river, it's just not him.'

'And, so…'

'So, what do I want from you?' she interrupted. 'I was wondering if you would… look into things… ask a few questions.'

'You think he was murdered?'

The last word came out as a whisper.

'I do,' she nodded.

Adam felt uneasy. It wasn't that he didn't want to help her, God knows she was obviously hurting. It's just that, he wasn't qualified. He was a gardener, not a private investigator.

'I can pay you,' she said, reaching into her purse, as if sensing his reluctance.

'No,' he said, waving his hand. 'Look, I'll ask around but I can't promise anything.'

She smiled warmly at him, tears threatening to wet her eyes. In order to appear somewhat capable, Adam asked for some background information on Matthew and his death. Fifteen minutes later, Elena rose from her seat and left the café.

Adam sat for a few minutes, digesting the information he'd been given and cursing himself for agreeing to help. He pushed himself out of his seat and walked to the counter, where he ordered two muffins.

When he had finished stuffing his face, he walked out into the dying daylight and pulled out his phone. If he was investigating, he'd need his trusty partner. He found his best friend's number and pressed call, knowing that he'd be keen for another adventure.

4

ELENA HENDERSON'S THEORY EXPLORED

'ABSOLUTELY NOT,' said Colin.

He listened to Adam witter away on the other end of the phone, barely pausing for breath. When Colin tried to interject, Adam simply spoke over him. When he could take no more, he pressed the red button and cut the call. He stuffed the phone back into his locker and left the staff room, annoyed that the phone call had taken up most of his short break.

He walked down the steps and made his way into the lounge of the Stonebridge Retirement Home, his place of work. He'd been here for a number of years and loved the place—or more correctly, the people. Their bodies may be failing, but their minds weren't. They were still razor sharp and desperately funny and Colin loved each and every one of them.

Most of the residents were sitting in their seats, watching an episode of The Antiques Roadshow.

'What are you saying, Mary?' asked Fred.

Mary studied the object currently being scrutinised by the expert on TV—a willow patterned jug.

'Hundred quid,' she guessed.

'Mary says a hundred,' Fred announced, writing her guess down on a pad of paper. 'Any other takers?'

The room erupted into a cacophony of noise, each eager to get their figure heard before the expert cast his judgement, while Fred tried his hardest to note down everyone's estimates. After a minute, he hushed the room in anticipation of the specialist's ruling.

'Thirty-six pounds.' Fred laughed. 'Barry, you were bang on!'

Barry shrugged nonchalantly, though a small smile spread across his face.

'What Barry isn't telling you is that this episode is a repeat of the one him and me watched last week,' Colin said. 'He's seen it before.'

'You prick!' Fred shouted at Barry, who laughed riotously as he raised his middle finger at the group.

The noise died down as Fiona Bruce appeared on screen to introduce the next item. Barry pushed himself out of his seat and followed Colin into a smaller room which was primarily used for craft sessions.

'Rebus, I can't believe you just sold me out,' he laughed.

Since finding out about the role Colin had played in solving Danny Costello's murder a few weeks ago, Barry had stopped calling him by his real name and instead addressed him with a different detective's name whenever the two spoke.

Colin supposed he was doing it to show off how well read he was, and he secretly liked it.

'I can't believe you were trying to deceive those nice ladies in there,' Colin winked.

Barry sat down on one of the wingback chairs and watched Colin clear the table.

'You seem preoccupied, Foley,' Barry said.

'Foley?' Colin replied. 'I've not heard that one before.'

'My daughter has got me into these audiobooks. It means I can lie in my bed like a lazy bugger and have some celebrity read the story to me. This latest one is a cracker. I can't remember the name of it, though. Something about trees by a fella called Bob Barker.'

'Isn't he the American game show host?'

'I might be getting the names mixed up,' Barry shrugged. 'Anyway, don't change the subject. What's eating you?'

'I've just had a phone call from Adam. He's trying to talk me into helping him out with something.'

'Something interesting?'

'Potentially. Do you remember that body they found a few weeks ago in the river?'

Barry nodded. Colin considered how much information to relinquish. He knew that Barry didn't have a hold of his tongue and whatever he told him would be passed around the other residents like wildfire.

'Well, apparently his wife called Adam today and told him that she thinks the death was suspicious, even though the police don't. She's asked him to look into it and he's asked me to help.'

'And you're not going to?'

Barry seemed surprised.

'Why would I?'

'Son, I hope you don't mind me saying, but you spend your days with a load of old farts who have one foot in the grave and another on a banana skin. If I'm right, you don't have a lassie either, so where is the excitement in your life?'

Colin shrugged.

'Exactly. You want my advice? Go and help your friend. It might come to nothing, but at least it'll get you off the GameBoy.'

'Alright. I'll call him back and tell him I'm in. If anyone asks, I've gone to the toilet, alright?'

Barry winked at him as he left the room.

THIS WAS THE first time Colin had been in The Otter since it had been refurbished. They'd done a decent job—the character of the place remained; the brickwork and the fireplaces endured but your feet didn't stick to the carpet anymore. It was win-win.

Adam was sitting at their usual table in the corner of the room, as was a fizzing pint of lager. Colin plonked himself down in the chair and took a swift sup.

'So,' he said, replacing his glass on the table. 'What have we got?'

Adam explained what had happened, starting with the phone call from Elena and ending with the muffins.

'Two?' Colin said, more preoccupied with his friend's greed than the dead man.

'I was stressed and I couldn't decide which flavour to get, so I got both. Don't judge me.'

'So, what's next?'

'Well, after I met with Elena, I rang Daz.'

Darren Ringley was their friend and member of the Police Service of Northern Ireland.

'And what did Daz have to say?'

'I asked him about the circumstances around the discovery of the body—when he was found, when they thought he had died, all that stuff. Elena reported him missing on the 17th September and his body was found on the 19th. The injuries were consistent with those usually suffered after a fall—bruising on the arse and legs and a broken coccyx. He also had a gash on his head from where he bashed it on a rock on his way into the water. They think it probably knocked him out—that's why they reckon he drowned. Apparently, he was a pretty good swimmer and would've stood a good chance of getting out, even with the currents.'

'It sounds accidental to me,' Colin said, having weighed up the information.

'It sounds it, but when you think of the timing, it's hard to know. The boat race is only a few weeks away…'

'You can't think that someone would've killed Matthew just to win a race though?'

'Stranger things have happened,' Adam said.

'In ganglands, maybe, but not in Stonebridge.'

'Look, it could be nothing, but Elena seemed pretty sure that foul play was involved. She kept going on about how safety conscious he was and stuff.'

Colin took another pull from his pint.

'Okay, I suppose it can't hurt to look into it. Where do we start?'

'That's the spirit,' Adam said, clapping him on the back. 'I've got a few ideas, but I think we need to see where he fell in. Elena said he was always the last one at the rowing sheds, making sure the equipment was all locked away safely and what have you. I say we pay a little visit there—that'll help us decide if the investigation has legs.'

With no other information currently available, talk turned to football and one pint became two, and two became too many. At last orders, they arranged a time to meet at the sheds, had one more pint and then made their unsteady way home.

5

DOWN TO THE RIVER

ADAM GROANED AS the sound of his ringtone clattered around his head. He rolled over, grabbed the phone off his bedside table and answered it without checking who it was.

'Still on for this morning?' Colin asked.

'Yep,' Adam croaked, stifling a yawn and hearing the thickness in his voice. 'I'm just about to get in the car.'

Colin laughed.

'You're such a bad liar. You're still in your pit, aren't you? Do you want to push it back an hour?'

Adam agreed that that course of action would probably be for the best before hanging up and falling back onto his pillow. His eyes were beginning to close when his phone rang again. He put it to his ear.

'Get up, now,' Colin said, and hung up.

IT WAS A crisp Autumn day and Colin was sitting on a bench that overlooked the grey, fast flowing river. He pulled the hood of his coat up against the wind and finished checking a few things on his phone as a car pulled into the rowing club's car park.

He watched as Adam pulled his rusty Clio into a space and dragged himself out of it, before traipsing over to the bench. He pointed at the other car in the car park, a sporty Fiesta, and Colin shrugged.

'I'm going teetotal,' Adam said as he plonked himself onto the seat and massaging his temples.

'We only had five pints.'

Instead of answering, Adam took in a deep, mollifying breath of fresh air.

'So,' Colin said, 'what is it that we're looking for?'

'We need to decide whether or not it's possible that Matthew could have simply fallen in. I just want a look around to see how steep the bank is, how close the building is to the water, that kind of thing.'

With that, they pushed themselves from the bench and walked towards the rowing centre.

It was a two-storey building. The bottom half was made from red brick and had three huge, metallic shuttered doors along its front, facing onto the bank of the river. Presumably this is where the rowing boats were stored.

The top half was smoothly rendered and painted white, though some time ago. Large windows overlooked the body of water and a balcony jutted out, housing a number of tables and chairs.

Colin tried the front door but it was locked, as were all the others.

Good, he thought, *less chance of being disturbed.*

They circled the building and met at the side facing the water. The bank wasn't steep and the water was far enough away from the building that a trip would've resulted in a fall onto concrete, rather than into water.

'I checked the weather on the date Elena told you,' Colin said. 'On the 17th September, it was sunny, as were the days leading up to it. Even if he was mucking about down near the water, the grass would've been dry, so the chances of slipping would've been minimal.'

Adam nodded and Colin followed him out onto the wooden jetty which sat above the river. They watched their broken reflections in the water for a while before Adam spoke.

'There are no cameras on the building, so we have no hope of any CCTV.'

'So, what are you thinking?'

Adam puffed out his cheeks.

'It's hard to know. It seems unlikely that a safety freak could've accidentally fallen in, given how far away the building is. The water doesn't get deep for a while either, so if he'd slipped in, the water would've been shallow enough for him to simply get up from.'

'Unless he was dead before he was dropped in?'

'No,' Adam said, shaking his head. 'Daz said that the official cause of death was drowning. His lungs were full of water. So, if someone else was involved, they dumped him in the river while he was still alive.'

'That might account for the bruises. Maybe he had a fight with someone on the bank and was knocked out. Maybe whoever it was thought they'd killed him and panicked, so threw him in the water and let the river carry him away.'

'Or, it could just be a horrible accident.'

Disappointed that the answer wasn't being made clearer by the environment, they left the jetty and returned to the car park.

A tall, dark haired man with glasses slipping down the bridge of his nose was standing by the Fiesta, key in hand. He looked around when he heard Colin and Adam approach and gave them a friendly wave.

'How are you, lads?'

'Alright, thanks,' Colin answered. 'Yourself?'

'Been better. I had a few too many last night at the social club,' he pointed at the top half of the building. 'I reckon I'm just about safe to drive now.'

'Are you part of the rowing team?'

The man nodded.

'Theo Jamieson,' he said, extending a hand which they both shook while introducing themselves.

'Theo,' said Colin. 'Do you mind if we ask you a few questions?'

THOUGH HE DIDN'T like the taste of it, the smell of brewing coffee behind the counter of the café was making Adam feel almost human again and he nearly pounced on the waiter when he delivered his hot chocolate.

He took a small sip and felt the sugar take hold immediately.

Theo sat opposite them making it feel and look like a job interview.

Perhaps not the best way to put him at ease, thought Adam.

'Thanks for agreeing to chat to us,' Adam said with a smile. 'We just have a few questions about Matthew.'

Theo's face fell.

'What about him? Are you the police?'

'We're not with the police, no, but we are looking into what happened to him.'

'Didn't the police say that it was accidental drowning?'

'They did,' Colin said. 'But we may have a different opinion.'

'Well, fire away,' Theo answered.

'How did you know Matthew?'

'Through the club. I only joined last year so this would've been my first race. I was proper looking forward to it, but it looks like it's going to be cancelled.'

'Did you socialise?'

'Not really. We'd sometimes have a few pints after training, but the sessions were so intense, I'd usually prefer to go home and have a hot bath. Made it easier on the muscles the next day. Sometimes, as captain, he'd make us stay for a drink. For team bonding and whatnot.'

'And what was Matthew like?'

Theo's eyes fell to the table and he began to chew his bottom lip.

'Umm… he was, alright.'

'But not really?' Colin prodded.

'Well, I don't want to speak ill of the dead, but it seemed like being captain gave him some sort of ego trip. He wasn't well liked because he spoke down to people. As the new boy, I took it with a pinch of salt, got my head down and worked hard, but others weren't so forgiving.'

'How do you mean?'

'He handled situations badly. Anytime he felt like someone was trying to undermine him, or if he thought someone wasn't pulling their weight, he went off on one. That kind of thing wears you down over time. There have been a couple of drunken fights—nothing bad—but a few punches have been thrown in the heat of the moment.'

'Anyone in particular?'

'Most have had a run in with him at some stage, but recently it's been mainly Craig and Simon who've taken the brunt of it.'

'Do you think either of them would've…' Adam lowered his voice. '…killed him?'

'Bloody hell,' said Theo, his cheeks reddening. 'No, people don't get murdered in Stonebridge. Look, he was always the one there at the end of the practice sessions. He was the one who put the boats away and made sure everything was locked up. He probably slipped on the jetty, that's all there is to it.'

Theo lifted his coffee cup and drank the remainder in one gulp.

'I wouldn't waste any more of your time looking into it,' he said, before bidding Colin and Adam farewell and making his way to the door. They watched him walk past the window and disappear.

'Bit of an abrupt ending,' Colin said.

'Yeah, it seemed like he realised he'd said too much.'

They sat for a few silent minutes, lost in their own thoughts. In Adam's mind, Matthew's death was not the cut and dry accident that it appeared to be. Resentful team mates and fist fights were not commonplace in any team he'd been part of and definitely hinted that something wasn't right here.

'What next?' Colin asked.

'We find Craig and Simon and hope that they talk to us.'

6

LEGWORK

AN EPISODE OF Sherlock Adam had seen a million times was playing in the background as he leafed through the Stonebridge Regatta commemorative programme from 2019.

The glossy magazine belonged to his mum's collection. She hadn't missed one in twenty-four years and was excited to collect her twenty-fifth in a few weeks' time.

If it went ahead, of course.

He flipped to the middle pages where the teams for that year's race were displayed. Photographs of each member stared out at him. Some smiling with a twinkle in their eye. Others with a slight scowl on their face, as if trying to intimidate the opposition.

Adam surveyed the Stonebridge team.

Matthew Henderson was in the middle, holding the gleaming cup they'd won the previous year, with a huge grin plastered across his face. Intense, dark eyes peered out from under a heavy brow.

Beside the picture, some information was listed. Things like how many years he'd been part of the team and what his proudest moment was. Alongside it was some trivia. Bland stuff, really. What his favourite restaurant was (The Ramore) and what he'd do with one million pounds (buy a Ferrari and move to LA).

Adam moved his attention to the other rowers.

Among them, were Craig and Simon.

Adam studied their smirking faces and turned his attention to the trivia section, hoping something would leap out that could give him an *in*.

Which, for Craig, it did.

He pulled out his phone and dialled Colin's number.

'Meet me at Lucky's tonight,' he said when the phone had been answered.

'Why?'

'Because I've got a plan.'

LUCKY'S WAS THE sports bar in the centre of Stonebridge. The owners had a huge love for all things American and had decked out the interior of the bar with anything starred or striped.

The walls were decorated with licence plates from all fifty states as well as promotional drink signs featuring American sporting royalty. Guest lagers from the US, with their exotic flavours and their colourful pump clips, filled the beer pumps frequently.

Amongst all of this were a number of huge plasma televisions, showing sport constantly. Tonight, a pivotal Premier League match between table topping Liverpool and second placed Manchester City was being shown.

Which was handy, because Craig not only worked at the bar, but also supported Liverpool.

As did Adam.

COLIN AND ADAM met outside the bar. Colin raised an eyebrow at what his friend was wearing—the newest kit the Reds had put out.

'How much did that set you back?' Colin asked.

'Seventy quid.'

'Jesus. I thought you were broke?'

'Well, Mrs Jones gave me a wee bonus for trimming her bush for her, so I thought I'd treat myself. And, you've not even seen the best bit yet.'

Adam shrugged off his coat and turned around to show Colin the pièce de résistance. The gale of laughter was not the reaction he'd expected.

'Who gets the names of players on the back of their shirts anymore? What are you? Seven years old?'

'He was our top scorer last year.'

'Did you have to pay extra for that?'

Adam replied quietly.

'What was that?' Colin said, cupping his ear.

'I said it was an extra fifteen quid.'

'Good God, you are a sad act. Put your coat on so no one sees what you've done or I'm not going in with you.'

Colin waited until Adam had done as he was asked before pushing the door open.

THEY MADE THEIR way through the crowd and squeezed into a booth that not only offered them a good view of a television, but also of the bar.

Craig was there behind it, pouring a pint and talking animatedly to the waiting customer. His dark hair, widows peak and pale complexion combined to make him look like Dracula.

Adam tore his eyes away from the barman and looked through the American themed menu.

'I think I might have a milkshake,' Adam said.

'You're here to question a possible murder suspect,' replied Colin. 'If you go up to him wearing your ridiculous football top with your favourite player on the back and order a milkshake instead of a beer, he might mistake you for a child and turf you out.'

'But my head is still sore from last night.'

Colin fixed him with a glare that left the matter resolved.

Beer it was.

Adam shuffled along the squeaky leather seat and left the booth. He walked to the bar and stood with one arm atop it, his eyes on the television mounted above the spirits. The pundit's lively voice boomed through the speakers, announcing which players had made the team sheet.

'Can I get you anything, mate?'

Adam lowered his gaze to meet Craig's.

'Two pints of Harp, please.'

As Craig poured the first pint, Adam unzipped his jacket slightly. He noticed the barman's eyes drift to his new t-shirt.

'Nice top, man,' Craig said. 'I like the bit of green on it.'

'Yeah, Nike have done a good job. Better than last year's kit, anyway.'

Craig flipped the handle of the pump and handed the full pint glass across the bar. He placed the empty below the pump and pushed the handle again.

'What do you think of our chances tonight?' Adam asked.

'I've got a fiver on us to win 2-1, so I've got my fingers crossed.'

Adam saw an in.

'Ah, betting man. What do you reckon about this year's rowing race then? Who do you fancy?'

Craig puffed out his chest proudly.

'I'm actually on the Stonebridge team, so I couldn't bet if I wanted to. Smart man's money is on the other team.'

'Why?' Adam asked, playing ignorant.

Craig looked at him like he'd sprouted a second head.

'Have you been living under a rock? Our captain fell in the river and drowned. We've had to appoint a temporary captain while we find a full-time replacement. It's been chaos.'

'Sorry to hear,' Adam said, taking a sip from his pint. 'Now that you mention it, the story is coming back to me. I've heard a few rumours that Michael…'

'Matthew.'

'Matthew, that's it. I've heard rumours that say he might not have fallen in. That he was maybe… pushed.'

'Bollocks,' said Craig.

'You don't think anyone would want to hurt him?'

'There's a difference between hurting and killing. I imagine quite a few of the team wouldn't have minded a free swing at him.'

'Why?'

'He was hard on us. He wanted to win, no matter the cost. He didn't care about friendships. As a matter of fact, him and me were best friends until he became captain.'

'Why would that stop you being friends?'

'He became paranoid that I wanted to take the title from him. Strange, really. He stopped talking to me and moved my position in the boat so that I was far away from him.'

Craig peeled away to pour a drink for another customer before returning. Adam wasn't sure why he was being so open with him. Maybe it was cathartic to talk about his friend, or ex-friend's, death.

'You see,' he continued. 'The captain gets the biggest share of the prize money. That's why he was so eager to hold onto the role.'

'Why wouldn't the money be split equally?'

'The captain does a load more work than anyone else. All the admin, the training plans and the organising. The first year the prize money was introduced, that's what the team decided and it stuck.'

Could someone have pushed Matthew to his death for a bit more money?

'Who became captain after Matthew's death?' Adam asked.

'A guy called Simon. One of the long-serving members.'

At that, a large group of raucous lads burst in through the door and made a beeline for the bar. Adam wished Craig luck with his bet before walking back to the booth.

'I thought you were brewing the beer yourself you took so long,' Colin said as he took his pint. 'I take it he told you some stuff?'

Adam spent a few minutes relaying the information he'd just received to his friend.

'So,' Colin said. 'Simon might benefit financially from Matthew's death?

Adam nodded.

'Sounds like we might need to have a chat with him.'

7

THE SHIP HAS AN ANCHOR AND THE CAPTAIN IS A …

MOST OF THE residents had retired to their rooms with a bellyful of food, ready for a mid-afternoon nap while a few had hung around in the main room with their eyes glued to the television.

Colin was using the downtime to crack on with some paperwork. He loved his job and he loved the people, but the incessant filling in of forms was a definite downside. Though, of course, he knew why he had to do it. He'd watched the horrible exposés where someone had gone undercover at a care home and filmed the abuse doled out by bullies who had somehow got a job there.

It made him sick to his stomach.

A knock on the door jerked him back to reality and he smiled at Barry as he made his way into the room and lowered himself slowly into a chair on the other side of the desk.

'How are you, mucker?' Colin asked.

'Not too bad, Poirot. I was just wondering if you've got a case on your hands or not.'

'We just might. Still trying to work out whether or not someone pushed him into the river. We've met a few shady characters and we've been pointed in the direction of another one.'

Barry sat up a bit in his seat, the excitement getting to him.

'Are you going to question him?'

'I'm going to go and have a word.'

Colin had been thinking about how best to approach Simon Holland and had finally settled on a course of action. He told Barry of his plans and watched a little smile form under the old man's moustache as he nodded his approval.

'I didn't realise you were such a devious fella,' he laughed. 'I'll have to keep an eye on you from now on. I can half-imagine you swiping my daily pills and flogging them to needy lads on street corners.'

COLIN PULLED INTO a space in the car park and got out, aware that the town's shops would soon be locking their doors for the day. He hurried through the narrow alleyway and emerged in the centre of Stonebridge, making his way quickly towards the far end of town.

Holland & Morrow Estate Agents held a small office which was sandwiched between a newsagent that had been in the town forever and a café that seemed to change ownership weekly.

Being a small university town, Stonebridge had a lot of student housing, which was Holland & Morrow's speciality. They also had a stronghold on lodgings for the single professional.

Which was the angle Colin was hoping to use.

While pretending to look at the pictures of houses in the window, he snuck a few glances inside. Simon Holland was sitting at a desk at the back, a phone clamped between his shoulder and ear. His mouth was moving at a mile a minute, no doubt chewing someone's ear off in order to secure a sale.

Colin pushed the door open and walked in.

Simon looked up from his computer screen and flashed a toothy smile at him. He pointed first to the phone and then his watch, before rolling his eyes. He then turned his attention back to his computer screen.

Immediately, Colin formed a dislike for the man. The perfectly tailored suit jacket, the overwhelming stench of aftershave and his Wall Street attitude were all so overblown considering he was running a boutique estate agency in a small town.

While Simon finished his phone call, Colin spent the time looking around the office. It was as if the two owners had decided to divvy up the walls and decorate them how they saw fit. Mr Morrow's half was basic. A few framed certificates were nailed to the wall and a calendar showing the Giant's Causeway hung just behind his tidy desk.

Simon's half on the other hand was like a shrine to himself. Newspaper cuttings about the company fought for space among the many pictures of himself in rowing gear. He was clearly very proud of the Stonebridge team's achievements over the past few years.

'How can I help you, young man?' he asked, as he replaced the receiver.

'I'm looking to move out of my parent's house. I need a bit of space, you know?'

'Ah, I do indeed remember how that felt and how great it was to get a foot on the ladder. You've come to the right place.'

He wheeled himself over to the computer and began typing furiously on the keyboard. His jacket sleeves rode up slightly, revealing gold cufflinks. An S in one cuff and an H in the other.

'Just going to take a few details and then we can begin a bespoke search for your prospective new property.'

Bespoke? thought Colin. *Jesus.*

He answered a series of questions and gave his house search criteria. Truth be told, he had been thinking of moving out for a while. He'd managed to save a healthy amount from his job, and his dad had often said he'd help top up the deposit if needed, so he gave an honest list of things that he would like—may as well kill two birds with one stone.

'Ok,' Simon said. 'Let's see what we've got.'

As he waited for the computer to work its magic, Colin seized his chance. He nodded to the pictures.

'You keen on rowing, then?'

'You could say that. This year will be my tenth with the Stonebridge team—providing it still goes ahead.'

'Are you confident of the win?'

'We were. Before what happened to Matthew.'

Colin nodded sympathetically.

'I imagine what happened must have cast a shadow on everything.'

Simon shrugged, his eyes scanning the monitor, his tongue protruding slightly between his teeth.

'Yeah. He'd been captain for the last few years. It won't be the same without him, but we're determined to win it in his honour.'

'A lot of responsibility on the new captain, I'd imagine.'

'I'm the new captain and I eat responsibility for breakfast.'

Colin let that statement settle, hoping Simon could hear how stupid it sounded.

'There was chat from someone I know that there had been some pretty big bust-ups lately.'

Simon stared resolutely at the computer, though it was clear that he wasn't focussed on the details on the screen. His cheeks had turned rather red, despite the cool temperature.

'Who told you that? Theo?'

Colin remained silent.

'I take that as a yes,' Simon continued. 'Everyone had clashes with everyone, especially on the run up to the actual race. If you didn't think the person beside you or in front of you was putting an honest shift in, you'd tell them. And they'd tell you. That's normal. You want to win so you demand the best from everyone around you.'

'Did Matthew get at you?'

'Course he did. And I got at him. We had a massive barney the night of his death. Like I said, it was normal. We argued and then we made up. It's Theo's first year and I'd honestly be surprised if he comes back. The lad's too wet for this game.'

Colin was aware that this was beginning to sound like a police interrogation so changed his tone. More agony aunt than Gestapo.

'That must be horrible—you having an argument and then him dying.'

'I've made my peace with it. He knew and I knew that it was solely for the good of the team. What happened was… unfortunate.'

Colin nodded.

'Like I said, we're going to win in his honour,' Simon said. 'Despite the antics of those knobs from Meadowfield.'

'What do you mean?'

'They are a bunch of hick farmers who have been trying for months to disrupt our training…' He suddenly looked alarmed. 'Oh, God, you're not from there, are you?'

Colin shook his head.

'Thank God. Well, they call them pranks, and at first, they were small funny things, but at times they've overstepped the mark. Matthew was convinced they were going to end up hurting one of us.'

As Colin was about to press him on what kinds of things the other team had been doing, Simon's computer emitted a small ping. He turned the monitor around so that Colin could see the various properties that fitted his price range and conditions.

They scrolled through a number of pages and Colin picked three that he liked. He checked his shifts at work and booked in viewings with Simon. If the houses came to nothing, it at least gave him more time to question the estate agent.

He left the office feeling as if he'd taken another step in the direction of adulthood.

8

THE WOOD EMPORIUM

ADAM SET DOWN the hedge trimmers and stretched. All the overhead work meant looking up, which meant he'd end up with a sore neck if he wasn't careful. He walked the length the holly bush, cursing when he realised how much more he had to do.

'What was that, dear?' said Mrs Stanley, who must've snuck into the garden on the other side of the holly without Adam noticing.

'Uh… I said I thought I heard a duck.'

'Not round these parts, pet. Maybe a goose flying overhead.'

'Maybe,' Adam said, snatching up the shears again. He replaced his earphones and pressed play on his phone, the harsh metal music immediately attacking his eardrums.

He closed Spotify and noticed a WhatsApp message from his mum which she had sent over two hours ago, according to the time stamp.

Phone me.

Adam's heart began to race. His mum rarely sent messages and when she did, they were lengthy compositions that took an age to trawl through.

Something must be wrong.

He pulled the earphones out of his ears again and phoned his mum straight away. She answered after a few rings.

'Mum, what's wrong?'

'Nothing, dear. Why?'

'Because your short message sounded like something someone might send if they'd managed to escape their kidnapper and didn't have very much time.'

'But, I just wanted you to phone me when you had a minute. What else was I supposed to say?'

'I dunno. Something like "I hope you're having a nice day. When you get a minute, would you mind phoning me. It's nothing important, and I'm definitely not in any mortal danger."'

'What a waste of time.'

'What is?'

'This conversation. All I wanted to do was ask you if you fancied meeting up for lunch today?'

Adam checked the time.

'I'll probably be done here in the next couple of hours, so I could meet you at around one?'

'Perfect,' his mum said, before the line went dead.

Who did she think she was hanging up like that, Jack Bauer? Adam thought as he stuffed the phone back into his pocket and carried on with his work.

THE SQUARE WAS his mum's café of choice—had been since he was a little boy. They'd come every Saturday, sit by the first-floor window and watch the world go by below them.

When he'd entered his teens, the café visits had become less regular. In fact, he couldn't remember the last time the two of them had been here. He smiled across the table at the woman who had raised him single-handedly, on account of his dad leaving one day and never coming back.

He resolved to make more time for her.

The waiter came and set a jacket potato smothered with cheese in front of his mum and a mouth-watering pulled pork panini on Adam's placemat.

Adam wolfed down his food, only realising as he picked up the meat-filled bread just how hungry he had been. His mum took a little longer and when she set down her cutlery, she cleared her throat.

'Adam, I just want to say how proud I am of you for giving something a go. The gardening thing really seems to be taking off and I think it's great that you are showing so much passion for it.'

'Thanks, mum,' he managed through a particularly full mouth. 'Means a lot.'

'I've been reading a hygge book…'

'A what?' Adam interrupted. He didn't know the word she had just said, but it sounded like she was choking on phlegm.

'Hygge. It's a Danish thing, all about recognising how good life is. Anyway, it's got a bit about sleep and de-cluttering and how having lots of electrical things in your bedroom is bad for sleep patterns.'

'Sounds like someone has too much time on their hands.'

'Thank you, Sigmund Freud. I was just telling you this because I thought you might like to turn the third bedroom into an office, you know, to do your invoicing and what have you. You could put your tele and games things in there too and really sort out your bedroom.'

Adam quite liked the thought of sitting at a desk, figuring out how much people owed him. He could sit with his chair tipped back and his feet on the desk, sipping a beer like they did in Mad Men.

'Sounds good. Nice idea, mum.'

'I thought we could go over to The Wood Emporium and have a gander. I bet he's got some nice desks and he's got a sale on at the minute.'

'When does that man *not* have a sale on. He's like a local DFS.'

'Is that a yes?' she asked, rising from her seat.

'It is indeed,' he replied, pulling out the bank card from his pocket. 'Here, let me get this.'

PERCY WOOD WAS the man you came to see if you wanted furniture. His shop was a landmark in Stonebridge—one of the longest serving family businesses left. Only old man Tucker's car garage topped it in terms of longevity, and he was without son. The Tucker name would soon pass, and Wood would take the title.

A little bell above the door tinkled as they entered. The shop was narrow, but long, and housed a wide assortment of furniture. From kitchen tables to oak sideboards, pine wardrobes to sets of drawers, Percy always had whatever you were looking for.

As they made their way past the counter, Adam was relieved to see that the patriarch of the store was not behind it. In his place was his son, Jacob Wood.

Adam could never pin down exactly why he had such an aversion to Percy. If he thought about it, part of it was because he reminded him of Ollivander from the Harry Potter books.

Percy had the same frazzled grey hair and dapper dress sense. He also always seemed to be lurking in the shadows, ready to appear from nowhere so that he could lead you to your chosen piece of furniture.

Jacob was much more lackadaisical, as evidenced by him barely glancing up from his book as Adam and his mum walked past.

'If you need any help, just give me a shout,' Jacob muttered, while turning a page of some pretentious looking tome.

They made their way to the desks and Adam pushed one of the wheely chairs over, taking his place behind a number of tables and pretending to type.

He'd always fancied one of those lights with a brass body and a green glass shade, and so chose the desk he thought it would look best sitting on. It was made of mahogany and he thought the dark wood would really make the light stand out.

'You're sure?' his mum asked, checking for a price tag.

He sized it up one more time, looked quickly at the others and nodded. This beast was the one for him.

They made their way to the counter.

'How can I help you?' asked Jacob, folding the corner of the page he had reached before setting the book down.

'We'd like to buy a desk,' Adam said. 'It's the mahogany one at the back.'

'The one with three drawers?'

Adam confirmed that that was indeed the one he had set his heart on.

While he was sorting the payment and insurance forms, Adam's mum tried to engage Jacob in conversation.

'How is your dad doing?'

'Ah, he's grand. He loves this time of year, what with the boat race and the fête and whatnot so he's taken a bit of time off.'

'Is he presenting the trophy again this year?'

Jacob nodded.

'He is. I think that's the only reason he offered to sponsor the race. Five thousand pounds just to hand over a cup. People must think he's mad.'

'I think it's a good business move,' said Adam. 'Surely most of Stonebridge associate this place with the race weekend.'

'They do, but it doesn't mean they all shop here. A certain Scandinavian outlet in the capital has seen to that. They may be cheaper but they don't have our quality. It's why we constantly seem to have a sale on—we have to do something to compete.'

Silence filled the musty shop.

'Sorry,' Jacob said, rubbing his greying temples. 'I'm ranting. It's just stressful trying to run the business in the age of smartphones and click and collects. Dad expects us to be as prolific as ever, but sadly, brand loyalty is not a thing anymore.'

'Well, you'll always be my first choice for furniture,' Adam's mum said.

Jacob's features rearranged themselves into something resembling a smile, as if the muscles hadn't been forced into this particular formation in quite a long time.

'I appreciate it. Thank you, you've brightened my day.'

And it seemed, they had. For after that, he led them to the back of the shop where a variety of office chairs sat, and offered them a good deal on whichever one Adam fancied.

With delivery arranged and payment made, they left the shop.

'Maybe he'd appreciate a lesson in hygge,' Adam said.

His mum slapped him on the arm.

'Don't be sarcastic with me,' she replied. 'And it's you who is going to need a lesson soon, because it's your job to clear out the back room ready for your new desk.'

9

TÊTE-À-TÊTE

COLIN PUSHED OPEN Adam's bedroom door and was met with an unusual sight. The mounds of dirty clothes that were a mainstay on the floor were gone. As was the widescreen television and the PlayStation. And the beer fridge…

Something wasn't right here.

He heard his name being called from the landing and left the room to find Adam peeking at him from the behind the door in the back bedroom. He walked across the hallway and entered the bedroom, amazed at the transformation.

On nights when the two of them would have a sleepover, drinking beer and playing Football Manager late into the night, this was Colin's bedroom. Usually, a single bed was pushed against one wall and a set of drawers sat against the wall opposite.

Today, it was totally different. Both bits of furniture were gone.

In their place was a sturdy desk made of dark wood, upon which sat Adam's laptop and some files. The flatscreen tv was mounted to the wall above it and a comfortable sofa bed filled most of the rest of the space.

Adam sat in a high-backed leather office chair.

'Nice place you got here,' Colin said, sinking into the sofa.

'Mum is on some hygge thing. She suggested decluttering my room for a better sleeping experience.'

'My dad was talking about that the other day. Is someone trying to brainwash us?'

'Not sure, but I spent yesterday breaking up the bed and getting everything tidy in here. Jacob Wood delivered the desk this morning. Kept going on about customer service. I think he was expecting a tip.'

'Well, I think it looks great in here. Well done, man.'

'Thanks,' said Adam. 'How did it go with Simon?'

'He's an idiot. Bloody loves himself. He's got pictures of himself all over the office walls and possibly worse than that—gold cufflinks with his initials on.'

'That is dreadful,' Adam agreed.

'He told me that him and Matthew had a massive argument the night he died and he didn't seem particularly cut up about the fact they ended their friendship on a sour note. He also said that the Meadowfield team were doing things to try and interfere with their training. Apparently, Matthew was convinced they were going to go too far and end up hurting one of them.'

Adam mulled over the new information silently.

'So, you think his death might've been a prank gone wrong?'

Colin shrugged.

'Who knew rowing could be so rowdy?' Adam laughed. 'Fist fights, arguments, inter-town warfare… next year the regatta will have ultras with flares standing by the riverbank.'

'Aye, and pouring offal from the bridges into the boats. What do we do next?'

'We think, the only way we know how.'

Adam turned the PlayStation on and started a football game. He handed Colin a controller and the two picked their teams. They knocked a few ideas back and forth, each finding a hole in the other's scheme.

Suddenly, Adam gasped and paused the game.

'Oi,' Colin shouted. 'I was just about to score.'

'Never mind about that. I have an idea. One of us could infiltrate the Meadowfield team—go undercover. If we can do that, we'll know whether or not they had a hand in Matthew's death.'

'And when you say "one of us", I'm guessing you actually mean me.'

'Well, if we want to get in with them, it needs to be believable. They'd laugh me out of town, what with my weedy arms and little boy body. But, strapping young lad like you, they'd have you in an instant.'

Colin couldn't argue with the logic.

'What if they find out I'm from Stonebridge?'

'You just badmouth the town—that'll instantly get you brownie points and a one-way ticket onto their boat.'

Colin sighed.

'Okay,' he said, finally. 'I'll find out when their practice times are and head down, try to get in with them.'

'Good man,' said Adam, unpausing the game whilst Colin wasn't quite ready. His defender tackled Colin's striker and booted the ball to safety. Adam received a thump on the arm for his troubles.

'Worth it,' laughed Adam.

Colin quickly retrieved the ball back and set about attacking again.

'I forgot to say. I'm going to be looking at some houses. Well, flats, but still… Be cool to have a place of my own.'

'That's massive, man. Think of the house parties! Is Simon showing you around?'

'Yeah, be a good chance to spend a bit more time with him. Reckon he might let a bit more slip if he feels he is in control of the situation. Get him on his own patch, so to speak.'

'Great idea.'

'So,' Colin said. 'I'm joining a rowing team and spending time house shopping with the captain of my soon-to-be rivals. I feel like I'm doing the heavy lifting here. What's your next move?'

'I'm going to go and visit Elena Henderson at home, see if I can learn a little bit more about Matthew. We still don't know if something fishy actually went on—it could've been an accident like the police thought. It could also be suicide.'

'I'd not thought about that.'

'Nor me, until yesterday. I want to see if there's any medication in the bathroom cabinet or something like that, something that might give us a hint.'

Plans set, attention turned in earnest to the pixelized players on the screen.

10

INITIATION

COLIN LEFT WORK the next day with a knot in his stomach.

As he walked to his car, he thought about his plans for the evening. The Meadowfield team were due to practice and they were expecting him. He'd managed to get in touch with a man called Jim who had intimated that they could do with all the help they could get.

Colin drove home, his thoughts on what he would say, how he would act and what persona he would put out to the Meadowfield team.

He was worried that they would know who he is. The towns were small and not that far away from each other—it was a part of the world where everybody seemed to know someone who knew someone who knew you.

There were no secrets.

Well, some. But not many.

He arrived home, ate dinner quickly and then went upstairs. For some reason, deciding what to wear was weighing heavy on his mind. He didn't want to look too keen, walking in dressed head to toe in sports gear. But he also didn't want to risk creating a bad first impression that would dissuade people from talking to him.

In the end, he chose tracksuit bottoms and a fitted T-shirt that showed off his toned arms. It was a warm night and if he could show that he may be an asset to the team, that might stand him in good stead.

He made his way back downstairs, fended off questions from his parents about where he was going and what he'd be doing, before finally escaping to the sanctuary of his car.

The journey to Meadowfield took about twenty minutes and he spent it all on the phone to Adam. They discussed what he might uncover and how he was potentially walking into a nest of vipers. He cut the call when he saw the sign for the neighbouring town's rowing shed and indicated, before turning down the narrow track.

No going back now, he thought.

HE PARKED HIS car alongside the others. Most had some sort of SUV or jeep and his hybrid Hyundai stuck out like a sore thumb. For a moment, he sat in the driver's seat, his stomach roiling and his head telling him to leave.

Leave now. Don't look back.

His almost jumped through the sunroof at the sound of someone knocking on his window. He glanced over to find an amused face peering through the glass. Colin held up a finger and made a show of collecting his bottle from the passenger footwell before climbing out of the car.

'Colin?' the man asked.

'That's me. And you're Jim?'

'Indeed. Thanks for the call today. It's great to have another set of hands on board. We're in desperate need of them.'

The two men shook hands and sized each other up.

Jim had a bushy moustache and greying eyebrows to match. His weather-beaten skin and lithe frame suggested that he had spent most of his working life outdoors and his friendly demeanour hinted that he was all the happier for it.

The callouses on his fingers scratched against Colin's smooth hands and he immediately felt self-conscious, as if his worth to the team could be judged by said softness.

'Shall we get started?' Colin asked, hoping to show how keen he was, despite his baby-smooth hands.

'Let's,' nodded Jim.

They walked towards the boat shed. It was smaller than the one in Stonebridge. The building was red brick and single storey. One garage-style door was open, giving the rest of the team access to the equipment stored inside.

Colin and Jim entered the room and were greeted with stony silence. The Meadowfield team sat on folding chairs, angled towards the door.

Towards him.

'Alright, pal?' one of the men said, while the rest held their silence. 'Where did you say you were from?'

Colin just had time to note the man's trimmed goatee and camouflaged shorts before the door slammed closed behind him, shrouding the room in darkness.

'I… umm,' Colin stammered, fear tightening a knot in his stomach.

What had he walked into?

Did they know that he was here with an ulterior motive? Had they somehow found out that he was from their rival town?

Suddenly, a light flashed into life above his head and the laughter commenced.

'Sorry, mate,' the man who had greeted him said, leaping up from his chair. 'We're just messing with you. My name is Ricky. Welcome to the team.'

'You prick,' Colin managed, as the two men shook hands to a chorus of laughter. He could hear the blood rushing in his ears as the adrenaline coursed through his body.

Ricky introduced him to the rest of the team and he was afforded a warm welcome from everyone.

Well, almost everyone.

Unlike the rest of the team who had left their chairs to introduce themselves, the man in the corner of the room had remained seated. His long, ginger hair was gathered on his shoulders and small, crab-like eyes seemed to penetrate Colin, as if searching for a secret.

Colin looked back at him, keen to appear aloof to the hostility. He even managed a weak smile, which wasn't returned. Instead, the man produced an E-cigarette from his pocket and took a long puff, exhaling a cloud of smoke that seemed to envelope him.

'Right,' shouted Jim. 'Let's get the boat in the water and do some bloody work. We've only got a week or so left until the race.'

The room became a hive of activity as the men moved with a practiced fluidity to where they were needed. Ricky's iron grip clamped down on Colin's shoulders and he led him outside while the rest of the team got ready.

'Everyone here is alright. Paddy in the corner there just got out of jail a few months ago and is a bit wary of new faces. He really is a solid geezer when you get to know him.'

Prison!

'What was he in prison for?' Colin asked.

'Never you mind,' came the reply. 'Just pull your weight, give your all and he will soon come round to you. Alright, sunshine?'

The rest of the team emerged from the boatshed; the long canoe hoisted above their heads. They walked to the riverbank and delicately placed the vessel on the water.

After a few minutes, the canoe was filled and Colin genuinely felt terrified. He was about to enter open water, trapped in a claustrophobic boat, with a man (or men) who could possibly be behind the murder of the rival team's captain, as well as an ex-con.

'Ready!' shouted Jim, and he used his oar to push the boat away from the safety of dry land.

Here goes nothing, thought Colin.

COLIN SAT IN the bar after, his muscles tired and his body cold, but his spirit high.

He couldn't remember the last time he'd had such fun.

Already a keen proponent of exercise, he had excelled in pushing his body to the limit. It had taken him a while to find his rhythm, but once he'd discovered it, he had revelled in helping push the small craft through the choppy water.

There was something primal about it.

The congratulatory pats on the back from the rest of the team had been a welcome surprise, as had the invitation to join them in the bar for a quick pint after the equipment had been safely stowed away.

He took a sip of his beer and listened to tales that had probably been told a hundred times before, but had been pulled out once more for the newcomer.

He laughed along at all the right parts and began to feel part of the team.

And that's when he noticed Paddy, sitting in the corner of the room with a sullen look on his face. He was looking out of the window at the rapidly deteriorating light.

Colin's instinct was to walk over and strike up conversation, though Ricky seemed to be able to telegraph his feelings.

'I wouldn't, mate,' he whispered. 'Besides, I've got something else in mind for you.'

He winked at a few of the others lads, who finished the dregs of their pints and got to their feet.

'Come with us. It's time for your initiation.'

COLIN HAD WATCHED footage of many a footballer croon a stone cold classic a cappella, murdering it in the process, as part of their initiation after a big money transfer.

That's what he thought the Meadowfield team had in mind for him. He'd even picked Sweet Caroline as his tune, hoping that the crowd participation parts would see him through.

Thoughts of Neil Diamond were quickly pushed from his mind as he was bundled into the back of a car which was driven off at high speed up the narrow track. The car raced on the familiar coast road between Meadowfield and Stonebridge, and Colin was surprised at how little time it had taken to make it back to his hometown.

He was even more surprised when they entered the car park behind the town centre. The barriers were up to signify that no payment was necessary.

And why would it be? It was nearly ten o'clock and all the shops were shut.

'Right,' Ricky said, tossing him a bag inside which something clinked together noisily. 'Your mission, should you choose to accept it, is to walk to the offices of one Mr Holland and graffiti his shutters.'

Colin glanced inside the bag and felt his mouth grow dry. Two paint canisters, red and blue, appeared to look back at him accusatorily.

'Why?' he spluttered.

'Why?' Ricky laughed. 'To show that you've got balls. To show that you hate these scumbags as much as we do. To give two fingers to the people of this crappy town.'

The two other men in the car laughed loudly.

'What should I write?'

A series of choice phrases were hurled his way.

'Any of those,' Ricky said. 'Or, if you're feeling creative, you can make something up. We won't be offended that you disregarded our suggestions.'

With a small nod of the head, Colin got out of the car. He walked towards the town centre, weighing up what he had been asked to do. If he was caught, which was unlikely given the time of day and how dark it was, it would have serious repercussions—one more serious than the rest.

He could lose his job.

And he didn't want that.

On the flip side, he was committed to holding up his end of the bargain. Adam had promised Elena Henderson that they would look into Matthew's death and for better or worse, this would help.

Surely, once he'd done this, the Meadowfield team couldn't question his commitment. He could start asking his questions in earnest.

Maybe even ex-prisoner Paddy would be impressed and let his guard down.

He sighed and skulked around the corner towards the estate agent's office. Aware that there were no CCTV cameras down this end of town that could capture what he was about to do, he ran to the metal shutters, pulled out a paint canister and sprayed a message as quickly as he could.

Once finished and without even bothering to check his handiwork, he threw the cans back into the bag and legged it down the street towards the car park. The muscles in his legs were burning when he rounded the last corner and he stared across the swathe of concrete in disbelief.

The car park was empty.

'Dicks,' said Colin to the desolation, before taking off at pace again, keen to put distance between himself and the vandalism he'd just been forced into.

When he'd gone far enough, he pulled his phone from his pocket and navigated to Adam's name, though his finger hovered over the number without pressing it. He wasn't sure he was ready to explain what had happened tonight; hadn't had time to process it himself yet, and Adam would have a million questions.

Instead, he dialled a taxi, shame at what he'd done causing his cheeks to burn.

11

NOTHING LIKE NARNIA

'THEY WANTED YOU to write *the C word* with spray paint?'

Adam couldn't believe what he was hearing. He increased the volume of his speakers and strained his ears to try and hear what Colin was saying over the whine of his car's engine.

'That, amongst other things.'

'And what *did* you write?'

'Meadowfield rules. With a Z. I thought that way the police, if they are called, wouldn't suspect a Stonebridge resident as the person behind it, and secondly, it might start some sort of civil war.'

'Where people get sloppy with their secrets... I like it. It was a risky thing you did, though, but a potential gamechanger. Well done, mate. The Meadowfield team will probably let their guard down now that they think they can trust you. Do you think any of them could be capable of drowning a man?'

'Maybe,' said Colin, his voice echoing around the car. 'There's another practice tonight so I'll see what I can dig up. From what I can tell, Jim is the point of contact but Ricky is in charge. He's the one all the lads look up to. He seems like a bit of a thug.'

'You're telling me. I can't believe what they made you do.'

'It's done. Let's not go on about it. There's this lad called Paddy, too—fresh out of prison and with some of the looks he was giving me; I'd suggest it won't be his last stretch either.'

'Prison? Jesus. We're in deep here, aren't we?' replied Adam. 'I'm just pulling up at Elena's house now so I'll have to go, but I'll chat to you tomorrow after tonight's practice for a proper catch up.'

He hung up and drove slowly down the street, scanning the numbers for the correct house. He hadn't wanted to give Elena prior warning of his visit, so that he would be able to question her without having given her time to rehearse her answers. But, he'd hit a snag.

He didn't know where she lived.

His mother had come up trumps, though, sieving through a pile of Stonebridge Gazettes and finding the obituary notice, which listed the address as part of the funeral arrangements.

It was odd, he thought, how much people of a certain age bloody loved the obituary section of a newspaper. His granny used to say that it was the only reason she bothered with the local paper at all.

His mum used to despair at her, and now she was exactly the same!

When he reached number 75, he was surprised to find two cars filling the narrow driveway. One, a sleek black Audi and the other a pink Mini.

He didn't want to block them in, so drove further up the street until he found a bit of unoccupied kerb. He performed a rather graceless parallel park and got out, sighing at how far away he was from the kerb, but not caring enough to do anything about it.

When he reached the Henderson household, he climbed the steps and rang the doorbell. He listened for the chime but couldn't hear it, wondering whether it was out of use, or just very quiet.

He waited a few minutes before knocking on the door, not wanting to appear too pushy if the doorbell had indeed sounded.

There was still no answer. He cast a stealthy glance over his shoulder and tried the handle, though, it didn't budge.

He considered leaving it. She was either out or busy. As he turned to leave, another thought struck him.

If someone *had* killed Matthew, could his recently widowed wife also be in the firing line? Perhaps this had nothing to do with rowing and everything to do with the Hendersons.

That's probably why she hired me in the first place, Adam thought. *To make sure she wasn't about to be chopped up into mincemeat by some maniac.*

He could feel his blood fizz. He simply couldn't walk away, could he?

He ran through his options. He could call the police, but if they came and it turned out she was simply at work, he could get done for wasting police time.

Calling Elena at her office was another option, though not a viable one as he was missing the key piece of information. He didn't know where she worked.

But surely if she was at work, she'd have gone in her car, which he assumed was the Mini.

Frustrated, he spent a few minutes looking around the outside of the house, before noticing that the back gate was off its latch. He walked into the back garden to find an overgrown lawn and flower beds being overrun by weeds.

A few months ago, he wouldn't have cared less, but the messy garden was getting to him. He decided that he'd offer to tidy it up for her, free of charge. It was the least he could do for the grieving widow.

He tried the back door handle, just in case, but it too was locked. Glancing around, something caught his eye. On the ground, just behind an empty plant pot, was a solitary smooth, grey stone.

He picked it up and turned it over in his hands, his suspicions confirmed. He'd seen one in a movie once, he couldn't remember which, but had thought it was an ingenious way of hiding a key.

He pressed the small button on the underside and slid the two halves of the "stone" apart, unearthing a key the same colour as the back door's handle.

Ordinarily, he wouldn't go barging into someone's house unannounced or uninvited, but he was worried that Elena was lying beyond the door, injured or worse.

He wiggled the key into the lock, turned it and pressed down on the handle. Surprised at how easy people made it to break into a house, he took a tentative step across the threshold into a modern kitchen.

'Mrs Henderson,' he called, though only silence greeted him.

He tried again, louder this time, though it ended in the same result.

He closed the door behind him and moved to the centre of the room, turning a full circle on his heels, hoping something would leap out at him.

Nothing did.

Unsure of what he was looking for, his search became more like an episode of "Through the Keyhole". He flung open drawers and had a look at the contents, before moving into the living room.

Everything in here was fairly standard – a couple of sofas, a television and a rather ornate fireplace.

Something bothered him, though. There was a lack of personal touches. Most couple's houses he'd been to had an annoying number of photos of themselves. It always struck him as rather vain.

This living room, on the other hand, had no photos whatsoever. It was as if Matthew had never lived here at all. Perhaps it was simply Elena's way of dealing with her grief, he thought.

Out of sight, out of mind, as they say.

He made his way cautiously up the stairs, keenly aware that the bloodied body of Elena Henderson may be waiting for him. The thought made him shiver.

Upon reaching the landing, he called out again.

He was surprised by the wobble in his voice, but unsurprised with the lack of reply.

Gathering his bravery, he shoved each door open with a swift push, breathing a sigh of relief as each room offered no bloodied body.

Safe in the knowledge that he wasn't contaminating a crime scene, he relaxed and thought about where to begin his search.

He remembered watching a black and white film about Joy Division a few years ago, and how Ian Curtis used to steal medication from medicine cabinets of people he would visit after school. Or something like that. It had been a few years since he'd seen it.

This memory led Adam to the bathroom. The room was painted a light green and was home to one of the most luxurious showers he'd ever seen. For a nanosecond, he considered trying it out, before remembering that this wasn't his house.

Instead, he turned to the mirrored cabinet above the sink and opened it. He was hoping that there might be a tube or two of tablets that might signal that Matthew was on some sort of anti-depressant. Sad though the thought was, it could've pointed the finger at suicide, rather than murder.

Sadly, for Adam, all that was to be found was a couple of tubes of toothpaste and some hair grips.

He closed the door of the bathroom and made his way to the master bedroom. An immaculately made king-sized bed took pride of place, surrounded by heavy wooden furniture.

As he was about to check the contents of the bedside tables, a noise from outside disturbed him—a car's brakes squealing as it came to a stop.

Adam ducked down underneath the windowsill and listened intently as he heard two doors slam closed. He could hear the drone of continued conversation and the clicking of heels getting closer to the house.

Not daring to breath, he snuck a peak out of the window, before ducking back down again and swearing continuously under his breath.

Elena and another person—a man—were walking up the path towards the house.

Panic was rolling through his body in waves as he ran through his options.

One, he could come clean and simply reveal himself. Though, explaining what he was doing in a widow's bedroom—having let himself in—could be tough to pull off.

Two, he could attempt to get down the stairs and out of the back door by the time Elena had let herself in the front.

This plan was dashed immediately as he heard the door at the bottom of the stairs open with a click and the two voices became clearer.

Which led Adam to plan three. Not the greatest of the trio, but the only one now available to him.

Hide.

He looked around the room and settled on the huge oak wardrobe. He crept over to it and pulled the door open slowly, before crawling into it and easing the door closed again.

His heart was hammering as he listened to the footsteps on the stairs and the voices grow closer. As the bedroom door opened, he tried to become zen—to be as still and as silent as it was possible or a human being to be.

What he heard chilled him to the bone.

Elena, and whoever the man was, instantly started kissing. He couldn't see it, thanks to the solid manufacture of the wardrobe, but he could sure as hell *hear* it. That horrible squelch of saliva swapping.

Who was this mystery man? Adam thought, trying to zone out the sounds of clothes being removed. *And why was Elena kissing him (and more) mere weeks after her husband had disappeared?*

What followed was the most uncomfortable and shameful twenty minutes of Adam's life. He could do nothing to ignore the grunts, the utterances of pleasure or the bedsprings proving their worth and was close to rocking backwards and forwards when the whole thing had come to a climax. Literally.

'Do you want me to have a look at it now?' the man asked, once clothes had, presumably, been reapplied.

'No, I best get back to the office,' came Elena's reply. 'You can do it another day. It's a good excuse for you to come back again.'

They giggled as they left and Adam emerged from the wardrobe a short while later, once he was sure that the coast was clear, feeling very much like a perverted Peter Pevensie emerging from a Narnian peep show. He was pretty sure that at some stage in his life, he'd recount this moment to a professional psychiatrist.

But he couldn't dwell on that now. He had a theory that he wanted to present to Colin, though he may omit the details on how he came by said information.

12

A VIEW TO A KILL

COLIN PULLED UP in front of the house. It was a simple two up, two down in an alright part of town. No fuss, no muss.

He stepped out of his car and walked to the porch, keen to get out of the mizzle that was starting to fall.

He checked the handle, but the door was locked so he pulled his coat a little tighter and turned his eyes to the road. He didn't have to wait long.

A minute or so later, a black BMW pulled into the street and screeched to a halt beside Colin's parked car. Simon Holland emerged from the driver's side; hands held aloft.

'Sorry I'm late, mate. I've had a right morning of it. First, the police and then I got held up with the last client.'

The estate agent flashed an apologetic smile.

'But, I'm here now and ready to show you this wonderful property. Now, I know we spoke mainly about flats, but I reckon with your budget, we can push to a lovely little house like this beauty. What do you say?'

Colin voiced his approval as he moved out of the way, allowing Simon to unlock the door. Colin followed him into a deceptively spacious living room.

As he was given the grand tour, Colin's attention kept wandering. Simon had mentioned the police and Colin was in no doubt as to why he had been in contact with the authorities.

He found himself walking around the house with his hands in his pockets, worried that there was a small smudge of paint he hadn't managed to scrub off, feeling very much like a modern-day Lady Macbeth.

He nodded at all the right times and tried to sound enthusiastic when he was shown a feature of the house Simon thought particularly pleasing, though he knew he wasn't fooling anyone.

'Not the house for you?' Simon said, when they returned to the front door.

Colin mumbled something non-committal and Simon laughed.

'The beautiful thing about houses,' he answered, 'is that there are hundreds of the buggers. We'll find the right one for you yet, Cinderella.'

He laughed at his own joke, before saying goodbye.

'I hope it's nothing too serious with the police,' Colin called after him.

'Nothing to worry about,' he said. 'Just some graffiti at the office.'

'That's a shame. Do you know who did it?'

'Some of those pricks from Meadowfield. There's no CCTV so we don't know who, but the police think it's probably someone from the rowing team trying to intimidate us, but it isn't going to work.'

'Yeah,' Colin answered. 'Don't let it get to you. I hope you beat them.'

'So do I, mate. I could do with the money. Also, could you imagine losing to a town who have two words for a patch of grass in their name. We'd never live it down.'

They bade each other farewell and, after a while, Colin's heartbeat returned to a normal speed. It seemed he had gotten away with his Banksy moment and in doing so, will have earned the trust and respect of the Meadowfield team.

He checked his watch.

It was nearly time to exploit that trust.

COLIN WALKED INTO the rowing shed with an annoyed look on his face. He didn't want the Meadowfield lads to think that he was a pushover, and making him break the law before abandoning him was a pretty low thing to do.

Most of the team were already there. They cheered when he entered and Colin took this to mean that the news of his initiation had been passed around and that he had been "accepted".

'Sorry, mate,' Ricky said, throwing his arm around Colin's shoulders. 'I know it was a dick move, driving away, but it's what we've done with all the others.'

Colin grunted before sitting down and getting changed for the upcoming session.

'I'll but you a pint to say sorry afterwards, alright?' Ricky said, and Colin nodded.

'AM I FORGIVEN?' Ricky asked.

Colin couldn't help but laugh at the ridiculous face the other man was pulling.

'I suppose so,' he said.

Ricky punched him softly on the arm.

'That's my boy. So, what's your deal?'

Colin gave some scant details of his life, keeping them as general as possible.

'How did you get involved in the Meadowfield team?' Colin asked.

'My family have always been involved. Of course, my father did it for the fun of it, whereas I'm quite money orientated. All the lads are. Five thousand pounds split between nine is alright compensation for winning a race.'

'Would you do it if there was no money involved?'

'Probably,' said Ricky. 'Like I say, it's a tradition in my family and it's always a chance to get one over those Stonebridge dicks.'

He paused to take a sip of his drink before elaborating.

'The money is a nice bonus, and of course, it acts as extra motivation. Since the prize money became a thing, the Meadowfield team have taken it more seriously, but we've still never won it. But, this is our year.'

'You sound sure of that.'

'Well, we have you for starters,' he laughed, squeezing Colin's bicep. 'But, to be honest, I doubt the race will even be held.'

A devious grin spread across Ricky's face.

'But, how can you win a race if it hasn't been held?' Colin asked, confused.

'It's in the rules that, if for some reason one of the towns cannot field a full team, it's counted as a forfeit and the opposing team are awarded the money.'

He took another gulp of his pint.

'We have a plan. We thought that what happened with their captain might force them into forfeiting in advance, but they appointed a new captain—the estate agent—and just carried on.'

'You didn't think they would?'

'No, any decent group of friends would surely abandon in the race in his memory. But not Stonebridge. They appointed another captain the very next day, I heard.'

'The captain gets an extra share of the money too.'

Ricky looked suspiciously at Colin.

'I think I read about it in the newspaper last year,' Colin muttered.

They descended into quiet for a minute or two.

'You mentioned before about a plan to force them to forfeit,' Colin said.

'Yeah. It's nothing bad or anything. What we thought we could do is try and target some of the members of the other team; intimidate them a bit so that they don't turn up on the day. That way, we win the money without even stepping into the boat.'

Colin could feel the question rising in his throat and when it emerged, it came out as a whisper.

'Did you have anything to do with Matthew Henderson's death?'

Ricky looked furious at the accusation and, as he was about to answer, the door to the bar flew open and Paddy walked in.

'Everything alright, here?' he asked, registering Ricky's scarlet cheeks.

Ricky stood up and walked over to his friend. He nodded in Colin's direction.

'Col here reckons we had something to do with Matty's drowning.'

'Oh aye?' Paddy said, raising an eyebrow. 'And what if we did?'

13

SUSPECTS

ADAM AND COLIN got in the car park's lift and descended three floors, emerging at street level. They walked past the gym, the butchers and the recently refurbished hair salon that Adam's auntie worked in, though he couldn't spot her through the window.

They entered The Jet—a huge hanger of a place that combined a cinema, soft play centre, arcade and a couple of restaurants. It was a Stonebridge favourite and was, as ever, very busy.

Colin booked the tickets for the film while Adam queued for the snacks. It was a time saving ritual they had perfected over for years.

'The 7 o'clock is sold out,' Colin said, as he approached his friend. 'But I got us the last tickets for the half past showing.'

They walked to the arcade and gravitated towards the shooting game. Colin inserted a few coins into the machine and they picked up the guns, as a computerised voice told them about their upcoming mission.

As the assignment began, they picked up the discussion they'd been having in the car about what Colin had learned from the Meadowfield practice sessions.

'What happened after Paddy came in, then?' Adam asked.

'I nearly pooed my pants, that's what happened. Ricky jumped up, saying I'd accused them of Matthew's murder. Paddy said something vaguely threatening and when I started to stammer and apologise, they both laughed. They were bloody well having me on.'

'I thought you said Paddy was a moody so and so?'

'He was the first night, but apparently my act of illegal vandalism was all it took for him to warm to me.'

'So, do you think they *could* have had anything to do with it?'

Colin considered this. He'd been turning it over in his mind since last night and he still hadn't come to a suitable conclusion.

'I think if any of them were behind it, it would be either Ricky or Paddy. The rest, aside from the two hyenas who were in the car with Ricky and me, seem to do the practice and head home. Ricky also talked about a plan to intimidate the Stonebridge team, so that not all of them would turn up and they'd be forced to forfeit. That way Meadowfield would win the money without lifting an oar.'

'Devious swine,' Adam replied, pointing his gun at the corner of the screen and taking out a Yakuza at point-blank range. 'So, we can put Ricky and Paddy on our mental case board.'

'And Simon, I reckon,' said Colin.

'Because he's an estate agent? Did you not like the house he showed you?'

'Shut up. Not just because he's an estate agent, and no, actually, I didn't like the house he showed me. But there is something off about him—taking the captaincy from your dead mate and not caring that he died while they were on bad terms shows that he's not a nice guy.'

'A nice guy—no. But a killer?'

'Maybe. Most people kill for one of three reasons—money, revenge or sex. And in this case, he stands to take home at least a grand, instead of a few hundred quid if his team wins.'

The game ended as Adam's risky move backfired and his character ended up splayed on the floor in a pool of pixelated blood.

'Speaking of sex…' Adam said, as they walked towards the seating area.

'If this involves you, I don't want to hear it.'

Adam fake laughed and then relayed his unsavoury wardrobe experience. Colin listened, aghast, to his friend's story and when he'd finished, he burst out laughing.

'You do know how to get yourself into some almightily weird situations.'

Adam punched him on the arm.

'In all seriousness, though,' Colin continued. 'There's something fishy there. Having it away with some unknown man weeks after your husband has died is strange behaviour.'

'I think she could have something to do with it. Maybe she and whoever the man is planned it together.'

'But why would she engage our services to find out who killed her husband if it was her and an accomplice. That makes no sense, except if she wanted to throw everyone off the scent.'

'But the police had already put it down as an accident. Why dredge it up again?'

'Maybe whoever the man she was… you know… doing the dirty with is the killer and he is trying to get close to Elena so that he doesn't look like a suspect, but in doing so, is making himself look very much like a suspect.'

'So, what's next?' Colin asked.

'You keep going with the Meadowfield lot. Maybe now that Prisoner Paddy has come on side he'll open up. And I'll try and find out who Elena is sleeping with.'

Colin checked his watch and realised that the film was about to start. He ushered Adam towards the correct screen, showed the employee his ticket and walked through.

While Adam was faffing, looking for his ticket, Colin pulled out his phone to put it on silent. He saw that he had a missed call and a text message from a number he didn't recognise.

Call me. Paddy.

He showed it to Adam, who had eventually located his ticket in his jacket pocket. Adam told him to ring immediately.

Colin walked a little way down the wide hallway, past posters of soon to be released films, and pressed dial.

'Hello?' said Paddy, answering on the second ring.

'It's Colin, how are you man?'

'Good,' came the swift reply. 'Rick and me have been down watching those Stonebridge lads practice. They look good and don't seem to be in the mind of giving up. So, we've come up with a plan. Be ready to stay a bit later after practice tomorrow night. See you then, pal.'

He hung up and Colin walked back towards the screen. Adam had already gone in and Colin stumbled towards the seat in the darkness. He apologised as he nearly knocked over a young girl's popcorn and almost fell into the lap of a rather annoyed looking man.

Finally, he slipped into the empty seat beside his friend.

'Well?' Adam whispered.

'Paddy says they are planning to do something to the Stonebridge team tomorrow night. I don't know what.'

14

A TWINKLE IN THE TORCHLIGHT

ADAM REPEATED THE journey to Elena Henderson's house, parking in a similar spot further up the street. He checked his watch. He'd intentionally chosen to arrive at a different time of the day; seven o'clock seemed perfect. Late enough that she would definitely be home from work, but early enough not to seem inappropriate.

He walked up to the door and knocked twice.

He heard movement from behind the door and was shocked when Elena opened the door.

She was wearing a red, figure hugging dress that was definitely too formal for a night in, alone. A pair of towering heels lent credence to the idea. In her hand, she was holding an unopened bottle of wine.

However shocked Adam was, it appeared she was more so. Her wide smile formed a perfect circle as she let out a gasp at the sight of him.

Clearly, she had been expecting someone else, though she managed to pull it together.

'Adam, how are you?' she said, adopting a more sombre tone which was at odds with the outfit choice. 'Do you have any news?'

'I'm okay,' Adam answered. 'No news, yet. We're still asking around. I was wondering if you wouldn't mind me asking a few questions.'

She took an almost imperceptible glance at her gold wristwatch and bit her lower lip.

'It won't take long,' Adam urged, and she relented.

She let him in and closed the door. He walked into the living room that he had been in, without her knowledge, just yesterday. It felt odd.

'Make yourself comfortable and I'll get you a drink,' she said, indicating to the sofa. 'Wine?'

'Just some water, thanks. I'm driving.'

She entered the kitchen while Adam took a seat. In the few minutes she was gone, he could hear a flurry of beeps which presumably were coming from her phone. He imagined her texting whoever she was expecting to tell them to delay their coming over.

Finally, she emerged with a tumbler of water and a half-filled glass of red wine. She set the water on the coffee table and sunk into a chair, cradling the wine glass.

'I'm not keeping you from something, am I?' Adam said.

'No,' she replied. 'I'm expecting a friend over; a woman from work who has very kindly offered to check on me.'

The emphasis she put on the company being female was so obviously a front. Adam almost pitied her, though he appeared to accept her story without question.

'I just wanted to ask a few questions about Matthew. We spoke to a few of his teammates and they suggested that the Meadowfield team were trying to do things to intimidate our team. I was wondering did Matthew ever mention anything about this?'

'No. He didn't really talk about the rowing thing at all. He knew I wasn't really interested, so he kept it to himself.'

Suddenly, she gasped loudly.

'Actually, I do remember something he said. We had this big fight because he blamed me for losing some of his equipment. I said he must've forgotten to bring it home one night, but he was adamant that it wasn't at the sheds. Over the weeks, more of the lads complained about losing things and they were convinced that someone was stealing from them.'

'Did he ever say who?'

'He mentioned a guy called Theo. He kept going on about him because he was new this year and he didn't know if he could be trusted. In the end, nothing was ever proven.'

'So, there was inter-team fighting?'

She nodded.

'To be honest, I don't think any of them really liked each other.'

'Was Matthew ever scared of going to training?'

'No,' she said. 'He was this big, burly man who wasn't scared of anything. He often compared being captain to one of those Attenborough documentaries; as soon as the young guns sense a bit of weakness, they pounce. That's why he always sort of ruled with an iron fist. It made him unpopular but it kept the others in line.'

Matthew didn't sound like a nice man. In fact, to Adam's mind, he sounded like an egotistical dictator when in fact all he was, was a captain of an amateur team of rowers.

Adam wouldn't be surprised if he *had* been pushed in. He sounded insufferable.

'Can I use your toilet?' he asked.

She nodded and directed him, though of course he already knew exactly where it was.

He walked up the stairs and went to the bathroom, but didn't enter. Instead, he closed the door loudly from the outside before tiptoeing to Elena's bedroom. It was the only room he didn't get a proper look around yesterday (having been mainly confined to the wardrobe), and he was keen to rectify that.

He took out his phone and turned on the torch.

The room was a bit messier than it was the last time he'd been here, but nowhere near as disordered as his own. Black trousers and a cream blouse, what Adam imagined must be her work clothes, were strewn on the bed alongside the contents of her handbag.

He passed the torch over the room, feeling his face redden at the sight of the wardrobe.

He pushed the thoughts of squeaking bedsprings out of his head, knowing he only had a minute at most before Elena would start to wonder where he was.

Pretty sure that there was nothing suspicious to be found, he moved to turn the torch off, when he saw something on the bedside table sparkling in its beam.

He moved as quietly as he could across the room and lifted the small object.

A cuff link; perhaps one of Matthew's that she kept by the bed for sentimental reasons, but more likely, Adam thought, belonging to the man she had invited to her bed yesterday.

And then, he realised exactly who it belonged to. He'd bet his house that the capital H stood for Holland. He remembered Colin tell him about the kitsch cufflinks that the estate agent had worn when he'd visited the office for the first time.

Simon Holland—that's who she was banging!

The cheek of the man, thought Adam. First, he took the captaincy freshly vacated by the recently deceased Matthew and now he was shagging his widow.

Simon Holland was doing nothing to improve the public's perception of his particular profession.

As Adam made his way to the bathroom and flushed the chain, he considered if Simon could be behind Matthew's murder. It made sense. He was in a position to take the lion's share of the prize money and, more importantly from what he knew of the man, he was the alpha male of the team. That status was probably more important to him than the cash.

He made his way downstairs, considering whether or not to bring up Simon.

In the end, he decided to keep that information under his hat for now. He thanked Elena for her time and returned to his car.

Instead of driving home, he circled around and parked his car in a space that gave him a clear view of her house. He didn't have to wait long at all for her visitor.

Adam was unsurprised when a tall man with dark hair, rather than a female colleague, emerged from the black BMW. He walked up to the door and kissed a laughing Elena on the cheek, before they both disappeared inside.

Did the estate agent pose a danger to her? Or could Simon and Elena really have planned this together?

15

A FAULTY ARM

ADAM'S EYES WERE hurting from concentrating on the screen. This was the side of business that he wasn't too hot on. Sure, he could slave away happily in a garden for the day, but an hour of VAT receipts and tax notes were beyond his skill level.

He was doing something about that, though. On the side of the desk were the stack of books about business he had invested in. He'd ordered them online and had secreted them under his bed when not in the house.

He was sort of used to bumbling through life and buying the books had felt like a very adult step. A ridiculous one at that.

His head kept telling him that Adam Whyte wouldn't amount to anything, let alone a successful businessman. Businessmen wore expensive, tailored suits and carried briefcases filled with important documents. They didn't toil in gardens and get their hands dirty. Literally.

Truth be told, he'd rather show his mum his dubious internet history than the covers of *Starting a Business for Dummies* or *Understanding Accounting*. Showing those to anyone else would mean admitting that he was serious about something. And he wasn't ready for that pressure. Yet.

The doorbell rang and he heard his mum groan out of her chair to answer it. He supposed it was a parcel delivery or one of her friends, but when he heard Colin's rumbling voice floating through the floorboard, he panicked. He lifted his pile of books and stuffed them as quickly as he could into the wardrobe, wincing as they clattered noisily onto the wooden base.

Colin appeared a minute later, just as Adam slammed the wardrobe closed.

'You're very red faced,' Colin said, hovering by the door. 'Have I caught you in the middle of something?'

'Shut up,' Adam replied. 'I was just doing some work.'

'Is that what you're calling it now?'

For the next few minutes, Adam filled Colin in on what information he'd gleaned from his house visit last night. When he'd finished, Colin looked shocked.

'So, Simon Holland is seeing Elena Henderson?'

'It certainly looked that way from last night. And sounded that way from the day before that…'

'Jesus.' Colin rubbed his chin with that back of his hand. 'It seems a bit soon to be moving on, doesn't it?'

'That's if she hadn't moved on before Matthew did.'

'You think she was doing the dirty on him before he died?'

'I'm not sure, and I'm not the grief police, but if my husband had died, I don't think I'd be ready to start something new a few weeks later. I think there may have been a period of cross-contamination.'

'What a horrible turn of phrase,' Colin said, throwing a sock he'd found at Adam.

As Adam went to bat it away, the arm of his chair separated from the leather upholstery, causing him to fall forward and faceplant onto the floor.

Colin roared with laughter as his friend picked himself up, holding the snapped plastic arm of the chair in one hand.

'I've only just bloody bought this,' he moaned, checking the damage to the chair. 'I've got a full day out and about tomorrow, so I'm going to have to take it back today. You fancy coming along?'

'Sorry, man,' Colin said. 'I have to get back to work. Some of us have set hours!'

The friends said goodbye and Adam shouted good luck down the stairs. Whatever Paddy was planning for tonight, Colin would need all the luck he could get.

THE WOOD EMPORIUM'S car park was empty when Adam pulled into it. He turned the engine off and walked around to the boot. From it, he manoeuvred the bulky chair, getting his angles just right as the chair slipped out. He grabbed the snapped piece of plastic and wheeled the chair inside.

The bell above the door had barely started tinkling when Percy sidled out of the shadows, uttering a greeting that made Adam swear aloud.

'Sorry for the fright,' Percy wheezed. 'How can I help you?'

Adam showed him the damaged chair and produced the receipt when asked. Percy apologised profusely as he waddled down the centre of the shop towards the computer and till.

With his tongue between his teeth, he logged onto the computer and clicked the mouse a few times. He blew out a mouthful of air, disturbing the dust that had settled on the desktop.

'I'm ever so sorry about this.'

Percy clicked a few more buttons and then turned the screen around so that Adam could see it. On it was a chair that looked almost the same as the one he had bought, but was several hundred pounds more expensive.

'They don't have the model you bought, and if they did, I wouldn't insult you by ordering the same one anyway, but they do have this one. Please allow me to exchange it for you, by way of apology.'

Adam tried to argue, and when that didn't work, he offered to pay at least some of the difference, but again his words fell on deaf ears.

'I think Jacob is up at the warehouse doing a stock check today, so I'll give him a ring and sort out delivery. He doesn't let me go up there anymore, on account of my back and I'm secretly glad. Stock checking is the most boring of all the jobs.'

He offered a small smile, before continuing.

'Anyway, I'm babbling. We'll be in touch. And once again, I'm very sorry for the inconvenience caused.'

Adam assured him one more time that it'd been no hassle, thanked him and walked out of the shop with a Wood Emporium Regatta weekend newsletter under his arm and a different opinion of the old man.

Percy Wood was alright, even if he had scared the bejeezus out of him at the start.

16

NEFARIOUS DEEDS

'YOU SEEM JUMPY, Colin.'

The words, spoken by Paddy, pulled Colin from his trance-like state in the back seat. He looked into the face of the ex-prisoner and forced a smile.

'Nah, man. I'm just a bit pissed that you won't tell me what we're about to do.'

'All in good time,' Paddy replied, while casting a glance at Ricky in the driver's seat.

Colin turned his attention back to the passing scenery. He rested his head against the cool glass and tried to slow his pulse by adopting some of the mindfulness techniques he'd been teaching the old folks at work.

It didn't work.

Try as he might, he couldn't shake the feeling that Paddy and Ricky were about to include him in something that may be the wrong side of legal. Not for the first time, he wondered if he should just bin the whole charade off. Paddy and Ricky were nutters and, not for the first time, he dreaded to think how this could impact his job and his life.

Colin observed the two of them, in the front, whispering and giggling. He felt sick.

He watched as the outskirts of Stonebridge came into view and listened as Ricky lambasted his hometown. It struck Colin as incredibly childish to be slagging off the architecture of a supermarket, but Ricky seemed to be enjoying himself.

A few minutes later, it became clear where they were going. Ricky indicated down the narrow road towards the Stonebridge rowing team's practice shed and swung the car into the track at high speed.

Instead of driving all the way down, he pulled into a lay-by that was mostly obscured by the overhanging branches of the surrounding forest.

'Out,' he ordered, as he turned the engine off.

Paddy obliged, pushing the door open and running around to the boot. From it, he pulled a black box with a carry handle.

'What's that?' Colin asked as he climbed out of the back seat.

'It's our toy for the evening,' Paddy laughed.

Ricky and Paddy set off walking down the track. The light was fading fast and the silence, punctuated only by the occasional cracking of a twig or a hoot from the forest, was unnerving.

When the building by the riverside came into sight, Ricky tugged the sleeve of Colin's jacket and pulled him into the edge of the treeline.

'Right, big man, here's the plan. We're going to go into their shed and cause some carnage. We've tried a few things now and nothing seems to be stopping them from competing, so it's time to up the ante.'

'Wasn't Matthew dying upping the ante?'

'For the last time,' Ricky snarled, 'we had nothing to do with that.'

Colin shrugged, trying to give off the impression that he didn't care one way or the other.

'Look man,' he said. 'All I want to do is have a share of the money, so let's do whatever crazy nonsense you have up your sleeves and get out of here.'

Colin wasn't sure if he sounded convincing or not, but Ricky and Paddy seemed to buy it. Before he knew it, they'd set off at pace towards the river. Colin followed them.

When he rounded the corner of the building, Ricky was already pushing a key into the padlock which held the metallic shutters tight to the ground. With a twist, they opened and Paddy began pushing them up into their holdings. The now uncovered door beneath was unlocked and they simply walked into the shed.

Inside, there wasn't much to see. Two canoes, stowed securely with the bottoms facing out, took up the back wall. A range of colourful kayaks filled another and a door on the bare wall led to the function room and bar area. A storage tub, filled with various sized oars, sat in the corner.

Paddy set the box he had retrieved from the boot of Ricky's car on the floor with a thump. A tinkle of metal sounded from within. The noise echoed off the concrete walls and floor.

'Shhh,' scolded Ricky.

'There's nobody within a mile of here,' Paddy shot back. 'Calm yourself.'

It was the first time Colin had seen a flare of anger from Paddy and it was an intimidating sight. The veins on his neck were popping and his teeth were bared like a wild animal.

'I'm calm,' said Ricky, holding his hands up in a placating manner.

Paddy, on his knees, undid the box's clasps and finally Colin set eyes on what was inside. He was, however, still clueless as to the actual intricacies of the plan.

Paddy lifted the drill out of the box and pressed the trigger. The end of the drill whirred into life. He lifted his eyebrows at Colin, as if expecting a compliment.

'What are you going to do with that?' Colin asked, confused.

In answer, Paddy pointed the drill at the canoes.

'We're going to drill a series of small holes into the bottom of the canoes, so that the Stonebridge team are unable to race. Therefore, they will have no choice but to forfeit.'

Ricky laughed. It sounded cold and cruel to Colin's ears.

'Imagine them at their next training session, when they realise there's water coming in. They'll not be able to point the finger at us because no one knows we have a key, and there'll be no sign of a break in. There won't be time to replace the canoes either, with the race being so close.'

Paddy was laughing now too. A high pitched, evil-sounding laugh.

Colin watched on as he carefully selected an appropriately sized drill bit and screwed it into place. He then got to his feet and approached the canoes.

Colin wracked his brains for some way to put a stop to this sabotage, but short of giving himself up, nothing came to mind.

Instead, he stood idly by as Paddy began drilling. The squeal of the metal drill bit penetrating the fibreglass was loud; almost disorientating. Colin clasped his temples and gritted his teeth, before nodding at the door to let Ricky know he was heading outside.

Once out in the fresh air, Colin took his phone out and was in the middle of composing a text to Adam when Ricky stepped outside too.

'Bloody noisy, isn't it?' he asked, as Colin quickly pocketed his phone.

'Horrible,' Colin answered.

'Look, I know all of this seems a bit extreme. But we need the money more than the Stonebridge team do. We know we can't beat them fairly, so this is the only way.'

'It doesn't sit well with me,' Colin said. 'I don't want anyone to get hurt.'

'They won't, mate. They'll put the canoe in the river and see that it's leaky immediately. It's an inconvenience at most.'

Colin deliberated on his next sentence, wondering how to word it best so as not to cause offence.

'Have you heard any whispers about what happened to Matthew?'

'This again? Look, all I know is from what the papers have said, that it was an accident. We had practice that night, so none of us could possibly have had anything to do with it.'

'Was Paddy at practice that night?'

Ricky took a few seconds.

'Come to think of it, no. He's only ever missed one and that was the night he wasn't there. But, I can assure you, he hadn't anything to do with it either. It was probably Matthew's missus that did it. Her, or he killed himself.'

'Why do you think that?'

'Ah, man. It's common knowledge that Matthew and Elena Henderson were heading for divorce. My brother worked with Matthew and he was proper down in the dumps for the last couple of months because of it. He was sure she was seeing someone behind his back.'

Well, hot dog, thought Colin.

As he was about to push Ricky for more information, Paddy poked his head out of the door.

'Oi, fishwives, we're done here.'

Ricky leapt into action, pulling the padlock from his coat pocket as Paddy rolled the shutters back down to the ground.

'Now, let's get out of here,' Paddy said, as they sprinted back to the car. As they clambered in and sped off, Paddy howled with adrenaline-fuelled laughter.

'Well, let's hope that does the trick.' Ricky said, entering the main road and decreasing his speed, so as not to stand out.

'Aye,' Paddy agreed. 'If not, we've only got one more thing up our sleeves and I'd prefer not to go there.'

17

A VIEWING AND A NO SHOW

A FEW DAYS had passed since Paddy's casual act of vandalism and Colin still wasn't sleeping well. Not well at all.

Every time he closed his eyes, the events in the boatshed kept playing on the back of his eyelids like some sort of drive-in cinema. He was worried sick that someone would find out he'd been involved, even under the guise of an undercover investigation. Which, he knew, would hold no weight with the police, and even less with his employers.

By the time the sun rose and it was time to get up, he had decided that night had been the final straw. He wouldn't be going back to the Meadowfield team. His undercover operation had come to an end with less than satisfactory results.

All he had learned was that Paddy and Ricky were fairly reprehensible characters and could well be behind Matthew's death, but were never going to admit it. He'd been coerced into taking part in their psychological games and been witness to physical sabotage of the other team's equipment. Both of them were closed books and were never going to admit to anything, so that was one dead end.

The other thing he had found out was that Matthew and Elena's relationship had been coming to a close before his passing. Perhaps that hinted at suicide. According to Ricky's brother's testimony, he'd been miserable for months. Maybe one night after practice, he'd finally had enough and thrown himself into the murky waters of the River Bann.

Or maybe Elena and Simon Holland were behind it. From what Adam had said, the two of them had seemed pretty cosy together. Maybe with Matthew out of the way, they were finally able to start a life they both wanted, but hadn't been able to have with Matthew alive.

Maybe Colin could lean on Simon a bit today during the viewing. Perhaps if he pretended to be super interested, the prospect of a sale may loosen the estate agent's tongue somewhat.

Speaking of which, if Colin didn't get a move on, there'd be no viewing!

THE HOUSE LOOKED promising from the outside. Even though it was a new build, it looked full of character—shutters on the side of the windows and a mint green door with a hefty lion head knocker.

It was in a nice part of town; affordable too, and he could imagine himself pulling up on the driveway after work and grabbing a beer from the fridge. Content, Colin sat on the steps outside with high hopes.

A few minutes later, a red Audi pulled up on the street outside and a suited man Colin recognised from the photos in the estate agents got out and walked towards him, hand extended.

'Jeffrey Morrow,' he said, wringing Colin's hand. 'Ever so sorry, but Simon couldn't make it today and he knew you were ever so keen on the property. We didn't want to let you down.'

Jeffrey led Colin into the house and showed him around. He enthusiastically pointed out features such as the south facing garden and the generously sized second bedroom, before inviting Colin to have a wander around on his own.

Having walked around it and got a feel for it, Colin fell in love with the house. The numbers worked for him and he was keen to do a deal, but first he wanted to know about Simon's absence. He walked back down the stairs towards the stand-in estate agent.

'I like it,' Colin said. 'I think I'd like to put an offer in.'

Jeffrey's face lit up. Colin's next words brought him back down to Earth.

'Since I've been dealing with Simon, I'd quite like to conclude my business with him though. Will he be in the office tomorrow?'

'Umm..' Jeffrey mumbled. Colin sensed that he was buying for time. He fixed him with a Paddington-style stare.

'The thing is… Simon hasn't been in the office for a couple of days and I can't get in touch with him. His phone is off. But,' he continued, regaining his professional mask, 'as partners, I can do exactly what he could. You're in safe hands.'

Jeffrey took a step towards the door, the look on his face suggesting that he couldn't wait another second to get back to the office and sign those papers.

'Exactly how long has Simon been missing?' Colin asked, as Jeffrey closed the door.

'He didn't come to work yesterday, nor today.'

'Have you phoned the police?'

Jeffrey actually chuckled.

'No, he's a big boy, who can look after himself. He's probably psyching himself up for the race. It's the day after tomorrow, you know?'

'Has he done this before?'

'No,' replied Jeffrey, absentmindedly. 'Though, it's his first year as captain. He has been snappier than usual in the office. I put in down to the added pressure. Anyway, shall we meet at the office and we can talk figures?'

Colin nodded and both men walked to their respective cars. As soon as he started the ignition, he dialled Adam's number.

JACK BAUER'S RINGTONE interrupted the music Adam was listening to. Yeah, the show hadn't been on TV for something like twelve years, but the *bloop bloop* of the tone always made him smile.

He pulled his headphones out, silenced the leaf blower and answered the phone.

'Good morrow, fair Colin,' he said, adopting a Ye Olde English accent.

His friend's reply was less friendly.

'Simon's gone missing. I'm going to ring Paddy and see if he knows anything, but he's unlikely to give anything away. Can you ring Elena and find out if he is at hers? There might be a perfectly reasonable explanation behind all of this, but with the race so close, something doesn't feel right.'

Adam confirmed he would, before hanging up. He found her number in his phone book and dialled.

'Hello,' she answered. She sounded angry.

'Hi, it's Adam Whyte.'

'I can see that on the phone display. What do you want?'

Adam was unperturbed. In his career with woman to date, he was used to them talking to him like something they'd stood on—if they'd even elected to speak to him in the first place.

'I was wondering if you'd spoken to Simon Holland recently?'

There was silence for a few seconds.

'Why would I be speaking to him?' she asked, finally, the venom of her last words replaced with a hint of confusion.

'Cards on the table, Elena. I saw him enter your house the other night after I'd left. I saw him kiss your cheek so I assume something is going on there.'

She attempted to interrupt, but he continued speaking.

'There's no judgement, okay? But I need you to answer me, have you spoken to him recently?'

There was more silence on the other end of the line, before a series of muffled sobs erupted in Adam's ear.

'No,' she said. 'I thought he was into me, but he's just like every other man. Once he got what he wanted, the communication stopped.'

'Can you remember the last time you did hear from him?' Adam said, attempting to interrupt her diatribe against men.

'Yesterday morning. We were arranging who was going to cook next and he was moaning about some damage to the canoes. We arranged to meet last night, but he never showed up and now my messages aren't delivering.'

'Elena, listen to me. We have reason to believe that something has happened to him. If you hear from him, please let me know.'

He hung up, phoned Colin back and relayed the conversation he'd just had with Elena.

'I don't think she's got anything to do with it. With Matthew or Simon. She was genuinely angry that he'd ghosted her.'

'Which leaves Paddy or Ricky,' replied Colin. 'Predictably, Paddy is denying any knowledge of Simon's disappearance. But, when we got back in the car the other night, he said he had one more idea up his sleeve in case the holes in the canoe didn't work.'

'And you think the contingency plan was kidnap?'

'With Paddy, who knows?'

18

A BREAKTHROUGH FROM AN UNLIKELY PLACE

ADAM LAY ON his bed, his mind whirring with thoughts he was finding hard to file in a helpful order.

They were at a sticking point. In his mind, Elena was innocent of any wrongdoing. Well, wrongdoing in the murder of her husband, anyway. And she probably had nothing to do with Simon's disappearance either.

Though the jury was out on whether her relationship with Simon Holland had started before or after Matthew's demise, that wasn't for Adam to concern himself with. Live and let live, as his mother said.

The troubling part was that Paddy and Ricky had had some sort of contingency plan in place, but wouldn't give any details as to what that plan was. It left Adam and Colin clueless, with a man's life potentially on the line.

Colin had spoken to Jeffrey Morrow again when he'd gone in to secure the house. Jeffrey hadn't appeared worried and was keen not to get the police involved, for fear of wasting their time, he'd said.

Adam and Colin had deliberated on the next step for a while earlier in the evening, but no real plan had emerged. Colin had suggested that they stake out the Meadowfield boatshed, just in case that's where Paddy and Ricky were keeping Simon. It had felt like a lot of effort for a maybe, considering both had work the next day.

In the end, they'd decided that what happened next was out of their hands. They'd been hired to investigate Matthew's death and, while there were still some suspicions, it was clear they weren't going to get any concrete answers tonight.

Adam had almost resigned himself to phoning Elena in the morning and telling her that they were going to stop investigating. And that, after another night of a no-show from Simon, it had probably become a police matter.

Sighing, he untangled his headphones and plugged them into the port on his phone. Recently, he'd been listening to podcasts before bed, as they seemed to relax him.

He found an episode he'd been half way through—*The Pitfalls of Business*—and pressed play. The American presenter's animated voice filled his ears as he fell back onto his pillow.

For a while he simply lay there, staring at the ceiling and listening as sleep crept up on him.

Suddenly, he shot up into a sitting position with a gasp. He unlocked his phone and rewound what he was listening to. The American had said something that had set off a series of thoughts in Adam's mind.

He listened again, to make sure that he had heard correctly.

"Debt can be the biggest driver towards not only your business failing, but towards you becoming someone who you don't like. It can make you do things you never thought you'd do, and treat people in a way that is not okay. It can turn you into a monster…"

Adam pulled the earphones out and went over to the desk. He pulled out the top drawer and found the plastic bag that contained the information he'd been given when he had bought the desk and chair from The Wood Emporium.

He laid his hand on what he needed and pulled it out.

The Wood Emporium Regatta newsletter.

He leafed through it and found the page he needed. Instead of an interview with then captain Matthew Henderson, there was a short celebration of his achievements, coupled with a mournful obituary.

Adam picked up his phone again and called Colin.

'I think I know where Simon is. And I think I know who killed Matthew Henderson.'

COLIN AND ADAM pulled up in a car park a short walk from the sprawling industrial estate. Adam pulled his coat on as they exited the car and they began walking towards the silhouetted warehouses.

'So, you think Jacob Wood is behind all this?' Colin asked.

'I do. When we went to buy my desk, he was slagging off his dad for sponsoring the race and putting up the prize money. He said they couldn't afford it and that his dad was putting sentimentality over the business. He also said that he was due to interview Matthew for the newsletter they put out. He was supposed to interview him on the night he died, but when Jacob got there, he claimed Matthew was nowhere to be seen.'

'You think Jacob did this to spite his dad?'

'No,' said Adam. 'I think he did it to try and have the race called off so that they wouldn't have to hand over five grand to the winning team. They've always got a sale on, so they must be in a pretty precarious financial position. I bet he thought that pushing Matthew into the river, if that's what he did, would put an end to this year's race.'

'But, it didn't,' Colin concluded. 'Instead, Stonebridge vowed to win it in his honour. So, Jacob had to go to plan B. You don't think he will have killed Simon?'

'I don't,' Adam confirmed. 'Too much heat for a small town. He'll have kidnapped him with the intention of freeing him as soon as the race was called off.'

'But, couldn't Simon just go to the police and tell them exactly who had him once he's been released?'

'I'm betting that Jacob somehow got to him without Simon knowing who it is. He was probably blindfolded and taken to the warehouse without knowing where he is.'

They were amongst the warehouses now. Adam could make out the one belonging to the Wood family, thanks to a small plaque to the side of the door that was being illuminated by the huge, neon sign of the cavernous Lyon's food service warehouse next door.

The front door of the Wood warehouse was shuttered, but a quick check around the perimeter of the building unearthed a back entrance.

Adam tried to jimmy the lock, but to no avail. It wouldn't budge.

Eventually, Colin took matters into his own hands and unleashed his size elevens. It only took a few kicks to free the door from its lock. Colin led the way.

IT WAS DARK inside the warehouse, the moon managing to provide only a small slice of light. Colin and Adam crept in quietly and listened.

At first, there was only silence.

And then, Adam heard it. The ragged breaths of someone close by.

He got out his phone, lit the torch and tiptoed towards where he thought the noises were coming from. The warehouse was full of wooden furniture and the layout reminded Adam of a maze. He wondered whether Jacob had laid it out like this on purpose.

The boys rounded a corner and there sat Simon Holland on a kitchen chair in a little alcove of the warehouse. He had a black bag over his head, though it was easy to identify him from the smart, pinstripe suit and chunky wristwatch.

'Who's there?' he uttered, the fear making his voice tremble.

'It's Colin McLaughlin.'

'The boy I'm trying to sell a house to?'

'Yeah,' Colin confirmed. 'Although, this is unrelated.'

He walked over to the estate agent and slipped the bag off his head. Simon's eyes narrowed at the beam of torchlight, which Adam quickly diverted away from him. Instead, he walked around the back of the chair and directed the light at the bindings, which Colin made short work of.

Free, Simon stood slowly on unsteady legs and massaged his raw wrists.

'Where am I?' he asked, his voice hoarse.

'Percy Wood's warehouse,' Colin answered. 'We think his son, Jacob, kidnapped you.'

'Bastard. Can I borrow your phone to call the police?'

Colin nodded and slipped his phone from his pocket. He unlocked it and handed it to Simon.

As he hit the third nine and hovered his thumb over the call button, a noise from outside stopped him. The industrial estate didn't get much passing traffic in the middle of the night, which meant that the roar of the engine must be approaching for a reason.

'No time for that,' Simon said, handing the phone back to Colin. 'But, I have an idea.'

They gathered around him as he revealed the details of his hastily put together plan, before getting into position.

19

CAN'T SEE THE WOOD FOR THE TREES

THE ENGINE NOISE got progressively louder until it sounded like the car might plough through the walls. Thankfully, it didn't. Instead, it swelled to a roar before stopping abruptly close to the front door, just like Simon thought it would.

Colin waited by one side of the door, crouched just underneath the light switch while Adam mirrored him on the other side. Simon stood in the aisle of the warehouse, the black bag back on his head. In the little light available, it was a terrifying sight.

Outside, the motorised hum of the shutters opening shattered the silence. Colin gave Adam a little nod to settle his nerves, which his friend returned.

How had they managed to get caught up in this? Adam thought.

The shutters clunked into their housing and keys jangled in the lock. With a click it opened and a hand appeared around the frame, fumbling for the light switch in the dark.

After a few attempts, he found it and with a flick, the room was illuminated.

Simon's plan immediately clicked into play. Jacob took one step into the warehouse and at the sight of the estate agent standing in the aisle with the bag over his head, let out a bloodcurdling shriek. At that, Colin rugby tackled Jacob from the side, taking him to the floor. While Colin secured his legs, Adam straddled his chest.

Simon pulled the bag from his head and walked over to the furniture seller. He bent over him and stared into his eyes.

'You prick,' he uttered, before tying his hands together and dragging him to a nearby chair.

WITH ASSURANCES THAT no one was going to hurt him (though Simon took some convincing), Jacob finally stopped whimpering. He pleaded to be untied, but was met with unsympathetic glares.

'Why did you kidnap me?' Simon asked, venom soaking every syllable.

'I thought that I could save the business that way. We're haemorrhaging money on rent and on good quality furniture that no one wants to buy. I thought that if the captain didn't turn up, the race would be called off and we'd have saved five thousand pounds.'

'Did you kill my friend?'

Jacob's chin sunk to his chest, his eyes fixed on the floor.

Simon took a threatening step towards him, but Colin intervened.

'Go outside and get some fresh air,' he said to Simon while handing him his mobile. 'And phone the police while you're at it.'

Simon looked like he wanted to dish out some stone-cold retribution, but Colin's level words seemed to sink in, as he turned and made his way through the open front door.

'Did you kill Matthew Henderson?'

Tears filled Jacob's eyes as he nodded once.

'I didn't mean to though. I was supposed to be interviewing him for the newsletter. Dad and I had just had a huge argument about our cash flow. He couldn't get it into his head that handing over five grand to the winner was a ludicrous thing to do in our situation.'

'So, you killed Matthew to stop the race?'

'Subconsciously, maybe,' Jacob admitted. 'I'd tried talking to Matthew a few weeks ago to try and get him to forego the prize money, but he'd said no. I thought he'd be sympathetic to our situation, but he couldn't have cared less. When I arrived at the boathouse to interview him, he goaded me straight away. He was so close to the water's edge and before I knew what I was doing, I'd hit him over the head. I immediately tried to grab him, but the currents were so strong that he was taken away before my very eyes.'

'And you didn't think about reporting it?' Colin asked, disgusted.

'I did. But then I thought better of it. I reckoned that with the team captain tragically dying, the race organisers might have made a compassionate call to cancel the race. When it didn't happen, I was livid. But I wasn't going to admit to murder. It looked like an accident and that's the way I thought it would stay.'

'Until you decided to kidnap the new captain?' Adam laughed. 'You realise that in a small town you were never going to get away with it?'

Jacob heaved a heavy sigh.

'Money makes you do crazy things. I was only ever trying to save the business and protect my family.'

'And in doing so, you've probably consigned your father's business to history. No one is going to want to buy furniture from a murderer.'

Jacob hung his head in shame as sirens filled the night sky.

20

THE STONEBRIDGE REGATTA

COLIN AND ADAM watched from the bridge as the canoes passed underneath. It was neck and neck with nothing to separate the two teams.

'You didn't fancy it in the end, then?' asked Adam.

'I think I might have suffered the same fate as poor Matthew had Paddy found out I was an undercover operative from Stonebridge!' laughed Colin.

In the distance, near the finish line of the race, a small stage had been set up next to a large screen, onto which live footage of the race was being projected. The boys followed the path by the river towards the finish line, eager to find out who'd won.

TEN MINUTES LATER, the judges were still deliberating over a photo finish. It was the closest race in the history of the regatta, and both teams were sat by the riverbank in two separate camps.

A microphone squeaked, causing many in the crowd to jump in surprise. Their attention was diverted to the stage, where the mayor of Stonebridge stood, with Percy Wood beside him.

'Ladies and gentleman, boys and girls,' started the mayor, doing his best impression of a circus ringmaster. 'The results are in. The winner of this year's Stonebridge Regatta is…'

He stopped, surveying the crowd with a wide smile, milking the moment.

'It's not bloody X factor, pal!' someone shouted near the front, causing a gale of laughter.

'Keep your hair on,' retorted the mayor with a smile. 'The winner is Meadowfield!'

A mixture of cheers and jeers filled the air as the Meadowfield team jumped to their feet and began a chorus of "Championes!"

The despondent Stonebridge team, led by Simon, got to their feet and formed a guard of honour for the winners to walk through on their way to the stage.

Percy Wood took to the microphone as the winning team received their medals.

'Congratulations to the Meadowfield team on a fine win. Before the trophy is presented, I would like to offer a sincere apology on behalf of the Wood family. My son's actions were not those of an honest man. What he did will haunt me to my dying day, and I only hope you do not associate his heinous actions with the family name.'

He gave a small sniff as the crowd applauded him.

'The business will be closing for good next week and I am delighted to hand over a cheque for five thousand to each team.'

The Stonebridge team's necks collectively whipped around at breakneck speed to look at the stage, to be sure that what they heard was correct.

And it was.

Percy was holding two oversized cheques, totalling ten thousand pounds.

As the celebrations began in earnest, Colin and Adam began walking home.

'That's two murders we've solved now,' Adam said. 'We're making a name for ourselves. I might give up the gardening and go full time.'

'Might be slow business—surely that's Stonebridge's excitement quota reached for a few more years.'

Adam nodded, and the two of them walked in silence.

'When do you get your new house?' Adam asked, after a while.

'Not sure,' Colin replied. 'Should be pretty quickly though. There's no chain to hold it up so it should be good to go in a few weeks' time.'

'I might be joining you.'

'In my house?' Colin asked.

'No, dickhead. In buying my own. Simon was so thankful to us for rescuing him that he told me he could get me a good deal on a flat in the centre of town.'

'Look at us moving up in the world,' Colin laughed. 'Our mothers will be so proud!'

-3-

MEAT IS MURDER

CHRIS MCDONALD

1

CHICKEN

A FINE EXAMPLE of Northern Ireland's famous summers was in full bloom—there had been an hour of glorious sunshine in the morning, followed by a biblical downpour.

Despite the rain, Tyler Love smiled as the padlock clicked into place. He gave his comrade, who was now chained to the fence, a pat on the shoulder before walking up the line of bodies like he was their military commander.

He grinned at each person in turn as he passed by, and doled out words of passion.

We are The History Makers.

That caused a cheer that gave Tyler a boost. Not that he needed one—he already felt like John Wayne.

Change is not a threat, it's an opportunity.

No cheer this time.

Hmm. Probably a bit too wordy for these simpletons, he thought.

He raised a fist and some of his crew gave him a stoic nod in return, their minds turning to the task at hand, though really there wasn't too much to think about. All they had to do was make sure that the owners of the abattoir and the investor whose teat they planned on suckling from couldn't access the property.

When Tyler got to the end of the line, he bent down and stroked the cheek of the last protester. Helena lifted her chin and met Tyler's eyes, fire blazing in her own. He pressed his lips against hers and then refocused himself on what he was here to do.

He marched to the gate of the abattoir and pulled the chain around his middle. It was thicker than the others, more heavy-duty. It wasn't needed, particularly, but it was an effective subliminal way of showing that he was making the biggest statement.

If it wasn't for this great hunk of metal holding me back, there'd be no chance for these butchers of death.

That's the message he wanted to give off.

Making sure it wasn't too tight, he slipped the padlock in between two links and pressed down, securing himself in place.

He looked down the line at his fellow bunch of rag-tags, all giving up their Saturday for the greater good. The T-shirts had been a great idea, though he had been loath to admit it—giving Willow praise always seemed to upset the power balance in the group. He didn't want to give her any ideas that he was willing to relinquish the leader role.

Still, each member of the group had a lettered shirt that spelled out MEAT IS MURDER. It was a powerful message, and one he hoped would make a difference. It would look great on the cover of the local newspaper, for a start.

He looked out at the small crowd that had gathered, and tried not to be too disheartened. He thought that their social media blitz, alongside the adverts they'd placed in the Stonebridge Chronicle, might've encouraged more of the town's residents to join their protest.

But, there was still time before the real action began. Some of the undecided might make their way to this side of town just in time.

He glanced to his left again and noticed Helena staring at him with a strange look on her face. He smiled at her and she returned it, though there was something in her look that was gnawing at him.

Was she still thinking about their argument last week?

He turned away from her. There was nothing he could do about that now and, besides, there were bigger fish to fry today.

Not that frying fish would go down well with this group.

Wanting to do something, he called for one of the protesters who had opted to carry a placard, having wimped out of being chained up, and asked them to pass him the megaphone.

He grabbed it off her and turned it on. It emitted a shrill screech that caused some of the onlookers to jump in shock.

'People of Stonebridge, we, The History Makers, are here today to make a change. McNulty's Meats has been in the news over the past few years for all the wrong reasons. There have been allegations of animal cruelty, poor working conditions and unfair redundancies. And now, perhaps the worst of all, Kevin and Ron McNulty, the owners of this abomination,' he stopped and turned his head to the grey blocky building behind him, 'are planning to sell to a multinational.'

He stopped to allow his words to sink in. The rumours had been swirling around the town for weeks that the McNulty brothers were planning on selling up. A huge business from England with a worldwide reach had apparently approached the two brothers with an offer they couldn't refuse.

When the murmurings had abated slightly, Tyler continued.

'Think what it'll do to our little town. Can you imagine some faceless owner, sitting in his fancy boardroom in London, giving a second thought to what happens to this place? They'll pollute our river, poison our air and build on whatever land they want if it means turning a profit.'

He was pleased to see that his words were causing a stir. Some of the crowd were muttering angrily while others had started a chant, which Tyler joined in with on the megaphone. The abattoir was in a small industrial estate, and some of the other warehouse doors had opened, the interest of their occupants piqued.

The noise suddenly died down as two sleek, black cars turned the corner of the road and pulled up on the kerb outside the gate.

Some of the crowd decided that now was the time to leave, their nerve deserting them, not wanting to be spotted by one of the McNulty brothers. The owners of the abattoir had a fearsome reputation.

As the engines died, the two brothers emerged from one of the cars. Kevin McNulty was the eldest. His wiry, prematurely grey hair was complemented with a matching moustache and his alert eyes were presided over by a slab of a forehead. He was well over six foot, though stocky.

Ron, the younger brother, was different in almost every way. His angular jaw was coated in designer stubble and his hair carefully gelled to the side. Though much shorter than his brother, his muscular frame was evident under his perfectly cut three-piece suit. He may have had the face, but Kevin had the brains.

The brothers noticed the protesters chained to their fence at the same time. Ron's eyes narrowed, while Kevin gave a playful laugh, trying to make light of the situation for their guest, who had just emerged from the second car.

'I thought you said there wouldn't be any bother,' the man said in a Cockney accent, as he approached the brothers.

'This?' Kevin said, motioning to the blocked gate. 'This is no bother. Nothing to worry about. Sure, why don't you head back to the hotel for a while and we'll sort this? We'll give you a bell when we're ready to start the tour.'

The Englishman nodded curtly and returned to his car, which took off as soon as he had closed the door. The McNultys watched it disappear around the corner before shooing the crowd. Most, including some of the protesters holding the placards, made the smart decision to vacate the vicinity.

When the area was mostly empty, the McNultys advanced towards the gate. Tyler could feel the sweat running down his back, though he tried to appear confident as the two men stopped in front of him.

'These hippies,' Ron said, pointing at the protesters chained to the fence, 'are a bit of an annoyance. But *you* are blocking the gate. That makes you, and you alone, the object of our attention.'

'Meat is murder!' shouted Tyler, though with no audience, save for his fellow protesters, the words seemed to lack any substance.

Kevin sniggered.

'Your little stunt didn't go down well with Mr Jones. He is a man who is very conscious of public perception. In fact, if we don't show him around this afternoon, the deal could be off.'

'Good,' spat Tyler.

Ron's face reddened and he nodded to his elder brother who delivered a hefty punch to Tyler's midriff with one of his ham-sized fists. Tyler gasped for air as pain flared through his body.

'Now,' said Ron, addressing the rest of the group. 'Who's going to make the smart decision and leave?'

Most of the protester's hands shot up. No one wanted to be on the receiving end of a McNulty fist.

'You lot are smarter than you look, which isn't saying much,' Ron laughed, before turning to Tyler. 'And what about you?'

Still fighting to pull air into his lungs, Tyler summoned enough saliva to spit into Ron's face.

The brother pulled away in disgust, using his tie to wipe the spit off his chin.

'You are going to bloody well pay for that,' he said.

As he swung his arm back in preparation for an almighty punch, the wail of sirens filled the air. A couple of police cars mounted the kerb and a number of uniformed officers rushed towards the scene.

'You just got very lucky,' Ron whispered. 'But your luck will run out.'

He moved towards Tyler like he was going to punch him, though stopped short and laughed when he cowered. Ron nodded at a police officer as he passed, and he and his brother walked away, back towards the car they'd arrived in. Tyler smirked as he watched them go.

Phase one had been a success.

Now, it was time to turn up the heat.

2

FEUER FREI!

ADAM WHYTE LIFTED the last of the tools out of his van and placed them carefully into his lock up. Since moving into his own place, he didn't have the space to keep all of his gardening tools, so had rented a small storage unit nearby.

Though it was a small thing, it made him feel that bit more professional. Six months ago, he had been happy to lie about on the sofa all day, alternating games of FIFA with episode after episode of Sherlock and asking his mum to make him sandwiches for lunch.

All that had changed when he and his friend, Colin McLaughlin, had inadvertently taken on the roles of amateur sleuths and had now helped solve two murder cases that the police had written off as accidents.

The feeling of pride he'd had at solving those cases had spurred him on to do something with his life. That something had turned out to be a garden maintenance business. It had started small; just him, his car, a lawnmower and a rickety trailer he'd managed to salvage from the dump.

Now, here he was, unloading tools from a van with his name and company logo on the side.

When he was sure that the van was empty, he pulled the roller door of the storage unit down and secured it with a heavy-duty padlock. He pulled at the handle and, content that it was secure, got in his van and started the engine.

The journey still felt odd.

He had only been living in his flat for the best part of three weeks and had found himself, more than once, driving in post-work autopilot towards the familiarity of his mum's house instead.

He navigated the quiet roads and pulled into the car park at the rear of his flat a few minutes later. Grabbing his bag from the passenger seat, he jumped out of the van and walked to the main door. He held it open for an elderly lady he didn't know, before climbing the stairs to the third floor and jamming the keys into the lock on his door.

His flat was on the small side, and sparsely furnished, but the rent was cheap and it offered a panoramic view of the town he'd lived in all his life. And what a view it was: during the day, a small town with narrow cobbled streets and pretty buildings, surrounded by lush green fields. Beyond that, an endless ocean stretched out like a turquoise carpet. At night, a blanket of inky blackness allowed galaxies of stars, lightyears away, to settle in for the night like old friends.

He threw his bag down beside the sofa in the living room and headed for the kitchen, only realising as he opened the fridge just how hungry he was.

He grabbed a ready meal and stuck it in the microwave, admonishing himself for being so unhealthy. Adam had always been weedy, no matter what he ate, but since turning his hand to the hard graft of his job, his body had started to change.

Muscles he didn't know the name of had started to announce themselves and even his best friend Colin, a regular gym-goer, was impressed with the results.

If I could only get the diet right, Adam thought as he pulled the piping hot, processed lasagne out of the microwave, passing it from hand to hand to avoid a scalding. He mentally added oven gloves to the list of things it would be handy to own.

He made his way back into the living room and sat at the dining table, flicking the television on. Scrolling through Netflix until he found what he was looking for, he grabbed his fork and tucked into his tomatoey meal.

As he finished, his phone rang.

'Hello,' he answered. 'Whyte's Gardening Services.'

'Do you have to answer your phone like that every time?' asked Colin on the other end of the line.

'You never know when a business opportunity is going to arrive.'

'Well, you should know that when it's my name on your display, I'm not calling for your services. Even if I had a garden, I wouldn't trust you with it.'

'What do you want?' Adam asked.

'FIFA?'

'Yep.'

TEN MINUTES LATER, Colin and Adam were sitting on the sofa, picking their teams.

Adam had met Colin at primary school and they had remained best friends for the ensuing twenty years. They'd seen each other at their best and at their worst, and were all the closer for it.

'How are the old folks doing?' Adam asked.

'They're all alright. Barry is scouring the paper every week, trying to find us leads to investigate,' Colin laughed.

Colin worked in the Stonebridge Retirement Home. Since solving the two murders they'd stumbled into investigating, the residents had come to view him as some sort of messiah and sworn protector. One of the residents, Barry, was actively trying to find him cases, even though Colin told him his investigating days were over.

'I don't think I could handle any more excitement,' Adam said.

'I don't think Stonebridge has any more to throw at us.'

'You say that, but did you hear what the hippies were up to?'

'Aye, I saw it on the news. Braver folk than me, going up against the McNulty brothers.'

'Brave? Stupid, more like!'

'Anyway, enough of the neighbourhood watch,' said Colin. 'Hurry up and pick your team.'

With teams picked and tactics sorted, the game began. The usual jibes were thrown back and forth and, with ten minutes on the clock, natural order was restored. Adam was 2-0 down.

As half-time approached, a bright flash followed by an almighty wall of noise from outside caught their attention. They paused the game and moved to the window.

'Looks like a fire,' Adam said.

'And a bloody big one,' Colin added.

'Shall we go and have a look?'

'We just talked about not getting involved in excitement…'

'It's just because you're 2-0 up, isn't it?'

Colin conceded that that might be part of it, along with the general area of where the fire was. It took Adam a few more minutes of arm-twisting to get him out of the flat and down the stairs.

By the time they'd driven there, the entrance to the industrial estate had been blocked off by an assortment of emergency vehicles.

From the road, Colin and Adam could see that a horde of firefighters were battling the blaze that was destroying the McNultys' abattoir, trying their best not to let the flames spread to the neighbouring buildings.

A black Audi skidded to a halt on the closed road and Ron McNulty got out. He ran to the police officer at the cordon and gesticulated wildly, pointing at his crumbling business. The chatter of the crowd prevented Colin and Adam hearing what he was saying, but he didn't look happy.

When another police officer came over, Ron held his hands up in a placating manner and took a few steps back, running his hands through his dark hair. A few minutes later, Kevin pulled up in his Honda and the two brothers retreated back from the police line and watched as their business disintegrated before their very eyes.

'You think the hippies have got anything to do with this?' Colin asked.

Adam shrugged his shoulders, hoping that for their own sake that they didn't.

3

THE AFTERMATH

COLIN RAN INTO the common room of the Stonebridge Retirement Home, his heart in his throat. From the adjoining office, he'd heard a huge commotion start and it had jolted him out of his chair—worst case scenario thoughts running through his head.

'What's the matter?' he asked Betty, who was sitting in the chair closest to the door.

'Just Barry having a tantrum,' she said, and Colin simultaneously laughed and breathed out a sigh of relief.

He walked over to the corner with the television in it and found Barry holding court, instructing everyone to look for the remote.

'What's with all the hubbub?' Colin asked.

Barry pointed to the television in way of explanation.

'I can't stand this bloody show with that idiot presenter talking to the machine like it's his mate. All the pleases and thank yous of the day. It's a bloody inanimate object!'

'He's just being polite,' Colin replied, struggling to keep the grin from his face. The *Tipping Point* complaints had become almost a daily occurrence.

'Polite to a bloody arcade machine!' Barry shouted, before realising that Colin was messing with him. 'Oh, ha ha.'

'You're too easy, Barry.'

With the remote found and the television turned off, quiet once again descended on the room. Barry grabbed a newspaper from the arm of the chair he'd been sitting on and followed Colin to the table that was commonly used for crafts but was currently unoccupied.

'What do you think about this?' Barry asked, handing the newspaper to Colin as they sat down.

Colin took the newspaper from him and scanned the front page. The headline was about the fire at the abattoir a few nights ago and a black and white photo of the blaze accompanied the piece.

'They've found a body,' Barry said, unable to keep the excitement out of his voice.

Colin folded the newspaper and set it down, knowing that Barry wouldn't give him peace to finish it.

'Oh yeah?' Colin said, trying to sound uninterested.

'Yes, indeed. It's that wee hippy fella who was the instigator of the protest.'

'Jesus,' Colin said. He knew Tyler Love from school, having been in the orchestra together, though he'd had been a few years younger than Colin. 'Have they arrested anyone?'

'Nope. And it doesn't look like they're going to either. They think he snuck in and started the fire himself. That it got out of hand quicker than expected and he couldn't escape in time.'

Colin hadn't been expecting that answer. He'd heard about the protest and had fully expected the McNultys to take some sort of revenge. Had the police got it wrong?

He glanced at Barry and could see immediately what the old man was hoping for.

When Colin had played a part in solving the murder case of their friend, Daniel Costello, Barry had been excited. He'd hounded Colin for every smidgeon of detail he could get. A few months later, when Colin had been involved in another amateur investigation, Barry was convinced that he was some sort of Sherlock-style genius.

'What do you think, Columbo?' Barry asked.

'I think the police probably know what they're talking about,' Colin answered. 'And I don't fancy getting into it with Kevin and Ron McNulty.'

Barry looked disappointed, though he did acknowledge that the two brothers were bother through and through.

'It's a shame the youth of today have to resort to violence and fighting when there's a disagreement,' Kenneth said, having been eavesdropping on the conversation from a nearby armchair.

'The youth of today?' Barry repeated.

'Yes,' Kenneth nodded. 'Tit for tat arguing and escalation. Why can't they just talk to each other like civilised beings?'

Barry shot Colin a bemused look before answering.

'Ken, when you were a youth, you were in the RAF during World War Two. Did you try and engage Hitler in polite conversation?'

'Well, no…' Kenneth answered, knowing full well that Barry had him beaten.

'Did you fly over Hamburg in your spitfire and drop kind words out of your plane?'

'No.'

'No,' Barry repeated. 'You dropped bombs. Bombs that exploded and took buildings and lives with them. So, don't try and make out that the youth of today are doing something different to what we did. You don't have a leg to stand on.'

'I know,' Kenneth winked at Colin, pulling up the hem of his trousers to reveal a length of his metallic prosthetic leg. 'I haven't had a leg to stand on for thirty years.'

ACROSS TOWN, Adam pulled his van into the driveway of a potential new client. He gathered his notepad and his keys from the passenger seat, stuck a pencil behind his ear and jumped out. Glancing around, he couldn't help but notice the weed-free path, well maintained flower beds and manicured lawn.

Looks like whoever lives here is doing alright by themselves, he thought.

He walked up the path and pressed the doorbell. He could see a blurred figure grow larger through the frosted glass and a few seconds later, the door opened to reveal a short woman with dark, shoulder length hair. Her cheeks were rosy and her eyes puffy. She looked at him quizzically.

'Hi, I'm Adam Whyte. I'm here about the garden.'

The woman nodded at him, seemingly remembering that she had in fact called him earlier in the day, and opened the door wider. Adam suspected that she was leading him to the back garden, so was surprised when she turned into a cosy living room and sat down on a sofa.

Adam sat down on a stripy armchair and opened his notebook. He glanced over at the woman and saw that she was staring blankly at a spot on the wall above his head.

'What is it that you'd like help with?' Adam said, hoping to spur her into action. 'I can have a look at it and price it up for you.'

Still, she didn't speak. Adam snuck another glance at her. It looked like she was building the courage to say something, which struck him as odd.

'Mr Whyte…' she started.

'Adam, please,' he interrupted.

'Adam, my name is Jennifer Love and I've called you today to see if you would be willing to look into my son's death.'

Love.

She hadn't told him her surname on the phone earlier, otherwise he might've put two and two together. That explained the red eyes and her distracted manner. When he didn't speak, she continued.

'The police have decided that Tyler broke into the abattoir a few nights ago and set fire to the place, killing himself in the process… I just can't believe he's gone!'

At that, she burst into huge, wracking sobs and waved a hand at him. She got to her feet and left the room. A moment later, he heard another door close and supposed that she had gone to the bathroom.

Alone, Adam didn't know what to think. He'd known about the fire, obviously, but he hadn't known that a body had been found. And he certainly hadn't known that the police had announced that they believed that lead hippy, Tyler, was behind it.

Adam wished he paid more attention to the news.

Forewarned would've been forearmed.

A few minutes later, Jennifer re-emerged, mumbling apologies which Adam batted away.

'Listen,' she said, as she sat down again, this time with a steely glint in her eye. 'Tyler was a good boy. He joined The History Makers to make a difference. A peaceful one. There's no way he would've broken in and set fire to the place – that's not the type of lad he was.'

She fixed him with a hard stare.

'The police have got it wrong, and I want you to get to the bottom of it. To clear his name.'

With her spiel finished, she sunk back into her chair, her energy spent, fresh tears ready to fall.

Adam wanted to say no. He didn't know anyone connected to the case, so had no idea how to get a foot in. He especially didn't want to get tangled up in a case involving the McNulty brothers. However, looking at the shell of a woman mourning her son, he couldn't help but think of his own mother.

His resolve crumbled.

'I'll ask around, but I can't promise anything.'

'I'd start with the McNulty lads,' she said, and Adam nodded the kind of nod that stupid people do when they agree to do something stupid.

A half-smile touched her face as a single tear slipped down her cheek.

4

THE HISTORY MAKERS

LIKE MOST BAD ideas, this one was dreamed up in a pub.

The Railway was an equidistant stumble between Adam and Colin's new houses, and therefore was the sensible choice as their local. They'd been a handful of times, and, though they were by far the youngest, they enjoyed the convivial atmosphere, the choice of lagers and the fact that live sport was shown most nights on the big screen televisions.

Adam walked back from the bar carrying two pints of Harp. He set them carefully on the table and slid one towards Colin, before throwing a packet of peanuts his way too.

Colin eyed the salty snack suspiciously. Adam was a notorious tight-arse, so he must've had a good reason for trying to sweeten Colin up.

The two friends engaged in small talk, discussing everything from their jobs to football to the lack of a female presence in their lives. Colin was surprised to learn that Adam had joined an internet dating site, and was unsurprised to learn that, so far, there'd been little to no success.

'Let me look at your profile,' Colin said.

'Why?'

'Because I'm thinking of joining one myself and I want to see how it works,' Colin lied.

Adam sighed deeply and slipped his phone out of his pocket. He thumbed his passcode in and found the app, before handing the phone to Colin.

Colin took a few moments looking through the profile, scrutinising the claims made in the 'About Me' section and checking which photos he'd used.

'You had a bit of a photoshoot at work, did you?' said Colin, turning the phone so that Adam could see the picture he was talking about. 'You look like you're in some sort of perfume advert. All you need is a sailor suit!'

Colin howled with laughter as Adam snatched the phone off him, his face crimson.

'Who took that photo, anyway?'

'Mrs Jenkins,' Adam said. 'I told her it was for the website.'

'And she didn't wonder why you came with gelled hair and an ironed T-shirt to pull out some weeds from her garden?'

'Anyway,' Adam pushed on, as if he hadn't heard his friend, 'I wanted to let you know that I had a chat with Mrs Love today…'

'Tyler's mum?' Colin interrupted, suddenly serious.

'Yeah. She said she couldn't believe that the police were trying to pin the fire on her son; that he would never do that kind of thing.'

'He did chain himself to the building to try and stop a takeover.'

'Yeah, but there's chaining yourself to a building to make a point, and then there's arson.'

'You don't think he did it?' Colin asked.

Adam took a sip of his pint and considered the question. He could see both sides of the coin—Tyler could well have burned down the building to make sure his protest and subsequent beating were not in vain. Fires were unpredictable and the smoke could easily have overpowered him, in the middle of his act of pyromania.

On the other hand, Adam had seen first-hand how vehemently Tyler's mother believed that he was not the guilty party here. That he had died at someone else's hands.

'I don't know,' Adam admitted. 'But, I'd like to find out. What do you say—are you up for a bit of Sherlocking?'

Colin thought about it. The previous "cases" *had* been fun, but this was a different kettle of fish. This one could put them in the firing line of a pair of psychopathic brothers.

'Is she paying us?' Colin replied.

'She's just lost her son, have a little respect,' Adam said, as a huge burp escaped his lips.

'Fine, stop tugging on my heartstrings, will you? I'm in. Where do we start?'

'With the hippies,' said Adam.

THE NEXT MORNING, Colin and Adam walked down the middle of the town centre and turned left at the newly renovated Starbucks. It was on this cobbled side street that the unofficial headquarters of The History Makers resided.

'Don't you think that they'll be annoyed if two strangers turn up to a memorial service?' Colin asked.

'They're hippies,' Adam answered. 'Their whole schtick is spreading the love. Anyone asks, we're there to pay our tributes to Tyler. We'll have wheedled them with their own stupid life motto.'

'I don't think we should call them hippies to their faces,' Colin said, fixing Adam with a look that said this was a command rather than a suggestion.

'As long as they keep their new age BS to themselves, we're all good,' Adam replied.

Colin had been worrying about not knowing which house was the HQ, but he needn't have. Thick tendrils of bluish smoke drifted from the open windows, furnishing the street with the sweet, piney smell synonymous with weed.

A man wearing green bell-bottomed trousers and a fluffy vest with no T-shirt underneath it approached the house from the opposite direction. He nodded at Adam and Colin as he pushed the door open gently and disappeared into the wall of smoke. It reminded Colin of the Stars In Their Eyes set.

'Tonight, Matthew, I'm going to be…' he started

'Stoned, against my will, by the looks of things,' Adam interrupted, as he followed the man wearing a vest into the house with a scowl.

A narrow corridor, plastered with posters of cannabis leaves and other drug paraphernalia, led to a small living room and an even smaller kitchen. As they made their way down the hallway, Adam wondered if one of the group owned the house or if they were renting. If it was the latter, the landlord would be furious with the state of the place.

They poked their heads in the living room, where a small rave seemed to be underway. Though the hour hand hadn't yet reached eleven o'clock in the morning, every single person in the room was holding a bottle of something alcoholic and dancing along to the thumping bass and chipmunk vocals being spewed out by a speaker in the corner of the room.

'We're not going to get much sense out of anyone in there,' Adam shouted over the thrum of the music.

They walked further down the hall and entered the kitchen. The atmosphere in here was much more subdued. Pictures of Tyler adorned the walls and a few unusually dressed people sat around on the rickety dining chairs, crying and swapping stories.

'Hi,' one of them said, rising from his seat to greet Adam and Colin, arm outstretched.

They both shook hands with the man who had introduced himself as Jay.

'Would you like to write down a memory?'

'A what?' Adam asked.

Jay motioned to the square dining table. On it was a small plastic box, a pile of paper and a few biros.

'We're collecting memories from everyone here. Their favourite memory of Tyler. We very much wanted today to be a celebration of his life, rather than something downbeat. He would've hated that.'

'That explains the disco next door, then,' Adam said.

'Yeah. I think…' Jay trailed off. 'I think maybe that's a step too far.'

'You think?' Adam laughed.

'Who organised this?' Colin asked, giving Adam a death stare. The full Paddington.

'Well, I thought it would be a nice idea to commemorate his life with a memorial service here. Tyler was my best friend, so I mostly took charge.

The memory thing was my big idea. Willow took it upon herself to organise the rave…' Jay said, casting an angry glance at the wall that divided the living room and kitchen.

'Who's Willow?'

'Our new leader, I guess. She was second in command to Tyler, but now that he's gone…' Jay dabbed at his eyes. 'Now that he's gone, Willow is in charge.'

'Is she in there?'

'Yeah, you can't miss her. She's got bright pink hair.'

'Of course she does,' Adam sighed.

They thanked Jay for his time and left the kitchen, making their way back into the living room. As Jay said, Willow was pretty easy to find. She was standing by the open window; eyes closed, a joint gripped between her lips as she swayed along to the music.

'She looks like she really misses him,' Adam said, noticing the smile on Willow's face.

Adam made to move but Colin put an arm across the door.

'I've got this,' he mouthed, noticing his friend's mounting annoyance.

5

AN UNWEEPING WILLOW

ADAM AND COLIN followed Willow up the stairs, away from the droning bass, trying not to look at her exposed G-string. She walked the length of the landing and wordlessly disappeared through the door at the end.

Adam shot Colin a confused look, which he answered with a shrug of his shoulders. Were they supposed to follow her in?

Thankfully, their confusion was short lived as Willow appeared in the doorway and beckoned them in with a flick of a finger. Adam pushed Colin in the back, gently, ushering him towards the door.

If Adam had been asked to sketch what he thought the inside of Willow's room looked like, he would've got about 90% right.

A couple of wicker peace signs dangled from nails above the headboard of her bed. Posters with drug puns such as "Don't drink and drive, smoke and fly" were stuck up on the other walls and on a desk facing the window, an overflowing ashtray sat alongside an old typewriter. Net curtains were being pushed into the room like holey ghosts by a gentle breeze coming through the open window.

Willow walked over to the desk and grabbed a cardboard packet, from which she pulled a single cigarette. She pushed some of the other things on the messy surface out of the way, searching for something.

'Lighter?' Colin said. He'd taken it off one of the care home residents earlier when they were threatening to light a recent prime minister's book on fire.

Willow looked at the translucent orange rectangle with disgust.

'Single use plastic?' she said, scornfully. 'No thanks.'

She eventually found the box of matches, and pulled one out, striking the stick along the side.

'Yeah, because cutting down trees to make matchsticks is so much better for the environment,' Adam muttered, though not loud enough for Willow to hear.

Smoking cigarette in hand, Willow crossed the room and sat down on the bed. She shifted backwards so that her back was against the wall, pulling her bare feet underneath her.

'I don't make a habit of letting two lads I don't know into my room,' she smiled. 'What can I do for you?'

'We were wondering if we could ask a few questions about Tyler?'

'Are you from the police?'

'No,' Colin said. 'The police have already said that Tyler's death was an accident.'

'So, you're what...? Private investigators?'

'Like I said, we just want to ask a few questions. We knew Tyler from school and him starting a fire and burning a business to the ground doesn't sound like something in his wheelhouse.'

'We were wondering if you could tell us anything about what happened that night at the abattoir,' elaborated Adam.

Willow tipped some ash into the glass ashtray and looked at them without expression.

'Well, I wasn't there, so I couldn't possibly know. I read in the paper that the police believe Tyler started the fire and then got himself trapped and died from smoke inhalation.'

'And does that sound plausible?'

'To be honest, yes. Truthfully, we didn't see eye to eye. The History Makers started as a group for good. We wanted to draw attention to things like climate change and show the town how little changes could make massive differences. When Tyler joined, he sort of assumed the leadership role and took us in a different direction.'

'What direction?'

'More... extreme. Like the protest that happened on the afternoon of his death. A couple of months ago, something like that would never have happened. He kept pushing and pushing us to show how much we wanted things to change.'

'He sounds... assertive,' Colin said, hoping that his apparent disapproval at Tyler's methods would keep Willow talking.

'Intimidating was more like it,' Willow said, extinguishing the cigarette in the ashtray. 'If you didn't do what he said, he belittled you in front of the group. He made out that no one cared as much as he did.'

'Sounds like a dick,' Adam chimed in.

'I never want to speak ill of the dead,' Willow replied. 'But he could be a dick. I mean, look at how he treated his girlfriend.'

'What do you mean?' Colin asked.

Willow's eyes widened as if she realised that she had started down a path she didn't want to continue. She took a few metaphorical steps back.

'Like I say, I don't want to speak ill of the dead. All I'll say is that he wasn't well liked.'

'By who?'

'By most of the group, but especially Ocean.'

Colin could see Adam struggling to keep a sarcastic comment under wraps, so barrelled straight in with another question.

'What happened after the protest at McNulty's Meats?'

'Well, those nutters who own the place turned up and gave us a chance to leave. Most of us did. I care about the environment, but I also care for my own safety. We got unchained from the fence, but Tyler stayed. We watched him take a punch or two before the police turned up. Before they could get to the gate, the brother who fancies himself whispered something in Tyler's ear.'

'Did Tyler say what?'

'No. After the protest we came back here. Tyler was fuming. He accused us all of wimping out on him, of selling him out. He trashed the kitchen, kept telling us how much we'd let him down. But he would've done the same to anyone of us. Tyler only ever looked out for Tyler.'

She rose from the bed and retrieved another cigarette from the desk, before retaking her spot against the wall.

'Do you think he lit the place on fire?'

'Well, he did say that he was going to pay them back for punching him. Once we'd managed to calm him down a bit, he sat in the front room, muttering to himself and getting himself worked up again. He left in the early evening without a word to anyone, never to be seen again.'

'And he didn't tell you what his payback was?' Colin asked.

Willow shook her head, causing ash to cover a section of the colourful duvet.

'He didn't tell me, but Helena went after him.' She looked up at the two blank faces. 'Helena was Tyler's girlfriend.'

'What happened when Tyler left?'

'To be honest, the rest of us saw the protest as a massive success. The English guy who is buying the factory left looking disappointed and the McNutters were furious, which meant we'd struck a nerve. We had a party to celebrate. Later, we saw on Twitter that the McNulty's Meats factory was on fire and we put two and two together.'

'Was anyone missing from the party?' Adam asked.

Willow squashed out the second cigarette and scratched at her fluorescent hair absent-mindedly. Finally, she nodded her head.

'Not everyone stuck around. It had been a long day and some people went home not long after Tyler left, but there's no way I could remember who was there and who wasn't.'

'You mentioned Ocean wasn't a fan of Tyler's…'

'You can say that again,' she interrupted with a snigger.

'Was she at the party?' Adam finished.

'Ocean is a guy,' Willow said. 'And, like I said, I can't be sure who was there. There were… substances being passed around, you know?'

'We'd quite like a chat with him. Is he here?'

'No,' she said, shaking her head. 'He's working.'

'Where?'

'At the Stonebridge Organic Food Store.'

'The *what?*' Adam exclaimed. He'd never heard of such a shop in his town.

Willow stood up, and made for the door.

'Can I go back to the memorial service now?' she asked.

Adam took in what she was wearing. Leopard print leggings and a black Slayer T-shirt; on the front of which a snake crawled out of a skull's empty eye sockets.

'Is that appropriate dress for a memorial service?' Adam asked.

Willow shrugged.

'At least I'm here… that's more than can be said for Helena.'

She raised her eyebrows suggestively before leaving the room, leaving Adam and Colin to mull over what they'd just uncovered.

6

AN OCEAN OF (UN)CALM

COLIN AND ADAM slipped down the stairs and left the house without another word to anyone. Any fresh air there'd been in the house had been pushed out by a heavy haze of green. Adam was spluttering as he crossed the threshold, though Colin was convinced it was for show.

'It's hardly Burning Man,' he said, 'chill out.'

'Chill out?' Adam coughed. 'Is that supposed to be funny? I'm so chilled out, against my will I might add, that my face is drooping.'

'That's just your jowls flapping from all the junk food.'

They ceased talking as Adam began lightly slapping his cheeks. Colin rolled his eyes and led them in the direction of what Adam called the "wrong" part of town.

Usually, the "wrong" part of a town or city would denote some sort of clear and present danger; the heart of the gangland territories, perhaps, or old sectarians doling out weapons to the new brigade in the hope of reigniting the dark days of the Troubles.

According to Adam, the wrong end of Stonebridge was worse.

To the casual observer turning into the offending street, the cause of Adam's chagrin might not be immediately obvious. It looked like any other street in the town. But, if Adam were to take you on a tour of his dislikes, he'd point you to Zen, the new age shop with a window display littered with crystals, glass skulls and tarot cards. Competing smells of incense drifted out through the bottom of the door, causing the street to stink of wood, flowers and spices.

Further along, a vegan café offered rabbit food to humans for a premium and, beside it, a clothes shop as dark as a nightclub catered for those who dared to dress differently.

Adam was all for people showing their personality through what they chose to wear (up to a point), but this was ridiculous. Opposite the boutique was the store they were here for.

A bell sounded as they pushed through the door. The lady on the till looked up from her magazine, smiled and offered her assistance. They assured her they were just here to browse, and she resumed her reading.

The shop wasn't very big and was bisected by a line of shelving. The smells of various vitamins and treatments mixed in the air, causing the room to smell a bit like a pet shop. Colin was going to mention this to Adam, though stopped himself in time. He needn't add more fuel to the fire.

At the back of the shop, a door flapped open and a man backed through it, carrying a stack of boxes. He lowered them to the ground and kneeled beside them, ready to start filling the shelves with their contents. Before he could start, Colin approached him.

'Excuse me, are you Ocean?'

The man pushed his dreadlocked hair out of his eyes and looked up at Colin.

'Yes, dude. How can I help you?'

Colin briefly explained who they were and what they were doing. When he finished, Ocean nodded once.

'I have a break in ten minutes. I was planning on eating in Renew, so if you want to nip across and grab a table, I'll meet you there.'

Colin thanked him, and he and Adam left the shop. As soon as they were outside, Adam's moaning began about the choice of eatery. A small smirk crept onto Colin's face, though he managed to hide it from his friend.

ADAM SIGHED AND picked up a menu, resigned to the fact that he was actually going to have to eat something. He didn't know how long Ocean would stay, but his stomach was already growling and he didn't think he could make it until they were finished their chat.

'There's nothing on here,' he muttered, after a minute.

'There's a sausage wrap.'

'Yeah, but the sausages aren't sausages, are they? They're Linda McCartney's idea of what a sausage is. And there's probably no gluten in the bread, which is the best bit.'

'You can't possibly know that gluten is the best bit of bread,' Colin replied, but this simply served to irritate Adam further.

His tirade against the café was stopped by the opening of the door and the appearance of Ocean. He was a hulking great figure; tall and muscular with dreadlocks dyed a light blue. A thick, dark beard covered the lower half of his face but, despite his intimidating size, his green eyes radiated a warmness. He seemed a walking contradiction—he *could* crush you, but wouldn't enjoy doing it.

'Alright,' he said, sliding into the booth beside Adam.

They both nodded their alright-ness as a waitress appeared.

'Hi Ocean. The usual?' she said.

Ocean nodded his assent and she turned to the two vegan noobs.

'What would you suggest?' Colin asked.

'The falafel wrap is really nice,' she replied.

Colin took her suggestion and added a glass of apple juice, while Adam succumbed to the call of fake sausages, though he still didn't look pleased.

'Does the orange juice have bits in it?' he asked.

'It's freshly squeezed, so yes,' she replied, as though this was a selling point.

'Course it does,' Adam muttered under his breath, before adding a glass of tap water to his order. The waitress smiled at them and touched Ocean lightly on the shoulder before turning and heading back towards the kitchen.

'How can I help you?' Ocean asked, now that they were alone.

'To be straight up, we've been asked to look into what happened to Tyler.'

'The police said he burned a business to the ground and killed himself in the process. Knowing Tyler as I do, or did, I'd say that sits perfectly well within the realms of possibility.'

'You weren't a fan?'

'Not overly, no. We both went to the same secondary school and he made my life miserable. He picked on me for my appearance, spreading rumours about my sexuality, that kind of thing. Things that matter a hell of a lot to a teenage boy who is trying to work out who he is.'

'That's tough. Sorry man,' Adam said.

'Thanks. I still get looked at for my hair, or for what I wear, but I don't care now. I'm older and I'm more confident, but those teenage years are hard enough with the devils on your shoulders, let alone having one in the flesh, taunting you daily.'

'So, how did you end up getting involved in the group?'

'Me? A few like-minded individuals figured Stonebridge needed a kickstart. So, we formed the group with the hope of showing the town, peacefully, that small changes can make big differences. We planned on leafleting and things like that. Non-invasive, not preachy, but just something, anything to try and help the planet.'

The food arrived as he finished speaking. The same waitress set the plates and drinks softly on the tabletop, before drifting out of sight again. For a few minutes, they ate in silence. Adam took a nibble from the corner of his sausage wrap and was pleasantly surprised by the burst of flavour.

He tried not to let it show on his face, though. If Colin caught sight of any hint of enjoyment, he'd never hear the end of it.

When the food had been seen to (Adam left a small bit on his plate just to make it look like he hadn't enjoyed it as much as he actually had) the questioning resumed.

'How did Tyler come to be involved then?' Adam asked.

'In his usual way. He caught wind of what we were doing and asked if he could help out. If I'd been there, I would've told him to do one. But, he was invited in and before we knew it, he'd assumed command and was making plans.'

'What kind of plans?'

'Plans that involved pushing the boundaries. Exactly what we had decided the group wouldn't be doing when we formed it. Like I said, we never wanted to ram our stuff down people's throats. But Tyler did, followed by a kick up the arse for good measure. The guy was a mercenary. He'd done this before with another group in the town, and they had the good sense to kick him out. Their leader is a scary bloke, though. We were all too nice to Tyler.'

Adam wrote the name of the group down in his phone with a reminder to look them up when he got home. Perhaps Tyler had done something awful in his previous group and the frightening leader had bided his time, choosing fire as a means of revenge.

'What about Helena?' asked Colin.

'She tagged along with Tyler, but you could tell her heart wasn't in it. It was like he was forcing her to be there.'

'Were they happy together?'

'Couldn't tell you, man. I tried to take as little notice of him as possible. Might be worth having a chat with her, though. He might've confided his plans to her. He didn't tell us diddly squat unless he was bossing us around.'

Ocean checked his watch and told them his lunch break was almost over. They slipped out of the booth and Adam told them he'd pay for lunch. Colin and Ocean walked outside, where the latter lit a roll-up cigarette.

Adam waited by the table and paid the waitress when she reappeared. He cast a conspiratorial glance over his shoulder, to make sure Colin hadn't sneaked in. When he saw that the coast was clear, he asked her a question.

'Do you do deliveries?'

7

A FURRY FRIEND

ADAM SPENT THE evening on the sofa. He'd finished some outstanding invoices for some of the council work he'd undertaken last month, and now came the really challenging part—getting them to pay.

Once the tedium of spreadsheets was done with, he stowed his laptop on the shelf under the coffee table and started the PlayStation. He navigated to Netflix and selected an episode of Peep Show he'd seen a billion times before. He only needed it on in the background, as he had another task to complete. This one, purely recreational.

He pulled out his phone and searched for information on the group Ocean had told them about earlier that day. It seems Stonebridge was fast becoming a political hotspot. The History Makers were campaigning for climate change and to stop capitalism, while rival group (if there could be rivals in trying to right the world's wrongs) Turn Back the Clock wanted to see less plastic in the seas.

He logged into Facebook and searched for this new group. It didn't take long to find their page.

Their mission statement was spelled out in the "About Me" section and there were a number of pictures showing a ragtag bunch at various protests and demonstrations. They were mostly women his age, though a tall man with tattooed arms and a buzzcut appeared in a number of them, too.

Even in the photographs Adam could sense the authoritarian in him. His stance, his soulless stare into the camera lens, the way he seemed to gather the female members of the group around him like a harem.

Perhaps he was being unfair to the man, though Ocean had hinted that he wasn't a very pleasant fella.

He dug a little deeper into the group and found a name—Mickey Dooley. Adam wrote the name down and started typing a text to Colin to discuss next steps, when his phone rang.

It was his mum.

'What are you doing tomorrow?' she asked.

'Hello to you, too. I'm fine, thanks for asking. How are you?' he laughed.

'Sorry, I'm just a bit excited. Are you free tomorrow?'

He checked his diary and told her that he had to cut Mrs Morrison's grass at some stage, but he was flexible with the time.

'Can you be here for 9?' she asked.

'In the morning? What's got you so excited?'

'You'll find out tomorrow,' she said. 'See you bright and breezy.'

With that, she hung up. His mum's phone habits were becoming more and more like a master spy. She'd tell you very little but leave your appetite whet. Sometimes, she didn't even say goodbye.

Adam wasn't fond of surprises and was dying to know what had got her knickers in a twist. He considered phoning her back, but knew she was like a steel trap when she wanted to be. Instead, he threw his phone to the other end of the sofa, sank back against the plump pillow and tried to take his mind of the many mysteries in his life by watching the finest comedy show ever committed to film.

WHEN ADAM PULLED up onto his mum's driveway the next morning, she was peering out from the window. Despite being a few minutes early, she had a scowl on her face.

Before he could undo his seatbelt, she was locking the front door behind her and making her way to the passenger side of his Clio.

'What kept you?' she asked, as she sat down beside him.

'What are you on about? It's not even nine yet.'

'It was by my clock. Anyway, let's not bicker. Guess where you are taking me?'

'I didn't know I was taking you anywhere.'

'Guess!' she said.

'The library?'

'Nope.'

'Stonebridge Retirement Home?'

'I don't know anyone there,' she replied, confused.

'I didn't say for visiting,' laughed Adam. 'I meant to get yourself a room!'

She slapped him playfully on the arm.

'We're going to the Dog's Trust! I'm getting a puppy!'

'Why?'

'Well, since you moved out, the house has been very quiet. I plod around on my own and last night, I saw an advert for this place and thought it would be nice to have a bit of company.'

Adam felt a pang of guilt as he thought of his mum being lonely without him. Perhaps a dog was a good idea.

He reversed out of the drive and asked his mum to type the postcode of where they were going into the sat nav. It had been a week or so since he'd seen his mum, and in between the robotic voice giving directions, they caught up. Adam told her about his busy gardening schedule and she told him about volunteering at the soup kitchen. His mum was just steering the conversation towards girls when a sign for their destination spared him having to tell her that there was nothing to tell.

They parked up and got out. A narrow gravel path led them up a small ridge towards the building. Barks and excited yelps could be heard before they'd even stepped foot inside.

The interior of the building was bright and welcoming. Smiling staff carrying bags of dog food strode with purpose towards the cacophony of woofs. It must've been breakfast time for the pooches.

A woman walked towards them and wanted to know if they needed help. Adam's mum explained their purpose here and the woman gave them both a rundown on how the adoption process worked. She showed them the way to the doggy showroom and left them with a promise that she'd be nearby if they needed her.

The sight that greeted them was both beautiful and sad. The far wall of the room was divided into eight small sections, each separated by a thin sheet of wood. Inside each section was a dog, waiting for someone to take them home.

Some were pacing around like a prisoner stomping the yard; some dashed this way and that, excited by the arrival of new humans while some simply lay in their beds, unfazed by the interest. Most were barking, as if trying to pull the attention of the visitors their way.

Adam and his mum strolled up and down the line, looking through the glass and reading the information that had been Blu-tacked to each partition. Adam could tell what his mum was thinking—she was wishing she could take every single one of them home. Probably would've done if he hadn't been here to keep her right.

At the end of the line, a little Shih Tzu caught her eye. A hair bobble kept its long hair out of its large, round eyes. It sniffed at the glass before putting one paw against it.

His mum instinctively reached out a hand and the deal was sealed.

The staff member from before must've been watching, as she came rushing over, delivering facts about the little dog. In a matter of minutes, they were outside watching her attach a lead to the dog's collar. She handed it to Adam's mum with a smile.

Adam and his mum circled the garden. The dog trotted along beside them, looking up every now and again as if to make sure this was actually happening. Adam's mum beamed the whole time and talked to the little hound in the way a new mother might talk to her new born. When the member of staff reappeared, it was to find that the dog was coming home with them.

They went inside and sorted the paperwork, arranging for a house visit the next day, just to make sure the dog was going home to a safe and secure home.

'You said his name was Daffodil?' Adam's mum said.

'Yeah, but he's young enough that if you wanted to change it, you could. He's a clever wee boy and he'll soon get used to something else.'

They bade farewell and Adam and his mum walked back to the car. She was fizzing with excitement.

'I can't wait to get him home with me. What do you think we should call him?'

Adam considered this while his mum spouted many different suggestions, ranging from musicians, to soap stars and everything in between.

'What's the guy's name from that Lord of The Rings thing you used to watch? They had some great names,' she said. 'Short fella. Starts with a D.'

'Umm…'

'Dildo!' she shouted suddenly. 'Is that it?'

Adam nearly crashed the car.

'Bilbo, mum. You definitely mean Bilbo.'

He quickly suggested more names, keen not to let her have Bilbo. He didn't want his subconscious to connect the poor dog with a sex toy every time he saw it. The little guy had been through enough already.

Adam spotted a petrol station, and pulled in to fill his tank. His mum told him that she would pay for it, and he tried to argue but it was like trying to take a restaurant bill off Mrs Doyle.

She disappeared into the shop and emerged a few minutes later, carrying the Stonebridge Chronicle under her arm. She got into the car and they pulled away from the pump. Adam glanced across at the paper draped over her knee and the headline caught his eye.

'What's that about mum?' he asked

She scanned the story briefly before replying.

'That company that were going to buy out the McNultys have found a new seller.'

'Does it say who?'

'You know I can't read in the car. It makes me feel sick.'

Adam considered this. Why was this English conglomerate so determined to set up camp in their small coastal town?

8

PLANS

'IT'S OPEN,' Adam shouted, in reply to the three knocks on the door. The handle turned in a ghostly fashion and the door opened, allowing Colin to enter. He walked down the short corridor and, upon reaching the living room, fell onto the sofa.

'I'm shattered today,' he said. 'The retirement home is getting a bit of a refurbishment and it's like bloody Piccadilly Circus!'

'Do you have to go back?'

'Aye, I only have an hour for lunch. What was so urgent?'

Adam explained about the newspaper article.

'Do you reckon it's Tanners?' Colin asked.

'Must be,' Adam replied. 'The article is vague, but it's the only other abattoir in town.'

Frank Tanner was the owner of Tanner's Meats. A very unimaginative name for a very unimaginative line of work. Founded in 1953 by Frank's father, Derek, it had been one of only two abattoirs in Stonebridge. When they were doing well enough, they'd expanded by opening a butcher's shop on the high street. On Saturdays, the queue for the freshest meat on the north coast wrapped around most of the town square.

This supposed success had not gone unnoticed. Like sharks drawn to spilled blood, the McNultys had sensed an opportunity to make a bit of money and really raised their game. Taking over from their father at the turn of the century, they'd poured serious investment into their business.

A business that was now in ruins.

'You think Frank had anything to do with the fire?' Colin asked.

'Maybe,' Adam nodded. 'I can imagine how he must've felt. He's been toiling away at the family business for all his life, and then these two McNulty yuppies wade in and are bought out for big money. It must sting a bit. Maybe he gets drunk one night and takes a torch to the place.'

'And kills Tyler by mistake.'

'Yeah. An accident. A dreadful one that he'll be put away for, but an accident nonetheless.'

'This is all conjecture at this point, though. We don't even know that it's Tanner at the centre of the new takeover,' Colin said.

Adam raised his eyebrows and Colin sensed the worst.

'I have a plan.'

Adam pulled his phone from his pocket and held up a picture. It showed the very professional website of the company who were behind the failed takeover of McNulty's.

'I'm going to pretend to be him,' Adam pointed at the boring looking man on the screen. 'Jonathan Jones. He was the one in charge of the buyout.'

'And say what?'

'Just you wait, mon frère.'

Adam found the number for Tanner's Meats and pressed dial, turning the phone to loudspeaker.

'Hello?' a man answered.

'O'wite mayte,' Adam started. 'It's John Jones 'ere. 'Ow you doin'?'

There was silence for a few seconds, that seemed to stretch out before them. Colin was about to curse his friend for ruining their chances of an in with Frank, when the man spoke.

'Mr Jones. Hello, I'm doing well, thank you. How are you?'

'A million dollars, pal. Listen, me secretary has only gone and lost some of the bladdy documents you sent across. Any chance you could fire 'em this way again?'

'Of course,' Frank said.

'And we're still on for next week?'

'Yes. I'll be there to greet you at the airport.'

'Cheers, pal. See you then,' said Adam, hanging up.

'What was that accent?' Colin asked.

'Cockney geezer, innit?'

'I don't think you'll be getting a part in EastEnders any time soon,' Colin laughed. 'But, good job. At least we know Tanner is the one set to make a fortune from the McNultys' misfortune.'

'Which means, he's just become our prime suspect.'

Colin nodded, rose from the sofa and walked towards the kitchen.

'Got anything to eat?' he asked, as he reached for the fridge door handle. Adam made a sort of strangled noise in return, that was mostly drowned out by the door opening.

'What did you say?' Colin asked.

'Nothing,' Adam answered, though he looked troubled.

Colin looked at him with a cocked eyebrow, before resuming his search for something to eat. His gaze settled upon a very out of place package on the bottom shelf. He smiled to himself, knowing that this branded, brown paper wrapped bundle was the source of Adam's reluctance to let him in the fridge.

'After all your moaning about the vegan café…' Colin said.

He shook his head in mock disappointment as he threw the offending packet of facon onto the kitchen worktop.

'Vegetarian bacon. Really?'

9

HEY MICKEY, YOU'RE SO FINE

IN THE CENTRE of town, just outside the Presbyterian church on the main street, a small crowd had gathered. It was mostly made up of teenagers, some dressed in Topman's uniform of skinny jeans and plain T-shirts, while the more out-there members of the group had pushed the boat out with some thrift-shop finery. Whatever their differences, they were united by one cause—listening to Mickey Dooley.

Colin watched from the doorway of a bookshop as the crowd nodded in agreement with the rhetoric that the man with the microphone was spouting. Disaffected youths, before his very eyes, were finding a cause to get behind. To find some meaning in their meandering teenage lives.

Who would've thought that the man shining that particular light would've been built like a tank with cropped hair like a soldier?

With a final bark urging the crowd to go forth and do right, he dispersed his disciples with a flick of the wrist. Some of the teens went left, some right. A couple started towards the local Starbucks. Evidently, sticking it to the man had no time constraints, and could wait until after their latte hit from a tax-evading multinational corporation.

Colin approached Mickey, who was busy packing up his microphone and portable speaker.

'Interesting stuff,' he said.

'Thanks, man,' Mickey replied. 'Are you interested in helping the environment?'

'As much as the next person. But, I'm actually here to talk to you about Tyler Love.'

Mickey looked momentarily wary, though his face quickly transformed itself into a mask of sadness.

'Poor Tyler,' he said. 'Horrible way to go.'

'I heard he used to be part of your group.'

'Well, firstly it's not my group, per se. Hierarchy breeds contempt and, as such, we instigated an egalitarian philosophy for Turn Back the Clock. We want everyone to be happy and willing to fight for a cause, so we subscribe to more democratic notions.'

'So, everyone is equal and you vote on ideas,' said Colin, trying to prise apart the political mumbo jumbo.

'Essentially, yes.'

'And, so, Tyler was once part of the group which you are also a member?'

'Yes, Tyler came to us a while back. As I said, we very much have an all-for-one type philosophy and so Tyler found ingratiating into the group… difficult.'

'Why?' Colin asked.

'Well, mainly because he wanted to be in control. If we said the sky was blue, he'd say it was green. Any vote that we did, he'd argue the outcome. He wanted to dictate, and we didn't let him.'

'What did he want, that you wouldn't do?' Colin asked.

'He wanted to adopt a more volatile practice than we had set out to use. He very much wanted to capture people's imaginations in the wrong way, often speaking about "big plans".'

'Like setting buildings on fire?'

Mickey gave a non-committal shrug.

'And so, you kicked him out?'

'Well, we uninvited him from the group and when he wouldn't accept, we had to be more direct?'

'Direct how?'

'Well, he and I had words.'

'And how did that go?'

'He gave me a black eye and damn well near shattered my skull. It was a cheap shot. He also smashed my car windows.'

'Jesus,' Colin said.

'Aye, I could've done with some of his divine intervention, to be fair.'

'Did you retaliate?'

'No, I didn't see the point. He'd already hurt me and trashed my car, if I'd goaded him further, who knows how it would've ended. I mean, I know I look handy, but I really deplore physical violence and am loathe to use it.'

Colin looked at his heavily tattooed, muscly arms and thought about the damage they could do if Mickey decided to free them. He also wondered if punching was off limits, but lighting a match wasn't. He didn't want to ask him outright, though.

'Do you think Tyler was capable of burning down a building? Colin asked, instead.

'Easily,' Mickey replied.

Colin thanked him for his time and started to walk away towards the car park, filing the conversation as inconclusive in his head. He thought the comment about hating physical violence was quite telling. Perhaps, after suffering at the hands of Tyler Love, he had simply bided his time until he could take some sort of revenge.

And that revenge had quickly spiralled out of control.

With these thoughts taking up most of his thinking space, it wasn't until he saw the sign for long defunct DVD rental shop that he realised that he'd walked in completely the wrong direction. Cursing himself, he was about to double back when his eyes fell onto a new shop.

The store, tucked between a bakery and a bookmaker, had recently been painted white and the slew of busy workmen suggested that time was of the essence in an attempt to get it open.

The front was anonymous, save for a pile of silver letters propped up against the wall, waiting to be fixed above the expanse of glass that would serve as a window for its wares, once the shop was open.

Colin was no countdown champion, but even he could work out that the jumble of letters would spell Tanner's once they had been correctly ordered.

He watched as a builder, covered in flecks of paint and dust, downed his drill just outside the door and took off his hi-vis jacket and helmet. He muttered something to another builder, who clapped him on the back and disappeared inside. The first builder walked in the direction of the café opposite.

Colin watched him go, before seizing the opportunity handed to him. Before anyone could notice what he was up to, he'd crossed the boundary and pulled the hard hat on, adjusting it so it covered as much of his face as possible. He shrugged the jacket on and stepped inside.

Colin didn't know much about butchers, but inside looked state of the art to him. Sloping silver display trays dominated the space, serving as a barrier between the area customers could wait in and where the butcher would work. The empty display, devoid of meat, looked strange. Weighing scales, knife racks and other paraphernalia filled the marble counters behind the display and a door on the back wall led to somewhere Colin couldn't see.

He imagined there was nothing to be gained by looking either.

One thing was certain, though. Tanner was already using the money from the takeover deal to expand his empire. Colin could only imagine how the McNultys were taking the news of their rival's windfall.

Perhaps Tanner *did* have something to do with the burning down of the McNultys' business. He was certainly profiting from it.

Colin reckoned it might be prudent to have a chat with the newly minted butcher.

He left the shop and set the hard hat and jacket where he had found them. He glanced up at the window of the café and saw the builder looking down at him, confusion creasing his wide face.

Colin took off in the other direction as quickly as he could. Since they were interviewing potential suspects in a possible murder enquiry, they were sure to make enemies and he didn't want to add an angry builder to the mix.

10

WHAT'S THE WORST THING I COULD SAY?

ADAM STOPPED MOWING the grass and wiped the sweat from his brow.

Summer was mostly a fanciful notion in Stonebridge. Usually, as the months that were tied to the season rolled around, talk turned excitedly to beach trips and outdoor activities.

The reality was that the sun would shine in a cloudless sky for about three days cumulatively, and the rest of the time was business as usual in Northern Ireland: heavy rain.

Today was one of the days where the sun beamed down and made everyone and everything seem happier. Mrs Young had been out not long ago to deliver him a glass of lemonade with the promise of a freshly baked cookie when he had finished his day's toil.

His work, however, had been interrupted by a ringing phone. He pulled his earphones out and looked at the unknown number that was flashing on his screen.

'Hello?' he answered.

'Is this Adam?'

He confirmed that it was whilst wracking his brains, trying to figure out if he's accidentally put his number onto his profile on the dating site. He didn't think he had.

'This is Helena. You messaged me on Facebook, asking me to get in touch with you.'

'Ah, I wasn't sure if you would. Thank you. Umm… I was wondering if you wouldn't mind me asking a few questions about Tyler.'

'Why?' she asked.

'Well, we're trying to find out what happened. His mum asked us to look into it.'

There was silence for a moment.

'I don't see the point in dragging all of that up again. It hurt too much telling the police what I knew first time around.'

He sensed she was about to hang up.

'Please,' he pleaded. 'Give me half an hour of your time and you'll never hear from me again.'

'Half an hour?' she repeated. 'That's more than most boys can promise.'

Adam was flustered by her flirty comment and mumbled something indistinctive. When she asked him to repeat what he'd said, he cleared his throat and tried to regain some composure.

They agreed to meet at Bar7 later that night.

'Don't be late,' she said, and then hung up before he could reply.

He sat down on Mrs Young's garden bench, his head spinning. Never mind the McNulty headcases, the hippies and the multinational corporations they were meddling with. It was Helena Bryer that was making him nervous.

He pocketed his phone, turned up the music and went back to work at double speed. He was going to need as much time to get ready as he could, if he wanted to impress Miss Bryer.

And he did want to impress her.

ADAM SAT AT a seat near the window in Bar7, overlooking the bustling promenade and, beyond that, the infinite sea.

Growing up, he'd sometimes been frustrated that all the action seemed to be confined to the capital, over an hour away. Bands he loved would never dare venture any further north than Belfast, so the only live music he'd been exposed to had been local bands playing tiny local venues.

Now, though, he realised just how lucky he was to live where he did. He'd finally recognised the beauty in the beaches, the ocean and the landmarks that tourists travelled thousands of miles to see.

His thoughts of his hometown were banished from his mind upon the arrival of Helena. Her dark, wavy hair spilled onto her shoulders and intelligent brown eyes scanned the room. She wore a strappy vest top with skinny jeans that stopped half way down her calf, exposing a small crescent moon tattoo just above her ankle.

Her eyes locked onto his and she gave a small wave, before starting towards him.

Adam could feel butterflies flutter in his stomach that had nothing to do with what he was about to ask her.

'Adam?' she asked, raising a hand hesitantly.

He nodded and, instead of shaking her hand like any normal person would, he grasped it lightly and raised it to his lips. He placed a delicate kiss on the back of her hand before the horror of the past few seconds had registered.

'I'm so sorry,' he stammered, practically hurling her own hand back at her. 'Uh, can I get you a drink?'

She laughed at his awkwardness and told him what she'd like. Adam excused himself, walked past the bar and into the toilets. He marched up to the sink, spun the handle on the tap and used his cupped hands to splash water onto his face, in the hope of regaining some composure.

When finished, he dabbed at his face with a paper towel and looked at himself in the mirror. He fiddled with his hair and ran a finger along his jaw, happy with the decision to shave off his scraggly beard before tonight's meeting. He looked good. But even at his best, he was still several leagues below Helena.

The momentary thought that flashed through his mind that she was now single, thanks to the death of her boyfriend, was laughable. Even if she wasn't in mourning, there was hardly a chance of romance there.

Delusions of grandeur, his granny would say.

He left the toilet feeling calmer. He stopped at the bar, ordered her a cocktail as well as a pint of Harp for himself, and then returned to the table.

He slid the cocktail in her direction and held his own glass aloft, which she clinked.

'Thanks for agreeing to meet me tonight,' he said.

'No problem. Sorry I was so reticent on the phone earlier. It's been hard, you know.'

Adam couldn't imagine what it would be like to lose a girlfriend in such tragic circumstances. Namely because he'd never had one. Still, he had to remind himself why he was here: she had been signposted by the hippies as a suspect. He couldn't let her good looks soften him.

'It must've been a very difficult time. I'll try to make my questions quick. Can you tell me about The History Makers?'

'They are a group of people who want to make a change.'

'And you are part of the group?'

'Was,' she corrected him. 'I only went because I was with Tyler. He dragged me along so that I would vote for whatever it was he wanted.'

'So, you weren't interested in their cause?'

'As much as the next person. Obviously, I care about the environment and would rather people recycled and drove electric cars, but going to weekly planning meetings on top of events was a wee bit overboard.'

'Sounds it,' Adam agreed.

'So, after what happened to Tyler, I haven't bothered anymore.'

Adam took a long sip of his pint as he tried to work out how to word the next question without sounding blasé about her ex-boyfriend's death. He set his glass down and licked some of the froth away from his lips.

'Can you tell me anything about the day of… the fire?'

At the mention of the fire, her face fell, and Adam's first thought was that he had ruined his chances of finding out more. His second was wondering if the look that had flickered across her features was one of guilt. She breathed out deeply, knocked the rest of her cocktail back in one go, and faced him again.

'We all went to the McNulty protest. It was Tyler's passion project. I think it was his way of showing the other members of the group that he had the balls to be head honcho. I mean, who else would go up against the Stonebridge Krays?'

She laughed, though it sounded empty.

'When that didn't quite go to plan, we all went back to HQ. He was fuming. At the McNultys, at the other group members and at himself. He'd shown weakness, you see? And so, he started mumbling to himself about showing everyone what he was really made of. Before anyone could calm him down or talk some sense into him, he'd gone.'

'What did you do?'

'I ran after him,' she replied. 'But, he told me that this was a one man mission and to run on home. We had a bit of a fight in the street, and then he left.'

'Was that unusual?'

'Fighting? No. It was quite a regular thing towards the end. We came very close to breaking up a load of times. I didn't like how much time he spent at the group, and he didn't like how much I moaned about it. One night, when he was drunk, he…'

She broke off, a sob escaping her.

'You don't have to tell me anything else,' Adam said, but she shook her head.

'No, it feels good to get it off my chest. He hit me—slapped me across the face. I told him that was it, but the next morning he came over with a bunch of flowers and apologised and, like an idiot, I fell for it.'

'I'm sorry to hear that,' Adam said, and considered placing a consoling hand on her bare arm, but instantly remembered the fumbling kiss at the start and thought better of any more unwanted contact. Instead, he said, 'can I ask one more question?'

She nodded.

'What did you do after your fight in the street?'

'I went home with my tail between my legs.'

'Home?'

'Yes,' she said, eyeing him suspiciously. 'I didn't have anything to do with what happened, if that's what you're thinking?'

Adam waved his hands in front of him, indicating that such a thought had never crossed his mind, when, in fact, that very idea was ringing sirens in his head right now.

When she offered to get the next round in, he convinced himself quite quickly that leaving now would look strange, and that he could use this time to acquire a bit of background info on her. Like a real private investigator would.

So, just like a real PI would, he accepted her offer and watched her make her way to the bar, along with every other set of male eyes in the place.

Another drink became a few and by the time they stumbled out at last orders, they were well acquainted. Adam had found out lots about her upbringing, her job and her interests and, in the process, developed a huge crush on her.

A crush on a possible murder suspect.

Just great.

11

MANFRED MANN

EVERY FIBRE IN Adam's being was currently dedicated to not throwing up inside Colin's car. If he did, he'd never hear the bloody end of it.

And, it wouldn't be a fair way to reply his friend's current kindness. When last night's "interview" with Helena had turned to serious drinking, he'd been forced to abandon his car. He and Helena had shared a taxi back to Stonebridge, though she'd gotten out at her own house, dashing any lewd hopes that had started whirling through Adam's drunken head.

Now, Colin was giving him a lift back to Portstewart to retrieve his car, though Adam was unsure if he was even under the limit yet. When he voiced this, Colin suggested they head for a fry up in The Atlantic. Even the thought of the smell of greasy food forced Adam to redouble his efforts in keeping last night's lager at bay.

When they reached the car park, Colin pulled into a space and they got out. They walked down the prom towards the café, Adam feeling very much like a wounded soldier, though receiving far less sympathy than he'd like.

They chose a table with a sea view and placed their orders (a full Ulster Fry for Colin and a slice of toast for Adam), before talk turned to where they were up to with the current case.

Colin told Adam all about his meeting with Mickey; how Tyler had physically assaulted him and then smashed his car up, just because he'd been asked to leave the group.

'So, there's definitely some motive there,' Adam said.

'Definitely,' Colin agreed. 'He claims he's not into physical violence but he's a scary-looking mofo, so I'm not sure I believe him. What about Helena?'

Adam told Colin what he'd learned; that Tyler had hit her, too. They foolishly had gotten back together, though were close to breaking up for good.

'Jesus,' Colin said, 'It's no wonder Tyler ended up the way he did. He was making enemies left, right and centre.'

'Yeah. So, we've got Willow who he pissed off by taking over the group; Ocean, who he pissed off by bullying at school and then taking over the group; Mickey, and Helena.'

'Don't forget the McNultys. He pretty much single-handedly stopped their business deal going through with his protest. Oh, and somehow Tanner benefits out of all this.'

Colin relayed the information about the new butcher shop in the middle of town.

'We need to start eliminating people,' Adam said, just as the breakfast came. 'What's next?'

'Well, I was speaking to my gran this morning and she was telling me about the McNultys' dad. Apparently, he's been looking for a retirement home. I thought I could go to the McNultys and pitch the home where I work, try that angle. If they see me as a friendly, they might let their guard down. And, more importantly, not batter me!'

'Good plan. How do grannies know so much?'

'I know,' Colin said, shovelling some soda bread into his mouth. 'It's like they have some sort of underground network for gossip.'

'I bet your gran would have this case sown up in no time at all. Maybe we should get her on board.'

'I don't think we could afford her. She'd bankrupt us on coffee alone.'

COLIN MADE HIS way up the street, the greasy food weighing heavily in his stomach, towards the McNultys' temporary office space. Their headquarters, which had been on the first floor of their warehouse, had obviously gone up in flames the night of the fire, so they had been forced into the centre of town.

In fact, their office space overlooked the shop currently being turned into Tanner's Butchers. Talk about adding insult to injury.

As Colin reached the office, he looked up to the first floor windows. The letters that had been painted on by the last owner, a tailor, were peeling and faded. But, this was not the reason for Colin's skyward glance.

It was the shouting.

Two male voices tumbled through the single-glazed window and out onto the street. Each response was upped a decibel until Colin was sure their argument could be heard at the other end of the town.

Suddenly, a loud bang sounded, presumably a door being slammed, followed by footsteps on uncarpeted stairs. A smartly dressed Ron McNulty emerged into the sunlight, his hair coiffed to perfection. He pulled a pair of sunglasses from his jacket pocket and put them on, glancing at Colin as he did so.

Colin watched him walk away, pulling a packet of cigarettes from a different pocket. Pushing Ron from his mind, Colin walked through the door and ascended the stairs, before rapping his knuckles on the flimsy door when he reached the top.

'It's open,' a voice called.

The door opened into a basic office. Two desks took up most of the space. The desk he assumed as Ron's was empty, save for a laptop that was charging, and a blue folder. Both items were positioned parallel to each other.

The other desk was messier, as if real work actually got done at it. Sheafs of paper jostled for position with binders and notebooks, rolls of receipts and a couple of mugs of gone-cold coffee.

Behind this desk sat Ron's older brother, Kevin; his grey hair falling onto his elongated forehead and his shirt sleeves rolled up against the heat.

'Who are you?' he said, without warmth.

Colin introduced himself, and told Kevin of the reason for his visit. He tried to sell the retirement home as genuinely as he could, explaining the benefits of assisted living and the activities laid on for the people who lived there. He passed a brochure across the table, which Kevin lifted and flicked through, stopping abruptly at the pricing page.

'Ah,' he said. 'Slight bump in the road there. Unfortunately, at the moment, myself and Ron are unable to fund this, as we are waiting for the insurance money to come through. I'm sure you are aware as to what happened.'

Colin nodded and mumbled his apologies.

'Unless you did it, you have nothing to apologise for. It was an act of arson by a small-time thug, and we may have missed out on the investment, but all shall come good. Sadly, our father's incarceration,' he flashed a small smile at the word, 'will have to wait until such times as our cash is flowing again.'

'Missed out?' Colin said, playing dumb.

'Yes, sadly it seems that Mr Tanner is rising from our ashes.'

Kevin raised his eyes towards the window, but didn't elaborate further. He stowed the brochure inside one of the desk's drawers and stood, offering his hand, seemingly in a manner that marked their meeting as over.

Colin shook it and left. As he neared the doorway that led back to the street, he heard someone speaking heatedly, apparently on the phone as the conversation was punctuated by silences.

Colin stayed listening for a minute, and was shocked by the anger in the man's voice. When the worry of being caught eavesdropping reached fever pitch, he made his way out onto the street. He was pleased to see that Ron McNulty's back was to him, and even more pleased when he caught the final words of the conversation before Ron replaced his phone into his trouser pocket and disappeared up the stairs Colin had just come down.

Colin hurried up the street and, when he was absolutely sure that he was out of earshot, phoned Adam who answered on the second ring.

The conversation didn't last long. Colin ordered Adam to meet him in town as soon as possible. Something was going down, tonight, and they needed to be there.

'What did he actually say?' Adam asked.

'Usual place. 6pm.'

'Which means?'

'Which means we have to follow him to wherever this usual place is, so get your arse into town. Now.'

12

A QUICK DETOUR

ADAM HUNG UP and checked the time on the dashboard. As ever, Colin was being a tad melodramatic—it wasn't even four o'clock yet. If he had to abandon his plan now, it'd be a while until he got round to it again, so he made the brave decision to ignore his best friend's urgency.

Instead, he climbed out of the car and walked up the driveway to the house Tyler Love had shared with his mum before his death.

He snuck a look through the net curtains as he passed the kitchen window, but could only make out his own reflection.

He made his way to the door and pressed the doorbell. It chimed a cheerful tune which felt horribly out of place, considering what he was here to do. As the tune faded out, he heard footsteps approaching and a few seconds later, he was face to face with Jennifer.

The saying "time heals all wounds" had clearly not been thought through enough. Perhaps, eventually, the passing of time may soothe Tyler's mother's grief, but here and now, it looked like she had aged decades since Adam had last seen her.

Dark bags hung heavily underneath bloodshot eyes and thin lines travelled down her face, as if the weight of the tears she'd shed had been so numerate that they'd carved narrow valleys into her cheeks. She tried, and failed, to give Adam a smile, and instead led him into the living room he'd sat in on his first visit here.

'Any updates?' she asked, as she sat down on the sofa.

'Not yet, I'm afraid,' he replied, and her shoulders slumped. 'But, we have spoken to a number of people and have some avenues we'd like to explore, so we're still working on it.'

He hated that he sounded like a character from a detective show, masking empty words with fancy phrasing, but giving it to her straight seemed worse somehow.

No, sorry. No progress yet aside from finding out that your son sounded like he was a bit of a prat to everyone, not to mention a woman beater and a thug.

Fancy phrasing would have to do at this stage.

'The reason I'm here is that I'd like to have a look around his room, if that's okay?'

'Why?' she asked.

'It's something that's worked before.'

He consciously left out the bit about hiding in a wardrobe like a voyeuristic Mr Tumnus while listening to a recent widow and her bit on the side have sex. Though he liked to think that it had been a maverick move, even he knew it sounded more like the behaviour of a sex pest. Not something the grieving mother sitting opposite him needed to hear right now.

Or anyone, ever, really.

If he could strike it from his own memory like the guy in Eternal Sunshine of the Spotless Mind, he would.

Pushing these thoughts from his brain, he realised that she was nodding. He listened to her directions and headed for the stairs, taking them two at a time. The flowery pattern underfoot reminded him of the carpet in his mum's house and a little knot of emotion formed in his throat when he thought of how she would handle losing him.

He resolved to put all ill-thought of Tyler to the back of his mind for the sake of Jennifer Love.

Upon reaching the top of the stairs, he turned left and took in the door in front of him. It was painted white, but had two slightly discoloured, sticky patches at about eye level, as if a poster or plaque had recently been taken down. The door was slightly ajar, giving it the air that the owner of the room had nipped out and never thought to close it fully one last time.

Adam pushed it open and was met with a tidy room. A bed took up the middle of the floor. A bookcase rested against one wall and a mahogany chest of drawers filled the other. A small television was mounted to the wall that faced the end of the bed. Adam imagined a buttock-shaped groove on the mattress, formed through countless hours of sitting playing FIFA.

Then, Adam remembered that he and Tyler were not cut from the same cloth. While Adam had been content to while away hours in front of the tele, Tyler had been out on the streets, fighting the good fight.

Or, if not "good", then at least fighting for something.

Adam didn't know what he was looking for particularly; perhaps he simply wanted to know a little more about Tyler in the hope that something might leap out at him.

He started by looking through the bedside cabinet, but nothing of note became apparent. It was mostly magazines; publications by Greenpeace, Planet Mindful and the like. He closed the drawer again and stood, looking around the room.

He searched through Tyler's clothes drawers, but aside from a few loose condoms in the sock compartment, again came away empty handed. He spun on the spot and his eyes settled on the book shelf.

It had five shelves altogether. The top four were dedicated to paperbacks; mostly crime, though interspersed with some YA fantasy. The bottom shelf, however, was filled with notebooks.

Adam crossed the room and got down on his hands and knees, pulling some of the spiral bound notebooks out onto the floor. His heart picked up its pace, and he wondered if the plan to ignite the McNultys' warehouse had been a plot weeks or months in the making.

When he'd spoken to the hippies, they'd suggested that he'd left the HQ that night seething, making it seem like the firebombing was a spur of the moment thing.

But what if they were wrong?

Adam flicked through page after page, aware that time was ticking on and Colin would be getting angrier by the second, so he skimmed faster. To his disappointment, the notebooks were mostly filled with journal entries about things that had happened, or plans for peaceful protests.

There was nothing to incriminate him.

Frustrated, Adam lifted the pile and shoved them back into the bottom shelf. The one at the end knocked against the wooden frame and fell out, opening as it did so, onto a bookmarked page Adam must've missed in his haste.

The page itself was unremarkable, but the item marking the page was certainly something. On it, was a scrawled mobile number and a little heart coloured-in black with biro.

Adam wondered if it was simply a remnant of when Tyler and Helena had first met, but surely he would just have typed her number into his phone's memory.

He pulled his phone from his pocket and found Helena's number, checking it against the one on the page to see if it matched.

It didn't.

He typed the number from the paper into his phone and was about to press the green button, when his ringtone erupted.

Colin.

'Where the hell are you?' he asked, as soon as Adam had answered.

'Keep your hair on, I'm two minutes away,' Adam lied, and hung up.

Making sure he had the number saved, he replaced the scrap of paper inside the notebook and set it back onto the bottom shelf. He cast one last rushed glance around the room, before hurrying down the stairs and saying a very brief goodbye to Jennifer.

He needed to find out who the phone number belonged to. It might be nothing, or it might be something.

However, he *had* to get to Colin in the next ten minutes. If he didn't, he might not be alive to guide the case to its conclusion.

With that thought in mind, he crossed the street in haste and wheelspun away from the kerb.

13

USUAL PLACE. 6PM.

COLIN THREW HIS phone onto the passenger seat in frustration and sat back sharply, smacking his head a little too hard on the headrest.

He assumed whatever Adam was up to was something to do with the case. Or hoped so, anyway. With a solid gold lead in the bag, he'd be very annoyed if Adam was doing something to jeopardise all the hard work they'd put in so far.

He glanced at the clock again, for the third time that minute, and sighed.

Colin had managed to find a spot to park his car that offered a dual view of what he needed. He had an unhindered sight of the main street, which allowed him to cast his beady eye over the comings and goings of the McNultys' temporary office. Not that there was much to see. Since Colin had left, Ron had re-entered and there had been no further activity.

The spot also allowed him to keep his eye on the entrance to the private car park that the row of shops used. At the first sight of Ron's Audi departing, he'd be after him like a shot, with or without Adam.

He looked at the clock, again. And swore, again.

Except, his curse word was cut short as something of note was happening out on the street.

Frank Tanner, tall and broad-shouldered, stepped out of his almost-finished butchers and looked up and down the street, as if trying to ascertain if his shop was in a good place for passing footfall.

Something a good businessman would have considered before putting pen to paper on the deeds, thought Colin. Was he simply taking in his empire? Or stalling on whatever he was about to do next?

In answer, he pulled a cigarette from behind his ear and shoved it into his mouth, before igniting the end of it with a disposable lighter. He took a deep suck in and exhaled a plume of smoke. When it cleared, Colin could see that his eyes were now fixed on the McNultys' office across the street.

Frank took a few more puffs before stubbing the cigarette out on top of a nearby bin and disposing of it. He marched across the street and disappeared through the doorway of his competitors.

Colin imagined the butcher bursting backwards through the upstairs window, shattered glass raining from the sky, bones breaking as Frank's body collided with the cobbles below.

It didn't take long for something to happen, though not quite the over-the-top imaginings going through Colin's mind.

Frank appeared first, emerging backwards. Initially, it looked like he was doing the moonwalk, which was a comic sight, until Ron appeared too. The McNulty brother was holding the other man by the scruff of his jacket, pushing him out of his office. They were exchanging words, and not kind words, judging by the disgusted faces of the little old ladies who happened to be passing at the wrong time.

Frank attempted to fight back, though that seemed to enrage Ron further. He shoved Frank up against the wall and delivered a fist to his gut, before releasing his grip. Frank dropped down the brickwork onto the floor, where he slumped over sideways, almost assuming the foetal position.

Ron shouted something inaudible to Colin, before retreating up the stairs and out of sight.

Frank lay for a little while longer, drawing a small crowd. Some crouched beside him, phones in hands, probably offering to phone the police, though the stricken man was shaking his head. In the end, he pulled himself to his feet and the crowd dispersed.

Frank cast an eye up the stairs, perhaps wondering if round two was worth pursuing. Evidently, he decided against it. Instead, he walked away, rubbing his stomach gingerly.

What had Colin just seen?

Did the McNultys believe Frank was behind the arson? And if he was, why would he go and visit them in their office? Surely, he would want to keep as much distance as humanly possible. Everyone knew what the psycho brothers were capable of.

Before he could make sense of the questions, the passenger door opened, and Colin jumped a foot in the air.

'What the hell?' he shouted.

'What's up with you?' Adam asked, as he slipped into the seat.

'Nothing, just…'

As he was about to explain what he'd just seen, the front end of a black Audi poked out of the car park. Using his mirror, Colin could see Ron's head swivelling as he looked for a break in the traffic.

Ahead of Colin, the traffic lights turned red and Ron seized his chance. Colin turned the key in the ignition and, once Ron and a few other cars had passed, indicated and started to drive.

'What's the plan, then?' Adam asked.

'We follow Ron to see who he is meeting at 6pm.'

COLIN HAD WATCHED a lot of cop shows on TV. They made it look easy to tail someone without being seen. They always seemed to stay a few cars behind and be able to read the bad guy's mind as to which direction he was going in.

In reality, it was hard work. Colin was nervous that he would lose Ron, thanks to changing traffic lights, straying too far behind and losing sight of him, or getting too close and spooking him.

Thankfully, Colin's car was a run of the mill Hyundai and was unlikely to stand out in amongst the town traffic.

The other thing that the cops seemed to have was a trusting relationship. The driver would be fully in control and his passenger would be 100% behind him.

Colin had Adam, who didn't seem to be 100% behind him. Instead, he nattered in his ear, giving "helpful" hints and tips and droning on about what he'd do. Colin could feel his normally cool demeanour slipping and was thankful that Adam seemed to notice it too, because the backseat driving came to a sudden halt.

They left the town behind and travelled on quieter roads a short distance before Ron indicated into Hamilton's Tavern, a pub just on the outskirts of Stonebridge.

As Ron turned into the car park, Colin stayed on the road, travelling by the pub as if on their way to Meadowfield—the next town over.

When they reached a lay-by, Colin pulled in and they waited a few minutes, before performing a three-point turn and heading back in the direction that they'd come from. When they reached the pub, they turned into the car park and saw Ron's car parked out front, so they chose a space in the bigger car park at the back.

'I can't go in,' Colin said, turning the engine off. 'He saw me earlier and if I just happen to turn up in the same out-of-town pub on the same day, it might around suspicion.'

'You think he'd remember you?' Adam asked.

'No point risking it.'

Secretly, Colin was glad at the prospect of sitting this one out. One encounter with a McNulty was quite enough for one day.

Resigned, Adam got out of the car and disappeared through the back door.

ADAM HAD MADE a fool of himself in Hamilton's more times than he'd care to remember. It was one of those pubs that the under-agers would visit on account of the landlord being a bit loose on the ol' legal age rule. Gordy Hamilton was a legend round these parts.

It had been a while since Adam had visited, though it seemed nothing had changed. The bar ran along one wall, the mirror behind the optics serving to make the place look double the size it actually was. The rest of the space was open plan with misshapen tables taking up much of the floor, though the pool table had been given a reverent place near the front door.

Walking to the bar, Adam clocked Ron McNulty sitting in a little alcove that afforded him an almost unhindered view of the whole room. He was alone, staring at a laptop screen and holding an orange juice. He glanced up at Adam, who gave him a small nod that went unreturned, before lowering his head to his work again.

Adam felt nervous.

He crossed the room, bought a pint, and chose a table as far out of Ron's eyeline as he could. He sat down heavily, playing the part of a tired man who'd just had a hectic day at work. He took a sip of his pint, and then pulled his phone from his pocket.

It was almost six.

With a bit of time on his hands, Adam considered the case so far. As far as he was concerned, Ocean and Willow were involved insomuch as they were part of the same group as Tyler and had both fallen out with him over strategy. As to his demise, Adam was pretty convinced that they had played no part. Sure, they had issues with the dead man, but their lifestyles didn't match up to the violence and hate needed to light a building on fire, knowing someone they knew was inside.

The McNultys weren't likely to set fire to their own property and screw themselves out of a lucrative takeover.

That left Frank Tanner, Mickey and Helena.

Frank had benefitted from the fire financially; Mickey had been assaulted, and worse, by Tyler; and Helena had also been physically abused.

Adam hoped against hope that Helena wasn't involved. He had barely stopped thinking about her since she'd left him alone in the taxi and had resolved to do something about his ongoing singleness (should she be proved innocent).

Thoughts of Helena were pushed from his head by the arrival of Mickey Dooley. He sauntered in through the front door, and stood for a second, surveying the scene in front of him like a cowboy visiting a potentially dangerous tavern for the first time.

Deciding that there was no immediate threat, he strode towards the bar where he chatted to the barmaid for a few minutes before choosing a table once his Guinness had settled. He sat down and pulled his phone out.

At no point did he ever glance over towards the waiting McNulty.

Adam couldn't understand why. Had Ron recognised Adam from somewhere, and called the meeting off? But, if he did that, why would Mickey show up anyway and act as if he didn't know him? Was Mickey waiting for some sort of hand delivered message on a piece of paper? If so, why didn't they just use text message or email? The only reason Adam could think of was that they didn't want to create a digital trail for the police to uncover later.

The scene didn't change for the next thirty minutes.

When it did, it was only because Mickey had finished his pint and decided to call it a night. He walked past Adam without a backwards glance and left via the same door he'd entered.

Adam was going to call it quits soon, too. He felt bad for Colin, having to waste a load of his time sitting in his car.

He tapped on his phone and pulled up his contacts with the intent of calling Colin to quietly relay what he'd seen and ask if they should call it a night. Instead, his eyes fell onto the number from the piece of paper in Tyler's room that he'd saved.

He considered texting but thought better of it. Texting gave someone a chance to block his number or come up with a lie as to who they were.

No. Phoning was the best way forward here. He tapped the number and put the phone to his ear.

'Hello,' a female voice answered after a few rings.

Adam hastily pushed himself out of his seat and walked out of the front door, having realised in the nick of time that declaring who he was and what he was doing within earshot of Ron McNulty would've been a very silly thing to do indeed.

'Hi,' he said, when he was sure he was safely out of range. 'My name is Adam, and I am investigating the death of Tyler Love.'

'I'm Emma,' she said.

'Hi Emma. I was wondering if we could meet to discuss a few things?'

'Are you the police?'

'No. I'm doing a favour for his mum.'

'I don't know anything about how he died.'

'That's fine, but it would still be good to meet. I need as much help as I can get.'

There was a short silence before she agreed.

Tomorrow night. Bar7 at 9pm.

He hung up and re-entered the bar. As he passed the alcove, he saw that Ron was gone.

14

SOLO WORK

THE CRAFT TABLE in the Stonebridge retirement home was a mess. Colin sighed, more for effect than anything. Sometimes it was like clearing up after a bunch of toddlers. He checked his watch and realised that the table had been hastily abandoned because it was time for The Chase—a unanimous favourite amongst the old folk.

As he swept the last of the mess into the bin, Barry approached.

'Alright, Sherlock?' he asked.

'All good,' replied Colin.

'Any news?'

'About the case? Not loads, to be honest. We've prospectively crossed the hippies off our suspect list, but everyone else remains under the spyglass.'

'Have you been up to the warehouse yet?'

'Isn't it still a crime scene?'

'No,' Barry said, shaking his head. 'My daughter drove past it this morning and said all the police tape was down. Might be worth a trip.'

'Don't you think the police will have gone over it with a fine-tooth comb?'

'Not if they only thought the boy killed himself. It was probably only cordoned off for insurance reasons, but I assume all of that has been sorted by now if they've taken their tape down.'

Colin considered this. Perhaps the old man was right—if the police were convinced that Tyler was a lone wolf, they might not have gone to the trouble of searching for another angle. There couldn't be much harm in heading up for a quick look around.

'Cover for me a minute, will you?' he asked.

'Oh, aye,' nodded Barry, tapping the side of his nose conspiratorially.

Colin left the room and ascended the stairs towards the staff room. He pulled his phone from his locker and dialled Adam's number. When he answered, Colin explained his thoughts on what he and Barry had discussed.

'Sounds like a good plan, but I can't do tonight. I'm meeting Emma.'

'No worries. I'll head up myself. I can't imagine there'll be anything to find, but it's worth a shot. Good luck with the girl.'

They hung up with the promise of filling each other in first thing in the morning.

ADAM CHOSE THE same seat by the window and looked up at the bartenders, wondering if they had him pegged as some sort of serial ladies' man. Highly doubtful, he thought, as he looked down at his creased T-shirt.

Like déjà vu, the door to Bar7 opened, though the girl who entered was almost the polar opposite to the one he'd met at the same table a few nights previously. She looked like a surfer, with short, spiky blonde hair, Hurley T-shirt, denim shorts and flip-flops.

She cast an appraising eye over the bar, and Adam stuck his hand in the air to catch her attention. She strolled over and sat down opposite him. Though she was trying her best to appear chilled out, Adam could tell she was nervous. Her eyes were already travelling towards the fire escape door, and her fingertips were drumming a rhythm on the arm of the chair.

'Can I get you a drink?' Adam asked.

She shook her head.

'No, let's just get this over with.' She winced. 'Sorry, that came out unkindly.'

'Not at all,' Adam said. 'It's an odd situation.'

'Actually, maybe I will have a drink,' she said. He watched her vault out of her chair and head to the bar. For a second, he thought she might do a runner, but thankfully she ordered and returned to the table with a half pint of lager.

'What can I do for you?' she asked, after a quick sip.

'Can you tell me how you knew Tyler?'

'We were seeing each other a bit. Nothing serious, no strings.'

'By seeing each other, what do you actually mean?'

She looked at him like he had just spouted two heads.

'What do you think I mean?' she asked.

'I assume… intercourse?'

'And I assume you're not getting any if you are calling it that. Yes, we had *intercourse* a few times. And it was usually when one of us was drunk. In reality, he annoyed the life out of me, but he was good in…'

'I think I've got the picture,' Adam interrupted, not wanting any more detail than he required. 'Did you ever join him at one of the protests?'

She shook her head.

'Why?'

'I've got a job and most of the protests were during the day. Also, I hate antagonising people and that was his whole set up. Even when we were just chilling out together, he'd be trying to turn a chat into a debate. It was exhausting.'

'Sounds it,' Adam nodded, absent-mindedly. His thoughts had drifted to Helena. 'Did you know he had a girlfriend?'

The look on Emma's face told him the answer—a resounding no.

'He never said,' she confirmed. 'Sometimes when we were arranging to see each other, he'd be cagey about his plans for that night, but I just assumed he was up to something with his History Makers group. God, I feel terrible for her. I'm such a bitch.'

Adam shook his head.

'It's not your fault,' he said, consolingly. 'You're not a mind reader. I don't suppose he told you any plans he had for the group?'

'No,' she said. 'He knew I didn't care, so he rarely spoke about it.'

Her tone suggested that she had nothing else to say. She downed her drink and stood up. Adam tried to reassure her that she was not the bad person here, and she nodded, though he could tell she didn't believe him.

He watched her leave and sat down again, considering what this new information meant. It certainly gave Helena more motive if she knew that Tyler had been playing away. Could she really have followed him to the warehouse and set it on fire?

He needed to talk to her again.

He looked at his watch and reckoned that the abrupt end to his meeting with Emma meant that he could meet up with Colin at the warehouse. As he walked to the car, he phoned his friend, and told him he was on his way.

UNDER COVER OF darkness, Colin crept into the skeletal remains of the warehouse. It had been a huge rectangular structure, built from brick in the Victorian times that had now been reduced to mostly rubble. Some of the brickwork did remain, though the walls were now uneven in height and one strong gust of wind away from crumbling completely.

Inside, the devastation caused by the fire was clear to see. The expensive machinery had been reduced to twisted clumps of metal and the floor was littered with warped pieces of wood and tiny fragments of glass that crunched under Colin's feet.

He stood in the vast expanse of destruction and turned a full circle, letting his eyes adjust to the darkness.

Really, as with most of the investigation, he didn't know what he was doing here. He was hoping that something would appear at his feet, or become luminous like in a video game, but he knew that wasn't going to happen, so he got busy.

He skirted the permitter of the building, and worked his way inward. Aside from stopping at various points to take in, up close, the wrath of the flames, he worked quickly.

Nothing jumped out at him.

As he crossed the floor towards what, at one stage, would've been an office, he froze. It might have been his imagination, but he could've sworn that he'd heard something move. He listened intently, though the only sound to break the silence was the roar of a motorbike or a scally in a car with a ridiculous exhaust some way away.

Probably rats, he supposed. The place must be full of them.

When he was happy that he was alone, he moved across the floor and into the office. Just like the main space, in here was destroyed too. What was once a metal filing cabinet was now just a charred husk in the corner of the room and, in the centre, a blackened desk stood on flimsy legs that looked like they could give at any second. Colin was amazed it was upright at all, considering what had happened here.

What had he expected to find? A signed confession from Frank Tanner? Statistical comparisons of how much the McNultys could earn if they claimed on insurance as opposed to agreeing to the multinational deal?

It had been something that Colin had been thinking about since his meeting with Kevin McNulty—how much the man was relying on this insurance pay out, though he knew that he was being unfair. Obviously, insurance existed for a reason, and this was the perfect example.

Kevin had been expecting a huge buyout, and now had to wait on the insurance company to pay out a far smaller sum of money, so that he could house his father in a retirement home and get on with his own life.

The thoughts of Frank, Kevin and insurance were wiped from his mind by another tinkling sound from behind. His mind zoomed back to marauding rodents, but before he could turn to check, all and any thought disappeared, as he was knocked unconscious. The last thing he heard was the sound of fading footsteps before he fell to the floor.

TEN MINUTES LATER, Adam pulled up at the warehouse and got out of his car, using the torch function on his phone to light his path. He climbed over a low wall of bricks and shouted his friend's name but got no answer.

He assumed Colin would've phoned if he'd found something or decided the search was pointless and gone home. Maybe someone had come and escorted Colin off the premises. After all, they were not the police's favourite duo, after solving two crimes the police had decided were accidents. He wondered if DI Whitelaw and his cronies were making sure they weren't bettered a third time.

Adam phoned his friend's number and listened intently. The opening guitar riff of *Back in Black* sounded from somewhere, and he followed Angus Young's tasty licks like a beacon through the darkness.

The music cut off when Colin's phone went to voicemail, but by then Adam's eyes had fallen on his friend.

Colin was lying in a side room surrounded by splintered wood, face down as if he had been dropped though the table from a great height.

Adam ran to his friend's side, and despite the blood (he was notoriously bad at dealing with claret), checked Colin's pulse. Thankfully, there was one. There was also a huge gash on the back of his head that required urgent attention.

Summoning all his courage, Adam hoisted Colin to his feet and put his arm around him. It looked like they were taking part in some sort of Battle Royale style three-legged race.

Halfway across the floor, Colin came to, though very groggily.

'Wha 'appen?' he asked, his speech slurred.

'We're getting you to the hospital,' Adam replied, before whispering to himself, 'and then I'm going to kill the son of a bitch who did this to you.'

15

THE OLD FAMILIAR STING

ADAM HAD ALWAYS hated hospitals.

The drab paintwork and the overhead strip lighting caused everyone to look ill, even if they weren't. His fear was always that a doctor would mistake him for a sick person and wrongfully administer some sort of drug. He knew that it was stupidly irrational and had never voiced it aloud.

The door of the waiting room flapped open and in walked another worried plus-one, who fell into a chair opposite him, offering no greeting, which suited Adam just fine. All his thoughts were taken up by the wellbeing of his friend.

Thankfully, Colin's mental capacities had improved in the car. He couldn't remember anything about who had attacked him, except that they must've been there since he'd arrived, since they had squirrelled themselves away in that side office where Adam had found him.

Colin had then faded into silence, focussed on holding one of the McDonald's napkins Adam had found in the passenger footwell to the cut on his head.

Adam had used the quiet to reflect on what had happened. Had whoever been hiding in the building been on a cover-up mission? Perhaps Frank Tanner had snuck in, just to make sure he'd left nothing incriminating behind that the police had missed.

Frustrated, Adam stood and left the room. He headed down the corridor towards the café, though it was shut when he got there. Instead, he turned to the bank of vending machines and chose a bar of chocolate and a bag of cheese and onion Tayto crisps. Until he tore the wrapper of his Twix, he hadn't realised how hungry he was.

He sat down on a nearby seat and munched his way through the snacks. His thoughts turned back to the McNultys. Colin had mentioned something about insurance, but Adam didn't buy that angle. It was too obvious. They were psychos, but they weren't stupid.

Which left Helena.

Could she have been the one wielding the length of wood that had caused Colin to black out?

Adam sighed and stood to put his rubbish in the bin. He looked back up the corridor and froze.

There she was.

Helena.

He spun around, planting his back against the wall like Solid Snake used to do in Metal Gear Solid. He peered out again, getting a better look at his target.

Helena's hair was tied up in a neat bun and she wore matching navy top and trousers. She was linked arm-in-arm with an old man wearing a gown and holding onto one of those portable poles with a fluid bag attached to the top.

Adam did the maths. Either she was pretending to be a nurse, sneaking in covertly to the hospital to finish putting Colin's lights out and was taking her undercover role very seriously, or she really was a nurse.

The last option sounded more plausible. She had probably mentioned it when they were drinking at Bar7, but the effects of the alcohol had more than likely been playing with his memory by that point.

Adam left his position and started to walk up the corridor towards her, pretending he hadn't noticed her. As he passed, he glanced up and saw the recognition in her eyes.

'Adam?' she said.

'Ah, Helena! How are you?' he asked, acting surprised.

'Is this your boyfriend?' the old man asked.

'I was about to ask her the same question,' Adam joked, eliciting a bark of laughter from the old man.

'No, just a friend,' she told him, before turning to Adam. 'Let me get Larry back to his room and then we'll catch up.'

Adam watched her slow journey towards the patient's ward. She pushed the door open and let the old man enter first. A few moments later, she reappeared, alone and beckoned Adam towards a side room.

'What are you doing here?' she asked. 'Is everything okay?'

'My friend got beaten up.'

'That's awful,' she said, raising her hands to her cheeks. 'Is this something to do with Tyler?'

'What time did you start working today?' he asked, instead of answering her question. Adam didn't know if he could trust her.

'I started at seven o'clock. I'm here for the night shift. And I know what you are thinking, and like I told you already, I didn't have anything to do with Tyler's death, nor did I have anything to do with your friend getting beaten up.'

'Sorry.'

'It's okay. I know you're trying to do a good thing, but I'm hurting too. Tyler and I were coming to the end of the line, but it doesn't mean I wanted anything bad to happen to him.'

Adam considered what he'd learned earlier, about Tyler and Emma getting together while he was still in a relationship with Helena. A few hours ago, Emma's news had put Helena firmly in the frame, but now that he knew she had nothing to do with hurting Colin, he also was convinced she wasn't involved in Tyler's death.

'What is it?' she asked, breaking the silence.

'I've got something to ask you that might be upsetting…' he replied.

'Go on.'

'Did you know that Tyler was cheating on you?'

'No,' she said, shaking her head sadly. 'Though, it would explain an awful lot. How did you find out?'

'I found a phone number in his room and met up with the owner tonight to ask some questions.'

'And you thought that if I knew he'd been cheating, that might be another reason why I'd want to kill him?'

Adam looked uneasy.

'Jesus,' she said. 'I need a drink.'

'Tomorrow night?' he asked, though he knew his timing wasn't the best. Asking someone out on a date soon after accusing them of murder and informing them that they'd been cheated on wasn't exactly ideal.

'I'm sorry,' she said, shaking her head. 'It's not a good time.'

With that, she opened the door and left him alone with his shame.

WHEN HE WAS sure that his cheeks weren't illuminated like beacons anymore, he walked out into the corridor and headed in the direction of the waiting room. To his surprise, Colin was sat in one of the chairs. His head was wrapped in a bandage, though he looked much more with it.

They left the hospital together and headed for Adam's car. The night air was crisp and served as a welcome respite to the stuffy, germ-filled air of the hospital.

Once they were seated, Adam spoke.

'I think we should give up. To my mind, the hippies aren't involved, and neither is Helena. Which leaves the McNultys, Frank Tanner or Mickey Dooley. They're all scary boys, and ones I don't think we should be messing with.'

'Nah,' Colin said, shaking his head. 'I want to find whichever bastard did this to me and teach them a lesson.'

'That's the concussion talking,' Adam said. 'Do you think your mum is going to let you keep going?'

'We're 25 Adam. I don't have to listen to my mum!'

16

NO REST FOR THE WICKED

COLIN HAD HAD a dreadful night's sleep. Each time, just as he'd get comfortable, pain flared through his head like a jolt of electricity. He'd cursed the weak painkillers he'd been given and had resigned himself to a night of being awake. Thankfully, at some stage, his need for rest had overruled the pain and now, he woke slowly with drool running down the side of his cheek.

He sat up slowly and took in his battered reflection in the mirror. The bandage wrapped around his head wasn't a great look, and the constellation of cuts on his face looked even worse. If there was a silver lining, it was that he hadn't lost any teeth.

Or died. *That* was probably the golden lining.

He got out of bed and went downstairs to get breakfast. It was on days like today that he was happy he no longer lived with his parents. If he did, the amount of explaining he'd have to do would be ridiculous. If he could only avoid them for a week or so, they might never have to find out about his beating.

He was also thankful that it was his day off. He planned on spending the day in bed, watching telly and resting. In fact, he was going to treat himself to jammy toast in bed. The only shame was that he'd have to make it himself. Or, he could call Adam…

No.

Having your friend bring you food in bed was too weird.

Once the toast was coated in strawberry jam, he took his plate and glass of orange juice up the stairs with him, propped the pillows up against the headboard and got in, pulling the duvet up to his neck.

He thought about what Adam said, about leaving the case be. It was definitely the smart move—the stitches in the back of his head were testament to that.

But, the ending felt close. The pool of suspects was being whittled down and Colin couldn't help but feel that the answer was close at hand. The throbbing in his head was arguing that they had perhaps got *too* close.

He breathed out deeply and resolved to spend today resting. The case would not enter his mind from now on.

As he thought this, his phone rang. He looked at the display and was dismayed to find that it was the retirement home.

'Hello,' he answered.

'Colin, it's Mary. I know it's your day off, but we've just had a viewing appointment booked and the man asked for you specifically.'

'Who is it?' Colin asked, though he already knew.

'Kevin McNulty.'

Colin assured Mary that he'd be in for the appointment at three before hanging up.

So much for a day of rest and not thinking about the case.

COLIN ARRIVED EARLY so that his colleagues and the old folk could get their shock at his appearance out of their systems.

He assured them that it had been caused by a freak accident, and that it wasn't as bad as it looked. In reality, now that he was up and about, it felt like a hangover from hell. It was only when he had a quiet moment alone with Barry that he admitted how rough he felt.

'You're getting somewhere, then,' the old man said.

'What do you mean?'

'Well, lashing out is the mark of a man who feels cornered. And someone certainly lashed out at you. And now we've got a visit from a McNulty. Do you think the two events are connected?'

'Doubtful,' Colin said. 'If he battered me, why would he ask for me to show him around?'

'Good point. That's why you're the detective and not me.'

Mary poked her head around the frame of the door and told Colin that the visitors were here.

'You need back up, you let me know,' Barry said, adopting a boxing stance, just as he descended into a huge coughing fit.

'Aye, I'll keep that in mind, Ali,' Colin said, as he left the room.

He met Kevin McNulty and his father, Raymond, at reception, greeting them with a handshake. Kevin glanced up at Colin's bandage, and Colin felt a silly impulse to apologise for how unsightly he looked.

'Did one of this lot do that to you?' Kevin asked with a smile, motioning to the roomful of OAPs.

'Yeah,' Colin said, 'Geraldine hates it when I'm late with her lunch. Isn't that right, Ger?'

'Too right,' she replied. 'Especially on lasagne day.'

Colin led Kevin and Raymond through the day room, chatting to them about the facilities, the range of activities on offer and introducing them to some of the folk who weren't asleep in one of the cosy armchairs dotted around the room.

He led them to the vacant bedroom that would be Raymond's if he wanted it. Raymond walked in, and the other two gave him some space and time. This part of the job often hit Colin like an emotional car crash. It was the point at which the elderly gent or lady knew that their independence was coming to an end. Some accepted it with a stoic nod, some saw it as a new adventure and looked genuinely excited at the prospect while others looked like a devastated child being abandoned on the first day of school.

Ray was the former. He glanced around dispassionately, pushing into the mattress with a balled fist to check its springiness before taking in the view from the window.

'Has the insurance money come through?' Colin asked Kevin.

'Not yet,' he said. 'But it should be any day now, and we thought it best to be prepared. I assume there will be some sort of administration involved on your end that could take a while so we thought we'd come and have a look around and start making decisions.'

Kevin's phone started ringing in his pocket, and he checked the display before excusing himself. Colin watched him walk down the corridor with purpose, before pushing through the doors at the end that led to reception.

'What do you think, then?' Colin asked, turning his attention to Raymond.

'It'll do,' he replied, sitting down on the desk chair.

'It's daunting at the start, but you'll soon make friends.'

He nodded, and Colin worried that he'd sounded patronising.

'I imagine your sons will come and visit often, too.'

The old man laughed. 'You must be joking. If you asked Ron who his father was, he'd tell you he didn't have one.'

'Why?' Colin blurted out, before he could help himself. 'Sorry, that's a bit personal.'

'You're fine, son. It's because you should never mix family and business. You see, when I was coming up to retirement age, I gave the business to the boys. It was my father's before me and his father's before that, and then it passed to me and my brother. Because I was older, I got 75% share.'

'Didn't that cause arguments?'

'Some, but it was a family tradition. Happened in every generation. My father once explained that it was so there was an outright leader. Someone who the buck stopped with. And, so, I continued it. Ron thought I might be the one to break the tradition, to split it 50/50.'

'But you didn't?'

'I didn't. Tradition is tradition.'

'So it's mostly Kevin who you see?'

'It's only Kevin I see,' Raymond said. 'Ron has effectively disowned me. Though, I suspect if their deal had gone through, and he'd made his fortune, he'd have got in touch to rub it in my face.'

'Were you upset that they were selling the business?'

He leaned back a little in the chair, his expression suggesting it was the first time he'd thought about it.

'I suppose I was. It's been in the family for generations now. One of the oldest butchers on the north coast, alongside Tanner's. It would've been a shame to see the abattoir with someone else's name on it.'

Colin's attention was stolen by the re-appearance of Kevin striding up the corridor. He smiled warmly and, when he reached them, poked his head around the door.

'Looks like you've got yourself settled already,' he said to his dad, who didn't bother to hide his eyeroll.

When Raymond had seen enough, Colin led them back to the reception area. Kevin told him that they'd be in touch soon and shook his hand. Raymond gave him a small smile and they departed.

Colin watched them go, keenly aware that Kevin could've been the one who'd bashed him over the head last night. He also couldn't wait to tell Adam what he'd managed to find out from Raymond.

He watched the McNultys climb into their car and leave the car park. When he was sure they were gone, Colin left too.

ADAM PUT DOWN the phone and thought about what Colin had just told him.

Colin's theory about insurance had been spinning through his mind all day. He'd sped through his work that morning, probably doing a horrific job on Mrs Kedie's flowerbeds, though she was partially blind, and he could nip back and fix them before she realised. Once he'd packed his gear into the van, he'd driven home and spent the day doing a bit of research.

He felt like Colin's information lent further credence to his idea, but it was like doing a jigsaw and finding that some crucial parts hadn't been cut quite right. Nothing was fitting together properly.

Yet.

But he had a plan.

If this were a film, there'd be a montage showing a flurry of action. In reality, Adam needed to print a few things and the sodding printer jammed. He spent a few minutes cursing it to high heaven in the hope that insults alone would jolt it into action, and when that didn't work, he turned it off and on again which only made the damned thing chew up his last few pieces of paper.

His gave it the middle finger, and in reply a notification flashed up informing him that it was out of ink.

He unplugged the leads from his laptop and gathered up anything else he'd need, before pulling out his phone and ringing Colin back.

'Are you at home?' he asked.

'I will be in five minutes.'

'Is your printer set up?'

'Yeah, why?'

'I need to print something, obviously, and mine is doing the devil's work. See you in fifteen.'

With that, he hung up, grabbed his keys from the sideboard and marched towards the door.

It was business time.

17

WHOLE LOTTA LUCK

'I THOUGHT YOU said yours was working?' Adam said. A purple vein was throbbing in his forehead.

'It was the last time I used it. It's you and your bad printer juju that making it go on the fritz.'

'Well, we need to print this off somehow so that we can present the information, but I can just show you for now.'

Adam turned the laptop screen towards his friend and talked through what he'd found. Colin listened intently, despite the throbbing pain in the back of his head. The information was coming thick and fast, though when Adam had finished, he was convinced that they'd arrived at the correct outcome.

'So what do we do now?' Colin asked.

'We somehow lure them to a meeting place. Somewhere public so that they can't hurt us.'

Colin left the room and walked to the kitchen. Hr grabbed a packet of paracetamol from the drawer and poured a glass of water, throwing the tablets back in quick order. He was impressed with Adam's investigating, but didn't want to let on too much. He could already feel his friend's ego swelling.

Keen to contribute, he racked his brain for a kernel of an idea. Something that could bridge the next step…

'I've got it,' he shouted, shocking himself.

'What?'

'I have an idea as to how we can get them to a meeting point.'

Colin explained his idea, and was annoyed when Adam pointed out the gaping holes. After a few minutes of knocking ideas back and forward, they'd figured how to paper over some of the cracks, though they'd still need a hell of a lot of luck.

Adam pulled his laptop towards him and started on his side of the plan while Colin grabbed his keys and headed to town.

AN HOUR LATER, they had what they needed.

Adam was in possession of two mobile phone numbers, which he had scribbled on a piece of paper. He slid it across the table to Colin, who picked it up and keyed the first number into the brand-new phone he was holding.

"Brand-new" in the fact that he had bought it within the last sixty minutes. It had cost fifteen quid from the exchange shop and would have been considered behind-the-times in 2002. Still, he only needed to send two messages and it was more than capable of that.

'Before I send this, are we sure that there isn't a more fool-proof way of getting them both there?'

'Nope,' Adam said, shaking his head. 'I tried to come up with something better when you were out, but nothing came.'

'Great.'

Typing on something other than an iPhone felt strange. The phone didn't have a touch screen so he had to use the number buttons to painstakingly spell out the words. It was like typing morse code.

He finished typing and passed the phone to Adam to check it before he pressed send. Adam read it aloud.

'I think someone is on to us. Usual place. 6pm. No contact until then.'

Adam looked up from the phone and nodded, though Colin could see that he still wasn't fully convinced. Before they could chicken out, Colin grabbed the phone off him and hit the send button. He then typed an identical message and sent it to the second number.

When he was sure the duplicate message had been delivered, he took the back off the phone and popped the battery and SIM card out. He shoved the former in the bin and snapped the latter in half.

He then set the phone onto the carpet and stood on it with a heavy boot.

'Who do you think you are? The SAS?' Adam laughed.

'Dunno. It feels like something Jack Bauer would do,' Colin shrugged. 'Now, we need a great big slice of luck.'

And, as if a message was being sent from the heavens, Colin's printer beeped to life and began delivering the pages Adam had sent an hour ago.

'Fate smiles upon us,' Adam said.

Colin rolled his eyes.

18

USUAL PLACE. 6PM. ENCORE.

COLIN AND ADAM pulled into Hamilton's at five o'clock, keen to get there early and secure a good seat.

The plan was set. The hope was that the two guilty men would think the other had texted them, and that they'd both show up to find out what intelligence the other had gathered. Then, Colin and Adam would swoop in.

So as not to arouse suspicion, they went to the bar and ordered a beer each, and some food. Colin opted for the fabled surf and turf, while Adam went for the burger. They carried their drinks to the corner table and waited.

A short while later, the food arrived and, just before six, the first of the men entered.

Ron McNulty went straight to the alcove and sat down, casting a sneaky glance around the room before pulling his laptop out. Adam assumed he was pretending to do work; something to make it look like he was here for a reason.

The barman brought a pint of lager to him, which he accepted with a fake smile, though it sat untouched on the table while Ron's eyes flicked towards the door every couple of seconds.

Ten minutes later, Colin and Adam's suspicions were confirmed to be true. The next man through the door was Frank Tanner. He glanced around furtively, before heading straight to the table occupied by Ron, sliding into the chair beside him.

Adam could hear irritated mutterings, though couldn't make out what they were saying.

'Time?' he said to Colin.

'None like the present.'

They got out of their seats and crossed the room. It was empty, aside from the four men, the barman, and a curly haired fella reading the newspaper with his back to them, oblivious to the fireworks that were about to be lit.

'Evening gents,' said Adam, summoning more nerve than he thought he had in him. 'Mind if we sit?'

Without waiting for an answer, he slid into the chair opposite Ron. Colin followed his lead, taking the last remaining seat.

'Gentlemen, we have much to discuss. You see, we know what you've got yourself muddled up in.'

'And what would that be?' asked Ron.

'Oh, let's see… we've uncovered insurance fraud and manslaughter so far, but who knows where that list ends.'

'Is this about the fire?' Ron asked. 'The fire that destroyed my business? I'm the victim here, Mr…?'

'Never you worry about our names for now. And labelling yourself the victim here is laughable. *He,*' Adam pointed at Frank, 'could be considered the victim, at a stretch, but only because he's got as many braincells as one of those chickens he makes his living from. But, you? I think *mastermind* might be the best label for you.'

Frank looked confused by what was going on. He stared dumbly at Ron, who seemed to be the mouthpiece of this alliance.

'And who do you think the police are going to believe? They were the ones that told me the fire was caused by that wee lad who died.'

'Tyler Love. We'll get to him,' Adam replied. 'He's the reason we got involved in the first place.'

'What are you? Private detectives?' Ron laughed. 'Dicks, they sometimes get called, don't they? Well, if the shoe fits...'

Adam ignored the childish jibe and set the manila folder on the table. Ron adopted a bored look, though Adam could tell his interest had been piqued.

'Here's what we'll do. I'll present my case, you tell me if I'm hot or cold, and at the end we'll see if I've won the speedboat.'

Ron looked bemused, not least by the Bullseye reference.

'Here goes. Tyler's mum asked us to look into his death. She didn't believe the police—told us he wasn't the type of boy to go around lighting fires. Now, I'll be honest, we talked to a fair few people about him and not many had positive words to say. Still, going from petty vandalism to arson is a leap, so we looked at other avenues.

'The stroke of luck came when we spoke to your father. He told us about the crappy deal you we're getting. twenty five percent of the family business because you were born a few years later than your brother is a bit of a bum deal. My words, not his. He fully stood by his decision, isn't that right, Colin?'

'Bang on,' Colin agreed.

'So, even with the multinational buying your business, you weren't going to make as much from it. Why take a quarter of that pie, when you could have half of another.'

Adam reached into the manila folder and pulled out a piece of paper.

'After your bit of street theatre the other day, when Frank came to speak to you at your office, we thought something was amiss. I mean, why would Frank be coming to speak to you? You hate each other, right?'

'Wrong, it would seem,' Colin continued. 'But you didn't want your brother to know that, so you took Frank out onto the street and gave him a bit of a fake duffing…'

'It wasn't fake,' Frank interjected. 'He smacked me in the bloody stomach.'

'Regardless,' Colin said. 'We figured you two were working together, so we looked into a few things. It seems that you, Ron, bought some shares in Frank's business not so long ago. Quite a lot, actually. Half of the company. And, you probably got quite a good deal when you told Frank of your plan.'

Ron didn't say anything, but Adam noted a look of fear cross his face for the first time. He was on the ropes.

'Now, all you needed to do was make sure the McNulty Meats deal didn't go through. So you burned your business to the ground.'

'Ah, that's where you're wrong,' he started, though Adam shut him down.

'Figure of speech. I should've said the business was burned to the ground. By Frank. You knew that if anyone saw you do it, the insurance wouldn't pay out. So, you instructed Frank to do it, and like an obedient little boy, he did.'

Neither Ron nor Frank said a word.

'So, now with McNulty Meats in ashes, the multinational moved onto the next biggest company in Stonebridge. What luck. Now, Ron and Frank are going to be rich, and Ron even has that 25% of the insurance pay out winging its way to him, too!'

'Tragically,' Colin said, taking up the story. 'Unbeknown to you, Tyler had broken into your factory and was tinkering with your machinery, or smashing windows or something. Revenge for you roughing him up at the protest. Frank chucks the petrol bomb in, Tyler can't escape, and a young man dies.'

'A thug,' Ron spits.

'A dead one. It must've been such a relief when the police blamed him. I bet you thought you were home and dry, eh? So, how did we do?'

'Clean sweep, if I'm honest, lads. What can I say? I was getting the crap end of the shovel with my father's outdated business decisions. I worked my fingers to the bone for the company, in the hope that he'd change his mind. When he didn't, I took matters into my own hands. Tyler's death was a mistake, but he shouldn't have broken into the warehouse.'

Ron lifted his pint for the first time and took a hearty slug, before slamming it roughly back onto the table. He wiped his top lip and smiled.

'Now, as interesting as that was, hearing you two boy scouts recounting my plan back to me, it was all for nothing. The police think Tyler did it, and just because I invested in another business does not show me as guilty. In fact, it showcases my entrepreneurial spirit and community-mindedness, if anything. Why are the police going to believe you two?'

AT THAT MOMENT, the curly haired man sitting at the bar folded his newspaper and spun round on the seat.

'I'd say hearing a full confession with my own ears might be reason enough,' Detective Inspector Whitelaw said. He spoke into the walkie-talkie that was attached to his shirt pocket, and suddenly the bar was swarming with police officers.

'One more question,' Colin said, while the two men were being handcuffed. 'Which one of you bashed me over the head?'

Ron and Frank both genuinely looked blank.

'Take them away,' Whitelaw ordered, before turning to Adam and Colin and offering congratulations, albeit begrudgingly.

WHEN THE MADNESS had died down, Colin and Adam retook their places at the corner table they'd chosen originally. They ordered fresh pints, and when they came, clinked them together.

'Surely,' Colin said, 'that's Stonebridge's quota of drama filled for the foreseeable future.'

'You'd think,' Adam agreed.

19

AN ANSWER AND A QUESTION

THEY WERE BOTH wrong. Stonebridge wasn't quite finished with them yet.

Colin walked down the street, glad that he and Adam had called it quits after pint four. His mum had Facetimed earlier that morning, and, forgetting that he looked like a battered potato, had pressed the green button.

Her gasp had shocked him. She'd been at once angry, confused, cross and weepy. She'd made him tell her everything, and admonished him for keeping it a secret. He'd felt bad, and had proposed meeting for lunch to tell her the whole story.

As he passed the town hall, he saw Mickey, and nodded. He was speaking into his microphone, trying to entice passers-by to listen, but no one seemed interested today. When Mickey saw Colin, he froze. For a second, Colin thought he was having one of those absence seizures, but then he dropped the microphone, causing the town square to fill with squealing feedback.

Mickey turned his PA system off and ran over to Colin.

'Dude,' he said. 'I owe you an apology.'

Mickey told Colin how he had been up at the McNulty warehouse the other night, looking for any evidence that they'd been up to no good. After his and Colin's chat, he'd felt bad about dissing Tyler, so had set about trying to help Colin and Adam's investigation in order to exonerate his old foe.

Mickey had been in the office when he'd heard someone come in to the warehouse. He suspected it was one of the McNultys, so had armed himself with a table leg. He'd bashed Colin over the head with it, and ran.

He rained apologies down on Colin who waved them away. Colin assured Mickey that he would've done the same before giving Mickey a brief overview of what he and Adam had uncovered. After that, they bade each other goodbye.

Colin walked away, happy in the knowledge that the final mystery had been solved. He also determined never to get on Mickey's bad side!

ACROSS TOWN, Adam was regretting that fourth pint. His head was a mess.

He pulled himself out of bed and walked down the stairs, hunting for some paracetamol. He popped two out of the blister packet and set them on the counter, before reaching into the cupboard and pulling out a mug. He set it on the counter, too. As he pulled his hand away, something caught his eye.

There was movement inside the mug, so instinctively, he punched it, smashing it completely.

As the pain registered in his shrapnel-bitten hand, two things went through his mind. Firstly, that punching the mug because he thought a spider was inside it was a silly thing to do, and secondly, he was most likely going to need stitches.

Luckily, he'd fallen asleep in last night's clothes.

He grabbed a jacket off the coat hook and, summoning every ounce of bravery in his body, wrapped it around his bleeding hand, putting as much pressure on it as he could stand. He made his way to the car and drove carefully to the hospital.

When he got there, he paid through the nose for a car parking ticket, sticking it begrudgingly onto his windscreen before making his way into A&E. He told the receptionist why he was here, and she told him to take a seat; that someone would be with him shortly.

He strolled to the seat, hungover, trying not to think about how much blood he was losing. Things couldn't get any worse, he thought, glumly.

'Adam?'

Ah! Things *could* get worse, it would seem.

Helena stood in the doorway of one of the treatment rooms. Even in her work garb, she looked beautiful. Adam cursed the universe.

She beckoned him towards her and led him into the room. He unfurled the jacket and showed her his injury, explaining what had happened. His face was burning with embarrassment.

'Adam, this is a bit extreme,' she winked. 'If you wanted to ask me out again, you could've just phoned.'

MEAT IS MURDER

-4-

THE CASE OF THE MISSING FIREFLY

CHRIS MCDONALD

Stonebridge Radio Hallowe'en Party

You are cordially invited to the
Stonebridge Radio Annual Hallowe'en Bash
on Winkle Isle.

comprising a sumptuous meal,
a few scares and an evening of Murder Mystery.

I do hope you can join us.

A. Fernsby

RSVP by 6th October to guarantee your place.
No cost.

1

NO MONEY, MORE PROBLEMS

ALBERT FERNSBY RUBBED his weary eyes and reached for the tumbler that sat on his office desk.

It used to be he'd only drink on special occasions. Then, there'd been a few years where he'd elevated minor wins to full blown celebrations, just so that he could justify the heft of a full glass in his hand. Now, it had become a nightly thing. A glass of wine with dinner. A few fingers of whiskey while he worked in the evening. Sometimes, even a small glass of port before bed.

He was sure Margaret had noticed, but if she had, she hadn't said anything. It wasn't like he was doing it solely in the confines of his office.

It was hard to keep secrets after more than forty years of marriage, and he was hoping that she might see the drinking as a cry for help, rather than for what it actually was—a distraction.

He strained his ears and heard her padding around upstairs, the floorboards creaking under her feet in the bedroom.

He listened for a few more seconds and, when he was happy that he wouldn't be disturbed, pulled out the blue folder from the filing cabinet.

It was innocuous enough. It looked like the dozens of other files and folders in his office, the ones that lined the shelves and held evidence of his business prowess. Receipts of advertising deals and good decisions made at the right time.

The blue file in his hand showed exactly the opposite.

He set the folder in front of him, front and centre on his desk. He glared at it with contempt and thought that a steaming pile of fresh cow dung would be more welcome on his desk than *this*.

Perhaps it was his advancing years or perhaps it was the changing world, he didn't know, but the past year had been a ruinous one. Financially.

Running a radio station was hard work.

Running a local radio station was even harder.

Stonebridge Radio had started with his father all those years ago. Albert looked at the framed pictures on the walls of his office and smiled. The muscles in his face protested; it had been a while since they'd been pulled into this unfamiliar position.

He took in the black-and-white photos of his father, of the newly founded radio station, of presenters who had started small and either gone on to great things in the capital or faded into the obscurity that stacking supermarket shelves offers.

His smile faded at the more recent photos. He knew that he had taken the radio station as far as it could go. The rise of social media, streaming services, podcasting and a certain fruity corporation had been the death knell of local radio.

The businesses who had once relied on the radio for advertising spots had found other means of reaching their customers; viral videos and celebrity endorsements rendering the advertising service at the station all but useless.

Income had fallen and outgoings had risen, and now they were on the brink. The loan repayment letters and the overdraft statements in the folder were testament to that.

He puffed out his cheeks and took a sip of the amber liquid in his glass. It smarted as it dripped down his throat; the cheap supermarket stuff nowhere near as smooth as his favoured brand. A brand that was beyond his means, at the moment.

Beggars can't be choosers.

He rubbed a hand over a couple of days of stubble and sighed.

He'd have to come clean to his wife. She deserved to know that they were having financial difficulties. He knew they were a team and that whatever happened to them, they'd face it together.

Still, admitting defeat was a bitter pill to swallow.

He sighed again as it became clear what he'd have to do. What he'd been trying to circumnavigate for the past few months but now, there was no other option.

The station would have to close.

He thought of his staff—of the lives he'd be throwing into turmoil with his decision. He thought of his poor father, and what he'd think if he were alive to see it.

He was so caught up in his thoughts, that he didn't hear his office door open. He jumped as he caught sight of his wife's recently dyed locks in the doorway.

'Are you alright?' she asked.

'The best,' he smiled.

He watched as her gaze fell first on the almost empty glass and then on the open file. She was a perceptive woman, and a kind one. Instead of commenting, she simply nodded.

'How's your leg feeling today?' she asked.

'A bit better,' he replied.

Albert had lost the bottom half of his right leg in a car accident a few years back. Learning to walk with the aid of a prosthetic limb had been hard on him, his pride dented with each pitying look he'd received. Last night, he'd complained about the stump rubbing. When she'd tended to it, it had been bright red and bleeding a little.

'Can I do anything for you?' she asked.

He shook his head, forced a smile.

'I'll leave you to it then, love. Are you all packed for the weekend?'

Albert sighed.

'I'll take that as a no,' she laughed.

'To be honest, I could do without it.'

'The annual Stonebridge Radio Bash used to be your favourite weekend of the year,' she replied.

'I'm an old man now. I like my own bed, my home comforts.'

'Well, *I'm* looking forward to it,' she said. 'You never know when it's your last one. And, I've always fancied a murder mystery evening—I'm good at guessing the bad guys when we watch Death in Paradise. I think I'll be a dab hand at being a detective. It'll be a laugh.'

Not with the bombshell I'm going to drop, Albert thought to himself.

2

ONTO THE ISLAND

THE WAVES SMASHED against the hull of the boat, slamming it this way and that. The hum of the engine was lost to the howling winds and the captain, when his voice sounded over the public address system, sounded panicked, though he tried to reassure those on board that they were almost at their destination.

Adam Whyte was furious. Not many things scared him (aside from clowns, the thought of a snake slithering up his toilet bowl while he was sat on it, being made into a meme, and the way daddy long legs buzzed around aimlessly while possessing the deadliest poison known to man), but the sea was truly frightening. The vastness of it, the fearsome sharks that lurked beneath the surface and the fact it had swallowed up a ship once deemed "unsinkable" were only a few of the factors that caused this fear.

He and his best friend, Colin McLaughlin, were sat near the back of the boat. Adam was gazing out the window, though he couldn't make out anything except a few twinkling stars that had broken through the blanket of cloud. He certainly couldn't see the island they were heading for.

'Remind me again why I'm here,' he said, turning to Colin.

'Because my mum is paying us both a hundred quid to set up a projector when we get there because her usual tech guy called in sick,' he replied.

Adam thought back to the proposition put to him a few days ago. At the time it had seemed like easy money—one hundred quid for a few minutes work certainly wasn't to be sniffed at. The fact that they had to stay on an island for two nights didn't bother him either, once he'd been assured there was WiFi. He could easily while away the weekend in the company of Cumberbatch and Freeman.

Of course, what hadn't been mentioned was the group of people he'd be having to share a boat ride with.

Colin's mum was an event co-ordinator and had been hired by the Stonebridge Radio team to organise a murder mystery night on Winkle Isle, a small island just off the coast of Stonebridge. Legend had it that the island was the most haunted place in Northern Ireland, which made it the perfect place to host such an event with a Hallowe'en theme.

Had Adam known about the group he'd been sharing the weekend with, he'd have declined instantly.

The Stonebridge Radio presenters were notorious in the area for their childish behaviour, pig-headedness and their absolute willing to do whatever it took to bag the best show. They'd gladly push a colleague in front of a bus if it meant they could climb a rung on the ladder towards the prime-time evening slot; a position currently held by Keith Starr.

At least the owner of the station, Albert Fernsby, was there too, Adam thought. Surely the presenters would be on their best behaviour if the man who paid their wages was on the island too.

'Right,' shouted Drive Time Dave above the cacophony of wind, waves and rain. 'As it's Halloween and everyone has put in a load of effort with their costumes… except for the boss…'

This raised a few sniggers, but not many.

'Here is my proposition,' he continued. 'For the entire weekend, you must keep your outfit on. That means, for the entirety of the time on the island, I will resemble Dracula. The first person to break this rule, will have to pay the drinks tab on Sunday night, and let's face it, that's going to be a bloody fortune! What do we say?'

Not wanting to appear like stick in the muds, the other presenters instantly held aloft a bottle of beer each and agreed.

'This is going to be so much fun,' squealed afternoon presenter Sophie Saunders, who was dressed as a sexy cat.

Adam stared at her. It always amazed him that some people, like her, saw Hallowe'en as an excuse to wear as little as possible. A year ago, his tongue would've been lolling on the floor at the sight of her low-cut top and sheer leggings, but not this year. The newly matured, spoken-for Adam Whyte was more worried about her catching hypothermia on this cold October night.

Adam noticed the other presenters didn't look as enthusiastic as Sophie. Keith Starr, dressed as a fat David Bowie, looked over at Gavin Callaway. Gavin was well over six feet tall, built like a tank and was currently squeezed into black spandex in an effort to look like a 90s wrestler. Gavin rolled his eyes. Keith did too.

Adam turned back to Colin.

'You're a dick for not mentioning who we were coming with.'

'Like it matters,' Colin shrugged. 'It's not like we're going to have to spend any time with them. We set up the projector in the main room and that's the last we see of them.'

'You'd best have brought good snacks.'

Colin zipped open his rucksack to reveal a treasure trove of sugary treats. 'By the end of the weekend, you'll be well on your way to having diabetes.'

'Good man,' laughed Adam, patting his friend on the back.

'You know,' Colin said, 'I was surprised when you agreed to come, if I'm honest.'

'Why?'

'Well, the island has this reputation as being the most haunted place in Northern Ireland…'

'And…?' Adam interrupted.

'Well, you're a bit of a scaredy cat, aren't you? You don't like blood, can't even watch it on telly without feeling faint, and as for horror movies…'

'I just don't see the fun in watching something designed to scare you. It's stupid. And there won't be any of that this weekend. You said it yourself—most of the weekend will be spent in a room, away from whatever it is these idiots get up to.'

Adam was still pontificating about how brave he was as the boat slowed and began to approach the wooden jetty that jutted out from a rocky alcove. The boat rotated and the engine died. There was some shouting as the captain communicated with one of the crew, who had leapt from the boat to the jetty to secure the vessel to land with a length of rope.

The gentle chatter of the guests was interrupted by a guttural scream from outside.

Sophie grabbed hold of Drive Time Dave's arm and Keith jumped a foot in the air, which was a surprising feat considering his girth.

As Adam adjusted himself to try and see what had happened, a sneering moustached face appeared in the circular porthole, almost nose to nose with him. Adam fell off the bench seat onto the floor, pain shooting up his back as his tailbone collided with the hard sole of the ship.

Swear words Colin had never heard before spilled out of his friend's mouth at a rate of knots, as the face disappeared from the window and the body it belonged to started to descend the steps at the front of the boat.

'So,' the tall man said, staring intently at each person in turn, 'you are the island's next victims, hmm?'

Before panic could descend, the tall man broke into a huge smile.

'Sorry about the drama,' he said, his eyes on Adam who was still lying on the floor. 'I am your host for the weekend, and I do like to make a theatrical entrance. Though we've never had someone actually collapse before.'

The guests all turned to where the tall man was looking. Adam's cheeks began to burn as the atmosphere changed. Laughter broke out at the scared young man. One of the DJs actually had tears rolling down his face.

'This is going to be fun,' shouted the tall man.

'This is going to be a bloody nightmare,' thought Adam.

3

THE OMEN

THE TALL MAN stood on the jetty, helping people off the boat and on to dry land. When Adam reached the front of the queue, he eyed the man with mistrust.

'Sorry about before, I didn't mean to frighten you,' the man said.

Adam scoffed.

'You didn't frighten me, you surprised me. There's a difference.'

'If you say so,' smiled the man.

He gripped Adam's hand tightly and pulled him onto the jetty, before moving onto the remaining passengers. As Colin and Adam marched off the rickety, wooden dock, they passed the crew member of the boat who had been tasked with securing the boat with the rope.

'Was it you that did the fake scream?' Adam asked.

'Yep,' the man confirmed, looking pleased with his part in the ruse.

'You're a prick,' said Adam, before walking away.

THE PATH THAT led up to the accommodation was stony and steep. Rain had started to fall not long ago and already the stones were slick and slippery. Up ahead of Adam and Colin, Sophie was begging one of the other presenters to give her a piggy back, as the high heels she had opted for were unsurprisingly ill fitting for the rugged terrain.

A moan of discomfort from behind caused Adam to turn. Albert, who must've been in his mid-sixties, was struggling to climb the hill.

'You need a hand?' Adam said, pointing to his case.

'That'd be very kind,' Albert replied, pointing to his right leg. 'It's this bloody thing, the prosthetic leg. I was in a car crash a few years ago and they had to amputate the bugger. Now, anything that isn't flat makes it feel like I'm climbing bloody Everest.'

Adam didn't want to pry, so took hold of the case wordlessly and dragged it onwards. Colin grabbed hold of Albert's wife's case without asking, for which she thanked him through chattering teeth. They walked a few more steps, when, from nowhere, the tall man appeared, hooking his arm around Adam's neck.

'For f…' Adam started, his heart leaping into his throat. 'Is there any chance that you could cough or something before you give me a bloody heart attack.'

'Sorry about that, I thought you'd seen me.'

'Well, I hadn't. What do you want?'

'Charming,' the tall man said, with a chuckle. 'I thought I'd introduce myself. That way, perhaps you won't have such a fear of me. My name is Damien, and it's lovely to meet you.'

'Damien? Are you being serious?'

'Maybe,' he said, conspiratorially, as he unhooked his arm and hurried on to the next group. Adam heard a swear word uttered in a deep voice from ahead of them. Clearly, Damien's presence had caught them by surprise too.

'Make sure you lock your door tonight,' Adam said to Colin. 'I'd bet you a hundred quid that at some point, that sneaky son of the devil will be standing over your bed with an axe in his hand.'

AT THE TOP of the hill was a narrow path that was presided over by gnarled trees. Trees that had probably been there for centuries and had endured storm after storm, unshielded from the lashing rain and wind. They were stooped over and made Adam feel claustrophobic as he passed under them. He was on edge. All he could think about was how Damien was probably stood behind one of the deformed trunks, waiting for him to pass so that he could scare him once more.

They reached the end of the path without incident. Emerging from the darkness, the group were presented with their lodgings. And they weren't too shabby at all.

It looked to Adam like a small castle. The thick cobblestone walls were illuminated by a number of uplights resting on the grass to the side of the building. Four turrets, at each corner of the square building, disappeared into the rapidly descending darkness and a gravel path bisected the gardens, leading to a pair of heavy oak doors. The rain was really starting to hammer down now, and the group rushed as fast as they could to the entrance. Adam felt sorry for the old man and his wife, who lagged behind. He could hear them bickering, their whispered words carried on the wind.

'Looks like there's a storm brewing,' said Damien, when they were all safely ensconced inside the entrance hall. As if to emphasize his point, a peal of thunder boomed in the distance.

'I'm soaked through,' said the man dressed as a wrestler.

'You're not going to take your outfit off though, are you?' asked Drive Time Dave.

'I don't want to pay for a weekend of booze, so no,' Gavin said. 'I'd rather get hypothermia.'

Damien led them through an impressive foyer, with a black and white tiled floor and expensively framed oil paintings hanging on the walls, into a cosy lounge. A roaring fire was being stoked by a man in a waistcoat, who Adam assumed worked here. The presenters swarmed around the warmth; hands held outstretched to the flames. Albert and his wife sank into a couple of upholstered armchairs, pleased for a moment of respite.

'Are you the technology experts?' the waistcoated man asked.

Colin told them that they were and he led them into a room that had been made up like a wedding function room. A long table was placed along one side of the room, laid with a crisp white table cloth and heavy silver cutlery. Ornate candlesticks were placed at intervals along the table, their flames flickering in the light draught that blew through the room.

A bar with a heavy oak counter top in the corner of the room was being cleaned by a woman in a white blouse, while a man was changing one of the optics affixed to the back wall.

A large, rectangular portion of the room was dedicated to what looked like a dancefloor. A rig of brightly coloured lights had been set up, and a makeshift DJ booth had been assembled and pushed to the side of the room. Beside this, was the equipment that Adam and Colin needed.

They hunkered down and got to work. Adam shoved plugs into sockets and cables into ports. The whirr of the projector coming to life sounded as Colin pulled the canvas down, creating the screen. They adjusted the focus and after five minutes, their job was done.

"Easiest hundred quid I've ever made,' Adam said, as they tidied up the cardboard boxes and hid them behind a long, velvet curtain.

They picked up their sopping backpacks and asked the waistcoated man where they would be staying. He led them out of the function room, into the foyer and up a flight of stairs.

The first floor was made up of one wide corridor with narrower passages branching off to the rooms. The plush carpet and golden, striped wallpaper combined to give it a regal air. They followed the man to the end of the corridor, where he showed them to adjacent rooms. They thanked him and he walked off with a slight nod of his head.

Adam's room was perfect. A double bed with a heavy wooden headboard rested against one wall; the deep red duvet and the laundered sheets looked very inviting to his weary eyes. A large television and a DVD player sat atop a sideboard opposite the bed and a radiator was fighting the chilly evening air.

This'll do nicely, he thought to himself.

He walked into the bathroom and closed the door behind him. He did his business and then washed his hands in the sink, taking in his appearance in the mirror. Gone were the straggly beard and dark circles under his eyes. Thanks to an exercise routine, a job he loved and caring about what he ate, he had never looked healthier. He unlocked the door and jumped when he entered the main bedroom again.

Damien was sitting on the edge of his bed.

'Your door was ajar so I thought I'd let myself in,' Damien explained, seeing Adam's perplexed look.

'No, it wasn't,' Adam shot back.

'Maybe I walked through the wall then, I can't quite remember. Anyway, we're going on a ghost walk. The island has many legends and it's a tradition for newcomers to hear them.'

Adam didn't care too much for ghosts.

Or Damien.

'We're not really with the party downstairs…' he started, though Damien quickly cut across him.

'Nonsense! You're a guest of the island.'

'Colin mentioned earlier that he wasn't feeling too well, so I'll have to see what he thinks.'

'Already taken care of, my friend,' Damien smiled. 'He's well up for it.'

'Great,' Adam said through gritted teeth. 'Just great.'

4

SPOOKY GOINGS ON

IF ANYONE HAPPENED to be passing by the island on a boat (impossible because of the vicious waves and roiling storm) or somehow zoomed in on it with a telescope, they'd be greeted by an odd sight.

Despite the lashing rain and rumbles of thunder; a vampire, a wrestler, a scantily-clad cat woman, an obese David Bowie and two young men wrapped up in thick coats (one of whom was having a terrible time) were huddled around a tall man dressed as a circus ringmaster.

So far, their tour guide had given them the history of their accommodation. According to him, it had been built by a wealthy family who wanted to get away from the hustle and bustle of city life in the 1700s. The construction had been plagued with difficulties and obstructions and when the house was finally finished, the family moved in, though they didn't stay for long. Historical documents, like Mr. Winkle's diary, tell of ghostly sightings and paranormal activity. When his wife awoke one morning to find her favourite pearl necklace missing, it was to be the final straw.

The family moved out and the property passed through many hands. Some stayed longer than others, but they all found a reason to leave for good in the end. In the mid-1800s, it had been used as an asylum, before passing out of use altogether when it was deemed the island was doing the lunatics more harm than good.

Finally, it had been taken over by a local entrepreneur who stripped it and made it what it was today. Sometimes, Damien said, you can still hear the screams of the unfortunate fellows who endured shock treatments and experimental medicines. Their pleas for mercy endured in the walls.

Adam hated this. He tried to act nonchalant, but tales of Winkle Island had been bandied around at school and had unsettled him then. Now that he was on the island with this ragtag bunch of presenters and the creepiest man he'd ever met, he regretted ever saying yes to the job.

They left the house behind and walked to the north of the island. The unrelenting rain felt like needles on any skin left exposed and Adam felt a pang of pity for Sophie, who must've realised by now that she had made a silly decision. At least the vampire, after some discussion about whether fancy dress rules were being broken, had given her his oversized cape to protect herself from the worst of the elements.

As they approached the cliffs, a small building swam into view. It wasn't much bigger than a garden shed and made from wooden logs, like a filming location from a Scandi Noir. Damien unhooked the snib on the front door and ushered everyone inside.

They stood in what would've been a circle, had there been space. Some stamped their feet on the stained concrete floor in order to get some blood flowing to their toes; others crossed their arms over their bodies and rubbed their arms. The vampire did this, and Adam didn't know if it was to get warm or to look the part.

'This is the chapel,' Damien said, his words coming out in a mist. 'When residents of the asylum sadly passed on, they were brought here for a religious ceremony before burial. Obviously, no one from the mainland attended, hence the size of the place. Their bodies were then taken down the path to the graveyard near the house. I like to end the tour there, so you will all get to see it.'

Great, Adam thought as they were ushered out into the cold once more. *The highlight of the island is a bloody graveyard.*

As they traipsed towards the graveyard, Damien pointed out a deep well just behind a thick wall of trees. The crumbling, circular brickwork was just visible and thankfully, they weren't expected to go for a closer look. Instead, Damien picked up the pace, his enthusiasm for the burial site evident in his long strides.

After a couple of minutes, they reached a rusty gate with a dirty sign attached, announcing this as sacred ground. Beyond the gate and chain link fence, identical rectangular headstones emerged from the ground. The uneven terrain made them look like teeth inside a mouth that hadn't ever been to the dentist. Some had fallen over, though most stood tall and proud, despite being there for over a century.

Adam gazed up at the house and saw Albert and his wife in one of the windows. He was jealous that Damien had accepted their advancing years as a suitable enough excuse to avoid the tour.

Damien ushered the rest of the group into the graveyard and they spent ten miserable minutes being led through the rows, listening to stories about infamous inmates of the asylum.

Adam didn't know if what Damien was telling them was true or not, but the stories chilled him anyway. Then he saw it.

A hand reaching from one of the graves. The fingernails caked with dirt and the knuckles bloodied and broken.

He let off a volley of curse words and as the presenters turned to him with confused faces, he pointed to the ground with a trembling finger. Sophie let out a yelp and Paul repeated some of Adam's choice words. Adam started to back away towards the gate, when he noticed Damien's smile.

He watched as the ringmaster bent down and pulled the prosthetic arm free of the dirt. He waved it around, much to the laughter of the group. Adam shook his head and started walking towards the warmth of the building, a perfectly cued flash of lightning lighting his way.

5

LA LUCIOLE VIOLETTE

ADAM LAY ON his bed, pleased to be feeling warm again. The shame of making a fool of himself in front of the other guests had washed away as the hot droplets from the showerhead had collided with his skin. He didn't owe them anything and, with any luck, he wouldn't have to set eyes on them for the rest of the weekend.

He opened his bag and pulled some fresh clothes out. He was happy to be free of the sodden jeans he'd been wearing before, and felt a pang of pity for the presenters who had agreed to wear the same clothes all weekend. They must be freezing after the tour.

He pulled a T-shirt, a pair of joggers and a hoodie on and stood by the radiator while he connected his laptop to the television. After a minute of fiddling, his computer screen was duplicated on the wide screen of the TV.

Let the weekend begin, he thought to himself.

He opened up a browser window and typed in the WiFi code he'd been given earlier. Once connected, he navigated to Netflix and chose an episode of Sherlock—the one where Moriarty appears for the first time.

Andrew Scott, to his mind, was the best actor to have played Sherlock's arch nemesis. Colin liked Natalie Dormer's portrayal in Elementary, but Adam reckoned that was only because he fancied her.

He threw himself onto the bed just as a brisk knock on the door sounded.

'If that's Damien,' Adam said. 'You can do one. Anyone else, come in!'

Colin poked his head around the door, a smile spreading across his face at the theme tune for his favourite show.

'Fancy an ep?' Adam asked, shuffling over to one side of the bed.

'Yeah, later. We've been invited for dinner.'

'But, we've got our weekend supplies right here.'

Adam pointed to the bag of food. Sausage rolls, Thai sweet chilli crisps and enough chocolate to rot both their teeth. Not to mention the bottles of Coke.

'I know,' Colin said. 'But, they've got a roast dinner going on downstairs. Chicken, spuds, gravy and a spread of desserts for after.'

'It'll mean mingling with those dicks, though,' said Adam.

'Worth it for a free feast.'

Adam weighed it up in his mind. He was already sold, but he needed Colin to know that he was putting up a real fight.

'Okay,' he said, standing up. 'But, if I end up next to the creepy guy, I'm leaving.'

SITTING NEXT TO the creepy guy might've been better than how it had ended up. Adam sat with Colin on one side, which was fine, but with Gavin's bulk on the other. As a six foot something, twenty-stone man, dressed in wrestling garb, it meant certain areas of his body were left exposed. Like the armpits, which were right next to Adam's face.

Worse than that, though, was that Damien was directly opposite him. Which meant intense eye contact that Adam was trying hard to avoid, but could feel boring into him.

As they waited for the food to be served, Keith stood up.

Adam had to give it to him—he had balls. He had tried hard to pull off the Bowie look. He'd squeezed himself into a sparkly silver catsuit and painted the colourful lightning bolt onto his face. However, with his straggly dark hair and considerable girth, he looked more like Rab C. Nesbitt.

He held a glass aloft. Adam thought that he had taken it upon himself to be the group's leader. Perhaps that was one of the expectations of having the prime-time slot.

'I thought it might be nice to go around the table and say what we are thankful for. It's become something of a tradition.' He glanced around at his audience. 'I'll start. This year, I am thankful for the continued opportunity to entertain the people of Stonebridge and to once more have the top-listened to show.'

He sat down and looked to his right.

'My beautiful wife,' said Albert, motioning to the lady sitting beside him.

'Getting to spend the weekend with you lot,' said Drive Time Dave.

'Love,' said Sophie.

'Love?' repeated some of the members around the table.

'Have you met someone?'

'You've kept that quiet,' said Gavin, looking put out.

'I've not told anyone because it's early days,' Sophie said. 'I don't know if it's going to go anywhere but it's feeling good.'

'So, who is the poor chap?' asked Keith.

'That, I cannot divulge. Yet,' she added, as a chorus of boos filled the room.

'Go on,' Gavin said.

'Leave the poor girl alone,' Albert said, and any more cross examination was quelled by the arrival of food. Conversation died as plates were loaded and eating commenced.

ADAM AND COLIN stood by the bar, pints in hand. It had been a long day and Adam could feel the tiredness begin to creep behind his eyes. One more pint and he'd call it a night.

The presenters were getting a bit rowdy. They'd had a few cocktails during dinner, and now that the food was gone, the drinking had begun in earnest. They sat in groups at the table, chatting and laughing while Albert fiddled with the computer at the side of the room.

A media file appeared on the fabric screen and Albert tapped a knife against the stem of his wine glass. He cleared his throat as a hush descended in the room and attention was turned to the station's owner.

'I've prepared a short video for us to watch, before I say a few words.'

He pressed play on the video and grainy black and white footage began. It showed a small building with smashed windows and missing roof tiles. A man was smiling happily at the camera, one hand on the ramshackle building as if it was his pride and joy.

Then, colour bloomed. The footage leapt on a generation. On screen was Albert, forty years ago, with thick sideburns creeping down his cheeks, wearing a flowery shirt and bell-bottom trousers. Next, some footage of Albert sitting behind a mixing desk, talking into a microphone. You couldn't hear what he was saying, but he looked like he was having a great time.

The footage continued in this vein; fond memories at Stonebridge Radio Station over the year. Laughter sounded in the room as a much younger and thinner Keith Starr walked through shot, his fingers pointing like guns at the camera.

Adam watched as present day Keith shook his head and chuckled.

The footage finished with a picture of the current stock of presenters. Albert closed the video and cleared his throat again as the presenters looked at him expectantly.

'Right, well, first of all, I want to say thank you for coming. I know we do something for Hallowe'en every year, and this feels fitting. I'm looking forward to tomorrow evening's murder mystery, and I'll expect you young ones are looking forward to a bit of a boogie after I'm done…'

Adam could see the beads of sweat forming on his forehead. It felt like he was circling what he wanted to say, as if he was building up to something.

'Unfortunately, I have some bad news. I have made the tough decision to close down the station. Revenue has been down year on year. Streaming services are taking over and there is sadly no room for local radio anymore.'

The room exploded into a storm of words. Questioning him. Cursing his decision. Cries for clemency.

Albert tried to placate them, assuring them that it was a decision forced on him by money. He was losing a lot of it, and he didn't have a lot to spare in the first place.

As the noise threatened to overwhelm again, Gavin barked at everyone to quieten. He pointed a thick finger at Albert's wife, who was sitting quietly at the end of the table. Her face was ashen.

'What about that necklace?' he said. 'Great big diamond like that's bound to be worth something. Sell it and keep the station going.'

Instinctively, Margaret's fingers flew to her jewellery. Gavin was right—it was worth a lot. The thin silver chain was valuable on its own, but the real prize was the firefly pendant. The ornate thorax of the insect was a single cut purple diamond, while the silver wings were studded with smaller purple sapphires.

Margaret held the glittering insect in a balled fist.

Albert's face reddened.

'Now, listen here. I do not owe any of you a living. That necklace is family heirloom and it's none of your business how much it's worth. I'm coming up to retirement age as it is, so you would've been out on your ears in a year's time anyway,' he said. He took a moment to compose himself and when he did speak again, his voice was softer. 'I don't want to ruin the weekend, so please, have fun and enjoy the time you have together.'

He held his hand out and his wife followed him out of the room, taking the firefly with her. The cacophony of noise started up again as Adam and Colin finished their pints.

'JESUS,' COLIN SAID as they walked up the stairs. 'A mass firing! A bit of drama for the evening.'

'And even weirder that they were all dressed in their costumes.'

'I wonder if the murder mystery will still go ahead?'

'Who cares? I plan on not leaving my room again until the boat arrives.'

They walked the length of the corridor, bade each other goodnight and entered their respective rooms. Adam's head had barely touched the pillow before he'd fallen asleep.

6

MURDER MYSTERY

COLIN AWOKE WITH a start.

It felt like he hadn't really been asleep for any considerable amount of time. The heavy thump of bass had carried through the house from the presenter's disco, though he must've drifted off, as he couldn't remember hearing the party reach an end.

The room was pitch black and the storm was roaring on outside, but aside from that, the house was quiet. He wondered what had caused him to wake. A crash of thunder? He didn't know, but a smashing sound was lingering in his thoughts. Perhaps, it was a bad dream, he thought as he rolled over.

As he pulled the duvet tightly around him, a scream sliced through the howl of the wind. He sat upright again and strained his ears. He couldn't tell whether it had come from inside or out, but surely no one would be daft enough to be outside in weather like this, especially at this time of night.

As he pushed the duvet off to go and have a peek out the window, he froze. There was another shout. A man's shout this time. It had come from down the corridor.

He reached to the bedside table and picked up his phone. It was just past three o'clock. What was going on?

He tried to ring Adam, but there was no signal, so he ran to his room instead. He knocked quietly on the door.

'Who is it?' Adam whispered from behind the heavy oak.

'Colin. Let me in.'

Adam opened the door slightly and peered out.

'You hearing this?' he said.

'Yeah, what do you think…?'

Colin's question was cut off by a noise further down the corridor. They both stopped talking to listen.

'Murder! There's been a murder!' someone screamed.

'Bloody hell,' said Adam. 'It's going to be that dickhead ringmaster doing some sort of SAS murder mystery. He's taking the piss if he thinks he can start this in the dead of night.'

Guttural cries for help sounded from behind a closed door at the end of the hallway. Colin took a few slow steps in the direction of the noise.

To his ears, the anguish in the shouts sounded too real to be those of an actor. Though, this place ran murder mysteries most weekends of the year, so those involved were probably pretty good at nailing the realism by now.

Still, this sounded too… raw.

When another shout pierced the blackness, Colin picked up the pace and arrived at the room he believed the noise was coming from. He turned the handle and burst in, half-expecting a fake crime scene, but not getting it.

This one was very real.

Albert was hovering over his wife, his hands pressed to a deep gash in her chest, trying to stem the flow of blood.

'Call an ambulance,' he yelled, and Colin took off at pace down the stairs to the reception. He figured if his mobile had no reception, then none of them would, but he'd spotted a landline behind reception when they we're checking in.

He rounded the desk and picked up the handset, dialling 999.

When it was answered, he told them the emergency and the location and was met with bad news. The storm would make it impossible for any help to arrive. It was too dangerous for boats to make the crossing and a helicopter would stand no chance of landing in the ferocious winds.

They had a short conversation about what he could do, before he hung up the phone and sprinted up the stairs again, three at a time.

He arrived to a gathering of people. A few of the presenters loitered in the doorway, swaying gently with unfocused eyes. It must've been one hell of a party.

Damien looked like he was giving a rather green looking Adam a pep talk in the corridor and, inside the room, Sophie was holding a thick towel to Margaret's wound. From the way the towel was stained a deep crimson, Colin knew it was too late.

On the floor, Albert was sitting with his back against the radiator with another towel pressed to his forearm. He looked up and saw Colin's expression, before breaking down in tears.

7

THE AFTERMATH

AN HOUR LATER, everyone had scattered.

Most had uttered their condolences and gone back to their rooms, locking the doors behind them. Adam had simply pointed to the blood-stained bed and backed out of the room.

Colin knew that a pinprick of blood was enough to send Adam woozy, so he didn't blame the guy for wanting to leave.

He did, however, think it was rather callous of the presenters not to stay and rally around their boss, supporting him in the aftermath of the murder of his wife.

But, then it dawned on him.

One of them must have been the one to have done this to him.

The island was remote and it was only the presenters, the staff and Damien here. Which meant it had to be someone in the house who had done this.

Colin made another cup of tea for the old man, who was sitting in the armchair with his eyes closed. He'd been that way for a while, and Colin hadn't wanted to disrupt him.

He had thrown a bedsheet over his wife's body so that Albert didn't have to stare at it. The vividness of the red and the ghostly white skin.

He didn't need the reminder of what had happened tonight there in front of him, though Colin was sure that the image would be stained behind Albert's eyelids for the rest of his life.

Colin set the cup of steaming tea on the circular table beside the old man, and sat on the other armchair. He angled the armchair slightly, so that when the old man opened his eyes, it would not seem like some intense interview scenario.

'How's your arm?' Colin said.

The old man responded with a shrug.

In the aftermath of what had happened, Colin had tended to the gash on Albert's arm. It was a couple of inches in length but thankfully not very deep. It would probably require a few stitches when back on the mainland, but for now, Colin had washed it as well as he could and secured it with a tight bandage.

The first aid training from his job at the Stonebridge Retirement Home had stood him in good stead.

At length, Albert opened his eyes. He glanced at Colin, then at his arm before settling on the body of his wife.

'I can't believe it,' he said, his voice hoarse and cracking. 'I just can't believe what has happened.'

His eyes never left the bed.

'Bad enough that they killed her, but they took the necklace, too. Heartless, heartless people,' he said, shaking his head. 'What did the police say?'

After attempts to stem the flow of blood had been unsuccessful and Margaret's death had been confirmed, Colin had descended the stairs once more and called the police.

They'd said the same thing as the ambulance service; the storm was too strong for any of their transport to deal with. They'd promised him that at the first sign of the storm's retreat, they'd get here. But, for now, the best that Colin could do was close the door to the room and keep the crime scene intact.

Colin had watched enough true crime shows to know that the immediate period after the crime had been committed was the most valuable. Police called it the golden hour, when material usable by the police is at its most readily available.

Judging by the weather forecast, the police were going to miss this window by a good twenty-four hours, at least.

Colin relayed the information back to the old man, who frowned and shook his head.

'They'll never catch who did this,' he said.

'Well, there's a bit of an advantage. The suspect pool is low, there can't be more than twelve people on the island. The police will ask their questions and…'

'And nothing,' Albert interrupted. 'All the evidence will have gone—whoever has done this will lie through their teeth and get away with it.'

'You sound like you don't have much faith in the police.'

He sighed.

'Over the years, the radio station has been broken into a number of times. Expensive things were stolen and I was constantly fobbed off with the "it's under investigation" line. Never heard a bloody thing back. So, no. I don't expect the police to do a damn thing about this.'

Colin knew that the police would treat a dead body differently to a set of stolen speakers, but bit his tongue. Albert didn't need to hear it. Instead, they sunk back into silence. Albert closed his eyes again.

Colin's heart went out to the man. In his job, he'd seen families attempt to deal with the death of a loved one. He'd comforted many a wife, husband, son and daughter, and seen first-hand the devastation caused by a natural death.

He couldn't imagine what this must be doing to poor Albert.

'You know,' Colin stared. 'Adam and myself have done a bit of investigating in our time.'

'I'm aware,' Albert replied. 'Your mother spoke about you when we were arranging this weekend. She's very proud of you.'

'If you like, we could ask a few questions. See if we can do anything until the police get here.'

He shrugged again.

'I just want to be left alone,' Albert said, as he began to cry.

Though it sounded like a rudely worded dismissal, Colin knew better. He'd been spoken to far worse in the past by grieving relatives.

'If you need anything, let me know,' Colin said.

He pushed himself out of the chair, opened the door and took one last look at Albert's heaving shoulders before leaving and walking to Adam's room.

IF THE SUN had risen, there would have been no way of knowing.

The already violent weather outside had seemingly stepped it up a notch, as if in retaliation against the human race's more base ideologies. Like, for example, one human life meant more than another, and so we're entitled to play God. Or, the Devil.

Rain attacked the window like mini battering rams and the dark clouds gathered and swirled, refusing to be moved on by the gale-force wind.

Adam let the curtain fall back into place, blocking out the sight of the outside world but not the sounds. He grabbed his laptop from the table and took it to the bed. He climbed in and pulled the duvet over him, prompting a shiver that had nothing to do with the cold.

He'd only ever seen one other body; that of his friend Daniel Costello who'd met his untimely end last year, though not anywhere near as violently as poor Mrs Fernsby. It was no secret Adam wasn't good with blood, though he doubted anyone on the island could bear witness to the aftermath of whatever happened in that room without the feeling that they needed to throw up.

He opened up his emails and typed the beginnings of Helena's address into the recipient box. He had no other way of getting in contact with his new girlfriend and thought that what had happened should be shared. He was midway through the body of the missive when a knock sounded on the door, before Colin made himself known.

Adam slid out of bed and unlocked the door, letting his friend in. He followed Colin to the bed and sat down on the edge.

'You okay, man?' he asked.

'Yeah. Trouble seems to follow us around.'

They both nodded, aware that empty words would do little for either of them. Something awful had happened here tonight.

Or, rather, someone had done something awful here tonight.

'I told Albert we might look into things. He told me that mum was banging on about our exploits when they met to discuss this weekend.'

Adam smiled a small smile in reply, before nodding.

'I feel bad for the old guy. And I assume we're grounded here until the storm passes. But, didn't the police say…'

'When have we ever listened to the police? They don't know their arse from their elbow in Stonebridge.'

'Fair point. Where do we start?

8

THE CRIME SCENE

ADAM HESITATED OUTSIDE the room. The heavy oak door was the perfect barrier between him and the bloody body, but he knew that he couldn't put it off forever. He gave Colin a nod and watched as his friend knocked three times on the door.

'Yes?'

The voice was broken and cracked.

'Albert, it's Colin and Adam. We're here to do the thing we discussed.'

Adam thought his wording was very clever. With the other presenters staying in rooms on the same landing, announcing a murder enquiry would've been unwise.

It also made Adam feel inadequate. Behind this door lay a still body and a man shattered by grief. A long marriage quite literally severed by a sharp blade and here were two lads who fancied themselves as detectives, turning up to ask questions.

Before he could convince Colin that they were perhaps not up to the task and that waiting twenty-four hours for the police to arrive might not be a bad thing, the lock clicked and the door swung slowly on its hinges.

Albert looked like he'd aged a hundred years in an hour. His eyes were sunken into dark holes and a patchwork of red crossed his face; the exertion of endless crying clear to see.

He turned wordlessly and shuffled back to his seat. Colin and Adam entered. Colin walked to the seat he'd sat in not long ago, while Adam closed and locked the door. Happy that the room was secure, he crossed the floor and stood beside his friend's chair; his back to the body on the bed.

Out of sight, out of mind, he reckoned.

Adam smiled at the old man, who accepted the silent sympathy with a nod of his head.

'Albert, we're going to ask around and see what we can find out. The necklace has to be somewhere on the island, so I'm sure it'll turn up.'

The old man nodded again.

'Albert, can you tell us what happened?'

The old man was silent for a further minute. Aside from his eyes, which glanced this way and that, the rest of his face remained still. It looked like a photograph gone wrong.

Finally, he found his voice.

'Well, after delivering the news that I'd be closing the station, myself and...' he stumbled over the word, 'myself and Margaret came up here. Too much excitement for one night. We got ourselves ready for bed and I told her to put the necklace in the safe, but she told me she was too tired and would do it in the morning.'

He asked for a glass of water and Colin rose from his seat to fetch one. He passed Albert the glass and the old man took a few loud gulps, his Adam's apple bobbing up and down, before setting it on the table beside his seat.

'We went to sleep and I woke up to a crashing sound. Like glass breaking. It was dark, and when I turned round, there was someone standing over my wife.'

'But you didn't see who?'

'No,' he said, shaking his head. 'The curtains were closed and it was very dark. I didn't have my glasses on either. No, it was more like I sensed them there, rather than seeing them. I could hear their breathing.'

'Anything you can remember about the size at all? Short, small?'

'No, sorry.'

'That's fine. What happened next?'

'Margaret screamed when she realised there was someone else in the room. I reached across, I don't know why really. Maybe to push him away, or to shield Margaret. I felt the knife go into my arm but it took a second or two for the pain to follow. I screamed when it did and fell out of bed. When I pulled myself up again, he'd stabbed Margaret and was heading for the window again.'

'You think it was a he?'

Albert shot them a confused look. Colin added to the question.

'Only you said "he'd stabbed Margaret".'

'Oh,' Albert said. 'Well, only because I assumed no woman could be capable of such an act.'

They didn't need to ask what had happened next. Colin had heard the smash of the window, and the shouting, and had run down the corridor, unable to prevent Death from snatching Margaret from Albert's grasp.

'I think that's all we need for now. Do you mind if we have a look around?'

'By all means,' Albert said, waving an open palm at the expanse of the room. 'I'm going to get a bit of fresh air.'

'You're not going out, are you? Have you seen the rain?'

'Just to the front door. I fancy a smoke.' He looked at the body, covered by the sheet. 'She was always trying to get me to give up. Said the cigarettes would be the death of me.'

He removed his raincoat from the radiator where it had just about dried after the walk from the boat. He pulled it on and winced as the fabric passed over his bandaged arm.

Watching this, Adam couldn't stop the tears coming to his eyes. Maybe the fact that he'd started going out with someone he genuinely cared about was softening him; or perhaps it was that the old man opposite him was dealing with two types of pain—the flesh and the heart.

He'd had a lucky escape and Adam's earlier concerns about tackling the case were washed away; now, he promised himself that he'd work tirelessly to get to the bottom of it.

For Albert.

For Margaret.

They watched the old man slouch out of the room, letting the door swing slowly shut behind him. It latched with a small click, and Adam and Colin got to work.

Not having gloves, they decided the best course of action was to simply have a look. It wouldn't look good when the police came and their prints were plastered all over the room like graffiti. If something caught their eye, they'd take a picture and that would be that.

They split up; as much as a pair can split up in a hotel room. What Adam meant when he suggested "splitting up" was that Colin took the side of the room with the body, and he would cover everywhere else.

He watched Colin walk towards the bed, and like The Cowardly Lion, wished he wasn't so much of a wimp sometimes.

COLIN INCHED TOWARDS the bed. Towards the unmoving mound of bedsheets.

Sometimes, he wished Adam wasn't so much of a wimp.

I mean, yeah, he got it: no one was enthralled about being in the presence of a dead body. But Adam was another case entirely.

He'd been the laughing stock at school on BCG day. The boys in his year group had been speculating on the size of the needle for weeks—someone had heard from his brother's friend's cousin that it was as thick as four normal needles.

On the day, Danny Costello had slipped an oversized joke needle to one of the nurses, who duly whipped it out after calling Adam's name. He'd vomited at the sight of it, before promptly fainting, causing a right old ruckus. The headmaster had told him to man up when he'd come to.

But, looking over at his friend now, Colin couldn't hope for a better partner. They were yin and yang and both brought different strengths.

The smell of expensive perfume wafting through the soiled sheets brought Colin back to the here and now. He knew he couldn't risk pulling back the sheets for another look at the body, so instead would bank on the images seared into his brain from the early hours.

He only needed the headline anyway. Margaret had been stabbed to death.

Instead, he cast his attention to what surrounded her. On the floor were her clothes from the night before; the bottle green dress and her low-heeled shoes. Albert had said that she was too tired to deposit the necklace in the safe, and how she discarded her expensive clothes certainly seemed to back that up.

The set of drawers beside her bed looked like they'd been here since the beginning of time. The flat top was scarred from years of objects being dragged across it and thrown on top of it.

On it now was a half-empty glass of water and a pair of glasses. Colin snapped a picture of the items, though doubted they meant anything. They'd have been there regardless of Margaret's fate.

Perhaps the water level might be lower were she still breathing, or the glasses perched atop her nose if she was having trouble sleeping and had decided to read instead.

On the floor, in the narrow gap between the drawers and the bed, lay a little silver strip of tablets, encased in miniature domes. Colin got on his hands and knees and inspected the packet as best he could. He didn't recognise the name that was printed in green over the foil packaging, but took a picture so that he could research it later.

ADAM WAS ENGROSSED in his own discoveries a few feet away.

He'd had a walk around the rest of the room, but all the action and evidence seemed to be on Margaret's side as Albert had said. Currently, he found himself on his hands and knees, staring at the carpet.

The carpet was cream, or rather, it used to be. Decades of different footsteps; some heavy and some light, had flattened and stained the once extravagantly thick shag. The flattened areas told their own stories; plotted journeys from bed to en-suite bathroom and back again.

But these lost footprints were not what was of interest to Adam. No, he was more concerned with the residual dirt left behind from a recent visitor. Not enough muck to leave a traceable footprint, but evidence enough that someone had climbed through the window with murder on their mind.

Or, if not murder, definitely money.

Adam had watched enough true crime shows to know that death was sometimes a secondary notion. Gain was usually the first—and in this case, the gain was the necklace. The money it would bring when it could be flogged on the mainland.

Adam followed the mucky tracks from the window to the bed (as close as he dared to the body) and back again. There wasn't anything more he could tell—no outline, no size nor tread that they could match should they request everyone hand in their shoes for examination.

He stood up when he got to the window and took in the ragged, shattered glass in the lower left-hand corner of the pane. Rain smashed against the glass and the wind poured through the hole, there in the room like an unknown presence were it not for the shrill whistle it brought along with it.

Looking down, Adam could see a trellis attached to the exterior wall. It was hard to make out any detail, such was the angle. This would require a trip outside, which, given the weather, was not an exciting prospect.

'Got what we need?' asked Colin, breaking their collective silence.

'Almost,' replied Adam, pointing outside.

They both groaned.

9

LOOKING IN

THEY LEFT ALBERT'S room and walked back up the corridor to their own rooms to collect their coats.

'You know,' Colin said as they reached their doors, 'it's kind of a one-man job, isn't it?'

'Is it?' Adam asked.

'Well, all one of us has to do is go and have a look at the trellis.'

'One of us…'

'Well, yeah.'

'And which one of us would that be?'

'Allow me to put my case forward for it being you. I was the first on scene at the murder. I helped with the first aid on Albert and I was the one who did the dirty work near the body, while you looked at some muck on the floor.'

Colin cocked an eyebrow at Adam, challenging him; though his friend couldn't muster much of a counter-argument. Instead, Adam nodded his head solemnly and reached for his door handle.

'Seriously, though,' Colin said. 'We've been up half the night, so it might be wise for each of us to have a rest. I'll get some sleep now while you do this, and in a while, we'll talk about our next move.'

'Sounds like a plan,' Adam said.

Colin disappeared into his room with a swift goodbye. Adam opened his own door and entered the room. He made use of the bathroom and then grabbed his still-wet coat from the hook by the door. He looked out his window, at the darkness that lay beyond, sighed, and closed the door again.

He walked down the hall, his eyes poring over the doors that lined the corridor as he went.

He thought about what awaited the occupants upon awakening, if they were asleep at all. Tragedy loomed; some, like sober Sophie, would awake knowing that she had played a small part in trying to save a life. She might feel like a hero, knowing she'd at least done something. Or, she might feel the total opposite; a failure who had been unable to prevent a soul from drifting away into the ether.

The other presenters might awake to the news like it's the first they've heard of it, despite all four of them standing in the doorway. Some might remember nothing at all, thanks to the amount of alcohol consumed. Some might rouse, snatching at a half-remembered dream until the reality came rushing in at the sight of Albert.

His injured arm.

His dead wife.

One person would wake with an expensive necklace secreted somewhere in their room, checking their hiding place nervously as they waited for the storm to abate.

Adam walked slowly down the stairs and across the foyer to the porch. Inside the porch, to the left of the door, was a shoe rack. On it, and next to it, were several pairs of shoes and the green wellies kept by the hotel for those travellers who had come ill-prepared for a walking tour.

Currently, there was a pair of wellies for each of the party who had been for the walk last night, save for Damien who had brought his own, and Gavin who was wearing a pair of huge Doc Martens as part of his wrestling get-up.

Adam found the pair he had discarded last night upon arriving back from the ghost walk, and winced as the wet soles immediately soaked his socks.

He pulled open the door and peeked outside. There was no sign of Albert. He must've finished his cigarette and gone back to his room, or, more likely, thought better of going outside when faced with the cold and rain.

Adam pulled the hood over his head, pulled the drawstrings so tight that he resembled Kenny from South Park, and stepped into the storm.

WITHIN SECONDS OF closing the door behind him, his cheeks were numb and his nose was bright red, though not luminous enough to make a dent in the darkness that surrounded him.

The wind felt like it was zeroing in on him and him alone; the gusts catching his hood like a parachute and forcing him backwards. He reckoned if anyone was looking out a window at him now, it wouldn't look too dissimilar to the video for Michael Jackson's Earth Song.

He fished his phone from his pocket and turned the torch on. He held it out in front of him, trying to protect the screen from the downpour as much as he could, and set off. He tried to hug the building as closely as possible, though it afforded little protection.

He edged past windows, slipping occasionally in the flowerbeds and grass which had more of the consistency of quicksand to it. Thankfully, childhood had always placed quite an importance on how to evade such granular matter, so it didn't hold him up for too long.

Finally, he arrived under Albert's window. Luckily, the light was still on and the curtains open, as they had been when he and Colin had left. This meant he could put his phone away and use the light from the room. It made him feel like he was on some divine quest, bathed in ethereal light from above.

Though, there was nothing divine about what he was doing, slinking about in the darkness and the mud, looking for clues that could lead to them finding a killer. If anything, it was a quest sent from Beelzebub.

He reached out and pulled at the trellis. It was made from a heavy wood and painted white, though a long time ago. The original oak colouring was shining through where the white had started to peel. Ivy crept up the wooden structure, spreading in a triangular shape as it stretched past the window and reached for the roof. The leaves dropped water on Adam's exposed hand like a waterfall, and he uttered a few curse words under his breath as his skin turned to ice.

The trellis was attached securely to the wall, barely moving at all when Adam shook it. He figured that it could easily support someone who wanted to climb it.

Adam was half-temped to try and climb it himself, but the wooden trellis and the ivy were slick with water and, if he fell, there was no telling how much damage he'd do to himself. And anyway, the door to Albert's bedroom had been locked from the inside and all the evidence pointed to the killer entering via the window above Adam's head.

Sherlock Holmes wouldn't need to climb the trellis to reach that conclusion, so neither did he.

Instead, he cast his eyes to the ground. The area underneath Albert's window was partially protected from the rain by an overhanging triangular section of roof. It hadn't done a lot to keep the ground dry, it was only slightly less marshy than the rest of the island, but it had helped with one thing.

In amongst the drowning flowers, was a footprint. It was facing towards the wall and looked like the print of a welly boot. The heel area had a firm imprint on the soil, though the toe area was not as defined.

Adam tried putting his foot beside it to gauge what size it might be in comparison to his size nine, though it was impossible to tell due to the front section that faded without an end. Glass crunched under the sole of his shoe, and for a second he was worried he'd impaled himself.

Still, at least he could tell conclusively that someone had come through the flowerbed, ascended the trellis, broken the window and killed, before making their escape the same way.

Adam got out his phone again and opened the camera app. He pressed the button to take a photo, and as the flash blossomed, something in the treeline opposite moved.

Adam killed the phone light and flattened himself hard against the wall, trying with all his might to sink through the brickwork like some sort of character from The X-Files.

He peered into the darkness, searching for any flicker of evidence that whatever had moved was coming his way. After a few minutes, when he had convinced himself that he had imagined it, or that it was simply an animal he had startled with his burst of light, he started to breathe audibly again.

Damien's stories swirled around his head. Branches and wind morphed into ghouls and banshee's wails. Adam counted to three in his head and ran as fast as he could to the front door, only pausing for breath once he was safely entrenched in the entrance hall.

His eyes briefly lingered on the wellies again, realising that he was no safer in here than out there. Though, in here, the monsters were real.

He set off again at full pace, up the stairs and down the corridor. He fumbled for his keys with his frozen hands, shoving them in the keyhole at the third time of asking.

He locked the door behind him and slid down the back of it.

Finally, he allowed himself a laugh.

What had they got themselves involved in this time?

10

THE BROTHERS OF DESTRUCTION AND THE MINISTRY OF DARKNESS

OUTSIDE, THE CLOUDS formed a black patchwork; its seams so tightly knitted they could not be seen. They rolled this way and that across the sky, an embargo mission against the sun's rays.

And they were bang up to the task.

Inside room number nine, whatever was happening outside was of no importance to Adam. If he could've, he'd gladly have locked his door from the inside and swallowed the key. He'd happily have waited for the police to kick down his door or, less fun, use a spare key from reception to free him from his haven; the killer having been apprehended and already on his way back to Stonebridge.

But that wasn't going to happen anytime soon.

It had taken quite a while for his heart to resume a normal rhythm inside his chest. He'd liked to have taken Colin's advice and get some shut-eye, but the slightest noise or rustle of curtain in the draught took him back outside, when he had pressed himself against the wall and waited for the killer to emerge from the treeline.

Instead of hiding under the duvet waiting for Johnny Nod, he was at his computer. He finished his email to Helena, providing her with a detailed account of his sleepless night, though he had hovered over the send button for long enough to know that sending it was a bad idea.

Without phone signal, it was cruel. To tell her he was essentially locked in a building with a thief and a killer who was unafraid to stab an elderly couple was a bad idea. To tell her that he was actively trying to find said rogue was even worse.

In the end, he'd deleted the email and had instead been using his time to gather as much background information on his potential quarry as possible.

Stonebridge wasn't exactly the centre of the universe and the presenters were definitely not household names. Information was taken from the Stonebridge Gazette's archives, the Stonebridge Radio Station's website or from their own social media accounts.

He scribbled down as much as he could, compiling a fact file on each. It wasn't much to go on, but something was better than nothing.

He'd then turned his attention to Damien, but without even knowing if it was his real name, he didn't get very far. There were a few photos of him on the website for this hotel; staring at the camera solemnly from the edge of group pictures, as if that week's party had asked him to be part of their memory and he couldn't think of anything worse, but couldn't decline either.

Adam closed the lid of his laptop, got up and walked across the room to the door. He summoned the courage to unlock it, took a deep breath and eased it open a few inches.

There was no one there.

He pulled it back further to reveal an empty corridor.

He slinked out of his own room and knocked on Colin's door. He waited a few minutes and knocked again, this time hearing his friend's annoyed mutterings.

A minute later, the door opened slowly to reveal a bleary-eyed Colin, his hair pointing in all directions like a malfunctioning compass. He checked his watch, though all it told him was that he hadn't had the amount of sleep he had wanted, before fixing his eyes on Adam.

'You've got a date with the wrestler,' Adam said, handing him the page containing the information he'd managed to find on one Gavin Callaway.

'Thanks,' Colin croaked.

'I'd say put some clothes on, but wrestlers tend to do their best work in not much more than boxers. It might be the way in to Gavin's world.'

Adam backed away before Colin could connect with the punch that was aimed at his arm.

FULLY DRESSED AND with a coffee down him, Colin was feeling more alive. Well, as alive as three hours sleep and a hit of caffeine can make you.

He dragged the spoon through the second milky coffee and set it on the table. He picked up the piece of paper Adam had given him and read over the notable and newsworthy parts of Gavin's life.

Which amounted to one main point; but quite a telling one.

He leaned back in his chair and supped at his drink, trying to prepare himself for his chat with Gavin. He didn't know how to broach the subject on the paper, and wasn't sure he wanted to in a room with just the two of them in it.

He puffed out his cheeks, stood up and walked towards the door. At least Adam knew that he was meeting the man dressed as the wrestler. If something were to happen to Colin, at least they'd have an answer to the question that they were poking at.

HAVING KNOCKED ON the door a number of times, Colin came to three conclusions.

One. That, behind the door, Gavin might be dead. Dispatched in the same way as poor Margaret Fernsby.

Two. That, behind the door, Gavin might be passed out drunk. Colin had heard the pulse of loud music long into the early hours of the morning and had seen Gavin swaying in Albert's doorway as Margaret's life had ebbed away. Such a sight might drive an already drunk man to more drink.

Three. That, behind the door, there was no Gavin. That he was simply somewhere else; safe, sound and doing all he could to drive the lingering remnants of alcohol from his bloodstream.

Colin thumped the door one last time and set off to find the missing man. The relentless thrum of rain on the roof told Colin that Gavin would more than likely be somewhere within the confines of the hotel.

Unless he was some sort of Bear Grylls type.

Which, it turns out, he wasn't.

Whereas the intrepid television explorer liked to drink his own urine from a recently hollowed out snake corpse, Gavin was much more of your deal-with-your-problems-with-a-stiff-drink type of guy.

Colin found him slumped against the bar, a hand curled around a small tumbler, and a bottle of whiskey his only company.

Colin cleared his throat to announce his arrival.

Though it was fairly dark in the room, Gavin took his chin off his hand and squinted at Colin with almost closed eyes.

Less about the amount of light and more about the numbers of me he's seeing, thought Colin.

Colin introduced himself and got a loud grunt in reply. Though, it seemed, the grunt was merely a precursor to Gavin pushing himself off the bar and hefting his enormous frame to its full height.

Gavin was truly something. On a normal day, he'd be tall. Today, with his platform boots on, he was pushing seven foot. His spandex vest and sheer tights showed a body once toned and cared for, but now let off the leash a bit. Long strands of hair from a black wig fell onto his wide shoulders. His get up fell somewhere between funny and threatening.

He held out a bear-like paw which he used to squash Colin's fingers into one single digit.

Still without words, he sat down on the bar stool he was calling home and held the glass aloft, wordlessly asking if Colin wanted to join him in a dram. Seeing an opportunity for getting his foot in the door, Colin nodded. Gavin reached over the bar and procured a clean glass, which he slid along the wooden bar top and into Colin's waiting hand.

Within a minute, he'd filled Colin's glass and refilled his own and was looking at Colin with bleary eyes.

'Who are you again?'

'Colin McLaughlin,' he replied. 'I was here to set up the screen and the computer and stuff for tonight's murder mystery.'

'Looks like you wasted a trip, brother. We got the real thing last night.'

He took a slug from his glass as if the mention of last night's events needed to be washed away.

'Dreadful, isn't it?'

'Just awful,' Gavin replied. 'You know, Margaret and Albert were very good to me a few years back. Gave me a chance when not many would've done.'

Colin already knew the story, thanks to Adam's research, but hearing it first hand, unprompted, would be even better.

'How do you mean?'

Gavin drained the glass before beginning his story.

'Well, as everyone knows everything about everyone in Stonebridge, I don't imagine I'm telling you anything new. But, I used to work in the city, doing pretty well for myself. I was in a club one night, and this weedy wee fella was cracking onto a girl and I could see that she was uncomfortable.'

'You got involved?'

'Aye. My sister would've been about that age and I had this vision of this creep doing the same thing to her. So, I told him to leave it. Polite, at first, but he gave a bit of mouth back. I asked him again, less polite this time, to back off. He swung for me, but I saw it coming a mile away. I moved out of the way and… retaliated.'

He didn't relay any more information, and didn't need to. Colin had seen the photo of the boy. He looked the cocky type, even with two black eyes and a couple of missing teeth.

'Anyway, I was sentenced to some jail time. Lost my job and my girl.'

He looked mournfully at the ceiling, as if trying to summon some retrospective divine intervention.

When none came, he pressed on.

'It was hell and, let me tell you, I paid for my mistakes in there. When I was released a few years back, I came back to Stonebridge. I was treated like a leper by my old "friends" and at one stage, I considered… you know…'

He pulled a finger swiftly across his throat.

'That's a dreadful thing to say, isn't it? Considering what has happened to poor Margaret, considering it was her and Albert that saved me.'

'How?' Colin asked.

'We got talking one day. Chance meeting in a coffee shop. I recognised him as the owner of the station, and I told him about how I got into radio presenting in prison. They try to teach you new skills and I was always into my music. Those weekly sessions really got me through. So, next thing I know, he's telling me that one of his presenters is having a baby and inviting me down to try out.'

'And it went well?'

'It went okay. I think he felt sorry for me, more than anything. There aren't many listeners on the 4am-7am show, so I think he thought I couldn't do too much wrong.'

Now that he'd got him loosened up and talking, Colin switched tack.

'You seemed quite angry last night.'

Gavin fixed Colin with a stare that would cause a statue to have bowel movements. Colin looked away as Gavin began to speak.

'Put yourself in my shoes, kid. Ex-con doing the graveyard shift on local radio. It's hardly the morning show on Radio One, is it? I'm not really raking it in, so when he told me he was essentially firing me, yeah, you could say I was angry. But, I had nothing to do with what happened, if that's what you're implying.'

'You pointed out the necklace.'

'You know what…' he said, raising himself up from his stool. 'I don't like what you're getting at here. Yeah, I pointed out the necklace. It doesn't take Mr Cartier to know that the necklace with huge purple diamonds might be worth a quid or two. Sell that, save the business is all I was pointing out.'

Colin couldn't help but notice the flecks of spittle that had taken residence in Gavin's thick beard. Or, the manic look in his eyes.

'Do you think one of the other presenters might have had something to do with what happened to Margaret?'

Now that he was out of the scope's sights, Gavin seemed to relax slightly. He once again fell onto his seat and topped up his glass. He swirled the contents, and the look may have had more gravitas if the amber liquid wasn't spilling with each flick of the wrist.

'You know, I barely know them. I know they are generally self-serving, ambitious people who would throw you overboard if it meant a shot at having a better show… Having the middle of the night slot has rendered me an unworthy friend.'

He took a sip, and stared at the glass, as if to question where the rest of the whiskey had gone.

'Do I think one of them could've killed Margaret and taken the necklace? Absolutely I do.'

He finished his glass, thumped it against the bar and got to his feet once more. He leaned in close to Colin, who got an uninhibited blast of the sweat and alcohol emptying from Gavin's pores.

'It might be worth having a word with Dave,' he said, before burping loudly. He wafted away the smell without apology. 'He was absent for quite a while from the party, and rumours have it that he could do with a bit of extra cash at the minute.'

He touched his nose conspiratorially, before marching off across the would-be dancefloor and out of the room.

Colin pushed his untouched glass away. He'd heard it said once that there was a special rung in Hell reserved for those who wasted good whiskey, but currently, he had his own devils to dance with.

He followed Gavin out of the room.

11

BAD BLOOD

DRACULA OPENED THE door and gave Adam a look.

Not an "I want to suck your blood" look. More a "who the hell are you and why are you knocking on my door" type.

But then, nothing about Drive Time Dave looked very much like a vampire. What was left of his dark hair was racing back from his forehead and a small mouth held captive oversized front teeth like some sort of prisoner of war camp; the conditions not quite up to scratch. He was about the same height as Adam, though slightly hunched, like sitting behind a mic all these years had wreaked havoc with his posture.

Instead of welcoming Adam in, or telling him where to get to, he simply left the door open and walked back to the bed. He picked up his mobile and held it to his ear.

Unsure of what to do, Adam hovered at the entrance for a minute or so, before coming to the conclusion that an open door was not a closed one, so walked into the room and shut the door behind him.

He stood leaning against the mahogany desk, watching Dave. A stream of consciousness rumbled from the phone, and Adam could only pick out a word or two here and there, before realising that it was commentary of a horse race.

'Is it not on TV?' Adam asked, only getting a wide-eyed glare for an answer.

Suddenly, the commentator got very excited, his words tumbling out now, causing Dave to assume a jockey like pose on the bed. He rocked his hips in time with the rhythm of the words and Adam started to feel uncomfortable at the strange show of obscenity.

'Arigato Shuko Sho!' the vampire suddenly thundered, jumping off the bed and holding Adam in a celebratory hug. He released Adam and crossed the room, pulled the mini bar's door open and retrieved himself a can of ice-cold beer.

'Celebrating?'

'Too right I am. Big win!'

'Isn't a bit early for horse racing to be kicking off?' Adam asked.

'Maybe here, but not in the land of the rising sun.'

'Japan?'

'Someone got their geography O-level,' Dave laughed, as he crossed the room again and settled on the bed. Adam reflected on the information he had acquired from the internet. This live demonstration of brokenness was a big fat tick of validity.

Drive Time Dave had a gambling problem.

He also had a drinking problem, too, if him necking a can of lager at this time of the morning was anything to go by.

Still, one problem at a time.

'Albert just wanted us to check if everyone was okay, after last night, you know?' Adam started. 'Obviously, he's in no fit state.'

'Yeah, totally. That was some messed up shiz.'

'He also asked us to do a little bit of digging into what happened. Did you know the firefly necklace is gone?'

'You're kidding? Oh, no. I mean, losing your wife is bad enough, but losing valuable jewellery… that's going overboard.'

'Valuable? How do you know?'

'Well… I assumed,' Dave said. 'They were fairly well to do and a big purple stone like that I assume cost a pretty penny.'

'It has to be somewhere on the island. Do you think any of your fellow employees could have taken it?'

Dave seemed to study the ingredients of his lager for a moment too long. When he looked up, there was fire in his eyes.

'Employees is a funny word, considering we've all just been let go.'

'You know what I mean.'

'Yeah, I do know. Anyone of that lot is capable of anything. Gavin is an untrustworthy jailbird, Keith is the star of the station and would not have taken kindly to being tossed to the kerb like the rest of us. And Sophie? She might be the worst of all.'

'Why?'

'She's a woman. And women are the devil.'

Quite a forthright view, Adam thought. He wondered if he could needle that point any further.

'What did she do?'

'Oh, you know, came in to the station with flesh showing, laughing at everything Albert said. Suddenly, she's got the afternoon show. I've been there for ten years, paying my dues, and she shoots up the ladder right past me.'

He held up a finger to Adam and scrolled through his phone, hurriedly pressing buttons. He shot up from the bed, grabbed his jacket from the back of the chair and made for the door.

'Everything okay?' Adam asked.

'Just lumping a few quid on Hotaru in the six fifteen. Japanese standard time that is, not GMT. Smoke,' he said, holding up a packet of cigarettes. 'I get nervous before a race and these calm me down a bit. You want one?'

Adam nodded. He wasn't a smoker; in fact, he hated cigarettes, but felt he was getting somewhere and didn't want to plug the reservoir as it was emptying.

Dressed in his vampire costume, Dave looked at home in the unlit wide corridors, as if he was made to lurk in shadows; the dimness of a radio studio, the dark corners of gambling debt. It was where he felt comfortable.

They descended the stairs and walked to the door. Dave pulled a cigarette from his pocket, unbent it and shoved it between his lips. He lit it with a disposable lighter and then opened the door.

Figuring he'd got the headline about the other presenters (the headline being no one could be trusted in the eyes of Drive Time Dave), Adam decided to change lane.

'You often bet on international horse racing?'

'Yeah, sometimes virtual horse racing if there are no real races on.'

'As in, computer generated horses? But, surely that's just luck. There can't be odds or anything.'

'It's all luck, friend,' Dave said, with a grimace. 'You soon realise that. The numbers stop meaning anything and you go with your gut.'

'And how's your gut?'

Dave considered the question for a while, his cigarette disappearing in a haze of ash and smoke. With a quarter of it left, he threw it on the ground outside the door, the weather doing a foot's job of extinguishing it fully. He pulled the door closed again and rubbed his arms, the international signal for "I'm a bit cold".

'My gut has not been great these past years. It's no secret that I'm in a lot of debt. My wife left, or rather, she kicked me out. She stayed in the house and I live in a crappy little flat on the outskirts of town. Jesus,' he laughed. 'I can't even afford a place in the centre of Stonebridge! That should show you just how bad things are.'

'So, I imagine the news of your unemployment made you pretty mad?'

'Don't think I can't see what you're doing,' he said, pulling another cigarette from his pocket and shoving it behind his ear. 'If you think I had something to do with this, you're barking up the wrong tree.'

'We're just trying to eliminate people. To help Albert. Someone said they saw you leave the party…'

'Screw Albert and screw whoever told you that,' the vampire spat. 'Yeah, I left the party. I didn't feel like dancing. If that's an offence, fire me. Oh, wait. You can't. I don't have a job.'

He's rattled, Adam thought. Time to go for broke.

'So, the necklace might come in handy?'

Without warning, the vampire launched at Adam, pinning him the wall with a forearm across the neck. Adam pulled at his restraint but to no avail. For a split second, Adam had the ridiculous notion that his neck was about to be pierced by two long fangs. Though, taking in the fury burning in Dave's eyes, maybe the idea wasn't so ridiculous after all.

'How many different languages do I have to say this in. I did not take the sodding necklace.'

They stared at each other for what seemed like an eternity, before Dave released his grip and walked away.

'Sorry, man,' Adam called after him, once he was sure his voice box was working. 'We're just trying to help.'

He watched the vampire skulk off to the stairs, where he was swallowed once more by the darkness.

Adam stayed in the entranceway for a while, rubbing his neck and thinking about Dave. He had a temper, that was for sure. And a very valid reason for stealing the necklace.

When he was sure that he'd left enough time for Nosferatu to return to his lair, Adam got to his feet and made for Colin's room for a catch up, taking the stairs three at a time.

12

BENEATH THE SHEETS

ADAM PULLED HIS coffee closer and let the warmth of it filter through his hands. He pulled a white sachet from the little tub of condiments on the table and tore the top off. Normally, one sugar would suffice, but today was not a normal day.

He stirred the granules into his drink, the tinkling of spoon on china the only sound to be heard in the hotel's cafeteria, save for footsteps of his returning friend.

'Better?' Adam asked.

'Are you asking me how my toilet experience was? Having a girlfriend really has changed you.'

Adam threw the empty sugar packet at his friend, but missed. He adopted a hushed voice.

'So, what did you find out?'

Before answering, Colin took a sip of his tea.

'Well, Gavin is a huge ex-con with an eye for jewellery it would seem, though he claimed it wouldn't take a dummy to realise that the firefly necklace was worth a penny or two. He may also be a functioning alcoholic.'

'Do you think he could've killed Margaret?'

'I wouldn't rule him out. Obviously, I'd like to believe in the justice system and the power of rehabilitation, but he is a bit scary. What about Dave?'

Adam relayed what he had learned about Drive Time Dave; drowning in debt, addicted to gambling, pissed off that he's been fired and more than capable of physical assault. Adam pulled down the neck of his T-shirt to show his friend the beginnings of a bruise.

'Quite the unlikeable bunch!' Colin laughed.

'I could've told you that before spending a weekend with them.'

'What's next?'

'We talk to the others—Sophie and Keith. Damien, too. I know he's not in their crew, but he's a creepy so and so.' Adam shivered at the memory of the circus ringmaster reclining on his bed.

'It might be worth having another word with Albert too,' Colin said. 'Maybe now that he's had a while to think about it, some new memory might have been shaken loose.'

'Who should we start with?'

'Sophie, I think. You mentioned that Dave reckons she is the most capable of all of them.'

'Aye,' Adam snorted, 'but that's only because she's a woman. His views would've been outdated in the fifties.'

'Well, we'll see what we can find out from her and Keith, and then we can go back to Albert with some findings.'

'Sorted, then,' said Adam. 'Now, where are the toilets?'

Colin gave directions and Adam followed them—out the main door, down the corridor, to the right and to the left. His steps led him the back of the building where he hadn't ventured before. The furnishing was in keeping with the rest of the place, wooden panelled walls and framed pictures of old dudes and places.

The toilets were much the same. Adam did his business, aware that he was feeling watched by a painting above the urinals with eyes that moved where you did. He half-expected some sort of Scooby-Doo stuff to happen—the painted eyes sliding away to reveal human peepers or something like that.

But it didn't, thankfully.

He washed his hands and made his way back into the corridor. He turned left and walked to the end of the hallway, realising with a start that he had turned the wrong way out of the toilet and was off reservation. As he began to turn, something caught his attention.

He was now at the back of the hotel. Outside the window, he could make out a small decking area with a number of chairs and tables on it. He figured they must be bolted down, as the gale force winds would surely have made playthings of them had they not been.

Beyond the decking was a wall of black cloud, though on a clear day, the view would probably be stunning.

All of these thoughts came later, however, as the thing that had snagged his attention was front and centre in his brain.

Lying in the small conservatory that led to the outside area was a mound of blankets.

He didn't have to look any closer to know that it was another body.

And he didn't look any closer.

In fact, within the blink of an eye, he was halfway down the corridor, aiming to put as much ground between him and the body as possible.

COLIN TOOK IN Adam's sweaty, pale face, the speed with which he crossed the room and his voice three octaves higher than it usually was.

'The toilets aren't that bad,' Colin said, with a smile, which Adam did not return.

Instead, he picked up a napkin and dabbed his forehead and top lip, wiping the sweat away.

He glanced around the room, like there might be something spooky hiding in the corner, before leaning across the table and whispering in Colin's ear.

'You what?' Colin whispered back.

Adam repeated his information.

'Albert's been murdered?' Colin repeated. He looked at his friend with doubt in his eyes.

Adam quickly told his friend what he had seen, though Colin still looked doubtful. The colour rose in Adam's cheeks and he pushed back his chair.

'I know what I've seen,' Adam muttered. 'Let's go find out.'

'I THOUGHT YOU said it was at the back of the hotel.'

They were walking up the stairs, away from the area where the body supposedly lay.

'Yeah, it bloody is, but I don't want to be the one to pull back the sheet and look into those glassy eyes, do you?' Adam asked.

'Fair point. So, what's the plan?'

'We knock on Albert's door. He's not going to answer. That's our proof.'

Colin looked doubtful.

'He might be asleep, or, he might be out and about.'

'Out and about? Where would he go? Down the high street? Cinema? We're on a bloody island, it's chucking it down and his wife has just died.'

'We'll see.'

They reached the top of the stairs and marched up the corridor. Adam hammered on the door.

Silence.

'See?' he mouthed at Colin.

Colin knocked again.

'Give me a minute,' came a voice from behind the door.

The sureness fell from Adam's face as the lock turned and the door opened. There stood Albert in all his faded glory.

'Everything okay, boys?' he asked.

'You're okay?'

'Well, my wife was killed not long ago, so not quite okay.'

While Colin engaged in small talk, Adam's mind drifted. If Albert was alive and well (or, if not quite *well*, alive at least), who was buried below the sheets?

'You did what?' Colin asked, bringing Adam out of his revery.

'Well, Keith suggested it. He said that it would be better if she was out of the room, because then at least I could get some rest. I thought it was a bad idea, like you said, the police wanted the body left where it was, but he told me that we would put her somewhere safe and respectful and that the authorities would understand.'

'So, you put her in the conservatory?'

Albert suddenly looked like a little boy who was being told off by his father for participating in a half-thought-out, hair-brained scheme. Adam felt a pang of pity, which didn't last for long, as the door was slammed in their faces.

13

CAT'S GOT CLAWS

ADAM AND COLIN were holed up in the latter's bedroom, one at the foot of the bed and the other in the hard-backed desk chair.

'Do you think Keith was really looking out for Albert's best interests or…' Adam started.

'Or did he suggest moving the body so that evidence is lost? We won't know until we talk to him, but the police are going to be pissed either way.'

'Surely a man with that gut has watched enough cop shows to know that the police want to see the body where the bad thing happened.'

Adam rolled the next steps around his head.

'So, we need to talk to Keith next?'

Colin shook his head.

'I think we stick to the plan. If we go straight to Keith, it'll tip him off that we know something and who knows what he'll do. I'll go talk to Sophie and see what she says, and then you can go talk to Keith afterwards.'

'Why do we need to speak to him at all?'

'Because, if we don't and he hears we've been talking to everyone else, he'll know were onto him. We'll simply be crossing our Ts and dotting our lower case Js, and then when the police arrive after this bloody storm dies down, we can tell them everything we know.'

Adam considered this, and found only one slight chink in the armour.

'So, let me get this straight. You get to go chat to the fit blonde, and I get to speak with the overweight murderer?'

'Apparent murderer. We don't know for certain yet. And, think of it as a favour that I'm doing you. Helena wouldn't like it if she heard rumours of you and another lady having a quiet chat in a locked room.'

'And how would those rumours possibly get out?'

Colin shrugged his shoulders, but the die was cast.

'Well,' Adam huffed. 'Off you go then. I'm going to try and get some more rest.'

'In my bed?' Colin asked. 'I'm aware of your level of hygiene. Go to your own.'

Adam gave him the middle finger in reply.

SOPHIE SAUNDERS OPENED the door with an air of inevitability. Her blonde hair was pulled back into a tight ponytail and an oversized black turtleneck jumper was tasked with keeping her warm.

Having spoken to half the presenters already, it was unlikely their investigation was going to remain under wraps for long.

'YOU HERE TO interrogate me?' she said.

The question sounded cold, despite the warm smile she had plastered on her face.

'I was wondering if you wouldn't mind answering a few questions,' he nodded.

'Sure, but not here.'

She grabbed a heavy raincoat from the back of her door and joined Colin in the corridor. Wordlessly, they walked down the stairs—Colin half a step behind—to the front door. The weather was still unforgiving, though Sophie didn't seem to mind. She stepped outside, accepted the storm's embrace, and marched up the path.

Colin swore under his breath and followed her, picking up his pace so that he could catch up with her.

'Where are we going?' he shouted, though the wind stole his words as they left his lips.

They retraced their steps from the night before. Before the heartache and the knife and the broken body. They walked past the graveyard, past the trees and eventually came to the small chapel. Sophie unhooked the snib and they went in.

The chapel at least offered shelter, if not warmth. Colin took off his jacket and threw it over the back of one of the two chairs in the room. The pitter-patter of dripping water seemed to echo in the confined space. Sophie kept hers on and slipped into the chair opposite.

'Why here?' Colin asked.

'It's the only place on the island with a roof aside from the hotel, and I can't be there at the minute. I keep thinking about the body. Her eyes. Staring…'

She puffed out her cheeks and closed her eyes, as if the images had followed the pair on the breeze and invaded the holy space.

'So, you're trying to get to the bottom of what happened then?'

Colin nodded.

'You know,' she went on, 'I've heard of the two of you. You're like the north coast's unofficial detective team. Where's the other one?'

'Sleeping,' he replied. 'It was quite a long night.'

'I'm glad it's you. I was hoping I'd get the handsome one.'

She cocked an eyebrow and Colin felt his face burn red.

'So, what do you want to know?' she asked.

'Do you know Albert and Margaret well?' he asked, knowing that it was a poor opener. He needed to regain his composure, ease himself in.

'Well, obviously Albert was my boss, so I knew him well. Margaret, not so much. She never really came to the station.'

'Was Albert a good boss?'

'He was a great boss,' she replied. 'He was passionate about the music, about the station and about making sure everyone was happy. Which we all were until last night.'

'Yeah, sorry about that,' Colin said. 'Can't be easy to find out you're getting fired like that.'

'Especially…' she started, though trailed off with a shake of her head.

Instead of jumping in, Colin waited, letting the silence expand between them. Someone had to fill it, and his money was on the one who talked for a living. If he was a betting man, he would've been celebrating ten seconds later.

'Especially,' she repeated, 'because he had just promoted me to the prime-time slot. I was due to start in the new year.'

'Is Keith leaving?'

'Nope, he was going to take my afternoon show.'

'Did he know?'

'I'm not sure Albert told him, but I did last night,' she shrugged. 'Albert told me in confidence, but now that the station is closing, it doesn't matter, does it?'

Colin tried to think about the wording of his next question carefully.

'Why you?'

'Why me what?' she said.

'Why did you get picked for the prime-time show? Dave and Gavin have both been there for longer, and Keith is nowhere near retirement age.'

'You think because I'm a woman I had to cast some sort of spell over poor old Albert? That there had to be some sort of deficiency in everyone else? How about the fact that I'm simply more talented than all those other losers?'

'That's a good enough reason for me.'

'You think I don't know what the others say about me? That I must be offering Albert "something" in return for the promotions. Gavin was in jail, Dave is up to his eyeballs in debt, and Keith is well past his sell by date. Seriously, the dude has never played a single record from this century! To be honest, I'm surprised it's taken this long for Albert to offer it to me.'

'You're angry with Albert?'

'Yes,' she nodded. 'I know it's only local radio, but prime-time still means something. It showed that my talents were being recognised. You should've heard Keith last night when I told him that he was going to be demoted. He was fuming!'

She laughed then. A shrill laugh with no humour in it. The wind buffeted their cliffside haven, causing the ancient windows to rattle in their frames. Sophie looked towards the glass, her stare momentarily vacant.

Colin gave her a minute, before asking: 'Do you think any of the others are capable of killing Margaret and stealing the necklace?'

He got to his feet while speaking. Their chat felt like it was coming to a natural end, and he was keen to get back to the warmth of the hotel.

'Yes,' she said. 'Like I said, Gavin beat a man half to death. His job prospects aren't exactly rosy, so I imagine a valuable necklace might come in handy for him. Dave is going to have loan sharks at his door soon. I can still picture the pound signs in his eyes when Gavin pointed the necklace out yesterday. And Keith? I don't know about him, but, he really was furious last night. People do crazy things when they're not thinking straight. Chuck in a load of booze and it's a bad mix.'

'Speaking of booze,' Colin said. 'You've taken your cat outfit off.'

'A woman died. You think I'm interested in some loser bet? I'd rather show my respects.'

Colin nodded to the door, but Sophie shook her head.

'I'm going to stay here a while. That hotel, man. The body.' She shivered. 'I'm going to spend as little time as I possibly can there.'

Colin nodded, thanked her for her time and left.

AT THE SAME moment as Colin asked his first question, inside the hotel, Adam's attention was pulled from the television by something moving outside.

Something white was making its way along the path. At first, Adam thought it was one of the presenters, but when he ran through their costumes, a ghost was not among them.

He looked outside again. The figure was definitely draped in white sheets, and a black belt was fastened around the midsection.

And then it hit him.

The figure *was* definitely draped in white sheets, but the belt was not a belt. It was a pair of hands, clasped around the spectre's waist.

Though, spectre was not the right word. Spectres aren't made of flesh and blood.

All at once, Adam realised that Margaret Fernsby's body was below the sheets. And was being moved against her will.

Adam pushed himself off the bed, grabbed his coat and sprinted to the door.

14

RESTING PLACE

ADAM PULLED THE door back and dashed outside, dressed in black with his hood up. He ran up the path, following the invisible footsteps left by whoever was transporting Margaret to pastures new.

When the path split, he hesitated. He could've played a quick game of eenie meenie miney moe and decided his fate that way, but a better idea sprang into mind.

He glanced left at the dense gathering of trees, at the perfect cover their thick trunks provided. He took one last look up the paths, saw that he was alone and ducked into the copse. He leaned his back against the trunk of a particularly large oak tree and waited for his breath to come back. Huge droplets of rain crashed from overhanging leaves, though since he was already soaked through, they made little difference.

After a few minutes, he heard movement. He could feel his heart thump against his chest as he willed himself to take a peek. He summoned the courage, took a final breath and poked his head out.

His cocked an eyebrow as he recognised the familiar gait of the traveller. Cupping his hand to his mouth, he proceeded to imitate the call of a bird. Quite well, if he did say so himself.

When the figure looked over, Adam waved a finger and Colin left the path, joining him behind the oak.

'What was that?' Colin asked. 'You scared the life out of me.'

'It was a wood pigeon's call.'

'More like the call of a strangled cat, you moron.'

'I didn't realise I was on the island with Bill Oddie,' Adam said. 'Anyway, enough about bloody nature, I thought you were talking to Sophie?'

'I was. We went to the chapel. Her idea. Said she couldn't be in the hotel knowing that the body was in there.'

'I think her problem has been solved,' Adam said, before going on to explain what he saw.

'Jesus,' Colin said, once the story of the moving body was finished. 'What do we do?'

'We wait. I figure that whoever is moving her will come back this way. It's the only path back to the hotel.'

And that is what they did.

With only the thick trunks, the bare branches and the darkness for protection from the weather and a conniving killer, they stood and kept watch, daring every so often to flick their heads out either side when they thought they'd heard something. To a casual observer, they may have looked like the most cautious meerkats in existence.

Adam was losing hope and was about to suggest abandoning their post, when he heard something. He looked at Colin, who was looking right back at him with wide eyes.

Adam nodded his head at Colin, who shook his and nodded back.

'Why me?' Adam mouthed.

'Why not?' Colin mouthed back.

With no good argument, Adam very slowly peered around the tree trunk, with fortuitous timing.

Emerging from the right-hand path was a tall figure, dressed from head to toe in black. The black gloves covered hands that swung at the end of long arms.

Adam watched the figure lope past them, eager by the looks of it to get back to the relative safety of the hotel. When he was sure the figure was too far away to hear them, Adam pulled back into the safety of the treeline.

'Well?' Colin whispered.

'Damien,' Adam replied, his voice shaky.

ONCE THE INFORMATION had washed over them, they formed a plan, which they were currently putting into practice.

When they were sure that Damien was happily ensconced in the hotel, Adam and Colin leapt from the treeline and ran up the right-hand path from where Damien had emerged. Chances were that he had dumped the body somewhere along this way.

All Colin and Adam had to do was find it and keep its whereabouts a secret until the police arrived. Presumably, the police would find it anyway when they combed the island on their arrival, but holding up a neon sign for them would be a time-saving and helpful step, evidence-wise.

They made their way up the path, Adam keeping an eye on the trees to the left, Colin the right. They were sure that the body would be buried deep within the wooded area, but a quick sweep now might save them time in the long run.

They arrived at the end of the path no wiser to the body's location. The view from the cliff top, where the path had led them, should've offered a stunning vista—endless ocean, unbroken sky and, on a good day, the rocky beginnings of Scotland. Today, all they got was a solid wall of grey.

'He could've thrown the body over the edge,' Colin said, pointing to the sheer drop below them.

'I don't fancy getting close enough to check,' Adam replied.

The grassy verge was slick with rainfall. One wrong foot placement and you could easily meet your maker on the jagged rocks below.

'We can assume that that's what happened if we don't find it back there,' Colin said, jerking his head in the direction of the woods that they'd just passed through.

They turned and were once again swallowed by the ancient trees on either side. They quickly cooked up a plan—they'd each take a side and venture in to the darkness. If one of them found the body, they'd shout as loudly as they could and hope that they could be heard over the wind.

They were about to split up when Colin saw something that rendered their plan unnecessary.

On his side, about twenty feet into the woods and nearly obscured by the trunks and weather, he could just make out a circular wall of crumbling bricks. Damien had even pointed it out to them on their tour last night.

Was that his plan all along? Nonchalantly point out his planned burial place? Had he dreamed about it on every tour he'd ever given, and finally the urge had smothered him—the sight of the expensive necklace too seductive to ignore?

Colin and Adam crept through the trees, pausing every time one of them stepped on a twig that snapped with the sound of a gun firing. An ominous sound if there ever was one.

When they got to the well, they each took a deep breath and Adam counted down from three with his fingers. When all he was left with was a balled fist, they looked over the top of the crumbling foundations.

And there she was.

Stained blankets covered the bottom of the narrow shaft, dirt accumulating on the sheets and mingling with the dried blood already present.

Underneath what Adam guessed were her feet, lay a long blade, the handle obscured. Blood coated the metal, a mixture of the deceased's and the lucky survivor. Though, Adam doubted if Albert would consider himself lucky. Losing your wife and an expensive necklace, as well as sustaining a significant injury yourself was hardly a day of the blessed.

'What do we do now?' Adam asked, once he was sure that the vomit he felt rising would not be making an appearance the moment he opened his mouth.

'I think we should let the police know what we've found.'

'They're not going to be happy that we've been digging around again. DI Whitelaw isn't exactly our biggest fan after making him look stupid on his last few cases.'

'We could phone Daz?'

Darren was a member of the PSNI and crucially, their friend. They could call him off the clock and have an unofficial chat. In return, he could use this information himself down the line and reap the rewards of Adam and Colin's hard work. It was a symbiotic relationship that had worked well in the past.

'Calling Daz is a good shout,' Adam nodded. 'I've got something I'd like to ask him to check out, too.'

'What?'

Adam prodded the tip of his nose twice with a frozen finger.

'I'd like to keep that to myself for now. It's a hunch, and might be nothing. You go talk to Keith, like we'd planned, and I'll have a chat with Daz.'

They left poor Margaret in her makeshift grave, and trudged back to the house, tired and wet.

THE MAN AT the front desk gave Adam permission to use the landline, before leaving so that he could have whatever conversation was to follow in private.

He found Daz's name in his mobile, copied the number onto the oversized buttons of the hotel's phone and pocketed his iPhone as ringing sounded from the handset pressed to his ear. After a few rings, Darren answered.

His chirpy tone disappeared as Adam launched into the story of murder, theft and his and Colin's subsequent investigation. When he was finished, Darren sounded annoyed.

'Why did you have to get involved? Again?' he asked.

Adam had no good answer to that question, so remained silent while Darren told him that he had done enough; that if he'd seen Damien walking away from where the body had been hidden, then that was a good start for the police when they arrived. He made it very clear, once more, that any further enquiries Colin and Adam felt they needed to conduct should not take place.

Adam confirmed that he understood, aware that Colin was talking to Keith upstairs at that very moment. Technically, the questioning of the Bowie-wannabe was already happening, so didn't fall under Darren's red tape jurisdiction.

'Before you go,' Adam said. 'Can you do me one favour?'

Adam explained said favour. It was met with a sigh.

'What did I just say about you investigating?'

'It wouldn't be me,' Adam said. 'It would be you. It might be nothing and it might be something, and if it is something, think of the kudos you'll get.'

He could hear his friend weigh it up on the other side of the phone. A moment later, the scales tipped in Adam's favour.

'Okay, I'll see what I can do,' Darren said. 'Forecast says the storm should pass by this evening, so we should be there by 8 o'clock or so.'

They bade each other goodbye, Daz reaffirming one final time they should put any Sherlockian tendencies on ice, and as Adam set the phone down, something in the corner of the room moved, making him jump.

'Sorry, mate,' Damien said, emerging like a shadow. 'Didn't mean to startle you.'

'You didn't,' Adam said, shrugging nonchalantly, though not quite pulling it off. He was panicking—how much of his conversation had the weirdo heard?

He reminded Adam of Johnny Depp's strange portrayal of Willy Wonka. The top hat, the velvet coat that hung to his calves, the crazy eyes.

'This is all very exciting,' Damien said. 'A real-life murder mystery.'

'I'd say tragic, rather than exciting.'

'Tomato, tomato. I hear you've been asking a few questions.'

'A few,' Adam agreed.

'You've not been to see me. Is that a good sign or a bad sign?'

'Good, I'd say. You've not aroused our suspicion. I can ask you a few questions now if it would make you feel better?'

'Please do,' Damien said, sitting on one of the plush chairs the spacious reception had to offer. He crossed his legs and adopted an innocent look, fluttering his long eyelashes.

'Did you see anything suspicious last night?'

'Nope. I stayed a while at their party, though it was lame, so I went to my room. Though, I see a lot of different groups coming through here, and these people are unstable. Did you see how they reacted to getting canned?'

'Wouldn't you say anger is normal?'

'Anger, yes. But berating a poor old man and telling him to sell a family heirloom? A bit much if you ask me.'

'Heirloom?'

'The necklace. I was chatting to Albert earlier today—popped in to offer my condolences. He was cut up about having to close the station, and even more upset that they couldn't see the sentimental value of the diamonds. It's been in his family for generations.'

'And he has no idea who took it?'

'No. Do you?'

'We're working on it. Where have you been today?'

'Why?' Damien asked, mock hurt in his features. 'You don't think I have anything to do with this?'

'Not at all,' Adam lied. 'It's just, you're soaking wet.'

'Oh, that. I went down to the boat to make sure it was still there and not damaged. Part of my duties. Dreadful storm,' he said, looking up as if the dark clouds were visible through the ceiling. 'Luckily, it's to die down soon.'

'And the boat is okay?'

'Ah, yeah,' he answered, waving a hand and shrugging, as if he didn't actually know.

'Well, thank you for your time,' Adam said, before making his excuses and leaving Damien dripping on the checkerboard flooring.

15

STARRMAN

TECHNICALLY, COLIN MCLAUGHLIN was flying without a licence. He'd nipped back to his room to change out of his sopping wet clothes and grab a quick snack, so therefore hadn't begun his questioning of Keith when Darren's instruction to cease and desist was ordered.

If life were a television drama, there'd be repercussions. As it was, our newly-clothed, recently replenished, and blissfully unaware amateur investigator walked down the hallway, unbound by law or order. When he reached Keith's door, he raised a hand but did not knock, for a sound on the other side of the divide acted as a pause button.

If anyone happened to come across Colin now, it would look like he was frozen in some sort of political stance; standing straight backed, fist raised against some unknown oppression, to which he was lending his silent support.

In fact, he was trying to make out what the sound was. Initially, it sounded like a vacuum cleaner with a broken fuse which caused the suction to start and stop every few seconds. He realised, quite quickly, that it was in fact Keith snoring.

Sounds like a deviated septum to me, thought Colin, as he hammered on the door, feeling a twinge of guilt in the process.

The strange whirring gave way to a bewildered shout, as Keith was pulled cruelly from his slumber. If time were not of the essence, Colin would perhaps have been kinder. As it was, they needed to hear what Keith had to say.

Heavy footsteps heralded Keith's progress across the room, and when the door was pulled back, Colin could easily imagine him as the faceless killer.

Dark rings surrounded his eyes and a few days' worth of growth clung to his jaw. He was still wearing his sequinned catsuit, though it was not quite as pristine as when he stepped onto the boat less than twenty-four hours ago.

He stared at Colin with a simmering rage.

'What?' he barked.

'I was wondering if I could have a quick chat?'

'I heard Sherlock Holmes was wandering the building.'

'Usually I'm considered the Watson character,' Colin said, hoping to soften Keith's expression with a self-effacing barb.

It didn't work. Keith's jaw remained set and rigid; his unblinking stare fixed on the bridge of Colin's nose. Eventually, he took a step back and motioned for Colin to follow him into the room.

'You woke me up, you know?' Keith asked, as he flopped down on the bed again.

'Sorry about that. I won't keep you long.'

'Get to the point, then.'

Colin watched as he unscrewed a bottle of water and poured it into a glass with smeared fingerprints covering it like graffiti. He took a series of loud gulps before turning his gaze back to Colin.

'You've known Albert a long time, right?'

'Yes,' Keith nodded. 'I've worked at that station for thirty years. Knew his father before him, and Albert has been a close friend for most of my life.'

'And you've been prime-time host for how long?'

'Oh, going on fifteen years now. I'm a very lucky man.'

'We spoke to Sophie earlier…' Colin started, and then stopped, noting Keith's expression. It was as if the mere mention of her name had caused the rainclouds from outside to drift through the window and plant themselves above his head. His cheeks reddened and his brow furrowed.

'I imagine that was a very illuminating chat,' he scoffed.

'Well, she told us about how you were being demoted.'

'Demoted? Is that what she said? Ha, the cheek of the woman. Honestly…' he said, before stopping, as if searching for the words that needed to follow. 'That woman has been nothing but trouble since she turned up.'

'How so?'

'Well, she came in on her first day with an ego—bear in mind she hadn't spoken a single word into the microphone at this stage. I took an instant dislike to her. After her first show, we gathered for cake to celebrate her debut broadcast. I looked across at her at one stage and she was staring at me like… like a witch from a fairy tale. Like she was letting me know she was coming for my job.'

'And she got it.'

'Yep. Didn't take her long once she turned on the charm with Albert.'

'Surely that's not the only reason she got the slot,' Colin said. 'You have to be good at what you do.'

'It helps to be good at what you do, of course, but you want to have seen the two of them round the station. A flirty comment here, a low-cut top there, a friendly hand on the knee in the break room. It was obvious she was using her womanly charms on Albert for her own benefit.'

Colin doubted that a man approaching retirement would be taken in by Sophie's charms, if indeed that was what she was doing.

'And what did Albert do?' he asked, in spite of himself.

'Well, he's a man, isn't he? An old man, but still a red-blooded male. He looked delighted at the attention. It wasn't long until he pulled me into his office and said that the station needed a shake up and that he was considering switching shows. I assumed I was safe…'

'But you weren't?'

'I thought I was, until last night when that harlot told me that she'd been promised my show.'

'And how did you take it?'

'Not well, especially hearing it from her. Vindictive cow. And when you think of all the help I've given him over the years.'

'Help?'

'Albert is notoriously bad with money. His father left him the business in good standing, but Albert made poor investment after poor investment. He's had to take out loans over the years, and then more loans to pay back the loans—that's how bad of a position he's been in. I've waived my salary for a few months to help him out here and there, but that all gets forgotten when a pretty blonde with an agenda turns up.'

'Is he okay now, money-wise?'

'No idea. I stopped taking an interest in anything to do with him. I'd stop turning up for work if it wasn't for my loyal listeners.'

He launched into another tirade against Albert, though Colin was only half-listening. From his tone, it felt like he had been waiting for an age to let this vitriol spill out into the world. Colin's attention was taken by these new revelations of lost money and poor investments.

Could this have something to do with Margaret's death?

When Keith had finished his lengthy diatribe, he leant back against the headboard, breathing heavily like a bull. His belly rose and fell, straining the fabric of his cheap jumpsuit.

'Were Albert and Margaret happy?'

'Yeah,' Keith nodded. 'They've been happily married for nearly forty years. When he had his car accident, she waited on him hand and foot. And I don't mean that in a jokey way, because he only had one foot after the crash.'

He may not have meant it as a joke, but he sure was pleased with it anyway, judging by the silly grin he was attempting to chase away.

'Who do you think killed Margaret?' Colin asked as he stood.

'No idea, I rather think that it's the police's job to find out,' Keith answered, giving Colin a look that suggested it would be an opinion best shared.

'You've been very helpful,' Colin said, taking a few steps towards the door. He reached for the handle, but spun around before taking it in his hand. 'Oh, one last thing.'

Keith nodded.

'Why did you tell Albert to move Margaret's body?'

'I didn't *tell* him to do anything,' Keith scoffed. 'I went to see him, to check how he was doing. The poor man was sitting on the bed, holding on to her cold hand. I suggested to him that he could do with some rest, and maybe having Margaret's body temporarily removed from the room would be for the best. As much as he's screwed me over, I still care for the old codger, in spite of it all.'

'And you didn't think about what the police would say?' Colin asked.

'Like I said, I still care for him. To hell with the fuzz.'

Keith sunk back onto his bed, keen to get a bit more shuteye in, and Colin left him to it.

16

EVIDENCE

FROM OUTSIDE THE bedroom window, it looked like two figures were locked in some sort of passionate Latin dance. Their silhouettes moved past each other, stopping suddenly, before moving back to their original position. Occasionally, one raised an arm.

If you were able to make your way inside and put your eye to the keyhole of room number 9, you'd realise that no rhythmic movement was occurring at all. In fact, the air was not thick with desire; rather, it was teeming with frustration.

'What are you doing?' asked Adam.

'Thinking,' replied Colin.

'Can't you do it sitting down?'

'Why?'

'Because we can't both be pacing up and down. It feels silly.'

Colin gave him a world-wearied sigh, but acquiesced to his request. The floor was now all Adam's, and boy did he intend to use it.

'Right,' he said. 'Where are we?'

'We've had a chat with everyone, and there seems to be no clear standout suspect—any one of them had reason to steal the necklace.'

He ran through the suspects, counting each on a finger.

Ex-prisoner Gavin, debt-riddled Dave, aggrieved-at-having-her-new-prime-time-slot-axed Sophie, and aggrieved-at-having-*his*-old-prime-time-slot-taken-off-him Keith.

'Don't forget Damien. We saw that freak actually walking away from the body.'

'Well, we saw him walk away from that general direction. The boat's captain backed up his story that he had been down at the jetty. He has a solid alibi.'

'Yeah, but, he is a freak, isn't he? He probably could have dumped the body and then turned into a bat and flown down to the dock.'

'Again,' Colin said. 'Let's stick to the realms of possibility.'

'I'll stick to your mum's realms of possibility.'

Colin let the immature comment go, before mentally turning back to the suspect list.

'What we need is evidence,' he said. 'The police have told us we're not allowed to go snooping in their rooms, in case we contaminate it for the forensic team.'

'Whoever's got the firefly necklace is unlikely to be keeping it in their room though, are they? Police turn up, find it straight away and that person is quickly arrested. No, if there were smart, it'd be hidden away somewhere on the island. They'd go and collect it just before the boat departs and dance off into the sunset.'

They both considered the places where it could be hidden for a moment, before Adam once again broke the silence.

'We're discounting one person here.'

'Who?'

'Albert.'

'Come on,' Colin laughed. 'The man's wife has been killed, he's lucky to have escaped with his life, too. Did you see how deep the gash on his arm was? And it's his necklace that's missing. His fortune. There's no need for him to steal it. And, if you need another reason, *he's* the one that asked *us* to investigate.'

'That's not true. You offered and he kinda agreed.'

'Well, he authorised it then, if we're getting into semantics.'

'I still think it's worth a look. He could've been playing us the whole day.'

'I guess it can't hurt to see the full deck of cards,' Colin agreed, somewhat reluctantly. 'But, we can't just go waltzing in to his room, telling him that he is on our list.'

'I've been thinking about this. We've heard his side of the story, but it would be good to have a look around his room, unsupervised. You offer to take him down for a coffee, and I'll hang back and have a nosey.'

'I don't like this,' Colin said.

'Me either, but it's where we are.'

ALBERT OPENED THE door, looking as tired as anyone had ever been. His eyes were red and bloodshot, and his chin quivered. It appeared as if they had caught him mid-cry.

The boys apologised for disturbing him, though he waved it away. He asked them for a moment while he pulled himself together, and closed the door lightly. They heard him muttering to himself and then blowing his nose and a minute later the door reopened.

'What can I do for you?' he said.

'I was wondering if you fancied some company,' Colin replied. 'I thought maybe I could buy you a coffee before dinner?'

'I don't know…'

'Come on. It'll be good for you to get out of the room and have a change of scenery.'

'I suppose,' the old man shrugged. 'It would be nice to go and sit with Margaret for a while, too.'

Colin shot a look at Adam, who simply nodded his head at Albert.

'That would be nice,' he said.

'Are you coming?' Albert asked, as he moved from his room into the corridor.

'Yeah,' Adam nodded.

Albert let go of the door and it began to swing closed. The three of them set off down the hallway and, when they were half way down the stairs, Adam feigned needing the toilet and ran back up the stairs. When he reached Albert's room, he shot a glance back the way he came, but he was alone.

When the old man had been blowing his nose, Adam had bent down and set his wallet against the inside frame of the door. It was dark and blended in with the carpet, so the old man hadn't noticed.

He stooped to pick it up and the closed the door behind him.

He surveyed the room and summoned all of his method acting skills, attempting to become more Daniel Day Lewis than he'd ever been.

If he were a diamond necklace, where would he be?

That's the insane thought that whirled around his head as he moved to the bedside table and pulled drawers out. In them, he found a well-thumbed Bible and a notepad, inside which no grand murder-slash-robbery scheme was written down.

Not that he had expected there to be, but something convenient like that *would* be nice once in a while. It would certainly save him a lot of leg work.

Once finished by the bedside, he got on his hands and knees and looked under the bed. Again, nothing of note.

He crawled around the rest of the room in the same position, hoping his lowly vantage might change the odds. He moved around like a sniffer dog, until he realised how silly this would look to an observer, and was about to push himself up when a sharp pain ripped through his body.

Grimacing, he stood and pulled up his trouser leg. He found the culprit; a thin wedge of glass had embedded itself in his knee. Thankfully, it was only a small shard and pulling it out wasn't too painful.

He went to the bathroom and unwound a large amount of toilet roll. He put the glass in the centre of the pile and wrapped the paper safely around the small shard, before pocketing it. The last thing he needed was the police finding the glass shaving with his blood on it on the floor.

Which, come to think of it, was quite empty.

The police had instructed the hotel staff and the guests not to clean up – to leave everything as it was. Obviously, Albert and Keith had disobeyed that already when they had decided to move the body, though, of course, a compassionate soul may see that as a reasonable thing to do.

But, had someone also swept up the glass? Adam cast an eye over what little glass remained on the floor and windowsill. He wondered if there had been such a pitiful amount when he had been here earlier in the day.

He looked again at the smashed pane, the placement of the handle to open the window, and again at the floor. Surely, a pane that size contained more glass than was currently strewn across the floor. He was about to look outside, when a knock on the door disturbed him.

Adam flattened himself comically against the wall like a mime artist might.

'Albert, are you in there?' a female voice said.

Another knock. And then another.

'We need to talk,' she said, before knocking one more time, and then seemingly giving up, as the knocking and talking stopped.

If this were a novel, Adam perhaps might've realised that he'd been holding his breath the whole time. As it was, his respiratory system had carried on as normal, collecting oxygen without his explicit command.

What he did do was flop to the ground and thank his lucky stars that she hadn't tried to turn the handle. He would've been caught red handed.

And then he saw it. Or rather, he saw something that turned out to be it.

He picked himself up off the floor, hurried across the room and retrieved the piece of paper that was sticking out of Albert's coat's inside pocket. He unfolded it and read it, before reading it again to make sure it was real. He pulled his phone out and snapped a few pictures, before folding the page again and putting it back where he found it.

It may not have been the necklace, but it was close to being the next best thing.

He cast one more glance around and headed for the door.

17

LAID BARE

ADAM HAD JUST finished his speech, detailing his plan of how best to go about not only announcing the killer, but unearthing the necklace too. Colin was still shaking his head a minute later.

'You don't think it's a good idea?' Adam asked, sensing his friend's reticence.

'Even your man-bun seems like a good idea compared to the one you've just told me.'

'What's wrong with it?'

'It went out of fashion a few years ago, it looks greasy, it…'

'The plan, ye numpty,' Adam interrupted. 'Not my hair.'

'Oh. Well, where do I start? For one, we don't have definite proof. It's like a badly done join-the-dots at this stage. Two, if you want us to go through with what you're suggesting and we're wrong, it's going to look like something from a Channel 5 blooper show.'

'And if we're right?'

'It's still not going to look great, is it?'

'So what?' Adam asked. 'If he gets hurt, it's something he should've thought about before killing an old lady and stealing her necklace. Also, we do have proof. I've shown you what I've got and you've kind've confirmed it with what you got.'

Colin considered this for a while.

'I guess you're right. The evidence does sort of point to them, doesn't it? And if we're wrong, screw it. We don't have to see these people again.'

They high-fived and Adam got to work on his computer. It didn't take long to achieve what he had set out to do. When he was finished, he sat back on his chair with a satisfied sigh and pulled his backpack towards him. He fished around inside it without looking, searching for a snack, when his fingers touched something he hadn't realised was in there.

It would probably come in handy, he thought, though the torment that Colin would bestow upon him afterwards might not be worth it. Quick as a flash, he pulled the item in question out and stuffed it into his back pocket, just as his friend came out of the bathroom.

Adam checked his watch. It was almost time for dinner, which would mean that the assembled cast would all be gathering around the table soon.

They ran through the plan quickly one last time, before Adam scooped his laptop up and they left the room together.

It was show time.

THE DINING ROOM had a more subdued air than the last time they'd all been here together. The good humour and convivial atmosphere had been stripped away, replaced instead with an impression of suspicion and wariness. Though tragedy had occurred, the smell of a roast dinner wafting through the corridors had beckoned everyone to the same room.

Alongside Colin and Adam, Gavin, Dave, Sophie and Keith now sat around the huge table, though none were talking. Each sat, as if forced to be here, their eyes on the door to the kitchen, in the hope that food would soon appear, so that they could eat and depart to the solitude and relative safety of their rooms.

As Colin and Adam had passed Albert's room, the old man had poked his head out and asked Colin to bring his food up to the bedroom as he couldn't bear to be in the same room as a murdering thief. In the end, they'd managed to convince him to come down with them, with a promise that they wouldn't let any further hurt occur.

Back in the room, Colin gave Adam a look. Now that they were here, in the presence of their suspected killer, the plan seemed less watertight to Adam than before. The words he'd spoken, and the certainty with which he had drummed them home, now seemed empty and untrustworthy in company.

However, he hadn't made a PowerPoint presentation for nothing. Also, the storm was beginning to subside and he wanted the credit for catching the baddie, rather than doing all the legwork just for the police to walk away with the kudos.

He stood, and all eyes moved to him.

'I've prepared a little something that I'd like to share with you all,' he said. 'In light of the station closing down, consider this a walk through time.'

He crossed the room and stroked his finger over the mousepad of the computer, which caused the screen to light up and the projector's beam to awaken. On the fabric screen was the beginning of the presentation. It showed a black and white picture of the station, which he had lifted directly from the presentation from the night before.

In fact, he'd lifted most of it from the presentation Albert had shown the night before. As the pages rolled on, groans sounded from the table.

Adam paused the slideshow.

'Okay,' he said. 'I realise it's very similar to the one you saw last night, but there's one almighty difference that I'm sure all of you will be very pleased to see. Well, almost everyone.'

Adam turned to Albert.

'Mr Fernsby, please could you join me?'

The old man shot him a quizzical look and then pushed himself up, before hobbling across the room to join Adam on the dancefloor.

'Albert, we've found out who killed your wife and stole the expensive firefly necklace.'

'Who?' he gasped.

The silence in the room seemed to swell, just as the slide that wasn't in last night's presentation appeared on the screen. Everyone's attention shifted to it as Adam pressed the freeze button to keep it locked in place.

'You can give up the act now,' Adam said.

'PREPOSTEROUS!' ALBERT SHOUTED, taking two steps back from Adam. 'Absolutely preposterous. My wife dies. No, not dies, is murdered, and a precious family heirloom stolen and you have the audacity to finger me?'

'Less of the drama,' Adam replied, quietly.

Colin's time to shine was about to arrive. He still couldn't believe what he was about to do. While silent chaos reigned, he got out of his seat, tiptoed across the dancefloor and got down on his hands and knees behind the old man.

He gave Adam a nod, and his friend did the rest.

ADAM NOTED COLIN'S nod and knew that it was his time to act. This part of the plan had seemed cool in theory, but now that he was in the here and now, it seemed kind of cruel.

Still, Colin was clearly committed so he would look stupid if he didn't hold up his end of the bargain.

With surprising speed, he closed the distance between himself and the old man, and shoved him in the chest with as much force as he could muster.

For a second, time seemed to slow. Adam felt the old man's bony ribs and registered the look of surprise on his face. He heard the shouts of the presenters, though they seemed a million miles away.

When time caught up with itself, he watched Albert topple over Colin's kneeling body and collide painfully with the floor. Adam had been subjected to this humiliation on the school's grounds many a time. It hurt your pride more than your body. But only just.

'What the…' Albert wheezed.

Adam held a finger across his own lips to silence the old man, before turning to the presenters who looked like they were about to stand up for their felled ex-boss.

'He's the killer and the thief,' he said, triumphantly. 'And here's the proof.'

Adam strode around the room, milking the moment. He heard Colin cough and, when Adam looked at his friend, he was giving him the “get on with it” look that he’d perfected over the years.

‘Okay, here we go. Firstly, the crime scene. Why, I ask you, would a supposedly exhausted woman who wanted to go to bed need a sleeping tablet? I’ll tell you why. Albert slipped it in her water to make sure she would drift off nice and quickly. And then he killed her. There never was anyone else in the room. He killed his wife and knifed himself to make it look like he’d been attacked too.’

‘What about the knife?’ Keith asked.

‘Well, after he’d finished being stabby-stabby, he smashed the window and threw it outside. You see, generally glass falls in the direction it’s pushed, and there wasn’t much on the carpet but there was loads outside. Also, the ivy on the trellis outside his room hadn’t been disturbed at all. That was his first silly mistake.’

‘What was his second?’

Adam pointed at the screen. On it was a picture of the piece of paper he’d found in Albert’s safe.

‘I present to you exhibit number two. And this really shows the man’s stupidity. This is a picture of a letter from his insurers, with whom he recently took out a policy for, you guessed it, a rather expensive necklace to cover damage and, you guessed it again, theft.’

He held his tongue for a while, giving everyone a chance to take in the contents of the letter and the eye-wateringly large sum of money Albert was in line to claim.

‘Of course,’ Adam continued, when he figured he had milked the moment long enough. ‘There might be one or two questions asked from the insurers when they cotton on to the policy being taken out very recently. What are the odds?’

‘This is all nonsense,’ Albert muttered. ‘I took the policy out not long after getting the firefly necklace valued. I hadn’t realised the amount of money that it was worth. I have the valuers report, dated a day before the new policy was taken out.’

‘Convenient, and very clever,’ Adam said. ‘And, of course, someone might buy that excuse if it weren’t for the fact you had an accomplice lined up to help you clear away your mess once you got here.’

A gasp went up around the room, as the presenters eyed each other with suspicion.

‘Sophie Saunders,’ Adam said. ‘She was your right-hand man, wasn’t she?’

Sophie began to deny it, but was cut off by Albert.

‘How did you know?’

It was the old man’s turn to look impressed.

'I'm glad you asked. Well, we figured you had help shifting the knife from outside your room when you'd dropped it through the window. When we got to thinking, there were a number of reasons.' He turned to Sophie. 'Firstly, your co-workers aren't all that impressed with your presenting ability. Fine for mid-morning drivel, but prime-time? Nah. So, there must've been another reason for your promotion.'

'Sex,' laughed Gavin, looking at Albert. 'At your age? You filthy old…'

'As much as it pains me to imagine it,' Adam interrupted, 'yes. But it wasn't just sex, was it? It was blackmail. You gave him a bit of the good stuff on the mainland and then you concocted the plan to kill off poor Margaret.'

'You were telling him in plain sight that he best not back out at the dinner last night. You were talking about love and threatening to expose who it was, but he cut you off,' Colin said, failing to look serious with the old man's legs still draped over his back.

'It was all her idea,' Albert said.

'Shut up,' Sophie shouted, and attempted to run out of the room. Gavin leapt up from his seat and caught her with his impossibly long arms.

'So, if these two are guilty, where is the necklace?' Keith asked.

This was the part Adam had been dreading, though his pride at throwing three darts and landing them all had increased his confidence. He marched across the floor and took Albert's prosthetic leg in his hand.

He looked the old man in the eye and yanked.

Adam realised how this must look. He could feel every eye on him. He tipped the hollow leg, and felt something move inside it. He angled it further and watched as the necklace tipped out, onto the wooden floor.

The purple firefly and diamonds glittered in the light.

'Busted,' Adam said, and swooped down on the old man. He slipped one of the handcuffs around Albert's wrists and motioned for Gavin to bring Sophie over. He cuffed her too.

Everyone stepped back to take in the defeated couple. Their attention was not fixed on the two criminals. Rather, what was holding them together.

After an awkward moment, Colin spoke.

'What the hell are those?'

'Handcuffs,' Adam answered quietly, his face growing red.

'I can see that. Pink, fluffy handcuffs. Why do you have them?'

Adam glanced around to find the groups' undivided attention fixed on him. 'Well, Helena and I, we…'

Damien chose the perfect moment to enter the room, the police trailing after him. He'd been waiting by the jetty for their arrival ever since the worst of the rain had stopped.

Detective Inspector Whitelaw stepped past the tour guide.

'What are those?' he asked.

Adam's burning face grew even redder.

18

ALL'S WELL THAT ENDS WELL

HELENA SET HER fork on the plate with a clatter and leaned back, rubbing her belly appreciatively. Adam's cooking had really come along in the past few months.

'And then what?' she asked.

He'd been telling her all about his crazy weekend.

The necklace.

The death.

Damien.

Although, in the aftermath of the police carting Albert and Sophie away, Adam and Colin had spent some time with Damien. He had, after all, played a small part in their plan by leading the police swiftly to the theatre of conflict.

They'd had a few beers together and underneath his creepy persona, they'd found a down to earth guy who loved his job. Namely, unsettling the bejesus out of unsuspecting guests. They'd exchanged numbers, and goodbyes had been punctuated by promises of drinks in Stonebridge.

Adam finished his story, stopping short of admitting that he used their handcuffs to apprehend the suspects.

They left their plates on the table and retreated to the sofa. Strictly was just starting, much to Adam's dismay.

'I'm thinking of dying my hair that colour,' Helena said, pointing to a flame-haired dancer. 'But I'm not sure.'

He listened to her weigh up the pros and cons of the dye job, offering his two pence when the opportunity presented itself. The rest of the evening passed in a haze of wine and as the night drew in, Adam's eyes grew heavy.

He suggested going to bed and she threw a suggestive look his way.

Christ, he thought, *I hope she's not expecting to be restrained tonight.*

And with that thought fresh in his mind, he trailed after her, towards the confines of the bedroom.

-5-

MISTLETOE AND CRIME

CHRIS MCDONALD

1

CHRISTMAS LIGHTS

THE CREDITS ROLLED on the Rom-Com Helena had chosen and, as the lights in the cinema grew brighter, she looked over at Adam. He had been reluctant to spend an evening watching good-looking actors saying cheesy things to each other, before the inevitable happy ending and overplayed Christmas hit to finish it all off, but had agreed after much persuasion.

To his surprise, he'd enjoyed it. He even found that a single tear was rolling down his cheek.

'Are you crying?' she laughed.

'Crying?' he scoffed, wiping his face covertly with his sleeve. 'Of course not! It's just so bloody dusty in here and I think some of it got lodged in my eye. In fact, I'm going to have a word with management on the way out, see if they can sort the cleaners out.'

'Uh huh. Nothing to do with the kiss at the end?'

'God, no. I saw that coming from the opening scene. What a load of tosh.'

He grabbed his hoodie and bottle of water off the floor and noticed Helena try her best to hide a smirk. They walked hand in hand down the steps and through the foyer, where a crowd had gathered by the doors.

The forecasters had been threatening it for almost a week, but seemingly the weather gods hadn't been listening, instead keeping a hold of their festive payload until they decided the moment was right. Which was now, apparently. The clouds had unleashed their frozen cargo, covering the ground in a thick layer of fresh snow.

Suddenly, the doors of the cinema had been flung open and an impromptu snowball fight was underway. Adam and Helena watched as civilised moviegoers went to war, popping out from behind bins and running for cover behind walls. An older gentleman walked though no man's land, seemingly oblivious to the chaos erupting around him. A snowball, thrown from a fair distance, arced in the air and pasted the old man square in the forehead.

The crowd froze.

The old man stumbled backwards a couple of steps, and a young woman with a scarf pulled tight around her neck darted towards him. He held a hand up to her, bent down as if to pick something up, and stood again with a huge snowball in his hand.

'Who was it?' he shouted, and the crowd burst into laughter.

Adam and Helena made a run for it, taking only a few direct hits, before emerging into the relative safety of the town square.

The town hall looked stunning. Jonathan McClane, the mayor, had really gone all out this year. Fairy lights twinkled in every window, and neon signs showing dancing bells and shooting stars were attached to the ancient stone walls, spilling their colourful light onto the cobblestones below. An immaculately decorated Christmas tree took centre stage in the square; perhaps the biggest one in recent history.

'I see McClane got his way,' Helena said.

'It's *so* him to get his knickers in a twist about what colour baubles to use, isn't it? I mean, who cares if someone wants a bit of blue on it?'

'People like tradition at this time of year. I think the gold and red looks nice.'

He looked at her hair shining in the moon's gleam and the lights from the tree reflecting in her electric blue eyes, and he'd never felt more in love.

'You look nice,' he said.

'Shut up,' she replied, digging him in the ribs with a playful elbow.

She hooked her arm in his and they walked towards the car park. The snow still fell heavily.

'Let's take the short cut,' he said.

'Oh, not down Burnside Way. It always smells of wee.'

'But it's so much quicker and I'm freezing. Just hold your nose and you'll be grand.'

They quickened their pace slightly and slipped into the alley between Baldwin's, the town's department store, and a new outdoor sportswear shop. The walls were daubed with many years' worth of graffiti, mostly faded, but some areas had been topped up by today's would-be artists. Exit signs from the shops cast a green hue over the alley, illuminating something near the other end.

'What's that?' Adam asked, pointing.

'Bags of rubbish?' Helena suggested, squinting through the falling snowflakes.

When they reached the pile, they had their answer. Lying in the snow was a man, who might easily be confused for Father Christmas, were it not for his sullied clothes and unsightly appearance.

His trousers were filthy at the knees and his coat was light and completely useless for the current blizzard—though since he was dead, that didn't really matter.

The snow around his head was stained red, and blood still spilled from a nasty gash in his forehead.

Adam had to look away. He'd never been good with blood, and already felt lightheaded at what he'd seen. Luckily, Helena was a nurse at the local hospital, so slipped straight into professional mode. Before disturbing the scene in any way, she took her phone from her pocket and snapped a picture. She then checked for a pulse and performed CPR, while shouting at Adam to call for an ambulance.

It arrived not long after, though the poor man was pronounced dead at the scene. They called the police and in no time at all, DI Whitelaw strode up the alleyway towards them, looking annoyed that he'd presumably had to leave his comfy pyjamas and crackling fire behind.

'Well, well, well. It wouldn't be a crime scene without Adam Whyte sticking his beak in. I thought you'd given up on the detective work.'

'I didn't think you needed me anymore, now that you've bucked your ideas up.'

'We *never* needed you. It's been over a year since that nonsense on Winkle Island. What are you doing here?'

'We were walking back from the cinema and stumbled across him.'

'Who?'

'Gerald Agnew,' Adam said, pointing at the body. 'Surely you must know Gerald?'

'Course I know Gerald. Bloody nuisance,' Whitelaw said, casting his eye over the body.

Gerald Agnew was a Stonebridge institution. Homeless as long as Adam had been alive, he'd refused help from any of the organisations who had offered their assistance. Instead, he roamed the town like he owned the place. He was friendly in the day, as long as you threw him the odd quid as you passed, and a drunken pest at night.

'Well, at least this one is cut and dried. Looks like the old man tripped or slipped and smacked his head on that concrete bollard. From the looks of it, he either had a heart attack or his brain simply shut off. Of course, I'm not a medical expert.' Whitelaw shrugged. 'Unfortunate, but that's the way the chips fall sometimes.'

'What a lovely sentiment. Are you free to do the eulogy at his funeral?' Adam said.

'Button it, you, unless you want to spend the night in the cells.'

Adam held his hands up and Whitelaw disappeared out of the alley, leaving a young constable in charge of taking his and Helena's statements, though there wasn't much to tell. The young constable thanked them and left, shaking snow from his shoulders as he went.

Adam and Helena walked to a nearby coffee shop that was open late, hoping to entice late-night shoppers in with the promise of a bit of warmth. They slipped into a booth, ordered two hot chocolates and reflected on what just happened. She, matter-of-fact and stoic; he, still a bit light-headed from the sight of the blood.

They drank their drinks quickly, and then made their way back towards the car.

2

OLD HABITS DIE HARD

COLIN MADE HIS way around the lounge of the retirement home where he worked, clearing up the left-over bots of coloured card and doing what he could about the glitter that had fallen on the floor and started a new life within the plush, recently-laid carpet. Karen, the owner wasn't going to be happy, but at least the old folks had had fun designing their own Christmas cards. Most of them had gone off for an afternoon nap now, and Colin was glad of the peace and quiet.

He was almost finished when Barry came hobbling over. His health was going downhill rapidly, but he still had a mischievous glint in his eye.

'Son,' he said. 'What's happening with you?'

'Not a lot,' Colin replied, signalling to the mess of cardboard and paint. 'Clearing up after you messy pups.'

'Jesus. This is what I keep saying to you—you want to leave us old fogies behind and get yourself a job with a bit of excitement.'

'And what do I keep saying to you? Giving you a sponge bath is all the excitement I need in my life.'

'I used to live vicariously through you,' Barry said, pointing at Colin. 'Remember when there was that spate of crimes and you and your wee pal went and sorted them all? That was keeping me young. How long has it been?'

'Over a year, now.'

'A whole year since that trouble with the radio station yuppies? Goodness. No wonder I'm looking this old.'

'Are you still working your way through the Mackay series?'

'Aye, and they're great, don't get me wrong. But what you were dealing with in Stonebridge was real!'

Barry slinked off, fell into his armchair and was asleep within minutes. Colin continued his cleaning up and admitted to himself that he kind of missed snooping around too.

After a number of embarrassing blunders, there was an investigation into the Stonebridge police force, which resulted in them taking crimes in the town a bit more seriously. This meant that the kinds of miscarriages and oversights that Adam and he had looked into had reduced in number, rendering the amateur detective duo obsolete.

That, coupled with the fact that Adam and Helena's relationship was becoming more serious, meant that the erstwhile detectives weren't seeing a lot of each other at the moment—though their FIFA playing exploits had simply moved online.

Colin felt his phone vibrate in his pocket. When he pulled it out and checked the screen, he laughed.

'Your ears burning, were they?'

'What do you mean?' Adam asked.

'Never mind. What's up?'

'I was wondering if you were free for lunch? Be good to catch up.'

'I've got a break in about twenty minutes. Is that too soon?'

'No, that's perfect. See you at Ground?'

'Plan.'

ADAM WATCHED COLIN through the window, waiting for the green man to cross the road, despite the lack of traffic, like a small child. When the traffic lights finally turned red, he dallied across the road and in through the café's door. He appeared five minutes later, holding a tray, rammed with goodies.

'I didn't know if you had eaten already, so I got a McLaughlin special.'

Adam *had* already eaten a panini before Colin arrived, but still dove into the sweet treats with abandon. He was nervous, and the usually delicious doughnut made him feel a bit sick. He set it down, disappointed with himself.

'Everything okay?' Colin asked. 'Still cut up about the Gerald incident?'

'No. I'm grand. It's not like we've never seen a body before.'

'Yeah, but it's still pretty messed up. A corpse is not to be trifled with. Especially you, you know, with your disposition.'

'My what?'

'Your scaredy-cat nature.'

Adam shrugged, knowing that Colin had him bang to rights, and tried forcing another chunk of doughnut down his throat.

'What is it, if it's not the body? Are you dying?' Colin said. 'I've never seen you have to set a treat down before.'

'Fittest I've ever been. Have you seen my guns at the minute?'

'Seriously, dude. I've known you for twenty years. I know something's wrong.'

'I'm going to ask Helena to marry me,' Adam blurted out. 'I know we've not been together long, but it feels right, you know?'

There followed a stunned silence, before Colin leapt off his chair and enveloped Adam in a bear hug.

'This is massive, dude. Congratulations!'

'You're the only person I've told, so radio silence. I thought maybe we could go looking for rings today. If you want to.'

'Of course!'

'And, you'll be my best man, right?'

Tears sprung into Colin's eyes. Their friendship was a long one. They'd met on the first day of primary school and had been inseparable ever since. It was built on solid foundations—a mutual love of FIFA, Thai sweet chilli crisps and live music, and showed no signs of ending.

'Too right I will.'

They shook hands and chowed down on the treats, Adam's appetite returning with a vengeance now that he'd gotten his news off his chest, and his best friend's support.

'Why now?' Colin asked.

'Well, I just got a tax rebate for five hundred quid, and I figure if I don't buy a ring, I'll probably end up buying the new PlayStation instead.'

'Safer with a ring, I reckon.'

'Definitely.'

They finished up, cleared their tray, and headed down the narrow steps, emerging onto Stonebridge's high street.

'Tiffany's or Cartier, sir?' Colin laughed.

'I said five hundred, not five grand.'

'I reckon you'd even struggle with that. Winston's?'

'That's what I was thinking.'

They walked up the cobbled main street towards the town's more affordable jeweller. Charles Winston was a Stonebridge cornerstone. His shop had survived fires, break-ins and IRA bombs during the height of The Troubles, while changing a multitude of lives in the process, thanks to his sparkling diamonds.

A bell trilled above their heads as they walked in, and Adam immediately felt overwhelmed by the sheer number of diamonds, rubies and emeralds facing him.

Luckily, Charles was on hand.

The old man placed a bookmark carefully into the crease in the pages and slowly closed his novel. He pushed himself out of the leather armchair he'd been reclining in, and peered over the top of the counter, adjusting his fitted waistcoat in the process.

He looked, to Colin's eyes, like a little old tortoise. His wrinkled skin, wizened eyes and hairless head combined to give him a reptilian look.

'How may I help you today, young sir?' he asked.

'I'd like to buy an engagement ring.'

'Well, we can certainly help you with that.'

For the next twenty minutes, he ushered them this way and that. A ring would be placed in Adam's hand and snatched away almost immediately again, Charles grumbling about something or other.

'I can tell when someone loves one of the rings from the moment they set eyes on it,' he said, shuffling towards a display case with white gold banded rings. 'You haven't loved anything yet, but we'll find it.'

Colin excused himself and went outside, returning a few minutes later.

'What's up?' Adam asked.

'I've asked work to cover me a while longer. This is much more important.'

Charles handed Adam another ring, and took a step back.

'I think we've found the one,' he said.

And he was right. Adam had a feeling in the pit of his stomach that this was the ring he'd been waiting for. The silver band was thin, and a small, perfectly cut diamond protruded from the top. It was understated and quite beautiful.

'How much is it?' he asked.

'£450, but I'll knock twenty quid off so that the two of you can go and celebrate with a couple of beers.'

Adam paid the money and shook the kindly owner's hand, before placing the ring box in the inside pocket of his jacket.

As they left the shop, a man with lank hair spilling from beneath a soiled beanie hat strode up to them, like he'd been waiting for them to emerge.

'You're the two wee lads who like to play detective, aren't you?' he said, his voice slurred and stinking of cheap booze.

Adam tried to walk on, but the man grabbed his arm.

'I'm not making fun, or anything. I swear. I need your help.'

'What's wrong?' Colin asked.

'My mate was killed.'

'Gerald?'

'Aye.'

'I found the body,' Adam said. 'The police said he slipped and bashed his head off the pole.'

'Nonsense,' the man spat. 'Gerald was like a cat. Nine lives, man. And he'd got himself off the drink, too. Least, that's what he told us. There's no way he slipped.'

Adam and Colin cast a dubious glance at each other. Their new friend didn't notice. He was too busy throwing a can of cider down his throat.

'What do you think happened, then?' Colin asked.

'I was nearby. I heard him arguing with someone.'

'And?'

'It was heated. Serious stuff, by the sounds of it.'

'Do you know who it was?'

'I think so, but I'm no grass, man.'

Adam went to walk on.

'What are you doing?' the man asked.

'You're giving us nothing to go on, dude. You can't expect us to help you out, when you won't tell us what you know. You're wasting our time.'

'Alright, alright. It was Marty Hesketh.'

'Jesus.'

'Aye. Now you know why I wanted to keep my mouth shut. He and Gerald were arguing, quietly. Intense, you know what I mean? I didn't know who it was at first, and I was going to go down and sort it out, but then I recognised the voice, so I scarpered. I don't want to be on Marty's bad side.'

'And you're sure it was Marty?'

'Well, I'm not 100%. But I assumed as much. He likes a fight, does Marty, and him and Gerald were two of the same.'

'But you can't be sure?'

'No,' he said, shaking his head.

'So, you heard them arguing?'

'Aye, and I scarpered. Like I just said. Heard a scream from the alley and then I saw the police and the ambulance and all sorts piling in not long after. Reckon they'd come to sort it all out, and then I find out that Gerry's died and the police have done nothing about it.'

'Were you drunk at the time?' Colin asked.

'Pished as a newt, aye,' he nodded.

'And you think Marty killed him?'

'Aye.'

'So why not go to the police?'

'And tell them what I know?' he laughed. 'Aye, they're going to take the word of a tramp and reopen a case. That would mean them getting off their fat arses and actually doing some work.'

'Why us?' Colin asked.

'Because you two boys get stuff done. I've read about you in the papers. Yous are like Batman and Robin. Yous hear about an injustice and yous get to the bottom of it.'

Adam looked at Colin.

'We can't promise anything,' his friend said.

'You've made my day for even considering it. God bless yous,' he said, and sloped off towards the town hall.

'We can't promise anything?' Adam repeated.

'It's a kind way of saying no,' Colin shrugged. 'You were there. Did anything seem off to you?'

'I don't think so.'

'There we are then.' Colin looked at his watch and swore. 'I'm going to be late for work. Congratulations again, dude. Let's have a beer tonight to celebrate.'

Adam watched him rush off, slipping comically a few times on the watery slush that was slowly turning to ice. He walked back to Ground and ordered a hot chocolate, before taking a corner seat and thinking about how best to propose.

But he couldn't focus, and his mind wandered to Gerald's body.

Something had been nagging him since Colin had asked if anything was 'off' about the scene in the alleyway.

The blood and the body had combined to immobilise Adam's senses at the time—the horror of it all taking up too much space in his mind. But, with the benefit of hindsight, the little sixth sense in his brain was picking something up, but couldn't quite pinpoint what *it* was.

He pulled out his phone and texted Helena, asking her to send through the photo she'd taken of the alleyway. She replied almost instantly, and the contents of his hot chocolate nearly resurfaced.

He put his thumb over the image of the body—out of sight, out of mind—and concentrated instead on the surroundings. The lighting wasn't great, rendering the image dark and grainy, though the flash from the camera had helped a little.

He studied the background and honed in on what he'd missed when he was actually there.

Footprints in the snow.

Footprints leading away from the messy body.

Either someone had used the alleyway as a shortcut, seen the body and walked on past without telling a single soul. Or, whoever the footprints belonged to had murdered Gerald Agnew and strolled away without a second thought.

3

THE HARDEST MAN IN STONEBRIDGE

ADAM WAS JITTERY. Had been all day since he'd bought the precious goods.

He imagined that the little box containing the ring, lodged in his jacket pocket, was giving off some sort of homing beacon signal, and every time Helena's eyes drifted towards it, he'd asked her what she was looking at. It seems he'd snapped at her too many times.

'What is up with you today?' she sighed, as she lifted his plate and took it to the dishwasher.

'Nothing. Sorry. I'm just tired.'

'Well, for everyone's sake, go to bed early. I've got yoga soon, so I'm going to go and get ready.'

She touched his shoulder gently as she walked past him on her way to the bedroom, and he flinched, thinking she was going to shake him down to find out what he was hiding.

Thankfully, she didn't notice.

When he looked at his phone, he saw a message from Colin, asking if he was still on for the pub later.

Just for one pint, he typed, before pocketing his phone.

'I'M GOING TO have to propose soon,' he said, lifting the glass and clinking it against Colin's. 'I'm going out of my bloody mind. I'm fully convinced she's ex-Spetsnaz and that she knows exactly what I'm up to.'

'Spetsnaz?'

'Russian Secret Service.'

'You've been playing too much Call of Duty.'

'Maybe,' he agreed. 'I'm just so worried she's going to go into my pocket to look for change or whatever, and find it. I need to get it done.'

'Get it done. Ever the romantic.'

'You know what I mean,' Adam laughed, throwing a pack of nuts at his friend's face and catching him square in the forehead.

They sank back in their seats and enjoyed the fire crackling heartily in the hearth. Fairy lights twinkled and lush garlands ran along the bar top. The atmosphere in the pub was jovial and Elton John was blasting through the sound system, urging everyone to *Step into Christmas*. A few would-be karaoke singers were mouthing along while some Strictly wannabes were already shaking their moneymakers on the dancefloor.

On his phone, Adam accessed the picture of the alleyway and pushed it across the table. Colin took it and gave it a brief look.

'Flip me, there's a lot of blood. Looks like a still from a noir film. What am I looking for?'

'The footprints.'

'What about them?'

'The fact they're there, and they shouldn't be.'

'But you were there.'

'Yeah, but we came from the side of the alley that we're standing on. Neither Helena or me had been past the body when she took the photo.'

'So those footprints belong to someone else.'

'Ding ding ding! We have a winner.'

'And I'm assuming you're thinking that they belong to the killer?'

'Why else would they be there? No one is going to walk past a body and not do anything about it.'

'Maybe whoever they belong to went to get help? Or find a phone in a shop or something?'

'Yeah, maybe. But there's an invention now called the mobile phone, and most people have one.'

Colin ignored the sarcasm. 'So, what are you going to do?'

'I think I'll show the photo to the police, see what they think.'

'Good idea.' Colin passed the phone back across the table. 'Now, back to the proposal. What are you thinking? Something elaborate? Hot air balloon, or a dove carrying it to her or something like that?'

'Nothing tacky. Just something simple.'

'Probably for the best.'

'Do you want me to be there for morale support?'

'Thanks, mate, but I reckon I'll be okay.'

They laughed and touched glasses together again, and Adam was reminded once again how good of a friend Colin was to him.

THE NEXT DAY, Adam sat in the uncomfortable seat, squirming. A heater blasted the room with everything it had, causing sweat to crusade down his forehead and pool in his armpits. He wondered if the copper sitting opposite him was using these techniques to make Adam feel uneasy. If he was, it was working.

'And what's this supposed to be exactly?' DI Whitelaw asked.

'It's a photo of the alleyway when we found Gerald's body.'

'Bloody reporter now, are you? The bit of detective work on the side not enough for you?'

'My girlfriend took it. She's a nurse and thought it could be helpful down the line.'

'Good of her. You hired her for your agency yet?'

'Look, I know I've made you and your team look stupid in the past,' Adam snapped, unable to stop himself. 'I just thought you might be interested in potential evidence.'

'Evidence? Of what?'

'Murder.'

'Don't talk daft, lad. We were all there. Drunk as a skunk, he was. You could smell the fumes from Meadowfield. Took a tumble and bashed his head. It's unfortunate, but there's certainly no foul play here.'

'And what about the footprints?'

'All they show is that someone else was in the alley at some stage. All sorts of drunks and scallies hang around there.'

'But…'

'Listen to me,' Whitelaw said. 'There is no crime. Do you hear me? Don't go kicking that hornet's nest, 'cos all you'll get is a big old sting, and no one needs that around Christmas time, do they?'

'Always a pleasure,' Adam said, as he stood up and walked towards the door.

'Oh, and delete that photo, would you? It's voyeuristic and weird that you've got a snuff picture on your phone.'

'A snuff picture? So, you're saying he *was* murdered?' Adam replied.

'What?'

'A snuff movie is where someone is murdered on screen. Are you now saying he *was* killed, or are you just trying to sound cool?'

'I got my words wrong, alright?' He shrugged. 'Now, delete it or I'll have you chucked in the cells, no questions asked.'

Adam knew Whitelaw was blowing hot air, but couldn't resist winding him up a bit more. 'For what?'

'Wasting police time.'

Adam left the police station and called Colin, who answered immediately.

'How'd it go?'

'As expected,' Adam replied. 'DI Whitelaw was incredibly helpful and courteous and I have full faith in his ability to take the case forward. It's lovely to see that he has turned over a new leaf.'

'I can hear the sarcasm dripping from here.'

'He dismissed it without any questions. I think we should have a little nosey into it.'

'That means talking to Marty.'

'Yeah, true. But it does look suspicious.'

'Fine,' Colin sighed. 'As always, Adam Whyte is right.'

'That could be my campaign slogan if I ever ran for mayor.'

'What's the plan, then?'

'Shall I meet you at eight o'clock tonight at Wilson's?'

'Wilson's? Jesus, have you a death wish?'

'It's where Marty will be,' Adam said.

'Alright. If we have to. But you're buying the drinks.'

WILSON'S BAR WAS on the wrong side of town, near the vegan food stores and hippy clothing bazaars. If you were ever hankering for an illicit high, this was the pub for you.

Colin pushed the door open, imagining he was an out-of-towner barging his way into a foreign saloon. The décor hadn't been changed since the place had opened, and that had been some time in the 70s. No attempt had been made at making the bar look even a little bit Christmassy. Heads swung around and brows furrowed at this newcomer who they'd never set eyes on before.

Colin stared back and walked to the bar, Adam cowering behind him.

'Two pints of lager, please.'

The bar man set down the filthy rag he was wiping the bar top with and sighed pointedly, like pouring drinks was a huge inconvenience or outside his skillset. When they were done, he pushed the glasses towards them, spilling a good amount from each one. Colin looked at the spillage, and then at the bar man.

'Are we going to have a problem here?' the bar man asked.

'No problem. No problem at all,' Adam said. 'Thank you so much for your service.'

The bar man grunted and started to turn away.

'Is Marty in tonight?' Colin said.

'Might be. Who wants to know?'

'I want to know.'

'He's in the back room, at the table. I doubt he'd want to be disturbed.'

Adam and Colin ambled off, making a point not to thank him. Colin abhorred rudeness, so felt a little bit bad, but also felt like the bar man deserved it. They pushed through a door that led to a narrow corridor, walked past the toilets (which were letting out an unholy stench) and stood outside a door with a sign proclaiming it as the room designated for staff use only.

Colin knew this was a lie.

The Back Room was part of Stonebridge folklore. All sorts of illegal activities took place behind this famous faded door, if the stories were to be believed. Drugs, gambling, bare-knuckle boxing. Their late friend, Danny Costello, once claimed to have been in there when a cock fight happened, though no one believed him.

Faced with this door, even the usually unflappable Colin was feeling nervous. He raised a shaking hand and knocked lightly. Inside, the screech of a chair scraping across stone flooring sounded and a few seconds later the door opened an inch. A beady brown eye appeared.

'What?'

'Can we have a word with Marty,' Colin said.

The man replied with words unprintable here, and went to shut the door.

'We think he'll want to hear what we have to say,' Adam said, pushing his foot into the gap, so that the door couldn't close.

'He can be the judge of that,' the voice inside scoffed. 'Now, move your foot before I remove it with force.'

The eye disappeared and a minute later, the door was thrown open. Marty Hesketh was even bigger than Colin remembered him to be. His hair was a matted mess and his eyes were bright blue and wild. He was wearing a vest, despite the Wintery chill in the air, and had to turn sideways to get through the door. His arms were covered in tattoos that looked like a blind man had inked them.

'What?' he asked, closing the door behind him.

'We've heard rumours that the police are wanting to speak to you about Gerald Agnew's death. We're having a look into it too, and were wondering if you could answer a few questions?'

'A few questions about what? I didn't do nothing.'

Adam wanted to point out the double-negative, but also wanted to keep his face the way it was.

'Look,' said Colin. 'We know you weren't involved, but if you could answer a couple of our questions, we can help clear you. Officially.'

'Are you detectives?'

'We kind of are, yeah.'

The big man studied their faces for a minute.

'Oh, I know who you two are now. I've seen you in the papers. The two lads who keep making the police look like idiots. Aye, I'll talk to you, but only because I'm due a cigarette break. Let's go outside.'

They walked down the corridor, Marty following behind them like the boulder in Raiders of the Lost Ark. They pushed the back door open, which led them to a smoking area and beer garden, though the term garden was rather grandiose for what it was.

They stood under a sloping roof to protect them from the drizzle. Marty used a huge hand to shelter the cigarette from the wind while he lit it.

'Ask away, fellas. I've nothing to hide,' he said, blowing a lungful of smoke into the atmosphere.

'Did you see Gerald the night he died?'

'I believe I might've.'

'In the alley next to Baldwin's?'

'Yep.'

'Why?'

'Because, he'd nicked my spot. Everyone who's homeless knows that that doorway is the best in the town. The pipes from the shop next door give out a wee bit of warmth and Brownley's throw all its unsold food in the big bin outside.'

'And you wanted it back?'

'Too right I did. Gerald was a legend in town, but that was *my* spot. I couldn't believe it when I saw him lying in it with all his stuff.'

'What happened?'

'I pulled him up by his shirt and we had it out. Verbally, I might add, detectives.' He added the last word with a little wink, before carrying on. 'We came to an arrangement. He could have the spot for the night, and I could have some of his wares.'

'Wares?'

'Aye. Gerald had started dabbling in the world of drug dealing. I told him it was a stupid idea. Everyone knows that Stu has a monopoly on the area, and isn't shy about dealing with anyone who thinks they can muscle in on his patch.'

'And what did he say?'

'Told me he was making good money through it, and that he'd be off the streets before Stu even got wind of what he was doing. I told him that Stu probably already did know what he was doing, and that if I were him, I'd throw the rest of the drugs in the river and plead innocence.'

The thought of Marty Hesketh being afraid of anyone was almost humorous, but the myths and legends of Stu Finnegan's behaviour circled around Stonebridge like a cautionary tale. Even the police were afraid of him.

'You think Stu could've killed Gerald?' Adam asked.

'Mmhmm. And afterwards, he would've walked away without so much as a second thought. We done here?'

'One more question,' Adam said. 'Was it snowing when you spoke to Gerald?'

'No, it was sunny. Why?'

'No reason. Thanks for your time, dude.'

Adam held up a fist for Marty to bump. Marty looked at the fist, snorted derisorily at the gesture, and sauntered back to whatever unlawful activity awaited him in The Back Room.

'Smooth,' Colin said, as they left via the back gate.

4

THE SMILES

'HOW DO WE get our hands on some drugs, then?'

This was the question Adam posed to Colin, who looked at him with a furrowed brow.

'Not for consumption, obviously, but we need to talk to Stu, and buying the cheapest, least illegal drugs he has for sale is the obvious way in.'

'You want to break the law, just to try and see if Gerald was murdered? The police aren't arsed about the case, but if Whitelaw hears that we've been asking around and buying drugs in the process, you can bet he's going to take a sudden interest in you.'

'And who's going to grass us up? Stu?'

'Maybe someone will see us talking to him and put two and two together.'

'We've braved Marty Hesketh. I think we can take Mr. Finnegan.'

Colin sighed. He'd been dragged through enough nonsense in the past that had put his job—which he loved—in jeopardy. And now that he was manager, he had a lot more to lose. Still, Gerald starting to deal drugs and ending up dead not long after *was* suspicious.

'Look,' he said, at length, 'if we see him, we'll ask him about it. If not, it's no skin off my nose.'

'Grand,' Adam nodded. 'Are you heading to The Pacific tomorrow night?'

'Jeez, has it been another year already?'

THE SMILES WERE a mainstay of the North Coast's burgeoning music scene, and their annual Christmas gig was a time-honoured tradition. No matter where old friends had disappeared to—uni, jobs across the water or even further afield, years out, or emigration to the other side of the planet—the same faces always showed up for this event.

The Pacific was the chosen venue for this year's gig. It was a grotty dive bar with sticky floors and toilets that would have Ray Mears thinking twice about using them, but it had heart. You knew what you were getting when you turned up—warm beer and loud music—and that was enough to keep people coming back.

'No Helena tonight?' Colin asked, as Adam jumped into his car.

'Nah, she's been called in to A&E. Christmas, apparently, is a time when the general public drink too much and have too many accidents. Who knew?'

Colin drifted off from the kerb, and pressed a button on the dashboard, flooding the car with sixstarhotel's latest album.

'It's a crying shame that they've never hit the big time,' Adam shouted above the galloping bass and duelling guitars. 'Better than ninety percent of the nonsense in the charts.'

He quietened then, opting to play air drums for the rest of the journey. The Christmas gig always took him back to feeling seventeen again.

No responsibilities.

No worrying about bills or jobs or debt.

When the only stress in life was wondering why it was taking the girl you were texting so long to reply, and how many x's to put on the end of the message.

Colin pulled into a space that overlooked the ocean. The dark water looked to have swallowed a blanket of stars; the pinpricks of light pulsing off the calm surface. They got out and walked the short journey to the bar along the seafront, stopping to look at the huge mural that had recently been painted in tribute to a fallen comrade on the side of the building.

Inside, it was already sweaty. The windows were fogged with condensation and the air thick with sweat. Gunther, one of the support bands, were already playing, amps turned up to eleven and currently blasting through a punk rock version of *We Wish You A Merry Christmas*. A tentative mosh pit had started, while an elderly lady and her husband made their way to the nearest exit at speed, hands pressed firmly over their ears.

Adam and Colin watched the stage for a while, and when the band put down their instruments, made their way to the bar and ordered some drinks.

'Why aren't you drinking tonight?' Adam asked, as the bar man slid a pint in his direction.

'I've got my annual review tomorrow morning. I can't mark my first year as manager by turning up stinking of booze.'

'Fair point.'

Conversation was cut off as local heroes Split The Sky took to the stage. They'd disbanded years ago and reformed for a one-night-only affair, much to the delight of everyone in the room. The floor space was filled before a single note had been played, and the singer looked thrilled with the reception. He led the crowd in an acapella verse, before the instruments rushed in on a wail of feedback.

It was joyous.

Colin and Adam stood by the bar and soaked up every note. Friends they hadn't seen in a while congregated around them, though catching up was saved for when the band had finished.

When relative silence had descended again—after a number of encores that forced the band to play songs they'd already played once—stories of work, kids, and engagements were swapped and more drinks were bought.

While it was lovely to see everyone, Adam kept his eyes peeled for the arrival of Stu Finnegan. The plan was simple: ask for the smallest amount of drugs possible and while he was sorting it, probe him subtly for information. Once the transaction was complete, he'd flush the contraband down the nearest toilet.

A quarter of an hour later, Colin nudged Adam's arm and nodded his head towards the back of the room, for there stood Stonebridge's supplier of illegal goods.

'You actually doing this?' Colin asked.

'I'm actually doing this'.

He walked on shaky legs across the room, trying to look as natural as he could. The casual onlooker, if they'd caught Adam's approach out of the corner of their eye, might've described him as looking *too* laid back—like a caricatured version of The Fonz.

When he reached Stu, he stood nearby and tried to catch his eye. Stu smiled, spotting Adam's coy glances.

'We're not at a primary school dance, dude.'

'Ha!' Adam laughed. 'Good one. I'm just not sure how all of this works, you know?'

'What kind of thing are you after?'

'I don't know, really. I've got a tenner. What will that get me?'

'Little bag of weed.'

'Good,' Adam nodded. 'Yeah. A couple of spliffs will do just fine.'

Stu fished into his pocket and produced a small clear packet from it. Adam slipped him the ten pound note and took the goods, pocketing them before anyone could see what he was up to. Instead of walking away, Adam loitered.

'Can I help you with anything else, dude?' Stu asked.

'I hear there's a rival in town,' Adam said, raising his eyebrows conspiratorially.

'A rival? What are you on about?'

'Another dealer. Though, from what I hear, he won't be much trouble to you anymore.'

'Speak English, dude.'

'Someone else was selling drugs in town, but they were killed.'

'Ah, now you mention it, it rings a bell.' Stu scratched at a scab on his cheek, which was perhaps evidence of a recent scuffle. Adam wondered if this was a tell. If it was, he'd make a horrible poker player. 'It's a shame, but that's usually what happens to someone who tries to muscle their way onto my patch.'

'Really?' Adam whispered.

'No! Jesus! I don't go around whacking people because they're trying to take customers off me. People in this town know I get the good stuff, as you'll find out yourself soon. I take it you're a virgin?'

'I most certainly am not. As it happens, I've been with a couple of…'

'With drugs, I mean,' Stu interrupted.

'Oh, right. Yeah. In that case, yes, I am a virgin.'

'As I said, you'll see that my product speaks for itself. I don't need to go around battering people or intimidating them.'

'So you never spoke to Gerald?'

'Oh, we had words, but nothing physical. Trust me on that.'

His tone suggested that that was all he had to say on the matter. Adam thanked him for the drugs, hurried off to the toilet where he tipped the sweet-smelling cannabis into the filthy bowl and flushed it away forever. He washed his hands like Lady Macbeth, making sure none of the smell lingered on his skin, and finally re-joined his friends just in time for The Smiles.

He held off telling Colin what had happened, instead letting every other concern slip away as the music started. Looking around at the familiar faces as he let the folky goodness wash over him, he was gripped by a sudden melancholy. All of this—the camaraderie, old friends, the bands that he loved—all of this would one day come to an end, and it might never occur to them that *this* was the last time.

'I love you, dude,' Adam said to Colin.

'Don't be weird,' Colin replied, though he was smiling. He stretched an arm around his friend and pulled him close, before punching him playfully on the arm.

5

THE PROPOSAL

COLIN WAS SWEATING.

He hated formal meetings and he wasn't keen on suits and ties and buttoned-up shirts that felt like a boa constrictor had taken up residence around your neck.

The room felt like it was set up to intimidate, though they probably hadn't meant it that way. He sat in a hard, plastic chair facing three older, unsmiling gentlemen, whose suits looked like they cost a whole lot more than Colin's annual salary.

He pulled at his collar again, and answered their question about how he'd found his year as manager. He'd told them that it was a lot more responsibility, but that he had very much enjoyed it. He liked being in charge. He liked making sure the service users (he hated that word, but that's how the suits referred to the wonderful residents and he thought he'd keep it professional) had the best day they could possibly have.

The suits nodded along and then the head suit broke out into a wide smile. It was rather disconcerting.

'Mr McLaughlin, the service users here are very fond of you. We conducted a number of interviews prior to our meeting and they couldn't speak highly enough of you. A Mr, uh—' he checked his notes, 'McCullough…'

'Barry,' Colin interjected.

'Yes, Mr. McCullough was adamant that we should give you a pay rise.'

'That's nice of him.'

'So, Mr McLaughlin, how would you feel about continuing in the role?'

'Continuing?' Colin repeated. 'But I thought it was fixed term. Isn't Cindy coming back?'

'We're afraid not. Sadly, she's still unwell and has handed in her notice, which we have accepted. We were going to put an advertisement in the paper this week, but it seems you are the man for the job. If you'd like it, of course.'

Forgetting the norms of an interview, Colin jumped from his seat and shook each of the men's hands in turn, thanking them.

'I take that as a yes?' the lead interviewer asked, laughing.

'A huge one.'

WITH THE FORMALITIES completed, Colin drifted out of the room on a cloud and made a beeline for Barry, who he hugged. It wasn't a normal patient/carer moment, and Colin was sure Barry—a ninety-year-old man who'd fought in World War II—probably felt rather uncomfortable with the level of affection bestowed upon him. For now, Colin didn't care.

'What's all this in aid of, then?' Barry asked, when Colin had released him.

'You, you beautiful man, just secured my job for me.'

'I only said what I thought, son. If I thought you were a prick, I would've said that too.'

'And I appreciate it so much. You're a hero, and I get a bonus! Don't tell the others yet, though. Management want to do an announcement, you know?'

'Don't they know it's a retirement home? The news of your job is already out and forgotten about—Doris knew before you did!'

Colin patted him on the shoulder, and walked off to get him his tablets. When he returned with the small, white container full of colourful pills and a glass of water, Barry thanked him and then leaned in, conspiratorially.

'I've got an early Christmas present for you, young man.'

'Oh aye? PlayStation 5?'

'Ha! You should be so lucky. It's some information, about your case.'

He leaned closer still.

'It seems old Gerald was going up in the world before his untimely demise.'

'How do you mean?'

'Well, word has it that he was due to be the Santa in Baldwin's department store this year. He'd been for the fitting and everything.'

'But that's Tom Little's gig. Has been since I was a wee boy.'

'Twenty-four years,' Barry agreed. 'Would've been the big twenty-five this year. I don't know what Baldwin was thinking, but that's the word on the street.'

'The street?'

'Doris,' Barry said, nodding his head at the old lady in the corner with the purple rinse and the mouth moving at a hundred miles a minute. 'Nothing gets past old Doris.'

'Did she say anything else?'

'Plenty. But I can only just take in the headlines before I lose interest. Might be worth having a chat with Baldwin, if you can. He must have his reasons. Maybe something he says will shake a bit of information loose?'

'Good man, Barry. I'll see what I can uncover.'

'And while you're at the store, a nice bottle of brandy wouldn't go amiss for your helpful pal!' Barry shouted after the retreating Colin.

ADAM WAS ON one knee in the bedroom, looking in the mirror with the ring held aloft.

He'd always imagined proposing under the moon and stars, a picnic blanket laid out with a bottle of champagne waiting, but that was never going to happen in Northern Ireland. If he managed to find a moment when it wasn't raining, the constant wind rattling in off the sea would blow the picnic away, so Adam had resigned himself to doing it indoors.

Of course, asking the big question inside, in public, was also a no-go, in case of a negative response or a dog stealing the ring at the vital moment or some other unforeseeable incident. Best to do it in the confines of your own home, where other rooms were readily available to sulk in, if the answer wasn't what you wanted to hear.

He'd written a short speech on a piece of paper that was now damp with perspiration. It had curled at the sides and the ink was smudged, but Adam had read and re-read the words so many times that they were engrained in his head.

Now, all he needed to do was say them out loud and wait for an answer. One way or the other.

He puffed out his cheeks, slipped the ring box into his back pocket and walked out into the living room, where the unsuspecting Helena was lying on the sofa, half-watching Tipping Point and half dozing after her night shift.

Adam stopped suddenly.

He detested Tipping Point with every fibre of his being, and wondered if it being on television at the very moment he was going to pop the question was a bad omen.

'You okay?' Helena asked, peering over the sofa.

'Ah, yeah. I'm just going to get a drink. You want anything?'

'Ribena, please.'

Adam scurried away to the kitchen to regroup. He poured a drink but wasn't concentrating and it slopped over the side of the glass and all over the counter. Cursing, he grabbed a tea towel off the oven door's handle and wiped the spillage.

He couldn't think straight.

Bloody Ben Shepherd was living rent free in his head.

He took a few calming breaths, but could still hear the presenter talking kindly to the machine.

This wouldn't do. Maybe he'd wait until after the show, march in, turn the television off, get down on one knee and say his speech, and then show her the ring.

Yeah, that would do.

Having finished mopping up the puddle of lemonade, he threw the tea towel in the wash and returned to the living room.

'What's all the swearing about?' she asked, as she took her Ribena from him.

'Ah, spilled a load.'

'Goodness, I thought from the words you were using, you'd discovered a body or something.'

'Nah, all good. How's she doing?' he asked, nodding at the TV.

'In line for a couple of grand, I reckon. Fumbled a few soap questions, but brought it back with some rugby knowledge.'

They watched the rest, Adam enjoying not a single moment of it. When the jackpot had been won and the credits began to roll, he turned the television off and turned to look at her.

'What's going on?' she asked.

'Helena,' he said, his voice betraying him. 'I know you and me haven't been going out *that* long, but...'

'Adam, you're being weird. Are you breaking up with me or something?'

'No, nothing like that,' he said. 'Just let me finish.'

He composed himself and as he opened his mouth, his phone (which he thought he'd put on silent) started to ring. He pulled it from his pocket and pressed the red button.

'Who was that?' she asked.

'Colin. I can speak to him later.'

'It might've been important.'

The phone rang again and Helena told him to answer it.

'But…' he started.

'I need a shower anyway. Talk to your friend.'

She got up from the sofa and walked to the bathroom, while an angry Adam put the phone to his ear.

'This better be bloody good,' he said through gritted teeth.

'Oh, it is,' answered Colin.

6

A LITTLE SLIP UP

ADAM WAS STILL feeling raw when he got into his car and wondered, not for the first time, whether running around town trying to solve a crime—if it was a crime at all—was a good idea.

He realised that perhaps the energy he had devoted to those other "cases" was because his life had been empty at the time. There'd been no real job, no relationship and he'd been living with his mother. The thought of solving a crime was exciting, but maybe it was only exciting when you had the time to do it and nothing to lose.

Now, here he was, trying to ask the most important question he'd ever ask anyone, and instead of being able to say it, he was being called away to question an old man who'd been snubbed for this year's department store Santa role.

He started the engine, and sat stewing while waiting for the blower to defrost the windscreen. When it finally worked its magic, he reversed carefully out of the space and made his way into town.

COLIN HUDDLED IN the corner booth of the coffee shop, trying to keep away from the cold wind whistling in through the automatic door that was almost exclusively open. One hand was wrapped around a steaming mug of hot chocolate and the other scrolled through pictures on his phone.

It felt strange, judging people solely on their looks and a few spartan lines about their lives, but such was the way with dating apps.

Things were looking up for Colin. He'd landed a managerial role in a job he cared deeply about, and he was living in a decent enough flat in a nice part of town. But, truth be told, he was lonely.

Since Adam had found Helena, he'd seen less of his friend. Which, of course, was natural. And he was happy for him, but sometimes he wished that after a long day at work, he could come home and lie on the sofa and tell his girlfriend about his day.

So, here he was, scrolling through photos of girls in the hope that one would catch his eye. A few had, already, and they'd exchanged some messages but the chat had quickly died out.

What he really wanted was to meet someone the old-fashioned way—technology free. He wanted someone to catch his eye across the bar, to bump into someone as they pushed through a door at the same time; the pile of papers she'd be carrying would scatter and they'd spend a few laughter filled moments collecting them, their hands brushing on the last sheet.

He'd told this to Adam once.

Adam, in return, had told him that if he'd knocked a load of important papers out of a girl's hands in real life, she'd call him a couple of choice names, refuse his help, and that'd be that.

He was probably right.

A breeze blew through the coffee shop again, and with it came an unhappy looking Adam.

'You alright?' Colin asked, as Adam took the seat opposite him.

'I was about to ask Helena to marry me when you phoned.'

'Ah, man. Sorry! You should've told me to do one!'

'It's okay,' Adam said, softening. 'It probably wasn't the best way to do it anyway. Ben Shepherd, you know?'

Colin didn't know.

'Having the ring in the house is making me feel uneasy, is all,' Adam continued. 'I just hate all the pussyfooting around.'

'I hear you. I really am sorry. If I'd known, I would never have called you.'

'It's fine, honestly. What have you got?'

'Barry found out that Tom Little isn't going to be the Baldwin's Santa this year?'

'What?' Adam was gobsmacked. 'But he's as close to the real thing as it's possible to get.'

'I know. And apparently it was going to be his twenty-fifth year.'

'A quarter of a century? A landmark! Have you spoken to him?'

'No, I thought we'd go and see him now.'

'You know where he lives?'

'No, but I know where he works.' Colin pointed across the street at the pound shop which had taken up the prestigious space once held by M&S.

'Stonebridge's Santa Claus to pound shop seasonal drone. What a fall from grace.'

'Right?'

'Does Barry know who was going to be the Baldwin's Santa this year?'

'I'll give you three guesses,' Colin said, as he grabbed his stuff and slid out of the booth.

THE STONEBRIDGE POUND shop was a depressing place to be at the best of times, but at Christmas it was like walking into the seventh circle of Hell itself. It was heaving with bodies; little old ladies who battered their way through the crowd with walking sticks, stressed-looking mothers with screaming children who wanted every toy they came across, and flustered, middle-aged men who were simply panic buying whatever they could get their hands on.

Adam and Colin fought through the sea of people, searching for old Tom.

They found him, trying to placate a woman whose face was as red as a tomato. Someone, apparently, had taken the last roll of Paw Patrol wrapping paper.

'We have Peppa Pig,' Tom said, holding up a roll to show her.

'And how is that going to help?' the woman shouted back. 'My kids only like Paw Patrol. It's the only thing they watch. So how is this Peppa Pig roll going to work?'

Tom apologised, despite not having done anything wrong, and when she sighed and turned her back, he raised a middle finger in her direction. He just about managed to get his hand to his nose, turning the rude salute into a passable impression of a scratch. She gave him the evil eye and made her way towards the exit.

Tom picked up a pile of mince pie boxes and started to stack the depleted shelves.

'Mr Little,' Adam said, approaching him through the crowd. 'Would it be possible to have a few minutes of your time?'

'I'm a bit busy,' he said, looking over his shoulder. 'What can I help you with?'

'We have a few questions we'd like you to answer.'

'I'm behind schedule here. Can you tell me what you're looking for and I can guide you to an aisle?'

'It's about Gerald Agnew.'

He dropped the mince pie boxes at the mention of the name, and turned to give the boys his full attention.

'I've got a break in about twenty minutes. It's a short one, mind. Meet me out the front.'

HE EMERGED TWENTY-FIVE minutes later, his blue shop vest replaced with a heavy overcoat. His thick, white hair was combed to the side and his bushy beard bobbed with each step he took. He nodded curtly at them and led them to a side street, where he pulled a cigarette packet out of his pocket and lit up.

Watching the only Father Christmas you've ever known inhale from the toxic stick was an odd sensation, and a little bit of Adam's childhood died with the flicker of the lighter.

'Shame about poor Gerald,' Tom said. 'He was an annoyance round town, always asking for money and that, but freezing to death is no way to go.'

'He didn't freeze to death,' Adam said. 'He was killed.'

Tom looked sceptical.

'That's not what it said in the paper. Anyway,' he glanced at his watch, 'I know the two of you—what you get up to. What's this got to do with me?'

'How did it feel being canned from the Santa gig?' Colin said.

'Canned? God, you boys watch too much American TV. Look, I'd had a good run at it.'

'But you expected it to be you again this year, right?'

'Well, I assumed I'd be picked again, yes. Baldwin was making all the right noises, but in the end, he chose Gerald.'

'And how did you feel about that?'

'What do you want me to say?' He laughed. 'I was annoyed, naturally.'

'Decent money being Santa,' Colin said.

'Not to mention the kudos,' Adam added. 'Making loads of kids happy. To go from that, to having to deal with the likes of that woman who treated you like a slug on the bottom of her shoe. That must sting.'

'I know what you're trying to get me to say, but you don't know the half of it.'

'You must've been angry.'

'Yeah, alright, I was angry. Happy? How would you have felt? You're the king of Christmas for all those years and now you're having to stack shelves for hours on end, at my age. I was angry, alright? But not with Gerald.'

'Baldwin?'

Tom nodded. 'I always thought Kyle Baldwin was a stand-up guy. His father had been, so I thought his son would follow in the same mould. Sure, I'd heard the stories of how he treats some of his workers and stuff like that, but he was always dead on with me. And then I hear that he's gone and hired Gerald. Second hand. Didn't even have the cajones to tell me to my face. Got that bimbo secretary of his to do it for him.'

'So, what did you do?' Adam asked.

'What did I do? I did what every self-respecting Northern Irishman does when faced with a hardship—I went to the nearest pub and had a drink, bitched about it a lot and then I moved on.'

'And that's that?'

'That's that,' he nodded. 'Look, I know you two see yourselves as mini-Sherlocks. I've read the papers. You're good, better than that idiot Whitelaw. But I doubt there's a case here. Gerald was your classic drunk. If he didn't freeze to death, like the papers said, his liver probably gave up on him. It's no way to go, but it's not like it he didn't bring it on himself.'

'There's a Santa gig going now,' Colin said.

'Aye, he's been on the phone to me, ol' Kyle. I told him he could shove the Santa job up his…'

The end of the sentence was left unfinished, as Tom's manager chose the opportune moment to find him and remind him that break was over and his shift was due to start again.

Tom nodded at them, and told them that they were wasting their time. He wished them a Merry Christmas and then followed his boss back to work.

'I think if I'd actually heard Santa say the word "arse" then, it would've ruined my Christmas,' Colin said, as they left the side street.

7

BALDWIN

THE TOWN OF Stonebridge may well have been built around Baldwin's department store; such was its longstanding role in the community. The vast, red-brick building held the best plot in the town—you *had* to walk past it wherever you were going.

The ground floor was cosmetics. Attractive men and women with no visible pores or blemishes used this space to casually assault shoppers with expensive bottles of perfumes and face creams. Whatever you came in for, you'd leave the shop smelling like a perfumer after a bad day in the lab.

If you managed to make it through unscathed, a set of escalators whisked you to the first floor, where you'd be greeted by an array of women's clothing. Mostly aimed at a woman of a certain vintage, though more boutiques were opening up that appealed to the younger generations. Their designs were daring and provocative and drew frowns and tuts from the purple-rinsed ladies who'd stopped in for a new plastic rain bonnet.

The second floor was chaos. Appealing odours drifted out from the café into the nursery section. Screams of pleasure (and displeasure) sounded from the ToyTown section, as children's wishes for a new action figure or remote-controlled car were granted or dashed. In the far corner, a harried looking woman was overseeing a calendar stall that looked both temporary and low on stock.

Every surface was covered in twinkling lights and a huge Christmas tree filled the centre of the floor. It looked overblown, and very much like the one in that episode of Mr. Bean where he visits Harrods.

'Do you see him?' Adam asked.

Colin scanned the second floor, but there was still no sign of Kyle.

'The office is in the back,' Colin suggested. 'But I suppose we can't really just walk in there.'

'We could try.'

They spent a few minutes looking around the top floor, and when there was still no trace of the store's owner, they set off towards a set of double doors with STAFF ONLY signs screwed into them.

The doors opened into a small waiting room, manned by a blonde woman sitting behind a desk. She assessed them with catlike eyes, though greeted them with a warm smile.

'Can I help you?' she asked.

Adam looked at Colin, who shrugged and looked right back.

'We're, uh…' Adam started.

'Oh, sorry. Silly me. You're obviously here for the emergency seasonal staff interviews, right?'

'Right,' Adam said, before his brain had time to truly compute what she'd said.

'Mr. Baldwin shouldn't be too much longer. Please, take a seat,' she said, waving a hand at the line of chairs that were sat along a faded cream wall.

'In fact, do you mind if I just nip to the toilet? I'm a bit nervous.' Adam rubbed his stomach and made a face.

'No problem.'

They walked back out of the door and Adam made for the stairs. Colin grabbed the back of his jacket.

'Where are you going?'

'Home?' Adam said.

'What about the interview?'

'What *about* the interview?' Adam repeated. 'Do *you* want a job here?'

'No, but I think you should.'

'What?'

'Think about it. Your gardening work is seasonal, so you have a load of time on your hands. This is a great way to get a bit of extra money, which you'll need for the wedding, and also a good way to keep an eye on Baldwin.'

'We don't even know he's involved.'

'But what if he is?' Colin said. 'This is the perfect way to keep tabs on him.'

Adam knew it was a good opportunity, but explaining it to Helena would be weird. It was the kind of thing they'd discuss first, but he supposed she had a lot of A&E shifts coming up, and he had some spare time. Colin's point about a bit of extra cash in the pocket was a good one, too.

'I haven't prepared anything for an interview, though,' Adam said.

'Just tell him you're willing to work whenever, in whatever department you're needed in. You'll work yourself to the bone for the duration of the Christmas period, and be fully committed to the role for as long as you are employed.'

'Are you sure you don't want the job? Adam laughed.

'Knock 'em dead, tiger.'

'That might be the weirdest thing you've ever said to me,' Adam said, before heading back towards the staff only door.

THE WOMAN BEHIND the desk nodded towards Adam's stomach as he reappeared.

'All okay down there?' she asked.

'All good, thanks.' He felt his face redden somewhat, as he took a seat and waited.

He lifted a battered copy of The Stonebridge Gazette that was lying on one of the other chairs and flicked through it, finding nothing noteworthy. He threw it down again and smiled when he saw the woman looking at him.

'Lauren, by the way,' she said. 'I'm Mr. Baldwin's PA.'

'Adam.'

'Has it been your dream to work in a department store at Christmas?' she laughed.

'For just about as long as I can remember, yeah,' Adam said.

'Tell him that and the job's yours,' she said, winking, before turning back to her laptop.

Lauren was an attractive girl. Adam put her around the thirty-year-old mark. Her long, blonde hair looked silky in the bright, overhead lights and her smile was perfect. Adam wondered if Colin had clocked her, and thought that if he did get the job, maybe he'd try and play matchmaker.

Helena had often commented that it would be nice to have more couples to hang out with.

Baldwin's office door creaked open and a confident looking interviewee walked out. He gave Adam a lingering glare, like a sporting star might give the opposition before a big game. Maybe this dude was trying to psyche Adam out.

Adam chuckled when the guy had gone. If he cared that much about the job, he was welcome to it.

Kyle Baldwin appeared in the doorway. Thick hair slicked back with too much gel, striped shirt straining against the paunch of his belly, the elbows of his designer suit rubbed shiny from overwearing. His tie had little Christmas trees with googly eyes on them, that looked like his wife (if he had one) had convinced him to put it on and he'd succumbed to save an argument.

He looked at Adam, then to Lauren, and back to Adam.

'Can I help you?' he said.

'He's here for the interview,' Lauren said.

'I thought we were done?'

'Apparently not,' she said, motioning to Adam as if unveiling a new car.

'In that case,' Kyle said, motioning to Adam, 'follow me.'

Adam pushed himself up from the chair and did as he was told.

Kyle's office reeked of self-congratulation. Framed photographs of the man himself filled most of the walls; a comprehensive history of his time in charge of the store. These were interspersed with newspaper clippings and magazine articles about his pride and joy. A large window overlooked the main street, and a heavy oak desk filled most of the space, looking out of place in the pokey room.

'Sit, please,' he said, as he squeezed past the desk and sank into his expensive leather chair. 'Can I get you a glass of water?'

'No, I'm okay, thank you,' Adam said.

'In that case, let's begin.'

The interview lasted longer than Adam had been expecting. It started with the basics. Adam apologised for forgetting to bring a CV with him, but talked through his employment to date. He could see Kyle was impressed when he mentioned starting his own business.

After that, it moved on to hypothetical workplace scenarios and what you'd do if they happened. You'd have to be a moron to say the wrong thing, and Adam told him what he wanted to hear.

He watched Kyle tick the sheet of paper on his desk as he spoke, and when he finished, the boss asked the question he'd obviously been dying to ask from the start.

'Why do you want to work at Baldwin's?'

Because I want to know more about why you hired a homeless man as your Santa and not Tom, as per the norm. I also want to spy on you, to see if you had anything to do with Gerald's untimely demise.

That was the real answer. Instead, Adam once again told him what he wanted to hear: That Baldwin's was a Stonebridge institution, and that to work in this great building would be a privilege, nay, an honour. It would allow him to become part of the fabric of a town he loved, even if the job was only for a few weeks.

Something like that, anyway. He might've gone a bit overboard, but it did the trick. Kyle nodded expansively and wiped something from his eye. The man had an ego. When Adam had finished waxing lyrical about the Baldwin empire, Kyle threw this hand out and offered him the job on the spot.

Adam thought of Mr. Psyche-Out and smiled as he shook Kyle's sweaty hand.

8

THE DRUGS DON'T WORK

COLIN'S REGULAR GAME of five-a-side was facing the usual festive disruption. They were increasingly relying on friends of friends to fill the spots at the last minute as Christmas drew nearer, which had its advantages and disadvantages.

It was a good way to meet new people, and most of the lads who played were sociable and good-natured. They saw the game for what it was: a bunch of old friends having a fun time. Sure, occasionally, the odd mistimed tackle caused a few cross words and a bit of handbags, but overall, it was a friendly game.

On the very odd occasion, someone turned up in studded boots (a no-no on the AstroTurf pitch), thinking that they were Stonebridge's answer to Messi. They always ended up souring the game and were never invited back. If you were the one who invited them, you were in the bad books too.

Nick was in the bad books tonight.

His mate Phil—Alice-band holding back longish hair and shin guards so small they may as well have been playing cards—was ruining the game by tackling late, rarely passing the ball, and mouthing off when things didn't go his way.

Colin was furious, and was trying his best not to let it show. He'd been caught by one of Phil's studs on the shin, and blood had been dribbling down his leg since. He wasn't one to let his emotions get the better of him, but he was biding his time until the chance for revenge reared its head.

With ten minutes left, Ross played a ball down the side of the pitch, and Colin saw his chance. As Phil collected the ball, he looked up to assess his options and was subsequently flattened against the wall. It was more of an ice hockey style tackle, and would've been a straight red in the Premier League.

Here, it received little complaint, and as Phil lay prone, trying to persuade air to enter his lungs, Colin received a few pats on the back as he walked away from the scene of the crime, ready to form a wall for the deserved free kick.

Phil got up a minute later, though his swagger was gone and he steered well clear of Colin for the rest of the game.

At the end, everyone made their way from the pitch to the bar for the customary post-match pint.

By now, with the edge of his competitiveness blunted and justice served, Colin felt bad. He approached Phil, who was sitting in a booth with Nick watching the Champion's League game on the big screen TV, and offered his apologies.

Phil waved them away graciously, though did take Colin up on the offer of a drink, which Colin ordered and brought back to the table.

'Cheers,' he said, clinking glasses.

Talk turned to the game on TV, and to the weekend fixtures, and to how much Phil had won on a bet the previous evening.

At this point, Phil took a packet out of his pocket and laid it on the table. He took some items from it, and Colin saw that he was setting about rolling a joint. The stench of the marijuana hit the back of Colin's nose, and he looked around the room to see if this blatant illegal activity was being clocked by anyone else.

Apparently, he was the only stick-in-the-mud, as everyone else had barely glanced before going on with their conversations. Colin couldn't believe that Phil was being so nonchalant about it.

'Aren't you worried someone will say something?' Colin said.

'Nah,' Phil replied. 'Everyone's at it, aren't they?'

He picked up a filter and placed it in the roll, before sprinkling the little buds in. Once he was finished, he cleared up the table and picked the joint up, placing it behind his ear for later.

'Do you buy from Stu?' Colin asked.

'Usually, aye. Funny story, actually. There was word around campus about a month ago that there was a new dealer on the block. Much cheaper. So, we went and found him, bought from him and went back to halls. The new stuff wasn't doing anything for us, and after a few joints we realised that the new guy had sold us tea. Can you believe that?' he laughed.

'That is ballsy. Did he not think you'd notice?'

'I don't know what he was thinking.' Phil took a sizeable gulp of his pint. 'But we thought we'd go and teach him a lesson. We were a hundred quid down.'

'I thought you said he was cheaper?'

'Twenty for a big bag is decent. Stu would be charging closer to forty. Should've known it was too good to be true. Anyway, me and my friends had been drinking, but we go looking for this geezer, plan to show him what's what.'

He took another hit of his pint, and Colin had the distinct impression that Phil had watched one too many Guy Ritchie films in his lifetime. He'd never heard someone from Stonebridge use the word geezer, but then he didn't run in circles that bought drugs and doled out punishments, either.

'And did you show him what's what?'

'We did. Gave him a bit of a duffing. Nothing too much, you know. When he was on the ground, we found his money and took back what he'd taken from us. And a wee bit more for the trouble he'd caused us.'

'Did you kill him?' Colin whispered.

'Oh, God no,' Phil said, looking sideways at him. 'Jesus, it was only twenty quid each. I'm not bloody Scarface.'

'You're sure he was alive when you left him?'

'Sure. He was pushing himself back up when we were leaving, turning the air blue with the names he was calling us.'

Colin didn't need to ask who the new dealer was. He assumed the stricken man was Gerald, and wouldn't put it past the fella to put tea in a bag and pass it off as weed. Not many people would go and challenge him when they figured they'd been tricked.

But, Phil's retribution had been a month ago. Gerald only died last week, so Colin figured that the pocket-Ronaldo next to him had nothing to do with his actual death.

It certainly begged a question, though.

Who else had Gerald Agnew wronged?

9

FIRST DAY JITTERS

ADAM POURED A bowl of cereal for himself, and one for Helena. He carried it from their kitchen to the living room, where his wife-to-be (if she said yes when he finally got around to asking the question) was sitting on the sofa.

He handed her the bowl and she pressed play on the next episode of Superstore. For the next twenty minutes, they watched and ate, before Adam got up.

'I still can't believe you got a job without telling me,' she laughed.

'It was all a bit quick,' he replied.

'You're telling me!'

'I just thought that the extra money wouldn't go amiss, you know? Plus, you're working all hours. At least this way I can't get myself into mischief.'

'More mischief, you mean. How is the case going?'

'Not sure, really. There are a couple of suspects who could've been behind it, but it's hard to narrow it down.'

'Stu?'

Adam had been filling Helena in on the breaking news as they got it.

'He's one of them,' Adam nodded. 'Didn't like that there was another dealer on his patch. Colin just told me about some lad he played football with last night who beat Gerald up a month or so ago, but I don't think he's in the frame. Then there is Tom Little, the regular Santa, and Kyle Baldwin.'

'Why would Kyle kill the man he'd only recently hired as his new Santa, though?'

'See?' Adam said, throwing his hands in the air. 'None of it makes sense. If it wasn't for the footprints in the picture you took, I'd be agreeing with the police that it was just a nasty accident.'

'But you don't think it is, right? So, what's next?'

'Not sure. I'm going to ask around at work, see if Kyle and Gerald had any beef. Maybe Kyle regretted what he'd done in not hiring Tom, went to tell Gerald he'd made a mistake, and the two got into an argument.'

'Sounds unlikely,' Helena said.

And she was right. None of it was seeming likely right now. They needed to either start asking the right questions, or accept that DI Whitelaw knew what he was doing. There was a first time for everything, after all.

He kissed her on the forehead and went to the bedroom to get dressed for his first day.

BY LUNCHTIME, he was regretting ever having walked into that backroom and accepting the job.

The crowds were mental.

His hands were hurting from folding so many clothes and he didn't know where anything was yet, so received many snooty remarks from little old ladies in a hurry, like he was some sort of usurper in their cherished store.

Whoever was in charge of the sound system had played the same five Christmas songs on loop. In his three hours of works, he'd heard *It's Beginning To Look A Lot Like Christmas* twelve times.

Twelve!

He was beginning to think that anyone who worked here could be behind Gerald Agnew's killing. Surely hearing that song that many times in one shift was enough to drive anyone to murder.

He was thankful when his break time came around. He escaped off the floor and into the staffroom, where three others were engaged in a heated debate. He shuffled past them and pulled his sandwiches from the fridge, and when he looked up all eyes were on him. An old lady with white hair, who introduced herself as Carol, had just finished talking and they looked like they expected him to join in.

'What are you talking about?' Adam asked, sitting down near them.

'We're discussing the weirdest body part,' Carol said. 'Nancy thinks it's body hair and I think it's the bones in your ear.'

'Which is ridiculous,' argued a young man with the beginnings of a moustache. 'They do a vital job. Whereas, the milk teeth are the stupidest thing known to man.'

'Explain.'

'Well, they hurt babies like a bitch and only last six years or something. And when they fall out it's equally as distressing.'

'So, what would you suggest as an alternative?' Carol asked.

'Metal teeth that last a lifetime,' concluded the moustachioed man.

Adam reckoned he had given this argument a lot of thought, and had practiced the finer points over a milkshake or two with his friends. If he had any, which Adam thought unlikely.

'So?' they said, rounding on him.

'I'm not sure, really. I'll give it some thought and get back to you.'

Silence descended upon the room, so Adam ate his food. When he had finished, he asked the others: 'What do you reckon to this business with Gerald Agnew?'

'Who?' the boy said.

Carol seemed to be in charge of this rag-tag group, as she spoke for them. She shushed the boy with a withering look.

'The people who work here were very confused as to what Kyle was thinking, though of course we'd never say that to him. We'd be out on our ears. We also felt very sorry for poor Tom, who would've been celebrating a landmark occasion had he been chosen. There was talk of walkouts, in solidarity, but…'

'You'd rather keep your job than show your support,' Adam said.

'Well, when you put it like that.'

'What's Kyle like?' Adam asked.

'He's a lovely man. Cares about the company.' She cast an eye around as if he might be listening through the walls, before whispering, 'But he will occasionally do things that raise an eyebrow.'

'And they always seem to come after he's had a meeting with his father, who is still on the board of directors,' added Nancy.

'What kinds of things?' Adam asked.

'Moving the boutiques around, which confuses the old dears. Changing the menu in the café, which also confuses the old dears,' Carol smiled. 'Generally upsetting the old dears, I suppose you could say.'

'No one here wanted Gerald to be the Santa,' Nancy chimed in, seemingly annoyed that Carol was pussyfooting around the issue. 'Tom was made for the role—natural beard, white hair, a bit round. Whereas, Gerald is a big stringy fella who reeks of BO. Hardly the message you want to send out to the children who come to visit.'

'But no one challenged him?' Adam asked, causing the three to look sheepish. He got up to leave. 'Oh, one last question. Who do I talk to about the playlist?'

LAUREN WAS WHERE she was last time Adam had seen her—behind the little desk outside Kyle's office. She wiped at her eyes as he pushed his way through the door, and greeted him with a smile that looked painted on.

'You okay?' he asked. 'Sorry, I didn't mean to barge in.'

'Oh, yeah. Sorry, just something silly. Don't worry.'

'You sure? Anything I can help with?'

'No, honestly, I'm grand,' she said. 'What's up with you? Don't tell me you're quitting already.'

'I might be if someone doesn't fix the playlist,' he replied.

'Ah, that. We have this argument every year. Kyle likes to keep the playlist short and sweet and on repeat. Thinks our demographic find the repetitive nature of the songs comforting.'

'Whereas the people who work here find it drives one of the unpacking knives closer to their wrists each time Justin Bieber's *Mistletoe* starts again.'

She laughed at that.

'Look, I'll see what I can do. I might be able to sneak one extra song a day in there. Gotta take it slow or he'll be onto us, although he's been a bit distracted the past week or so, so we might get away with it.'

'We?' Adam repeated.

'Well, yeah. I mean, *I'm* perfectly happy with the playlist.' She winked. 'But I'll change it for you, if it makes you happy.'

'It would,' he nodded. 'Start with The Darkness.'

'Oh, let's not go crazy. Some of our clientele might drop dead at the sound of wailing guitars. We'll compromise on *Wonderful Christmastime*.'

They laughed again, causing Kyle to open his door and check on the cause of the merriment. His suit was an outlandish red tartan today.

'What's going on?' he asked.

'Oh, Adam's just telling me about some of the shenanigans on the shop floor today.'

'You're enjoying it, then?' Kyle asked, suddenly beaming, and Adam nodded.

'Oh, before I go,' Adam said, turning back to Lauren. 'I meant to ask, if it's not too weird, if you're single? My friend, who I was in with yesterday, was very complimentary, is all.'

'That's very sweet,' she smiled.

Adam glanced across at Kyle, who was looking at her like he wanted to know the answer to the question, too, which struck him as a little creepy. The man was probably fifteen years her senior, and a little more on top. She glanced across at him before answering, like she'd been aware of his gaze.

'As it goes, I am,' she said.

10

THE SCENE OF THE CRIME (IF IT WAS A CRIME TO BEGIN WITH)

UNSURE OF WHAT to do next, Adam and Colin did what they normally do—filled their bellies and hoped the sheer amount of greasy breakfast food would lend them some inspiration.

It didn't.

All it did was make them sluggish.

Colin sat back in his chair and wished he could undo a button on his trousers.

'Do you think we just sack it all off?' Adam asked. 'It feels like it's going nowhere.'

'It does feel like that,' he agreed. 'But we've never given up on any of the others. Why this one?'

'With the others, it was clear that there was definitely a crime. With this… I don't know. Maybe he did just slip.'

'Maybe. But what about the footprints? They must count for something.'

'The footprints are the only thing stopping me from throwing the towel in, however much I want to.' Adam went to scoop a mouthful of beans into his mouth, but stopped halfway, setting the fork down again.

'We've been through the suspects again, but no one stands out. Maybe we go and have a look at the spot where you found him?'

'Could do. Won't the police have been through his stuff?'

'Not if they are as dim-witted as they usually are. If they were convinced what happened to him was an accident, I reckon they'll have left his bedding and stuff like that.'

'Worth a look,' Adam said.

They got up and paid at the till, before waddling out of the shop and heading towards the alley. On the way, Adam told Colin about Lauren's availability and, at first, Colin berated him for mentioning his name. However, the more Colin ruminated on that little nugget, the more he started to smile.

Kyle's PA was beautiful, and Adam said she seemed a bit of a laugh, too.

He apologised to Adam for going off on one, and asked for more details, of which there weren't many.

'Except,' Adam said, 'I got her number for you.'

He pulled out his phone and read the number aloud, while Colin typed the digits into his phonebook and saved it. He'd text her later, once he'd had time to think about what he was going to say.

The simple "hey" of yesteryear was seen as lazy. You needed a USP, at least in the world of online dating.

'What should I say?' he asked.

'Just ask her out for a drink or something,' Adam replied. 'Keep it simple.'

If he'd known ten years ago that Adam Whyte would be giving him dating advice, Colin might have ended it all there and then.

Still, he was thankful that his friend was being a good wingman. He thanked him again as they turned into the alley where Adam had almost stumbled over the body of Gerald Agnew.

THE ALLEY LOOKED different in the cold light of day.

Of course, that was, in large part, down to the fact that there was no body now. But there were other differences, too. The snow had melted, exposing the ground and the graffiti looked less urban and cool than it did at night; now it looked like the deranged scrawling of a talentless lunatic.

Adam and Colin walked up the narrow alley and stood by the pole. The blood had been washed off, but that wasn't what Adam was looking at—he was studying the ground.

Small metal studs surrounded the pole, driven into the ground. Adam had seen these before in areas where slippage might occur, and knew they were there to create friction with your shoe.

The snow that night had just fallen. It was fluffy and soft, so was in no way a slipping hazard. Adam pointed out the little metallic domes and explained his thinking. Colin nodded along.

'Let's have a look at where he was sleeping.'

They walked a few more steps down the alley and looked into the little nook where Gerald had been calling home.

There was a nervous looking old man in there, his earthly belongings scattered around a frayed and filthy sleeping bag. He appraised them with bloodshot, worried eyes and began to stammer.

'Don't make me move, officers. It's cosy and…'

Adam cut him off.

'We're not police. You're safe. We're just looking for Gerald's stuff.'

'Why?'

'We're looking into his death.'

'That's good of you boys,' he said. 'Gerald was a pal, and I know he'd be happy with me taking his place.'

'Isn't it Marty's place?'

'In a matter of speaking, but he won big at the poker and is treating himself to a couple of nights in a guest house. Said I could have his spot in exchange for a few ciggies. Nice for some, isn't it?'

'Has anyone been to look through Gerald's things? Police?'

'Nah, no one. And I'm an honest gentleman, you understand? I've not touched anything, except the fags, 'cos he's not going to need them where he's gone. Everything else is there as he left it.'

'What's your name?'

The man swept a hand through his thick mane and seemed to consider whether the question was a trick one. Seemingly, he didn't think so, though he still appeared cagey when he told them he was called Mick.

'Nice to meet you, Mick,' Adam said, as he began poking through the remnants of Gerald's life, which didn't amount to much.

There was a busking hat and a guitar with all but one of the strings missing. An old, tattered sleeping bag and an ancient MP3 player that had been drained of battery many moons ago. A heavy winter coat that the paramedics must've thought another homeless person could make use of, so tossed it back on his pile before they'd carted him off.

Adam peeled back the sleeping bag, and found a number of small bags of weed. Or what looked like weed, at least. It could well have been tea, going on Gerald's past form.

'Were there any more of these?' he asked.

'What are you trying to say?' Mick said, looking affronted.

'I'm not accusing you of anything, man. I'm only asking if these were all the drugs Gerald had.'

'As far as I know. I've been here constantly, pretty much since he died, and no one has touched anything, and I've certainly not. Marty wasn't even interested. He's into the harder stuff.'

'Haven't you considered selling it?'

'And have Stu Finnegan all over me? No thank you, sir. I'd rather keep my face the way it is.'

'Did he have words with Gerald, do you know?'

'Aye, he had words alright, but that was that, in fairness. Or so I was told. When we saw him coming down the road, we all scarpered. Gerald stood firm, and I think Stu could see that he wasn't going to need a duffing. That he was a reasonable man. That this was his turf.'

'And that was that?'

'Aye.'

'Do you know who Gerald was selling to?'

'He wasn't at it for very long. His heart wasn't in it, to be fair. Who is going to buy drugs off a tramp? He did sell some to a couple of the wee uni lads and did the dirty on them. Paid the price for that with a black eye and a couple of sore ribs.'

'And they left him after that?'

'Aye. That old man who used to be Santa came down a couple of times, but Gerald refused to sell to him. Thought 'cos he had taken his Baldwin's gig that the old Santa was trying to buy drugs and then get him in trouble, so he told the guy where to go.'

Adam thought about that for a while. They'd spoken to Tom and he'd never mentioned anything about visiting Gerald with the intention of buying drugs. Maybe they should speak to him again.

They thanked Mick for his help, and turned to leave.

'It's a shame poor Gerald has passed on. He seemed excited about the future, you know? Said he had irons in the fire and that, with any luck, he'd be off the streets by new year.'

'What did he mean?' Adam asked.

'Beats me,' Mick replied, cracking open a bottle of cheap cider.

They figured the fizz of the Frosty Jack's signalled the end of Mick's helpfulness, and left him to it.

11

ANOTHER LITTLE MEETING

TOM PUSHED HIS plate away and wiped his lips with a napkin, making sure to be thorough. Tomato soup was a no-go during his Santa days, for fear of spilling some onto his white beard. It wouldn't do well to greet a child warmly, only to be met with a horrified expression when their small little mind mistook soup for blood. Zombie Santa was not a good look.

Now that he wasn't bound with the chains of St. Nick, and with the cold weather zeroing in on his old bones, he could do whatever he liked, and that included having two bowls of forbidden soup at lunch if he wanted.

He smiled to himself and pulled the paper closer, though there wasn't much going on in the town. A few drink driving offenders were being made an example of in the run up to Christmas, which he saw as a good thing. Aside from that, the only thing that interested him was that Stonebridge FC had lost to local rivals (again) in football, and the manager was bullish about the prospects of being fired in his press conference.

The sooner he left, the better, Tom thought.

And then, all thoughts deserted him as two familiar faces walked into his little slice of sanctuary. He lifted the paper high, covering his face, in the hope that he hadn't been spotted.

ADAM AND COLIN closed the door behind them, keeping the cold breeze locked out. They'd watched Tom enter the café about twenty minutes ago and hoped to catch him on the way out, make it seem like it was a chance encounter.

Unfortunately, Adam had to get back to work, and thus Father Time had forced them to act.

They slipped into the chairs opposite and Tom lowered the paper, resignation plastered across his face.

'I assume this isn't a coincidence?' he asked, setting the paper aside.

'Correct,' Colin said. 'We thought another little chat might be useful. You see, we've heard whispers about you.'

Tom looked genuinely confused.

'Not here, lads. Too many ears,' he said. 'Let's go for a walk.'

Tom left them and approached the counter, paying his bill and putting on a jolly show for two small children who were sat near the till. He may not be the official Baldwin's Santa, but he was still the closest thing Stonebridge had. As he walked away, the children were positively vibrating in their seats and their mother had a huge grin plastered across her face.

'Shall we?' he asked, when he'd wrapped himself up.

They left the café, and the shrill bite of the wind was most unwelcome as they stepped out onto the bustling street.

'Last time you told us you had no beef with Gerald,' Colin said. 'That you hadn't been to see him.'

'Beef?'

'You know, no problems, no ill-feeling.'

'Ah. Why beef?'

'I don't know,' Adam shrugged.

'So, why were you visiting him?' Colin said, hoping not to get bogged down in the origin of slang.

'I wasn't. I hadn't,' Tom spluttered.

'It might look, to the police, let's say,' Colin shrugged, 'that you claiming you hadn't been anywhere near him and evidence emerging that you in fact *had* been to see him, as troublesome.'

'Evidence?'

'Eye-witness. Saw you a couple of times.'

'Okay, okay. I went to see him a few weeks after he'd been announced, but it wasn't on Santa business. It was to do with…' He looked around to make sure no one was nearby and listening in. '…Drugs.'

'Drugs?'

'I've got terrible glaucoma. I've been on all sorts of medication, and none of it is helping. I can feel my eyesight going, and it's a scary feeling—I wouldn't wish it on my worst enemy. One of the young boys in work was telling me that, in America, medical marijuana is prescribed for it. So, I thought I'd go and see him.'

'But he thought you were trying to frame him. Buy the drugs and then go grass him up.'

'And why would I do that?'

'Don't be naïve,' Colin laughed. 'You dob him in, he loses the job and the money, and you get your throne back.'

'Money?'

'Yeah, the money for being Santa.'

Tom laughed. 'Boys, I've been the big man for many years and I've not received a penny for my troubles. It's more of a pride thing.'

'But Gerald was getting paid for it. That's what we were told.'

'And look where it got him,' Tom sighed. 'And now, if there really is nothing else, I hope I don't see you two again in the near future.'

They watched him walk away towards his place of temporary work, and Adam pulled his coat sleeve up to check the time.

'Balls,' he said. 'I'm going to be late if I don't get a wiggle on.'

'No worries,' Colin said. 'I'll see you soon.'

Colin headed back towards the café they'd been in with Tom, his stomach rumbling at the thought of a big lunch. He sat down at the same table, which had now been cleared, and perused the menu.

When the waitress came, he ordered a Christmas dinner with all the trimmings, and then pulled his phone out.

He went to the messages and composed a new missive to Lauren. It took him a while to word it correctly, not wanting to come across as too keen or too aloof, and when he was happy, he re-read it a couple more times to make sure it was actually okay.

Before he could chicken out, he pressed send and then put his phone back in his pocket. He couldn't stand glancing at it every couple of seconds to see if the message had been read, or if there was a reply.

Instead, he picked up the paper and skimmed it. The smell of food wafting from the open kitchen was mouth-watering, and he wished it would hurry up, though upon flicking through a few more pages, the smell of meat and potatoes cooking was suddenly the last thing on his mind.

Buried deep within the paper was a mention of Stu Finnegan. There was no photo, but there were some details. Apparently, he had been caught beating up a student at Stonebridge University's campus. Stu claimed the guy owed him money, which turned out to be less than £20. The guy who owed the money was in hospital with a fractured eye-socket, though was also in trouble for buying drugs in the first place.

Talk about adding insult to injury.

Colin took a photo of the story and closed the paper.

Stu Finnegan had told Adam that he never needed to resort to violence, or something to that effect. He had definitely said he was in no way involved with what had happened to Gerald. Mick had backed that up, but had also been slurping from a giant bottle of cheap cider, so could they take his words as gospel?

Surely if Stu was willing to batter someone for the sake of seventeen pounds, he'd be more than ready to engage in physical violence with someone who was undercutting him and muscling in on his empire.

Colin didn't fancy broaching the subject with the maniac drug dealer, and hoped that the police might get a confession out of him while they were holding him in the cells.

His phone buzzed and what appeared on screen knocked all thoughts of Gerald, Stu and fractured bones out of his head.

He had a message from Lauren and it ended with two kisses.

12

THE PROPOSAL (PART DEUX)

THE GROUNDS OF The Rose Gardens were vast and beautiful. In the centre of the estate sat a large manor house, its balustrades, towers and turrets harking back to a grander time. Intricately carved grotesques guarded each corner of the old stone building. Inside was accessible by the wide, wooden door, currently being guarded by a National Trust volunteer who was shivering despite her thick woollen coat.

The endless blue sky and the light dusting of snow that coated the herbaceous borders and manicured lawns lent the scene a postcard quality, which pleased Adam enormously. It was the perfect scene to describe when answering the 'How did he propose?' question.

Adam and his unsuspecting wife-to-be took an easy stroll through the famous rose gardens. Of course, because it was winter, the vibrancy and definition of the flowers were not at peak beauty, but there was still something wonderful about the colours and the shapes.

There were other people milling about, scarves knotted around necks and coffees in hand, though Adam was trying his best to zone everyone else out.

While Helena was reading an information board about the formation of the gardens and how the owner nearly went bankrupt while trying to fulfil his dream, Adam patted his pocket and pulled the ring box out. With tears in his eyes, he lowered himself down on the grass behind her, the life-changing words on his lips. Something soft and wet squelched under his knee.

The stench of dog dirt reached his nose and made him retch. Thankfully, he had the presence of mind to stow the ring in his pocket before he choked audibly.

Helena turned around to find Adam on the ground, checking the soggy mess on his best trousers.

'What's up?' she asked, nose wrinkled.

'I was tying my bloody shoelace and I landed in this pile of…' Adam motioned to the immense stain. 'What a nightmare.'

'It's okay, we can go to the café and get you cleaned up. You can splash some soap onto it.'

More like set fire to them, he thought, though didn't argue. He needed to propose today, and if it meant doing it with slightly dirty trousers, that would have to do. Maybe it would be funny in those future retellings, though he didn't think so.

They walked back towards the more modern building which housed the café, and went in. The exposed metal work and glass walls allowed uninterrupted views of the landscape. Helena ordered a hot chocolate and settled in the corner, while Adam excused himself.

In the toilets, he pumped what felt like gallons of soap onto the desecrated area and wiped at it with a thick wad of cloth. Instead of coming off, the soap simply made the mess runnier and—if possible—smellier. Now it smelt like poo with top notes of harsh chemical.

Cursing, he held his knee to the air dryer for a while, spreading the stench of the muck around the confined space. He apologised to the other guy at the sink, who wrinkled his nose and left.

Helena grimaced as he sat down, and offered him a sip of her drink. He suggested they continue their walk, and she nodded. They walked outside, the stink following them, and bumped into Colin, who wasn't alone.

'What have we here, then?' Adam asked, introducing Helena to Lauren.

'He was very persistent,' Lauren said, rolling her eyes comically. Colin gave her a playful shove. It seemed they'd already become comfortable with one another.

'Thought we'd come for a wee walk,' Colin said. 'What happened to your knee?'

'He fell foul of dog excrement,' Helena answered.

'Nasty.' Colin pulled a face. 'You going home now?'

'We we're going to go for a walk too.' Helena said.

'We could make up a foursome?' Colin suggested.

Adam moved slightly behind Helena and shook his head, holding up his ring finger. Before Colin could reply, Lauren spoke.

'Aren't you supposed to be in work today, Adam?'

'I don't think so,' Adam said.

'The rota got changed. Didn't you get the email? Shirley was sick and Freddie jacked it in, so you were needed today, I think.' She pulled out her phone and scrolled through some emails, before holding it up to him. 'You're supposed to start at 1.'

'Balls,' he said, checking his watch. He only had an hour to get home, get changed and get to Baldwin's. Lauren apologised for being the bearer of bad news.

'Sorry,' he said to Helena, before bidding goodbye to Lauren and Colin and hightailing it back to the car.

HEAVY TRAFFIC AND slow walkers combined to make Adam late for work. He'd checked his watch nervously as he'd tried to shuffle his way past the walking dead of Stonebridge, and had decided that if he was going to be late, which he was, he'd simply slope onto the shop floor and pretend that he wasn't late at all—that'd he'd been here for a while and had forgotten to sign in.

Sadly, that plan was highjacked by Kyle, who was standing by the escalator looking at his own, much more expensive watch. Adam tried to glide past him on the moving stairs, but Kyle beckoned him back, causing Adam to have to walk backwards one step each time the stairs moved to keep stationary.

'What time do you call this?' he asked, as Adam lapsed into a sort of mechanical moonwalk.

'1:03pm.'

'And what time am I paying you from?'

'1pm.'

'Hmmm, that leaves me in a quandary,' Kyle said, adopting a pensive look. 'What to do? What to do?'

'Don't pay me for those three minutes,' Adam suggested.

'No, no. I'm an honest man and I'd rather give you the money than not.'

'There's no problem, then, is there?' Adam said, his mood darkening. He stopped treading the steps and let them sweep him up to the next floor. He stored his stuff in his locker and made his way to ladieswear, where he began mindlessly folding and hanging the clothes that had been abandoned after being tried on in the changing rooms.

He didn't have to be here. The job was a cover to get information about Kyle's involvement with Gerald Agnew, and he could jack it in right now. Tell the boss where to stick his job and his precious three minutes.

But, upon reflection, he felt like he hadn't made the most of the opportunities he'd been handed to their full potential. He had a wealth of workers here who knew Kyle better than most, and he'd barely spoken to any of them. Most employees had some sort of gripe against their boss, and it was time to exploit that.

For the rest of his shift, he broke the mould. He walked around, doing what he needed to do, but had a couple of insightful chats at the same time.

Tina in cookery implied Kyle had a temper.

Alison in home electronics conceded that, once, she'd heard Kyle scream at an employee in his office because his coffee was delivered cold.

Konrad in gardening cast a few furtive glances around, before telling Adam that Kyle was a straight-up… four letter word. Adam blushed as he thanked him for his insight.

It was helpful stuff, but then something occurred to him. Lauren would surely be a fount of knowledge—everyone bitched about their boss. He made a beeline for the back room, but Lauren's desk was empty. He made a mental note to catch her at some stage, and headed back to the shop floor.

And, as time ticked toward his shift ending, Adam felt a bit better. He had a background now, and he fully believed that Kyle had something to do with Gerald's death. It was too suspicious that the year he got picked to be Santa for the store, something bad happened to him. Especially when taking his chequered history into consideration.

Now, he just needed hard evidence.

On his way out, Kyle stopped him and apologised for being pedantic that afternoon. Stress, he said. This time of year always got to him. Adam held up a placating hand and told him he knew how it was, and not to worry, and that *he* was sorry for his tardiness. He started towards the door, before turning back.

'I'm assuming the Santa position is up for grabs now?'

'You're a bit young, son,' Kyle laughed, and Adam joined in, though it was a feeble attempt at humour.

'My granda said he might be interested, depending on the moolah.'

'Ah, sadly, we don't pay. Tom did it for two decades and was glad to do it for the pride of saying he was the Baldwin Santa.'

'Grand. It's just, I heard Gerald was getting some money for it.'

'Who told you that?' Kyle asked, tersely.

'Can't remember.'

'Look,' he said, softening. 'We didn't want it getting out, but we were paying Gerald to see if we could get him off the street. You know what they say about charity?'

'It begins at home?'

'Well, that, too. But I meant, if you broadcast it, it ain't charity. That's why we kept it quiet.'

He slapped Adam's face, twice. The first was light and playful and the second had a bit of venom behind it, or so it seemed. Perhaps Adam imagined it, but his cheek certainly stung as he made his way out into the darkening street.

'See you tomorrow,' Adam said.

13

FINNEGAN'S PLACE

COLIN'S FIRST DATE with Lauren went well. At least, *he* thought it did.

They'd stomped through acres of woodland before enjoying a slice of cake and a mug of tea in the café. Lauren was a good laugh and easy to talk to; didn't mind taking the mick out of herself, which Colin enjoyed. She was also beautiful, and after a few hours together, he could feel the excitement bubbling in his stomach, though he was trying to contain himself, in case she didn't feel the same way.

He'd suggested meeting up again as they'd got into their cars and she'd seemed keen. He'd suggested a few dates, and she'd said that she'd need to check her calendar as she knew she had a few nights out planned with old friends and things like that. Christmas is a busy time, you know how it is, she'd said. It wasn't a no, but a second date hadn't yet been confirmed.

Now, he sat at home, heating on full blast in an effort to get some warmth into his body. The television was on, but he wasn't really watching. He was thinking about his day. Little snapshots kept creeping into his mind, and his face hurt from smiling.

He flicked through the photos they'd taken, and found himself hoping that his camera roll would have more of them together. He'd even considered phoning his mum to tell her about his day, but reckoned he'd save the news until they'd seen each other a few more times.

He'd not thought about Gerald Agnew all day, though that changed when the photos he'd been scrolling through stopped being of snowy gardens and changed to the newspaper story he'd snapped a picture of—the student with the fractured eye socket and the detained dealer.

Stu Finnegan was never going to admit to laying a finger on the dead man, but perhaps there was some way to get him to talk when he got out of the police station. Maybe he'd see the light and turn his back on his criminal enterprises.

Yeah right, Colin thought.

And then he had another thought.

If Stu was incarcerated until his questioning was done with, maybe there was some sort of evidence in his flat or house or wherever he lived that would link him to the murder.

Maybe he'd made it look like he'd bashed Gerald's head off the pole in the alleyway, when actually he'd socked him over the head with a wrench and then made it look like the tramp had had a little slip and fall.

Breaking into Stu's house was madness, but Colin couldn't help but feel that the dealer was somehow involved. Also, he and Adam had spoken briefly this evening, and had arranged a gentleman's bet. Adam thought Kyle was the guilty party, while Colin was convinced it was Stu. Neither wanted to lose and sometimes, the urge to be the winner overpowers common sense.

Maybe the love of a woman was giving him a sense of confidence he usually didn't have. Whatever the case, he'd made up his mind. And anyway, Stu wasn't going to be there, so there'd be no danger involved.

Before that, though, there was something else he felt he should do.

THE HOSPITAL'S ATTEMPT to inject some Christmas cheer was half-hearted at best. Colin supposed that overworked doctors and nurses had been entrusted with the job, and it was the best they could do with the time they could spare.

He walked to the reception and asked where his friend was being kept. He'd memorised the name from the newspaper story and, when he held up a wrapped present and adopted a glum face, the nurse directed him to Joe's ward.

A waiting list for surgery had kept Joe in for more days than he'd have liked, judging by his expression when Colin walked in. It started with a morose look, that gave way to fear when he took in Colin's height and black clothes.

'Don't hurt me,' he said. 'I've paid. I've paid.'

'I'm not here to hurt you,' Colin soothed. 'I'm here to help.'

Colin introduced himself, before taking the chair beside the bed and setting the present on the side table.

'What's that?' Joe asked.

'It's only a couple of beers. But I reckon you could do with one after what you've been through.'

Colin nodded at his face, which was puffy around the nose and as black as night around the left eye. The lid drooped over the swollen skin, looking positively grotesque.

'Sore?' Colin asked.

'Was at the time, aye. That plank got me right and good.'

Joe spoke with a light Dublin lilt, and even when he was describing the attack to Colin, it sounded dreamlike. No wonder the Irish accent got voted sexiest in the world in so many polls.

'You had no idea he was going to get violent?'

'No idea at all. I'd sent him a few texts saying I was going to be getting money at Christmas from me ma, and that he'd get paid then. He said that was grand, and then he turns up one night and breaks my face.'

'No warning.'

'Nope. Right hook to me nose, couple of kicks to the head and it's goodnight, Irene. Took thirty quid out of my pocket while I was unconscious, too. Luckily, my mate saw what happened and videoed it from behind a wall. He apologised later for not running to my aid, but reckoned that having a film of it would be more helpful.'

'Looks like it has been.'

'Aye, the police have been. Said they got him, but that I'm in trouble too for buying. Me ma's going to be so impressed when she sees me!'

Joe's gloominess had given way to something approaching happiness during the time they spoke. Maybe it was sharing the story with someone who wasn't going to judge, or maybe something else. Colin was just glad that he was able to help in some small way.

Colin got up to leave, and before he did, told Joe what he was planning to do. Joe confirmed what Colin was thinking: that it was madness, but that it *could* yield results. Joe had read about Gerald, but told Colin that Stu had never mentioned his name, though why would he?

'Can I have your number?' Joe asked.

'Why?' Colin said.

'You've been kind to me, and I'd like to know that you're alive when the night's over.'

THE IMPULSE THAT something was to be discovered within the walls of Stu Finnegan's home was waning now that Colin was outside. Wisely, he'd walked—not trusting that he'd park up and actually do this if he'd taken the car.

He imagined Adam, lambasting him for doing something so stupid, but his friend was so convinced of Kyle Baldwin's guilt that Colin feared he'd chucked all his eggs in one basket.

He'd paced the street for the best part of twenty minutes and hadn't met another soul. On the last Friday before Christmas, most were at work parties or down the boozer with old friends they hadn't seen in a while.

And here was Colin, with only the waning moon, the glittering stars, and a grotty street full of terraced houses for company. He considered what he was doing one more time before walking up the steps to Stu's house and knocking.

He'd spoken to Gaz, their police officer friend earlier, who told him Stu was still behind bars. Colin hung up before Gaz could ask any more questions. He wasn't a fan of Adam and Colin's extra-curricular activities and certainly wouldn't approve of Colin's current plan.

Of course, a lot could happen in a few hours where the law is concerned. A minute after Colin had hung up, Stu could've been turned loose. If the front door opened and Stu appeared, Colin would run. That was his thinking.

However, the door did not open, so Colin hurried down an alley filled with bins and into the back garden, where he was met with a locked door and a window that had been left open. The stench of weed drifted out of it, and Colin supposed that Stu had left it open to air the place, intending to return a little while after. Instead, he'd battered someone half to death and the police had picked him up.

The garden had been left to rot and ruin—a gardener's hand had not been felt there since the trees had been planted. The bare branches stretched into the sky like spindly fingers, and did a good job of keeping nosy neighbours from being able to see very much at all. Add in the inky blackness of the night, and Colin may as well have been a ghost.

He cast a glance around, just to make sure there wasn't a hidden CCTV camera or a lurking rottweiler, though if there was, he'd probably have known about it by now. That particular breed of dog isn't renowned for its sneakiness.

Happy that he was alone, he swung a foot onto the windowsill and, using a gloved hand, pulled the window further open. He clambered in and landed with little grace in the living room.

It was a mess. Every surface was littered with empty beer cans and equipment used for weighing, bagging and selling drugs. The sofa was at an odd angle, as if there'd been a recent struggle, and a bright blue light from the television bathed the room in an alien hue.

Colin set to work, not really knowing what he was looking for, besides something incriminating. Of course, the room was full of incriminating things that could land Stu in lots of trouble, but after a fruitless search, Colin concluded that the murder weapon was not among them.

The knives in the kitchen were not soaked in Gerald's blood, and there was no hammer, or wrench, or screwdriver dripping with the dead man's DNA.

Colin ascended the stairs. The small landing was faced with three doors, all shut, which brought an uncomfortable level of darkness. He reached for his phone and accessed the torch function, which lit up the space quite intensely.

Colin nearly fell backwards down the stairs as the torch's beam illuminated a pair of bright green eyes. A steady stream of four lettered words spewed forth from Colin's mouth, even after he'd realised it was only a little tabby cat.

The cat, for his part, was unmoved and unoffended by Colin's profanities, neither their content nor the sheer volume. Colin supposed afterwards that the cat *was* living with a drug-addled maniac and was probably used to far worse.

Bending down, Colin reached out and stroked the cat's head. It accepted the fuss, before slinking past Colin's legs and making its way down the stairs. Colin watched it go and then searched each of the rooms, again to no avail.

It had been a stupid idea to come here. He closed the final bedroom door behind him and froze as he heard a key slide into the lock of the front door.

The lock clicked, the door swung open and slammed again a moment later. Heavy footsteps sounded on the wooden floorboards in the hallway and a voice drifted up the stairs.

Panic seized Colin in a vice-like grip. He looked around wildly, ruling out the bathroom and bedroom as hiding places. Stu was likely to use those in the near future. Instead, Colin quietly opened the door to the airing cupboard and squeezed himself in beside the boiler. He pulled the door closed again and waited.

A few minutes later, the voice grew louder. There were gaps in the conversation and Colin realised that Stu must've been on the phone. He strained his ears, and caught a snatch of the exchange.

'I needed a dump, so I've stopped off at Stu's… Aye, I know, but he's in jail…. Don't worry. He's not going to know that I've dropped a depth charge down his bog. Might not even flush. Merry Christmas, pal.'

Peals of deep, booming laughter filled the landing and Colin readied himself. He heard the bathroom door open and the lock click, and as the first splash sounded, he bounded from his hiding place and nearly took the stairs in one leap. He span left and ran to the front door, which thankfully the mystery man in the toilet had left unlocked.

He sprinted out of the gate, and kept running until his lungs turned against him and there were tears in his eyes. He hadn't dared to look back, but reckoned that whoever was in the bathroom had either stayed there or had been too slow to catch a sighting.

Colin shook his head at his own stupidity and walked home on mutinous legs.

14

LOOT

ADAM WOKE UP and thought about the slap. Though it hadn't been anywhere near hard enough to leave a mark, it did feel like remnants of Kyle's sausage fingers remained.

Had it been a warning?

Adam didn't know. Perhaps he was reading too much into it, but their terse exchange had come when discussing money, and more importantly, Gerald. Perhaps the slap had been a subliminal message to back off, and to stop all the questioning.

Kyle knew that Adam had done a bit of Sherlocking in the past, he'd alluded to the fact in the interview. Maybe he thought Adam was getting a bit too close for comfort, and was trying to keep him at arm's length, though it wouldn't work. Adam was like a shark with these things. Or if not a shark, at least a tenacious terrier. He couldn't let it go.

And so, he resolved to do something today that, he realised, could get him fired, but he didn't really care. The whole point in taking the job in the first place was to get access to Kyle Baldwin that he wouldn't normally have been able to.

Today was the day to use the free pass to the limit.

After making sure that Helena was still asleep, he got out of bed and, like some sort of crazed hobbit, checked the wedding ring box was still in its hiding place. Thankfully, it was.

He tiptoed out of the bedroom, made some breakfast and then thought a little about what he was planning to accomplish today. He concluded, after running several scenarios, that he'd need to get very lucky.

THE SHOP FLOOR WAS hellish, and Adam was tempted more than once to jack the whole thing in anyway. The stress of two abandoned proposals, coupled with rude customers and the repeated playlist (which hadn't been altered as promised), was really getting to him.

He was about to go and tell Lauren he was quitting when Lady Luck smiled upon him.

At three o'clock, he watched Kyle Baldwin make a beeline for the front door, car keys in hand. Adam assumed that meant he'd be gone for the rest of the day, which in theory meant he could have an uninterrupted snoop in the owner's office. If there was something to be found to link Kyle to Gerald's death, it was either going to be in there or at his home.

As casually as he could, he sloped away from the basket of clothes he was supposed to be hanging up and made his way towards the back. Unfortunately, his route to Kyle's office was blocked by Lauren, who sat at her desk.

'Alright, Adam? How's tricks?' she said.

'All good,' Adam replied. 'How are you?'

'Great, thanks to you. I had a class time with Colin yesterday, so cheers for introducing us.'

'You're grand. Are you seeing each other again?'

'I'd like to, yeah. Things are a bit manic at the moment, but we'll see how it goes.'

'Good to hear,' he smiled. 'Umm… Is Kyle here?'

'He's had to nip out. Did you need him?'

'Ah… Cathy said that there is something wrong with the front door. It's not opening automatically or something. Thought I should tell Kyle.'

'That bleedin' door,' she said, puffing out an indignant sigh. 'I've told him so many times to get it replaced, but he's too much of a skinflint. I'll go down and take a look, see if I need to call someone.'

She got up from behind her desk and Adam followed her out, before peeling off and standing behind a shelf of bathroom items, watching her make her way towards the escalator. When she'd vanished out of sight, he ran to the back.

Kyle had left in such a hurry that he'd not locked his door. Or, perhaps he never did. Adam knew he didn't have much time, so whirred around the office like a careful hurricane. He checked in the filing cabinet and the top of the desk. He rifled through notepads but was met only with order forms, HR reminders and pricing lists.

Lauren was bound to discover she'd been duped at any minute, and Adam gazed around hopelessly, when something jumped out at him.

Kyle's bottom drawer was the only one that had a lock on it, though the key was stuck in it, defeating the point of having a locking drawer entirely. Adam turned the key and found a stack of papers, which he flicked through rapidly. It was mostly more of the same, but two pieces amongst the pile caught his eye.

They'd been shoved in at different places; one near the middle of the stack and one near the bottom.

Both looked like they'd been handled a lot. The corners were dog-eared and uncared for. Adam folded them, shoved them in his pocket and was about to leave the office when he spotted something else.

A notepad on the desk he hadn't seen before. The corner of its pages were poking out from under an A3-sized envelope. He pulled it from its hiding place, and found that the top page had been torn off—remnants of it were caught in the spirals of metal. Whoever had written on it, though, was either in a hurry or angry, as the indentations on the next page down were clear as day.

Meet me tonight.

He took a photo of the page and hurried out onto the shop floor again, where he headed back to his bumper box of clothes, and not a moment too soon. He watched Lauren stride towards the back room, though couldn't see her expression. Hopefully, she'd assume that Adam or Cathy had made a mistake, or that the faulty door had righted itself without the need for intervention.

He kept his head down for the rest of his shift, and when it was time to clock off, texted Colin to ask him to meet in the pub.

It was time to discuss the contents of the pages.

'YOU DID WHAT?!' Adam practically shouted when Colin had finished his story about breaking into Stu Finnegan's house.

'Keep it down,' Colin whispered.

'Why?'

'Because one of his cronies could well be here and listening to you.'

Adam glanced around, and conceded the point. Colin was right. One of Stu's gang of local bandits could be in here, and discussing it at volume was probably a silly thing to do, so Adam lowered his voice but recommenced his tongue-lashing.

'Are you crazy?' he hissed.

'I just thought it would be helpful.'

'You getting yourself killed is pretty far from helpful."

'It's just, it's always you that finds the breakthrough. For once, I wanted to be the one to crack the case.'

'It's not always me that "finds the breakthrough",' Adam said, air quoting the final three words. 'We're a team.'

'I suppose.'

'And I need my best man's head still attached to his body if I ever get the bloody question asked, so promise me that you won't do anything as ridiculously dangerous as that ever again.'

'Scout's honour,' said Colin, holding up a hand with parted fingers.

'That's the Star Trek sign, you numpty!' Adam laughed.

He went to the bar and returned with a couple of drinks. When they'd both taken a few gulps, a corner booth was vacated by a group of lads, so Colin and Adam moved to the relative privacy afforded there.

Adam pulled the pages out and smoothed them on the table. Colin set his pint down and studied what Adam had found.

The scribbles on the first page were written in what looked like fountain pen ink. The paper had been torn from a spiral notebook, and had thin red lines on it. It said:

Jesus. What were you thinking?

The next message was written on a smaller piece of paper, and was tatty and torn in places. The writing was shakier, and looked more childlike. It said:

I'm going to need more. Remember what I know and who I could tell. GA.

'I'm assuming GA is Gerald Agnew,' Colin said.

'I'd say so.'

'So, he sent these to Kyle in the hope of getting more… what?'

'Money, I think, though of course there's no way of being certain.'

'Does it feel like blackmail to you?' Colin asked. 'First, asking Kyle for more money and then threatening him with telling someone something.'

'That's what I thought when I read it.'

'Which means that Kyle might have had something to do with his death? Maybe Kyle went to see Gerald, to pay him to shut up. Maybe things got heated and he ended up killing him by mistake.'

'Or he went to find him to shut him up once and for all, intentionally.'

'What about the first note?' Colin said, pointing to the more legible handwriting.

'They kinda link, I guess. "What were you thinking?"' Adam pointed to the more legible note, and then the scrawled one. '"Remember what I know." Maybe Gerald sent the first one to get Kyle's attention and the second to get him to pay.'

'But the writing is so different?'

'Maybe Gerald got a friend to write one of them so that they couldn't be linked if Kyle got the police involved.'

'What a mess,' Colin sighed. 'You think we should go to the police now?'

'For Whitelaw to tell us that we've been wasting our time and to take the evidence? I don't think so. You and me are going to see this through.'

Colin nodded.

'What's next, then?'

'Well,' Adam said, shoving the phone his way with the picture of the indented notebook on screen. 'Kyle is worried. And when someone is worried, they make mistakes. He's meeting someone tonight, and I think we should be there. Helena is on nights, so I thought we'd head over and stake out Kyle's house. We can follow him to wherever he's going. Maybe he's going to do something crazy.'

'Dude, I know we are finally making progress, but I have an early start at work tomorrow. Do you mind doing this one on your own?'

'No worries,' Adam shrugged. 'I'm sure it'll be a massive waste of time, but you never know.'

They finished their drinks and hit the road; Colin to his warm, comfortable bed and Adam to the confines of his trusty Renault Cleo.

15

YOU CAN TELL A MAN BY HOW HE LIFTS HIS HANDS

ADAM TURNED INTO Kyle Baldwin's street and pulled in between a couple of cars that were parked on the side of the road. It meant he had a clear view of his boss's house, but he was far enough away that he wouldn't be spotted.

He hoped.

The street was in the pricey area of Stonebridge. The houses were detached, the generous gardens well-maintained, and the cars that filled the driveways were a far cry from his own little rust bucket.

He'd swung by the garage before coming here, not knowing how long he'd be keeping a watch on Kyle. He'd hoped that whoever he was meeting was a fan of an early night, and the meeting would be over and done with by the time Match Of The Day started.

The curtains were drawn over Kyle's downstairs windows, though some light filtered out through some gaps in the fabric. Once or twice, a shadow flitted behind the glass, and Adam reckoned Kyle was alone. Perhaps he was getting ready, or summoning up the courage to go to his meeting.

While he sat watching the house, Adam wondered who he could be meeting with. Surely, if Kyle was behind Gerald's demise (and Adam was convinced he was), who could he possibly want to share the news with? If that's what he was doing. Maybe he thought the net was closing in on him; perhaps Adam's questions the other night had riled him and he was finding some way to negate his guilt. Maybe he was looking for a scapegoat.

Maybe someone else had ordered Gerald's killing and Kyle was simply a pawn. He doubted it, but he didn't know what to think.

Instead of running endless possibilities around his brain, his thoughts drifted to Colin and the stupidity he'd shown in breaking into Stu's house.

Colin was the one with the managerial role, the one who usually made the sensible choices. Adam wondered what was going on with him at the minute. Was he lonely? Was he trying to prove something by going on a daring, and illegal, mission without having discussed it with Adam first?

Adam reflected on his own behaviour. Since he'd been with Helena, he and Colin had remained close, whilst seeing less of each other. Maybe Adam was partly to blame for his friend's recklessness.

He resolved to make more time for Colin, outside of the cases they undertook. With any luck, this would be their last anyway, and they could simply spend time in the pub or with PlayStation controllers lodged in their hands, trading insults about each other's' FIFA prowess.

Adam's reveries were broken by a car passing by. He ducked down, not knowing why, and watched as the black Honda Jazz came to a stop outside Kyle's house. It idled for a while, before the engine cut and someone got out.

Adam was surprised to see that it was Lauren. As Kyle's PA, he assumed her role was confined to the 9-5 of working hours. Maybe her position called for late night brainstorming meetings, or maybe Adam had simply watched too much The Thick Of It.

What could the boss and his PA possibly have to meet up about?

Was it her that he gave the note to? And if so, why wouldn't he just tell her face to face. It wasn't like they didn't see each other during the day.

Was Lauren somehow linked to Gerald's death?

All of these questions were answered by what happened in the next minute. Adam watched her walk up the drive and ring the bell. She pulled her coat tightly around her and attempted to shelter from the howling wind.

Twenty seconds later, the door opened and Kyle appeared, wearing a white shirt and holding a bottle of wine by the neck. With his spare arm, he pulled her into a tight embrace that ended with a kiss.

And not a friendly kiss on the cheek. This was more akin to the climactic scene from a romcom, where the guy finally gets the girl and has a lot of pent up testosterone to share. Adam could feel the frisson of passion from his cold car.

He also felt the icy knife slip between his shoulder blades as Kyle's front door closed and the realisation hit that he was going to have to break it to Colin that his prospective new girlfriend was two-timing.

He was annoyed.

He thought that tonight would help wrap up, or at least push along, their investigation. But all he was being privy to was a hook-up between a boss and his closest employee.

He considered firing up the engine and going home, but thought that maybe she'd leave soon and he didn't want to miss what happened next, if anything did.

He resolved to stay a little while longer, and then made the mistake of closing his eyes.

THE EARLY MORNING sun made his eyes water and, when he finally managed to open them, he found that it wasn't only his eyes that were sore.

His whole body was in pain.

He'd somehow slept through the night in a cramped, cold car, and every muscle, ligament and tendon was letting him know. He opened the door and straightened his legs, while lying back on the passenger seat to really feel the burn.

His bladder was uncomfortably full and he had no sooner fired up his engine to head home, than Kyle's front door opened.

He killed his motor quickly and watched Lauren dash to her car and take off. Kyle stood and watched her go, leaning casually against the doorframe, before disappearing inside again.

Adam hadn't slept in a car all night to simply walk away from this nonsense.

He got out, locked the door and walked up Kyle's driveway. He pressed the bell, and heard footsteps from inside.

'Forgotten something?' Kyle asked, and then blanched when he saw who was standing in front of him.

'No, but I could do with a wee if you don't mind,' Adam said, pushing in past his trousers-less boss. Whatever was about to happen, one thing was certain—he was definitely losing his job, so he figured he could be as much of a prat as he wanted.

He walked upstairs and found the bathroom. For a single—or at least unmarried—man, the bathroom was surprisingly clean. The taps sparkled and the sink's porcelain shone. Adam did his business and then headed downstairs, finding Kyle in the living room, collapsed on the sofa. Thankfully, he'd found a pair of shorts from somewhere.

'Your PA? Seriously, dude. She's like half your age.'

'You won't tell anyone, will you?' Kyle whimpered.

'Well, considering she and my best friend have been on a date, I might just have to. Be honest with me, and we might be able to keep it between the three of us.'

'I'd appreciate that, you know…'

Adam cut him off by holding his hand up. He needed silence to think.

How he broached this could make or break the case. He decided to start casually.

'How long have you and Lauren been seeing each other?'

'Only for a few weeks. It's nothing serious, but if it gets out, I'll be in big trouble.'

'It doesn't look good, does it? A young, attractive girl in a relationship with the boss man. Some disgruntled employees might be worried about favouritism.'

'That's why it can't get out.'

Adam imagined the Baldwin business empire was flashing before Kyle's eyes. Adam pulled the two pieces of paper from his pocket and laid them on the sofa beside him. He picked one up, the one that said: "I'm going to need more. Remember what I know and who I could tell. GA."

'Tell me about this,' he said.

'Where did you…? Have you been…?'

'Yes, I've been through your office, but let me remind you that I'm the one asking the questions here. You give me an answer I don't like, and the police will be here before you know it.' Adam wafted the piece of paper. 'Tell me about this.'

Any fight left in Kyle Baldwin drifted out of him like a sad ghost. His shoulders slumped and his bottom lip jutted out.

'It's from Gerald, as you have probably guessed. He came in to talk about the Santa gig and saw Lauren and I… you know, on the table. He backed out, respectfully, and then came back the next day and threatened to go to the papers if I didn't give him some money.'

'And did you?'

'The amount he was asking for was a pittance, so I did. A few days later, he came back, asking for more. Out of principle, I said no. I told him that this little act could go on indefinitely, and where to go. His note arrived not long after.'

'So, what did you do?'

'I ignored it. I wasn't going to be bullied by Gerald bloody Agnew. I deal with bigger tossers than him on a daily basis, and I wasn't about to be blackmailed further by that lowlife.'

'And he went away?'

'No. he came back, in person, and had another word. Lauren got a little angry at him, which made him smile. He said some chauvinistic things to her, told me to cough up, and then left.'

'And then you killed him?'

'What?' Kyle actually had the good grace to look shocked. 'Kill him? Of course not.'

'What's this one about then?' Adam asked, holding up the other page. 'It feels vaguely incriminating.'

Jesus. What were you thinking?

'I wrote that one,' Kyle said, shaking his head. 'I realise now how stupid it was to put it down on paper, but at the time it made sense. It was either that or scream until my voice gave out.'

'What does it mean?'

'It was a note to Lauren. But I never gave it to her. I wrote it, and then filed it away.'

'And what *was* she thinking?' Adam asked.

'I don't know. But I'm telling the truth when I say it wasn't me that killed Gerald. It was her.'

'Bull!'

'I swear it. She came to me after she'd done it, in a blind panic. I told her to act like nothing had happened, and it would blow over.'

'What dreadful advice,' Adam laughed.

16

COLOUR THE MESS

BY TEN O'CLOCK, Colin was already clock watching.

Usually, he loved his work, but he knew at the end of today's shift, four long days of holiday were due to begin.

He was feeling burnt out. The endless Christmas songs, the long working hours, the investigation, the smouldering buzz of a potential new relationship. It was all getting on top of him.

Actually, that wasn't fair. The burgeoning relationship was one of the only things keeping him going at the minute, and his mind kept drifting to lovely Lauren as he went about his routine.

'You've got a spring in your step this morning, son,' Barry said. He was wearing a Santa hat and had the beginnings of a beard on his usually clean-shaven face.

'And you look like a hobo,' Colin laughed.

'I'm trying something new. Ladies love a bit of rough,' he said, scratching at the stubble.

'And who do you have your eye on?'

Barry glanced around. 'I'm thinking of inviting Doris for a wee dram on Christmas eve.'

'Doris? Wow. I didn't see that coming. I thought you said she talked too much.'

'Aye, she does a bit. But she's got all the good gossip. Helps pass the day in here.'

Colin had a massive soft spot for Barry, and was pleased that the old man was taking a gamble.

'Well, I'm sure she'll say yes to a wonderful gentleman.'

'A gentleman, probably, but what about me?' Barry chuckled.

Colin wished him luck, and told him to keep him in the loop. Barry walked away and settled in his favourite chair in front of the TV. Doris was nearby, doing some knitting and deep in conversation with Nancy. Colin would have liked to stay and watch, but he had things to do.

Once the retirement home was cleaned, he walked upstairs to the staff room to check his phone. He had a message from Lauren, asking him if he'd like to meet for lunch. He replied that he would, without trying to sound too excited.

He also had twelve missed calls from Adam, which was alarming. He supposed that Adam was ringing to brag that he'd been right all along, and that Kyle Baldwin was currently in a jail cell or in questioning.

Reluctantly, he called Adam back, who answered before the phone could even ring.

'Where have you been?' Adam asked.

'Working. I told you I was in early. What's up?'

Adam launched into the story of the past fourteen hours. Colin's heart sank when he heard about the kiss, and then sank further when he was told that Kyle was currently in police custody, but not for the murder. That, in fact, it was Colin's new flame that had been behind Gerald Agnew's death.

As hard as it was to hear, Colin thanked his friend. Only a true mate would be so honest, and though it hurt, Colin was glad he was finding out now. It wouldn't have done well to take a murderer back to meet the parents.

'She's just texted me, asking to meet for lunch. I'm assuming she hasn't realised that she's been rumbled, and I also assume the police will be looking for her.'

'I'd say so. You should call Whitelaw.'

'I should. Though maybe we can get to her before they do. Take the glory.'

'That's my boy!' Adam whooped.

COLIN AND LAUREN had arranged to meet at a café in the town centre, which told Colin that she was completely oblivious to Adam having rumbled her big secret.

The Town Street Fryer was quiet. It seemed everyone in the town was taking part in a shopping frenzy, abandoning their appetites for fear of missing out on the last action figure or Furby.

Maybe Colin's imagination was simply dredging up memories of watching *Jingle All The Way.*

As it was, they had the place more of less to themselves.

The smell of cooking bacon filled the air. Condensation frosted the front window, cutting off any view of outside. It had started to snow as Colin had parked his car, and he hoped the weather wouldn't stop his guests getting there.

One had already arrived.

Lauren was sitting opposite him, holding his hand across the table. He was trying to act as normally as possible, but was obviously finding it difficult as she kept asking what was wrong. He palmed it off as end of year tiredness, and it looked like she was buying it.

She told him about her night last night. How she'd gone round to her friend's house (Kiera, apparently) and they ended up watching a Christmas film and having a sleepover.

'What did you watch?' Colin asked.

'Love, Actually.'

'I've never seen it.'

'What?' She seemed genuinely shocked. 'That's ridiculous! We should watch it. How about tonight?'

'I can't tonight.'

'Oh. Tomorrow?'

'Let's cut the crap,' Colin whispered, unable to keep up the façade. 'I know about what you did. I know you are seeing Kyle and I know you killed Gerald.'

'What?' she laughed.

'I know,' Colin nodded. 'Adam watched you go into Kyle's house last night and leave this morning. He talked to Kyle, who told him the same story he is probably telling to the police right now.'

'Colin, I'm sorry…'

'Why didn't you just say no when Adam asked if you were single?'

'I thought it would be a good cover. If everyone thought I had a boyfriend, no one would suspect I was with Kyle. People were starting to talk at work, rumours were flying around.'

'Jesus. You've been using me to cover your own arse, and on top of that, you're a bloody murderer.'

'It was an accident,' she shrieked.

The banging and crashing from the kitchen went quiet and one of the chefs' heads appeared through the small serving hole. Colin gave him the thumbs up and he disappeared again.

'It was an accident,' Lauren repeated, quieter this time. 'He was trying to blackmail Kyle. He walked in on us once, and thought he could lord it over us. Kyle and me weren't serious, but the thought of my mum and dad finding out scared me. They wouldn't understand. So, I went and tried to talk to Gerald.'

'And it didn't go well.'

'I tried to talk some sense into him. Told him that the money Kyle was giving him was enough to make a change to his life, and that greediness would get him nowhere. He tried to intimidate me, then. Told me where to get off to. I was about to leave, and he told me that he could give me what Kyle is giving me and more.'

Lauren was crying now.

'He blocked my way out of the alley, and I was scared. It was snowy, and he was that drunk he kept slipping over. The last time he fell, he fell onto his knees. Right near the pole. I grabbed him by the hair and smacked his face into it. I thought it would daze him, give me some time to get away. But I knew from the way he fell I'd hit him too hard.'

'And Kyle covered for you?'

'I told him about it, and he said that it would probably look like an accident. Drunken old fool on slips on a cold night and bangs his head, you know?'

'And then we started looking into it.'

She nods. 'I thought if I could get pally with you, you wouldn't suspect me.'

The door opened at that point, and a set of heavy footsteps sounded on the cheap linoleum flooring. They stopped when they got to Colin's table, and DI Whitelaw slipped into the seat beside him.

'She's all yours,' Colin said, and walked out of the café without a backwards glance.

17

ALIGN THE PLANETS

ADAM AND HELENA clinked their glasses and saluted the incoming new year. They'd eschewed the heaving nightclubs and overpriced taxis and settled for a nice meal at their favourite restaurant and Jools Holland.

They'd got dressed up in their finery, though Adam wished he'd chosen something with a little give in the waist department. The burger and chips had been enough, but he could never resist the honeycomb cheesecake when he came here.

Which was weekly.

As the crooner in the cheap three-piece suit began to murder Sinatra, Adam paid the bill and they left. His hands were sweaty on the steering wheel and when he pulled into their parking space, the butterflies were beating their wings in a frenzy inside his stomach.

'You okay?' Helena asked.

'All good. Just full,' he nodded.

'Tell me about it,' she said, patting her stomach.

They got out, Adam making sure to walk ahead. He led her up the stairs to their flat and put the key in the lock, hoping Colin had been able to put their plan into action.

He turned the key, pushed the door open and heard Helena gasp behind him.

Colin, as ever, had come through.

Every surface of the living room, aside from the flammable ones, had been covered with tealights. Their little flames danced in the draught from the open door. Rose petals formed a sort of red carpet, that led Adam and Helena to a small table, where a bottle of champagne rested in a cooler and two flute glasses awaited. Imogen Heap's Speeding Cars was playing gently on the wireless speaker Adam had got for Christmas.

'What's all this?' Helena asked.

Adam sucked in a deep breath, trying to keep the emotion at bay. He faced her and took her hands in his. He managed to get through most of the speech he'd prepared, though his voice cracked near the end and instead of trying to finish it, he simply got down on one knee and took the ring out of his pocket.

Helena's hand sprung to her mouth as tears began to form in the corners of her eyes.

'Helena Bryer, will you marry me?' he asked.

He knew that he'd remember the small nod of her head and the tight embrace they'd shared after he'd slipped the ring on her finger for the rest of his life.

18

BE A PHOENIX

COLIN SMILED FOR the first time in what felt like days.

Aside from lighting what felt like a million little candles in Adam's house, he'd spent a lonely New Year's in his own home. He hadn't even bothered waiting up to see the new year in.

Hearing Adam gush down the phone that he was engaged, and how impressed Helena had been with the state of the flat, had brightened his outlook somewhat, and as he hung up, he resolved to banish the blues and change his outlook.

Now, he found himself back at work.

'Be a phoenix, son' Barry said. 'It's the first day of a new year and you need to forget that you were courting a murderer. Arise from the ashes, young man, and good things will come.'

'Like you did?'

'Aye, well, I bottled out of asking Doris for a drink, but if you stop moping, maybe I'll get round to it.'

'Deal,' Colin laughed.

He looked around the room.

'Oi, Doris,' he shouted. The old lady looked over the top of her magazine. 'Barry here fancies you and wants to know if you want a drink.'

Barry slapped Colin's leg with a rolled-up newspaper, before looking at Doris expectantly.

'I'd be delighted. Your place or mine?' she laughed, before going back to her photos of the latest celeb to get married.

'Easy as that,' Barry shrugged, and Colin laughed.

He left the lovebirds to it and headed for reception. A new resident was moving in today, and as manager, he wanted to be there to welcome them.

They arrived a short while later. Ken walked in with the aid of a walking stick, and surveyed his surroundings. Colin had met him on a few of the pre-visits, and shook his hand warmly. His family fussed over him, though something in Ken's eyes convinced Colin that he was ready for his next adventure.

Colin walked with him to his room, where they got to know each other for a little while. His daughter and two sons brought a few suitcases and personal belongings in, and Colin was about to leave them to it when a girl popped her head around the door that stopped him in his tracks.

Her long hair was the colour of a tropical beach, and her eyes the colour of the sea that washed upon it. She smiled at Colin, who heard Barry's words reverberate around his head.

'Be a phoenix, son.'

-6-

ALL AT SEA

CHRIS MCDONALD

1

DISASTER

ADAM HATED PACKING. Always had done. Always would do.

Of course, he was looking forward to what came after—the cruise. Eight nights on the open water, stopping at various European cities before docking in Venice. A short train journey later, he'd be on the banks of Lake Garda, marrying the love of his life.

His mother had been slightly disappointed by the fact that they'd decided on a destination wedding, but neither Adam nor Helena wanted a big fuss. They'd rather spend their money on a small ceremony with a stunning backdrop than fill a tent with second cousins and great aunts who they hadn't spoken to in ten years, and probably would never see again.

No. Tying the knot in front of people they actually cared about was far preferable, and doing it with the Italian sun on their faces even more so.

They'd flown out a couple of times, to assess the location, sort out the paperwork, and meet the vicar who would be performing the ceremony. Each time, Adam's heart had soared at the view from the medieval castle on the shore of Malcesine; the endless stretch of water, the snow-capped mountains that seemed to scratch the sky, the pretty Mediterranean houses with those terracotta rooftops he loved so much.

It was all so perfect.

The plan had been to fly there a few days before the ceremony to give them time to sort the last-minute things out, but then Adam's mum had surprised them with a once in a lifetime opportunity.

Two first class tickets aboard The Elysian.

Adam had scolded her at first, castigating her for spending what he presumed was an unholy amount of money, especially since she'd already chipped in for the wedding. But, no argument with a woman of a certain age about money gets won, especially if that woman is Northern Irish—the sweetest old lady in the land can turn into Deborah Meaden at the mention of cash.

And so, Adam found himself packing for the trip. As well as what he needed for the wedding (suit, tie, smart shoes), he was now also having to think about the journey by boat.

Would it be cold while they were journeying, or hot? Would he need a woolly hat or shorts? These were questions he couldn't answer, so he found himself randomly opening drawers, gazing in with little enthusiasm before closing them again.

Helena would know.

She was like The Flash with this stuff. Set her off, and before you knew it, your case was packed, zipped and labelled.

Adam threw down a pair of goggles he'd somehow acquired, despite not having swum for the best part of a decade (probably in one of Mr McCall's horrific PE lessons at school—even now, the thought of the cold, chlorinated water made him shiver). He made his way to the living room to ask for Helena's advice.

Except, Helena was in no condition to give advice.

She was lying on the sofa, cheeks stained black by running mascara. She looked like one of the band members from My Chemical Romance, though of course he didn't mention that particular thought. Instead, he rushed to her side.

'What's wrong?' he asked, taking hold of her hand.

'That was the dress shop,' she mumbled between sobs. 'The lady who does the alterations called in sick today, and won't be back until the start of the week. They can't get anyone else which means my dress won't be ready before the cruise.'

'They know your measurements, though. Mum can grab it and bring it with her on the plane.' Even as he said it, Adam knew he was underestimating the enormity of this particular disaster.

Helena shook her head.

'The thought of the dress not fitting on the day is awful. I'd be thinking about it the whole time we were on the boat. I need to go to the fitting.'

Adam nodded. He'd heard horror stories of how usually reasonable women became monsters during the run up to their wedding. Thankfully, Helena had remained her cool, normal self, and so he knew how much the dress meant to her if she was reacting like this.

'It's cool. I'll phone the company and see if we can rearrange the cruise.'

He was pulled into a tight hug and felt Helena's lips on his cheek. He returned to the bedroom to find his phone, and pulled up the email confirmation. Finding the customer services number, he dialled.

The company had chosen a lullaby version of a Foo Fighters song for their hold music, causing Adam to feel simultaneously impressed at their taste in music, and sleepy.

After a short wait, the music was replaced by a slightly accented voice—Nordic, he thought. Adam relayed his plight, and though the voice on the other side of the phone was sympathetic, they were also firm on their stance.

Because the planned journey was only a few days away, there was nothing that could be done.

Adam thanked the man on the other end of the phone and hung up, before delivering the news to Helena, who reacted by crying again.

'I'm so sorry,' she managed between sobs. 'You must think I'm a nightmare.'

'Not at all,' he placated her, stroking the back of her hand softly.

After a few minutes, she calmed enough to suggest an alternative.

'Do you think Colin would go with you?'

'I'm sure Colin wouldn't say no to a free cruise,' Adam laughed. 'The big man loves the sea.'

'You should call him,' she said. 'If he can't go, then I'll just have to trust the dress will be okay. I don't want to waste your mum's money.'

Adam once again reached for his phone, this time dialling the number of his best friend and one-time partner in crime (solving).

Over the past couple of years, they'd taken on the somewhat unlikely role of unofficial Stonebridge detectives, when people had come to them with problems that the police had written off as unworthy of their time.

Adam and Colin had solved five cases in their career to date, but hadn't been called upon in nearly six months, not since last Christmas. Adam was partly thankful, as he'd had a lot on his plate, what with the wedding and running his own business. Still, there was something exhilarating about the tangled web of a case that he missed.

He and Colin had a short conversation, that ended with his friend agreeing to come on the cruise, as long as Adam was willing to accept some money in return. He also offered to change the name on his flight to Helena's so that she could fly to Italy with Colin's girlfriend, Anna, who would make sure she got to the alter on time.

'Everything has worked out,' Adam said to Helena, setting the phone on the table and relaying the content of their conversation.

'Just promise me you won't get into any trouble,' she replied.

Adam laughed, and promised her that he certainly wouldn't be looking for any.

The unfortunate truth, however, was that trouble often found Adam, whether he went looking for it or not.

2

BON VOYAGE

THE ELYSIAN WAS breath-taking.

Though the ship was a few years old, it looked like it had sailed here straight from the shipyard it had just been built in. The town's harbour was usually reserved for small fishing vessels and the occasional jet skier, so the sight of this huge ocean liner was almost laughable. It was like something from another planet. The vast body was painted glacier white, and gleamed in the Stonebridge sunshine. The various decks rose high into the sky, and Colin could hear jolly music and laughter as he waited to board with Adam. Spirits were high, even with the keen-eyed seagulls squawking above their heads, hoping that such a large gathering of people might yield a decent return in the dropped food department.

Once boarding began, the operation was sleek and well-oiled, and before they knew it, their cases had been whisked away at the check-in desk, and they were quickly led away by a friendly, uniformed worker with a Claudia Winkleman fringe.

The interior of the ship was breathtaking, opulence dripping from every square millimetre. The place was polished to within an inch of its life; the white marble underfoot dazzling. Huge spiral staircases led to higher floors, each step emitting a soft white glow, the central column made up of thousands of twinkling LEDs. A smattering of chandeliers filled the space with light, the biggest and most lavish taking up most of the centre of the ceiling, itself painted in an imitation of Michelangelo's most famous work—The Creation of Adam.

They could have stood for a couple more hours and not managed to take in every detail of the decadence. Adam nodded at faux-Claudia and she ushered them across the cavernous space towards a bank of lifts.

They entered the lift, which was purposefully decorated in an art deco style; wooden panelled, complete with a shuttered door and one of those circular handles instead of buttons. It made Adam think of the Titanic, which was not a comforting notion at all. Claudia worked the handle, and the lift started to ascend, taking them noiselessly to the top deck. From here, they could see every detail of their town and beyond.

They leaned against the barrier, waved a dramatic goodbye and pretended to cry, hugging each other as if leaving for war, as Claudia looked on, not knowing what to do.

'Gentlemen, if you'll follow me,' she said, eventually, with a slight tremor in her voice.

Colin and Adam followed her to the stern of the ship, and stopped behind her when she pulled a key card from her pocket. She tapped it on the sensor beside a cabin door, which slid open.

'Your quarters for the next eight nights,' she said, handing the key to Adam, before bowing (bowing!) and backing away from them.

'Quarters' was underselling it, by some distance.

The Bridal Suite of The Elysian could've been lifted straight from one of the world's six-star hotels. The door opened into an enormous living space. The walls were painted a tasteful cream, letting the furniture do the talking. A purple, velvet sofa and accompanying armchair presided over a marble table, upon which sat a few classic novels, artfully arranged as if for a photoshoot. The room opened up into a well-appointed kitchen which looked a bit more modern, but still classy. The room was stunning, yet it didn't compare to the bedroom.

The king-sized bed was placed so that, upon waking, one could survey the endless ocean through a wall of glass. A little balcony could be accessed by another door, upon which sat a small table and a couple of chairs. The en-suite bathroom was the size of Adam's kitchen at home, and when he stood inspecting his kingdom, a little pang of sadness snagged at his chest at the thought of his wife-to-be missing out on such an adventure.

'I'm happy with the sofa,' Colin said, poking his head into the bedroom.

'I'm happy with you on the sofa, too,' Adam laughed. 'I don't want those cheesy feet stinking out a room this good!'

'Shut up,' Colin laughed, flinging a plump pillow in Adam's direction. 'Did you know you were going to be living in this much luxury?'

'No. Mum undersold it. Probably knew I'd make her take it back if I had've done!'

'Well, selfishly, I'm pleased she kept it hidden.'

They left the bedroom and sat down in the living space. On the table, beside the books, was a bottle of champagne in a frosted bucket, and two flutes. Adam had always feared popping a cork, as he thought it might result in losing an eye, so left Colin in charge. Ever reliable, he managed to release the cork with minimal effort, and without spilling a single drop.

Glasses full, they toasted their trip.

'Here's to you and Helena,' Colin said, raising a glass.

'And staying out of trouble,' Adam added.

After a few sips, they noted an invite on the table. Apparently, there was to be a tasting menu for first class passengers laid on in the Augustine Lounge that evening.

'A tasting menu?' Adam sighed. 'It's going to be all fancy crap and tiny portions, isn't it?'

ENTERING THE AUGUSTINE Lounge felt like walking into a room at Buckingham Palace, or so Adam imagined. He felt like a pleb from the get go.

In his mind, the cruise was going to be a relaxing time, filled with endless days on a sun lounger, punctuated only by trips to the bar or the on-board cinema. And, so he had packed accordingly. His suitcase had been filled with T-shirts, shorts and not much else. On the off chance he'd fancied getting dressed up (and mostly at Helena's insistence), he'd thrown in a pair of jeans and a flannel shirt, both of which he was wearing now.

Everyone else was either wearing an expensive-looking suit or a fancy evening gown. Some of the women even had fascinators perched on their heads, like they were heading to a day at the races.

The only saving grace was that Colin was also sporting a casual look. They looked like a pair of party crashers, and Adam was sure they were going to be asked for identification sooner rather than later.

A man in a full tuxedo sat behind a grand piano, tickling the ivories, while the first-class passengers sipped from wine glasses and got to know each other. Adam accepted his own glass from a passing waiter, and passed one to Colin.

'Maybe if we get drunk quickly, this will be less awkward,' Adam suggested, before raising the glass to his lips, downing the contents and fighting to keep an enormous burp at bay.

'That's one way to do it,' Colin said, before following suit and grabbing two more glasses from a different waiter.

From the front of the grand room, the ting of silverware striking the stem of a glass sounded, and the chatter died away. All eyes turned to the man responsible.

'Hello, everyone,' said the man. 'My name is Edd Graham-Hyde, and I am the captain of the ship. I want to wish you all a pleasant journey on board The Elysian, and want you to know that no request shall go unanswered. If we can do something to make your stay with us unforgettable, we will. We'll go overboard for you, though, not literally.'

This joke, that Adam assumed he said during every introduction, produced a hearty laugh from around the room. The man was tall and spoke with a hint of a German accent, and seemed to have finished his short toast, as he gave a small salute before leaving the front of the room and beginning to mingle.

A short while later, the assembled guests were asked to take a seat at one of the circular tables. Each table seated eight, and Adam and Colin simply picked the one they were closest to. The rest of the seats filled, and Adam suppressed a sigh.

Of course, he'd been saddled with the crazy lady.

He'd noticed her while boarding earlier in the day. Her mane of white hair and kooky pastel glasses were more than enough to make her stand out, but even stranger was the fact she had been carrying a framed painting. The same framed painting which stood on a portable easel beside Adam now.

As they waited for the first course to arrive, they took it in turns to introduce themselves, though one in particular needed no such introduction.

Vaughn McClusky was in many movies Adam loved—mostly action, though he'd shown he could turn in a good comedic performance, too. He seemed to be constantly on the cusp of a huge starring role that, sadly, had never come. Adam had often presumed that actors looked good thanks to make up and a range of tonics, but up close, he could see that Vaughn's good looks were thanks to an angular jaw and striking green eyes.

The man next to him was small and wiry, probably in his fifties, and was positively buzzing with nervous energy. A bushy moustache obscured most of his mouth, and when he spoke, his words poured forth in an American drawl. He introduced himself as Tex Rivera. Adam supposed it was a false name.

Henry Carver-Clark was next. His suit looked like the most expensive in the room, and when he spoke, he sounded like Prince Charles, despite being in his early 20s. He was tall and bony and, from the sounds of it, had never been told 'no' as a child. He made some quip about how the piano player was sticking to the tried and tested same-old, same-old, and only got a few grunts in reply. Adam didn't much like him.

He *did*, however, very much like the next two.

Isiah Lookman wore his suit casually. No tie, top button open. Adam would bet no socks, too, which he wasn't usually a fan of, but got the feeling that this guy could pull it off. His hair was shaved tight to his scalp, except for a strip up the middle which was dyed a bright red. Isiah cracked a little joke at his own expense, and the table laughed. He had an easy air about him.

And if Isiah was easy to like, Sean O'Connell was doubly so. He spoke with a thick Southern Irish accent and looked somewhat out of his element. The suit he wore looked cheap and shabby; shiny around the elbows and stained on the lapels. He sat at an angle, with one arm draped over the back of the chair. He occasionally tucked a stray strand of his curly ginger hair behind an ear, and looked like he was already a few Guinness's deep.

Adam and Colin were the last to introduce themselves, and finished just in time. The first courses were arriving.

Adam winced at what was set in front of him.

'Cèpe mushroom with Jerusalem artichoke and truffle,' the waiter said with a bow. Seconds later, the sommelier made an appearance and filled their glasses with a perfectly paired red wine, while giving them information about the type of grape used and the process of manufacture of this particular variety.

All Adam wanted was a can of coke and a cheeseburger. It was going to be a long night.

As the scant offerings were devoured by the rest of the table and picked at by Adam, Tex brought up the painting.

'What's with the print of Grachten?' he said.

'Grachten? Isn't that one of the chicks from Mean Girls?' Isiah quipped.

'That's Gretchen Wieners, you ignoramus,' Sean said, causing the table to howl with laughter.

'You know it?' Maggie asked Tex, in reply to his original question.

'I'm an art dealer, of course I know it! It was Otto Van Schaik's masterpiece, though of course it was sold shortly after the time of painting, having spent only a matter of months in a gallery.'

'Seems like you know your stuff,' the old lady smiled. 'Why not take a closer look?'

Tex got up and moved around the table. He peered closely at the details of the painting, from the signature in the bottom right-hand corner to the turquoise-coloured canals depicted in thick brushstrokes.

'You're kidding me,' he muttered, before turning to Maggie. 'You *own* it?!'

'It's been in my family for generations.'

'And you just, what, carry it about with you?'

'Yes. It makes me smile every time I look at it. What's the point of keeping it in storage, or at home? It's an excellent conversation starter, too.'

'It is magnificent,' Tex agreed. 'But, do you know how much it's worth?'

'Something like four million,' she said, breezily. 'At least, that's what the last valuation said.'

The table erupted in a quiet furore at the casualness with which the figure was said, like it was no more than loose change, and Adam wondered if she'd made a mistake in disclosing the princely sum.

The rest of the night passed quickly. Wine flowed and so did conversation, and before long, Adam found himself tipsily stumbling into the huge bed. Out of the windows, he watched the stars twinkle and swirl, before closing his eyes and letting sleep claim him.

3

THE INEVITABLE BOTHER

COLIN AWOKE WITH a start.

The room was dark and when he checked his watch, he saw that it was shortly after three in the morning. His head swam a little from the sheer amount of wine consumed a couple of hours previously, his mouth was dry and he couldn't figure what had woken him up.

He wracked his brain, and remembered a dream that ended in a scream. Had the scream been real? Was Adam in trouble?

Quickly, he pushed himself off the luxurious sofa, staggered across to the bedroom and turned the handle. He snuck in to find Adam on his side, snoring loudly with one arm hanging down the side of the bed, dead to the world.

Colin pulled the door closed again and looked around. Maybe it *had* been his dream that had woken him, but a feeling was tugging at his chest, telling him that something was wrong.

He checked the rest of the suite, before opening the door and heading outside onto the deck. He leaned against the barrier for a while and took a moment to appreciate the star-filled sky, the lack of land and the sheer vastness of the sea. The cool wind felt nice against his clammy skin, and he basked in it for a few more minutes, before turning back to his room.

Except, as he turned, something caught his eye.

The door to the next cabin along was open, which struck him as odd at this time of night. He walked over to it, and gasped at what he saw.

Lying on the thick carpeted floor of the suite was Maggie.

Her arms were above her head, like she'd been frozen in the middle of a Mexican Wave, and her monogramed silk pyjamas had ridden up, revealing a little tattoo to the left of her bellybutton. Her face was frozen in a rictus of pain, and Colin fell to his knees beside her and checked for a pulse.

Luckily, the faint throb of flowing blood was present at her wrist, and after thirty seconds, Colin let her hand fall gently to the floor. He wracked his brain for what to do next.

He didn't want to move her in case she had suffered spinal injuries, and knew the best thing to do was leave her where she was. The wind blowing in off the ocean was cold though, so he went to her bedroom and pulled the heavy duvet off, placing it over her where she lay.

As he was about to go and get Adam, the old lady began muttering groggily. She opened one eye slowly, and then the other, and cried out in fear when she saw Colin.

'It's okay,' he said, soothingly, holding up his hands like an arrested man. 'You've had a fall. It's Colin, we met at the dinner earlier. Do you remember? I'm trying to help you.'

'No… no…' She tried to push herself up and away from him.

'Try to stay relaxed,' he whispered. 'In a minute, I'm going to go and find someone who can check you over.'

He kneeled down beside her and stroked her hair, as one would a small child who was distressed. She closed her eyes again.

'Do you remember what happened?' Colin asked. 'Were you on your way out for a little midnight stroll?'

'A knock,' she muttered. 'A knock.'

'Someone knocked on your door?'

'Mmhmm.'

'And you answered it?'

'Yes.'

'Who was it?' Colin asked.

'Didn't see them. Too dark. Dressed in black. They shoved me and I think I banged my head. Next thing, you've woken me up.'

'Did they say anything?'

'No. As soon as I opened it, they pushed me over. That's all I can remember.'

Colin could see the old lady didn't know what happened next, and didn't want to cause any more distress by pushing her further. As he tried to keep her calm, he wondered why anyone would ram an old lady over in the middle of the night.

And then it hit him.

It was obvious.

The painting.

He pushed himself up from the floor and walked further into the room. The easel was standing near her bed, but the framed painting was nowhere to be seen.

He went to the kitchen and poured water into a glass, and took it to Maggie.

'It's gone, isn't it?' she said, when she'd taken a sip.

'Yes,' Colin nodded.

Her eyes immediately began to well and she started to sob, tear tracks travelling down her wrinkled skin. Colin rubbed her shoulder, and in a moment of being unsure how best to comfort her, said: 'The police will find it.'

She shook her head. 'I was told about that before I came on the boat. My son warned me. Told me I was being stupid taking it with me, that because it's international waters, there won't be much the police can do.'

'But, it's a boat. It's not like whoever took it can have got very far. Surely the captain can just search everyone's rooms.'

She stayed quiet, so Colin spoke again.

'Look, Adam and I have solved a few crimes back home. We'll find the painting for you.'

'No,' she said, 'I wouldn't want to put you through any bother. Besides, where would you even start?' she asked.

Colin was thinking about their dinner table. It was clear that Maggie wasn't in possession of the painting, and neither were he or Adam, which left the five men who they'd been sat with.

'You worry about getting better,' Colin said, squeezing her hand. 'And let us worry about the painting.'

The rest of the night passed in a flurry of activity.

Colin woke Adam up and made him go and get a doctor, who turned up quickly and checked on Maggie. Happy that no lasting damage had been caused, aside from the possibility of concussion, they helped her up off the floor and guided her to her bed. The doctor said he'd look after her, to make sure she stayed awake so that he could monitor her further.

Adam and Colin returned to their suite and Colin relayed what had happened, starting with the waking up and ending with the promise to investigate the missing painting.

Adam looked concerned.

'What is it?' Colin asked.

'Well, I'm supposed to be staying out of trouble.'

'An old lady has just been attacked and robbed, man,' Colin replied, barely keeping the disgust out of his voice.

'I know. Sorry. That was a stupid thing to say. Where do we start?'

4

BREAKFAST AND BLOODY MARYS

AFTER ALL THE excitement, Adam and Colin managed a few more broken hours sleep.

Upon waking, the first thing Adam noticed was the change in Colin. Usually, his best friend was easy-going and carefree, however, this morning he was charged and tense.

'What's up?' Adam asked.

'How could some scummy prick push an old woman over like that and steal from her? It's not right.'

Adam assumed that because Colin was the manager of a retirement home, a job he absolutely loved, he felt a certain affinity with poor Maggie. He was probably imagining someone doing the same to one of the old folks that he looked after.

'We'll find it,' Adam assured him. 'Luckily, there's only so many places someone can hide something on a boat. Even if this particular boat is bloody massive.'

They left their room and knocked on Maggie's door gently. The weary doctor answered and told them that Maggie was sleeping, and that he was pretty sure she wasn't concussed, but was staying with her to make sure she was safe. They thanked him, and told him they would return later.

They made their way down the stairs and into the food hall, the smells of fried eggs and succulent bacon causing their stomachs to growl with hunger. Having not eaten very much of the extravagant menu the previous evening, they piled their plates high with greasy breakfast food and sat down at a table.

Once their food had been eaten, and seconds had been collected, talk turned to the theft.

'At least the suspect pool is fairly narrow,' Adam said, shoving a fourth sausage into his mouth. 'Only five other people really knew about the value of the painting, and unless one of those five blabbed to someone else, and why would they, it has to be one of them.'

Colin nodded. 'Now we just need to figure out who.'

AFTER THEY'D FINISHED gorging themselves, they walked back up towards their room, where Maggie intercepted them.

She'd changed out of her pyjamas into a flowing black dress, a huge contrast from her multi-coloured garb from the night before. Her hair was pulled back into a tight bun and it looked as though she was in mourning.

'I just wanted to say thank you for last night,' she said, clutching Colin's arm.

'It's no problem at all,' he smiled. 'It's good to see you up and about. How are you feeling?'

'Okay. The back of my head is sore, but other than that and a few bruises, I'm right as rain. The doctor was a nice man and stayed with me to make sure I was grand. He said you called round on your way to breakfast.'

'We did. I know it's not the best time, but would you mind if we asked you a couple of questions?'

'Please do, though I'm not sure how much help I'll be.'

She ushered them into her suite and sat down on the sofa. Colin sat opposite her on the armchair while Adam lingered by the door like security.

'We won't keep you long,' Colin said. 'I was just wondering if anything had come back to you, about last night.'

'Sorry,' she said, shaking her head and wincing at the pain. 'Still the same. I opened the door, was pushed over, and woke up with you tending to me. You don't know how much that meant to me. Anything could've happened if it weren't for you.'

Colin waved the praise away. 'What about at dinner? Did anyone seem overly enamoured with the painting?'

'Well, the American was naturally interested in it, but that's his job. Once he examined it, he sat back down and conversation moved on. The well-to-do boy, the posh one, asked a few more questions about it, and I caught the others glancing at it every so often, but I guess that's only natural when you know how much it's worth.'

'No one asked about buying it or anything like that?'

'Lord, no,' she laughed. 'If all five of them bundled together, they still couldn't afford it. Well, maybe the actor could. It was valued at four million nearly ten years ago. Goodness knows what it's worth now.'

'And you've never thought about selling it?'

'Never,' she said, shaking her head. 'It has huge sentimental value, and I'd never considered selling it at any time of my life.'

'Thank you,' Colin said, getting up. 'We'll ask around and see what we can come up with.'

She pulled something from a handbag that was sitting beside her feet and tried to pass it to Colin.

'Your money is no good, here,' he said, pushing the notes back towards her and dismissed her protestations with a kind: 'Now, make sure you get some rest.'

They left her to it, with promises that they would update her with any developments. They walked back to their room to draw up their plan of attack, and quickly settled on locating one person.

THOUGH THE ELYSIAN was certainly big, thankfully it wasn't one of those ridiculous city-on-the-sea type affairs, and they managed to find Henry relatively quickly.

Despite the early hour, he was sat in the ship's casino, pushing coloured chips onto the roulette board. He was wearing a velvet smoking jacket, a crisp white shirt and a pair of tan chinos, and looked positively down in the dumps.

'Lady luck not smiling, eh?' Adam asked, as they approached him.

'You could say that. The pile doth diminish,' Henry half-smiled.

They watched the little white ball zoom around the roulette wheel, before bouncing and slowing, eventually settling in a red section. The croupier gave Henry a slightly pitying look as he raked up the remainder of the chips.

'And that's that, chaps,' Henry said, slapping his thigh and pushing himself up from the stool. They followed him to the bar, where he ordered the three of them a Bloody Mary each without asking, and led them to a table. The room was dark, and the small lamp on the table did little to alleviate that. When Henry spoke, it looked like he was doing that Hallowe'en trick of holding a torch underneath your chin.

'How are things, fellas?' he said. 'Enjoy dinner?'

'Not really my type of food,' Adam said.

'I quite agree,' nodded Henry. 'I thought it was okay, but when you've eaten fresh Beluga Caviar on the shores of the Caspian Sea, this mass-produced stuff like last night's fare pales in comparison.'

'Henry…' started Adam.

'Hazza. Please, call me Hazza. All my close friends do.'

'Okay. Hazza. You know Maggie?'

'Mmhmm, the old dear from our table last night?'

'Aye. Well, she was attacked last night in her room, and her painting was stolen. We were wondering if you knew anything about it?'

'That's bloody awful,' he gasped. 'She seemed like a spiffing sort.'

'She is,' Colin said. 'You don't happen to know anything about it, do you?'

'I'm hearing it for the first time from you, old sport. What could I possibly know about it?'

'We've heard that when we left the dinner last night, you were asking a few questions about the painting.'

'I did art history as a degree,' Hazza shrugged. 'In Florence, no less. I was simply interested in seeing a genuine masterpiece in the flesh. If showing an interest and making conversation is a crime, arrest me now.'

He held out his wrists and chortled.

'And where were you last night at three o'clock?' Adam asked, without humour.

'Chaps, forgive me if I'm gazing in the wrong direction here, but it seems to me like you are levelling accusations my way.'

'Not at all,' Adam said. 'We offered to help find the painting and naturally the people on our table from last night are the first people we're speaking to. We're simply trying to narrow down who could have taken it. Surely, you'd want to see the old lady reunited with her prized possession.'

'Obviously,' he said. 'Yes, obviously. Well, if you must know, I tried to chat up a waitress and failed spectacularly, so went back to my bunk alone.'

'And you stayed there all night?'

'Yes. All night, on my lonesome. Then, I woke up, showered, shaved, dressed and came straight here.'

'Did anyone at the table last night arouse your suspicions?' Adam asked.

'I think Tex is the only one, aside from myself, who understood the importance of the painting. The others probably saw a canvas and a gold frame and weren't that bothered, whereas I saw the effort, the love and all that comes with the creation of something special. Tex asked some questions about it, and obviously as an art dealer, he showed an interest in it, but nothing untoward.'

'Thanks for answering our questions, mate,' Colin said, before assuming a less authoritative air and gesturing to the roulette table. 'How much did you lose?'

'Oh, about a grand,' Hazza said. He tried to pass it off as if it wasn't very much, but Colin could see worry behind his eyes.

'Rough,' he said.

'Oh, luck comes and goes,' Hazza said, gazing around the room. 'Roulette wasn't my friend, but perhaps Blackjack will be. Now, if you'll excuse me, fellas.'

He patted them each on the shoulder two times, as if he'd learned his social cues from sleazy politicians, and strode off towards the card table with his chin in the air.

5

EBBS AND FLOWS

THE BOYS RETREATED to their room, and spent a while lounging about, discussing Hazza. The conclusion was that he either had too much money and didn't mind frittering it away in the name of fun, or that he was low on money and thought he could get a quick win on the roulette table to boost his balance. The latter seemed more plausible, considering the worried expression and the fact he was down a grand (at least) by eleven in the morning.

'I think Tex should be next on the list,' Colin said.

'Good shout,' Adam said. 'Let's go.'

'Hold up. I'm going to do some research on him first. Gimme ten.'

'That's why you're the best,' Adam said. 'I'm going to go and check in with Helena. See how she's getting on with that bloody dress.'

He went into his bedroom and closed the door, leaving Colin on the huge sofa. Colin pulled his phone from his pocket and searched for Tex Rivera. To his surprise, a rather official looking website for The Rivera Art Dealership appeared at the top of the page.

The background was black and the swirling logo for the company was tastefully rendered in silver. Below the banner, a photo of Tex standing beside a framed painting in a pristine gallery stayed for a few seconds, before being replaced by another very similar looking one. Different suit, different painting, same smug look. Colin imagined the wide smile was on account of the pretty penny he'd just made by flogging the painting he was standing in front of.

He found information on the company on one of the links. Tex had set it up a decade ago and had built it steadily, netting more than a million pounds in his first year and growing from there. It claimed he started the dealership out of his kitchen in San Antonio, Texas, before going global, with offices in no less than three continents.

It looked like things had been going well for Tex, right up until about three years ago.

On another page, there was a list of every painting Tex's company had been involved in the sale of. The entries were steady, and then seemed to dry up around 2019. Since then, only a handful of paintings had been sold, and even then, not for a lot. Certainly not enough to keep up what Colin imagined had been a lavish lifestyle.

'Adam!' Colin shouted, and his friend appeared.

'Got something?' he asked.

'I think I do.'

IT TOOK THEM a while to find Tex, but eventually, they did. He was reclining in a deck chair at the prow of the ship, his eyes hidden behind a pair of thick sunglasses. At first, Colin and Adam were unsure as to whether he was awake or not, and jumped when he spoke after a minute of them standing in front of them.

'Can I help you guys?' he drawled.

'Hi, Tex. It's Colin and Adam. We were at your table last night.'

'Right, right. Yeah, I remember. How are you guys doing?'

'We're alright,' Colin nodded. 'You mind if we sit?'

'Not at all,' Tex smiled. 'You want a drink?'

'We're fine for now, thanks.' Colin took a seat on one side of the American, and Adam sat on the other. Tex focussed his attention on Colin. 'You mind if we ask you a few questions about last night?'

'About what?'

'About Maggie's painting. It's gone missing.'

'No way,' Tex gasped. 'That's sad, man. She okay?'

'She's not taking it well,' Adam said. 'We're trying to help her.'

'Right on. That's good of you. Ask me anything, I'll do anything I can to help, too.'

Colin pulled a notebook from his pocket that he'd taken from the coffee table in their suite. At the sight of it and the Elysian embossed pen, Tex sat up a little straighter.

'You cops?' he asked.

Colin shook his head, suppressing a laugh. 'No, just a couple of do-gooders. But, we've found from experience that having notes of what people have said has come in handy. You don't mind, do you?'

'Of course not,' he said, though he looked like he didn't mean it.

'Can you tell us about last night?'

'You were there, man,' Tex said.

'We were, but it's good to hear events from a different perspective.'

'Okay. Well, I asked Maggie about the painting, had dinner and when Maggie left, Henry and I retired to a quieter bar for a nightcap.'

'Time?'

'Maggie left at about eleven. We all stayed at the table until midnight, then the others made their excuses. Henry, or Hazza as he insisted I call him, offered to pay for a decent brandy, and who am I to say no?'

'So you two went off to a bar. What time did you stay 'til?'

'We only stayed for one drink, and I was happily tucked up in bed by one thirty.'

'And Henry?'

'We left together. Far as I know he went to bed, too.'

'Did he try and chat up a barmaid?'

'He was trying to chat up anyone. Men like him, with money in the bank, think that's enough to pull whoever you want into the sheets.' There was disgust in his voice. 'Thankfully, everyone he tried said no.'

'Did you talk about the painting?' Colin asked.

'It came up,' Tex shrugged. 'Not every day you see something worth that amount of money.'

'What did you say about it?'

'I said nothing. Henry was asking the questions—was it really worth that much and who on earth would pay it? Those kinds of things. I told him it was definitely worth that much, and probably more than what poor Maggie thinks. Four million seems a bit low to me. As for who would buy it, there are art galleries and private collectors all over the globe who would pay that in a heartbeat.'

'And you have those connections?' Adam asked.

'Now, hold up. I hope that wasn't an accusation? Yes, I do have those connections, but purely professionally, you hear me, boy?'

Adam held up a pair of placating hands and nodded.

'I ain't got nothing to do with the theft, you hear?' Tex boomed again.

'We hear you. Adam didn't mean to make it sound accusatory, did you?' Colin said, and Adam shook his head.

'Fine,' Tex said, though he didn't look happy.

'Tell me about your business,' Colin said, trying to get back on to a level footing.

'Not much to tell. It's my baby, and I travel the world doing what I love. Not many people can say that.'

'I saw on the web that you've had a rough couple of years.'

'Ebbs and flows, my boy.' Tex smiled, but his words came out tersely. Colin could tell their chat was coming to an end. 'Truth is, art goes in waves. Sometimes, collectors fall over themselves to buy. Sometimes, it's like trying to sell ice to Eskimos. Or Inuits, or whatever you're supposed to call them now so as to not offend. What I'm saying is, you gotta plan for this. You have a bumper year, you be wise with your money. You hold on to some funds for when the lean year rolls around.'

Colin made to move, thinking Tex's business advice was the full stop in their conversation, but he was wrong.

'Matter of fact, this cruise isn't all for pleasure, it's for business, too. I've got an opportunity in Lisbon, when we stop tomorrow. I sell a painting there, I'm good for another couple of months. Like I say, ebbs and flows.'

6

LISBON, PORTUGAL

ADAM AND COLIN stood by the huge bedroom window, watching the City of Seven Hills grow larger as the ship was guided towards the port with military precision.

'So, you don't think we should try and get into his room?' Adam asked.

'I don't think so,' Colin shrugged. 'He's hardly going to tell us that he's going to sell a painting in the city, and it turn out to be the one taken from Maggie. If he was going to do that, he'd have kept schtum.'

'Yeah, you're probably right.'

Though frustrated with the lack of progress in the hunt for the missing art, Adam was excited about visiting a new city. He was Stonebridge born and raised, and had rarely ventured beyond the border of Northern Ireland, so he resolved to forget about their latest case while visiting Portugal's capital, and enjoy the city.

As the ship came to a halt, they grabbed their backpacks and made their way towards the gangplank.

AFTER TEN MINUTES of walking, the heat was stifling. Coupled with the vertiginous terrain, Adam was finding it tough to breathe. He motioned to Colin that he needed to sit down for a minute, and the two of them took solace on a nearby bench, bolted into the ground at a near forty-five degree angle.

'Why would anyone in their right mind build a city on such a hilly place?' Adam moaned.

'For the view?' Colin suggested, motioning to the expanse of ocean.

'Yeah, but at what cost? Everyone must be so knackered all the time that they can't be bothered to take in the view.'

'Not everyone is as unfit as you.'

'Shut up.'

As if to drive the point home, a little old lady with snow-white hair, marched past them while pushing a fabric shopping trolley. She smiled at them as she passed, and didn't look like a bead of sweat had been spilled with effort.

Adam jumped to his feet with renewed vigour, keen to show the show-off octogenarian that he could keep up, though they trailed in her wake as she made steady progress up the hill.

'Wow, you're really showing her,' Colin laughed.

Adam was too out of puff to even think of an appropriate rebuttal.

At the summit, they found themselves in a wide, cobbled courtyard. A couple of bars were welcoming their first customers of the day, while a line snaked out of a bakery and around the corner of the building.

'Beer or bread?' Colin asked.

'After that climb? Beer, I reckon,' said Adam.

They made their way to an outside table with a wide parasol that sheltered them from the blazing afternoon sun. They consulted a menu and, after a few minutes, a waiter in a casual shirt and a dainty fedora approached and took their order.

When their drinks had been deposited on the beermats in front of them, both Adam and Colin relaxed back in their seats and savoured the day. A light breeze blew through the square, and the frothy beer did a wonderful job of cooling them down further.

Talk turned to the wedding, and to Colin's own blossoming relationship. When they'd been growing up, they'd both been unlucky in love: unlucky in the sense that the opposite sex had generally considered them invisible. Now, things were looking up, and both were very positive about what was to come.

And then, ten minutes later, something stopped the conversation between them. Or rather, someone.

Tex Rivera, suited and with a tan Stetson perched atop his head, appeared over the brow of the hill. He was holding a large brown envelope. Sweat plummeted down his brow like a waterfall, and he walked with laser-like precision to the mouth of a street nestled between the bar and the bakery, eyes never once deviating from his course, and disappeared from view.

Adam jumped out of his seat and walked carefully to the lip of the street. He stood with his back against the stone building, and chanced a glance. The street was narrow, and opened onto a labyrinth of other smaller alleys and thoroughfares. Adam cursed, before quickly realising that they probably hadn't lost him at all. About a third of the way down the street was a small shop with a sign hanging above its door, proclaiming it to be the oldest art dealership in the country.

Adam hotfooted it back to the table, and relayed the information back to Colin.

'What do we do?' Adam asked.

'We wait.'

Adam ordered two more drinks, non-alcoholic this time, while Colin tinkered on his phone. It didn't take long for Tex to reappear, and when he did, he seemed to have an extra bounce in his step.

'Now what?'

'We go and visit the art dealer,' Colin said.

They quickly finished their drinks, left a tip on the table and made their way down the alley.

Muñoz Carvalho's shop looked small from the outside. The narrow window showcased a framed painting in the style of pointillism, and a carefully sculpted bronze figure that appeared to be mid-ballet move. It was tastefully done, to Adam's (very) untrained eye. Colin pushed the door open, and a little bell tinkling above their heads signalled their arrival.

A short, round man with weathered skin and a beautiful combover appeared from the back and greeted them warmly in English.

'Is it that obvious?' Adam laughed.

'Yes, my friend. You look like human milk bottle. Now, how may I help today?'

'I'm a huge art fan, and I've been looking forward to visiting your shop for many years,' Colin smiled, casting an admiring glance around the space.

The old man looked pleased.

Adam looked confused.

Colin continued. 'I've read about it, of course, in ARTnews. Quite a coup. The oldest shop in the city.'

'In all of Portugal,' the old man beamed.

'Of course, my mistake,' Colin said, marvelling at the four decorated walls. 'It's an honour to meet you, Mr Carvalho.'

'The honour is mine. Can I show you around?'

'Please.'

Muñoz showed an entranced Colin and a bemused Adam around his small shop, talking at length about the artwork that adorned the walls. He was passionate, and occasionally lapsed into rapid-fire Portuguese, before he corrected himself with an apology.

'Your English is very good,' Colin said, once all the paintings had been appraised.

'I work with dealers from all over the world. Middle-Easterns, Japanese…'

'American?' Colin interrupted.

'Sim,' he nodded.

'We just saw Tex Rivera out in the courtyard and we couldn't believe our eyes… well, I say we. This one,' Colin patted Adam's chest, 'wouldn't know the difference between a Picasso and a Pollock.'

Colin and Muñoz laughed heartily.

'Sim, Mr Rivera is a good man. He is respected in the art community for having a good eye. He bring me…'

The old man held a finger up and disappeared into the back.

'Oi, why are you making me sound like an idiot?' Adam hissed.

Before Colin could answer, the old man was back, holding a frame. He turned it to reveal a watercolour of snowy mountains and pink blossoms drifting from spindly trees.

'Glorious, no?'

'Yes, it's wonderful.'

'Like I say, Mr Rivera has good eye. It's not often a Kobayashi comes on the market.'

'Is that all he brought?'

'Sim. This is worth a lot of money. Though, he did mention that he has another painting that he had recently come into contact with, but he was saving it for one of the more renowned galleries in Venice.'

Adam and Colin exchanged a glance.

'Did he say anything else about it?'

'No, senhor. Just that it was out of my price range.'

Colin thanked him for the tour, and for his hospitality, before leaving his shop.

'When did you become a bloody expert on art?' Adam said.

'Took a quick Google crash course on Mr Carvalho while you were ordering the drinks. And good thing I did, too, because it looks like we have a lead.'

7

THERE'S NO BUSINESS LIKE SHOWBUSINESS

ADAM AND COLIN sat in the first-class bar, sipping at a glass of expensive champagne that was entirely lost on both of them.

'Are you supposed to just know if it's good or not?' Adam asked. 'Tastes like paint stripper to me.'

'Not sure,' Colin replied, looking at the bubbles fizzing in the glass. 'Probably. I mean, not everyone can go to wine school or whatever it's called.'

'Maybe our taste buds have been wiped away from all the coke and crisps we've eaten.'

'Aye, or maybe we're just not cultured enough to appreciate the intricacies of such fancy drinks.'

'I barely know what the word intricacies means, so you're probably right.'

They clinked glasses anyway and downed the rest of the contents, much to the horror of an elderly couple who were watching on from a nearby table.

'So, what do you reckon then?' Colin asked.

'About Tex?'

'Aye.'

'Well, it seems pretty cut and dried. It looks like he's going to save the stolen painting for a more exclusive gallery in Venice, who can pay bigger bucks and who can probably provide a little more discretion.'

'But what if the painting he told Muñoz about wasn't the stolen one? It's just a better one than the one he sold in Lisbon.'

'The old man said that Tex told him that he'd recently come into contact with it,' Adam shrugged.

'That could've been a week before he boarded the ship.'

'So, what are you suggesting?'

'I think we should assume that Tex has the painting, and alert the Venetian authorities when we get a bit closer so that they can apprehend him upon arrival,' Colin said. 'However, I also think we should also make sure that we don't put all our chickens in one basket…'

'Eggs,' Adam interjected.

'Huh?'

'You put eggs in a basket, not chickens.'

'Is that what I said?' Colin laughed. 'Well, whatever nonsense I'm talking still stands. We focus on Tex, but make sure we keep an eye on the others too.'

'Why don't we just go all-out on Tex? Barge into his room, find the painting and all this ends.'

'Because you told me that you were supposed to be staying out of trouble,' Colin said. 'So, let's leave it to the authorities, who will catch him red-handed when he is trying to get off the boat with stolen goods. Meanwhile, let's try to enjoy ourselves.'

At that moment, the door to the bar flew open and in walked a smouldering Vaughn McClusky. He marched up to the bar and ordered a large glass of expensive whisky, before stalking off to a table near the back of the room where he sat with his head in his hands, long fingers scratching at his scalp.

'He looks troubled,' Adam said.

'Maybe we should go and lend a sympathetic ear,' Colin suggested.

'To the star of such hits as Dead In The Grave, Maximum Extermination and I'll Be Back Before I'm Dead?'

'Is that seriously the name of his biggest films?'

'Yeah.'

'No wonder he's not hit the big time yet!' Colin laughed. 'All I'm saying is, remember what we said about keeping our options open? You never know, he could have the painting safely stowed away in his room. This performance he's putting on could be a sign of guilt.'

'He's an actor, dumbass. If he'd stolen the painting, he'd be acting like he hadn't.'

'Could be double-bluffing.'

'You're an idiot,' Adam said. 'I know you want to help the old lady, so do I, but Vaughn is not our man. Though, because I'm a nosey so and so, I do want to know what's upset him.'

'Me too,' Colin said. 'Let's go.'

They picked up their drinks and sauntered across the room. As they approached him, Adam gazed at the actor's tailored blazer and fitted chinos, and wondered what it would be like to have enough money that nothing would ever be a worry again.

He asked Colin, who shrugged.

'Your worries become different, don't they?' he said, sagely. 'Instead of stressing about your next pay packet or mortgage payment, you probably start worrying about a stray grey hair or a deepening wrinkle. Show Business is a fickle game.'

'Goodness. I didn't realise I was talking to Aristotle!'

'I'm a font of knowledge,' Colin said. 'You should ask me big philosophical questions more often.'

'Will I ever be truly happy?' Adam asked.

'For a while next Saturday, aye, but then after that, naw. It's all downhill from the alter, my friend.'

They laughed as they weaved through the tables, though stopped as they came to Vaughn's. When he looked up, Adam noticed a vein popping in his forehead and blotchy marks under his eyes.

'Can I help you?' he asked.

'We were at the table with you the other night for dinner. Adam and Colin,' Adam said, waving his hands as a children's television presenter might, feeling like a prize idiot.

Colin grimaced, and took over. 'May we join you?'

Vaughn looked like he wanted to say no, but was probably imagining the headlines in Heat and The Daily Fail if a guest who was sitting close by ratted him out for not having time for his fans.

'Please, do,' he said, motioning to the seats.

'Quite a ship, eh?' Adam said.

'Yeah, it's big alright.'

'I've gotta say, I loved you in He's Behind You. It's about time the comedy detective genre was started up again, and you are the perfect man to get it going.'

'Thank you,' Vaughn said, graciously.

'Any plans for a sequel?'

'There's some talk of one, yes, but you never know in this business.'

'And what are you working on at the minute?' Adam asked.

'Well, I'm between projects, but I'm heading to Venice to have a chat with a producer about something big. Could be the one that takes me to the next level.'

'That's cool,' said Colin, trying to counteract Adam's over-the-topness by going the other way. 'You don't seem overly pumped by it. Is everything okay?'

'It will be. Hopefully. As with everything in this business, nothing is ever done until it's on a cinema screen. Right up until that moment, nothing is certain. Take this one, for example. The guy I'm going to meet thinks we have the funding to get started within the next three months. We have the hottest script in town, we have a director who has just won the best newcomer at Cannes, we've got a location with tax breaks. We have it all.'

'Except?'

Just then, Vaughn's phone beeped, and he instinctively reached a hand into his jacket pocket. From it, he produced one of those pill boxes that separate medication into days or doses, and popped two circular tablets from today's section. He threw them in his mouth and washed them down with the whisky.

'Probably a no-no,' he laughed. 'Sorry about that. What was I saying?'

'You were about to tell us why your next project isn't set in stone.'

'Oh yeah. We have it all, except the backing. The guy who was putting the money up dropped out this morning. He has "reservations", apparently,' Vaughn said, using his hands to make air quotes.

'And it can't get made unless he's on board?'

'Well, not necessarily him, but someone with money. We're talking multi-millions here. Not pocket money.' He took a hearty slug from his glass and wiped his top lip. 'I woke up this morning so bloody excited, and then he phoned. It's a soul-destroying business.'

'Something will come up, surely,' Colin smiled. 'Like you say, all the other pieces of the jigsaw are in place. Keep the faith.'

Vaughn smiled sincerely for the first time since they'd sat down. He reached out his hand and Colin shook it.

'You ever thought about going into life coaching?' Vaughn laughed. 'You'd make a bloody fortune in LA. Half the town would pay you a small fortune for the little pep talk you just gave me.'

'Now there's an idea,' Colin chuckled. 'Look, we've taken up enough of your time. We'll leave you to it.'

Vaughn thanked them, and as they walked away, he shouted after Adam.

'You're a fan, right?'

'Yeah.'

'I'm sorry for being a grump. Tomorrow night, let's have a proper drink and I'll be less of a dick. I promise.'

Adam nodded as casually as he could, but practically skipped from the room as soon as he was out of sight of the actor.

8

A BRIDGE OVER TROUBLED WATER

ADAM AWOKE THE next morning to the same shimmering sunshine, and the same stunning view of sea and sky. Yet this time, he found he wasn't enjoying it.

He checked the time, and was pretty sure that Colin would be up by now, so pulled on a T-shirt and a pair of shorts, and made his way into the lounge to find his friend reclined on the sofa, reading a book.

'Good morning,' Colin said.

'It's morning, but I don't know if it's a good one.'

'Oh, I don't know about that. We're in the middle of the ocean on a big old ship, en route to Barcelona where I thought we might pay a visit to the Nou Camp, and not long after that, we'll be in Venice and on to Lake Garda, and you'll be mumbling your vows to the woman you love.'

'Well, when you put it like that,' Adam smiled, and sat down on the other sofa. 'I just can't help thinking of poor Maggie, and it's sort of ruining the trip for me.'

'I know what you mean,' Colin nodded.

'So, I've got a plan.'

'Oh, no. I know that look.'

'What look?'

'That look in your eyes. You're going to suggest something that goes against everything you promised Helena before you left.'

'Yeah, but it's to help an old lady who has been robbed. And, if we can do that, the stress I'm feeling will disappear and I'll be able to enjoy the rest of the trip and the wedding.'

Colin stroked his chin. 'Tell me your plan.'

For the next few minutes, Adam talked and Colin listened, and when the talking was finished, Colin shook his head and said: 'That's insane.'

ADAM AGREED THAT the plan was insane. Of course it was.

But, he wanted this case to be over with, and so, desperate times called for desperate measures.

The boys got themselves dressed for the day and made their way down to breakfast. They grabbed a plate, filled it and sat down, casting their eyes around for their intended target, who was nowhere to be seen.

Unfazed, they began eating, discussing the finer points of the plan in hushed voices. Adam noticed Sean and Isiah, the two lads they hadn't managed to speak to yet, at a table by the door. They were laughing and joking like they had been pals for years, each clutching either an orange juice or a Mimosa. Probably the latter, Adam thought, judging by their joviality.

'We should chat to them at some point, too,' Colin said, following Adam's gaze. 'They look thick as thieves.'

Adam agreed.

Any further discussion on that point was cut off by the appearance of their man.

Tex Rivera.

He walked to the breakfast bar with the air of a man with the world at his feet. Despite the early hour, he was dressed to the nines; a gold blazer and crocodile skin loafers.

Adam gave him the thumbs up, and when he'd sorted his food, the art dealer made a beeline for their table. He sat down with a little groan, and greeted them with a firm handshake.

'What's with the get up?' Colin asked.

'Oh, this?' he said, pulling at one of the lapels. 'You know how Tiger Woods always wears a red tee on the final day of a tournament? Well, I always wear this the day after a big sale. It's become something of a tradition.'

'Ah, balls,' Adam said, suddenly. 'Do either of you have the time?'

'It's just gone eight thirty,' said Tex, checking an expensive Rolex.

'Sorry, gents. I'm going to have to love you and leave you for a minute,' Adam said, pushing himself up from the table. 'I said I'd phone Helena before she heads to work. Excuse me.'

Adam heard Colin mention a ball and chain, and Tex's raucous laughter followed him as he left the restaurant.

That's right, pal. Laugh it up, thought Adam as he made his way back to his room.

BACK IN HIS bedroom, Adam opened the door to the balcony. In the past twenty-four hours, he'd realised two things of note:

Firstly, the balcony doors could not be locked. Adam presumed it was to stop you locking yourself on the balcony, unable to get back into the room to contact help. It was a safety feature that was about to work to his advantage.

The second thing he'd noticed was that Tex's room was right next door to his.

Now, obviously they couldn't just knock on his door and ask for a look around. He was sure to close the door in their faces. But, a little nosey without supervision would surely yield results. So, Adam's plan was thus.

1. Climb from his balcony to Tex's
2. Have a look around the room
3. Uncover the stolen painting
4. Turn Tex over to the authorities at the next available opportunity
5. Enjoy the rest of the holiday

When he'd dreamt up his plan, the gap between the balconies had seemed smaller. Looking at them now, the chasm between them seemed comparable to the Grand Canyon. Coupled with the sheer drop, the frothing waves and deep blue sea below, not to mention the sharp-toothed things sure to be lurking down there, he felt terror stir in his bowels.

Literally.

He rushed back inside and made it to the toilet, just in time.

Back outside, he looked at the gap and wondered if he really cared this much? Was it worth putting his life on the line, and the happiness of his bride-to-be, just to get some stupid painting back?

Except, it wasn't just some stupid painting. It was a masterpiece. And, more than that—it was the very idea that someone thought they could take whatever they wanted, even if that something was from an elderly lady.

Buoyed, Adam tentatively climbed onto the railing, swung his leg over the wooden handrail and reached out, ever so carefully, towards Tex's balcony.

Suddenly, the boat lurched sideways as it crested a wave, and Adam felt for sure that he was a goner. He gripped onto the rail with all his strength, his knuckles white from the effort of clinging on, and when the boat righted itself, found that he was still alive.

As quickly and as carefully as he could, he clambered over the top of the balcony and fell onto the ivory tiles on his back, panting with exertion and relief. He took a few minutes to compose himself, before getting up and making his way into Tex's room.

It wasn't quite up to the same standard as the Bridal Suite, but it wasn't far off. Adam surveyed the space, cursing the fact that the painting wasn't there in the centre of the room, propped on an easel with a spotlight focussed on it.

No, that would be *far* too easy.

Instead of wallowing, and aware that his time alone was running out, he tore through the main room and the bedroom like a Tasmanian Devil. He scooped up the sheets to check under the bed, he checked behind the sofa and in the kitchen cupboards, but came away empty handed.

And then he realised where it would be.

In Adam's own bedroom—or cabin he supposed it was called on a ship—there was a huge safe concealed within the wardrobe. In Tex's room, the same turned out to be true. Behind the wardrobe's mirrored door, sat a metal box with a small digital display and a keypad. It was built so ruggedly that it looked like a stick of dynamite would barely make a singe mark.

Adam supposed that there was nothing else for it.

He didn't want to guess the code, in case the police who investigated dusted the place for prints. He realised that he'd touched other places in the room, but surely they wouldn't be dusting the bottom of a valance.

Reluctantly, he slid the wardrobe closed again and made his way out of the room. At the door, he cast one last glance back, before slinking out, content at hearing it click locked behind him; but frustrated that he'd left the American's room empty handed.

9

LUCKY'S

ADAM AND COLIN cut frustrated figures as they sat on the sofa in their suite, facing each other.

'In reality, it doesn't change much,' Colin shrugged. 'Does it?'

'I guess not,' Adam said, though the disappointment of not finding the painting was etched on his face. He'd been looking forward to bringing the case to a close and getting on with his pre-wedding trip. 'Tell me again what you chatted about.'

'Nothing, really. He told me about selling the painting in Lisbon…'

'And you didn't ask about the one he plans to sell in Venice?'

'How could I?' Colin said. 'If he knew that we knew that, he'd know we were snooping around after him.'

'True. Good point, well made. What else?'

'Future plans. I told him about you getting married, he told me that he's going to fly home from Italy and spend some time with his family.'

'And he didn't seem on edge, or anything?'

'No,' Colin said, shaking his head. 'Cool as a cucumber. Made me doubt our hypothesis a bit, actually.'

'You don't think it's him?'

'I don't know. But I think we should get on with chatting to the others. We've spoken to Hazza, Tex and Vaughn, which leaves two more.'

'Sean and Isiah.'

'Indeed. So, I'm thinking we head out for a walk and see if we can bump into either of them. See if they know anything.'

'Plan. Gimme ten,' Adam said, and made for the bedroom.

ADAM PLUGGED HIS phone into the charger and waited for it to power up. He thought that chatting to the other two cold would be a waste of time, but maybe with a bit of information about them, the conversations could yield some results. (He'd been impressed when Colin had done it before entering the art gallery in Lisbon, and wanted to be similarly prepared.)

When the phone flashed, he snatched it up and opened Safari. He typed in Isiah's name, and was dismayed by the lack of results. It appeared that Isiah was like Adam, and was staying in first class by the grace of God (or thanks to the kindness of a family member). There was no evidence to link him to a famous family, or a business, or a won fortune.

Unlike Sean O'Connell, who it transpired was the son of an Irish businessman called Trevor.

Adam read an interview on the Financial Time's website, all about how Trevor's business was dealing with the fallout from Brexit. Amongst the doom and gloom of export prices and European red tape, there was a little golden nugget.

It appeared that Trevor thought Sean was an unsuitable candidate to take over the running of the business when the time came. Apparently, Sean did not possess the business acumen required to step into the role of heir apparent. When pushed, Trevor had hinted that his son wasn't good at budgeting, before moving the interview on.

Adam set the phone down and thought about what that meant. Could his father's public ire and disappointment have turned Sean into a thief? Had he stolen the painting in the hope of selling it on, and showing his father just how good he was with money?

It seemed a bit far-fetched, but that was where they were. Adam left his phone where it was, filled Colin in with what he had found, and set off in search of their prey.

IT TURNED OUT Sean was to be located relatively easy. They found him slouched over a bar, though not in the first-class lounge.

Lucky's was an Irish-themed pub in the middle of the boat. The décor was tacky, as if the person in charge had googled "Irish themed pub" and ordered anything and everything that they'd seen. Bunting with pots of gold and leprechauns hung overhead, green bulbs bathed the room in a sickly glow, and antique Guinness signs were plastered over every available surface.

As Colin and Adam took a seat on either side of Sean, The Dropkick Murphy's "I'm Shipping Up To Boston" gave way to "Dirty Old Town" by The Pogues, perhaps setting the tone for their chat.

Sean pushed his fiery red curls behind his ears and assessed his guests with bleary eyes.

'Right, lads?' he asked.

Adam nodded and introduced them both, in case Sean had forgotten who they were, or was too inebriated to remember.

'I remember ye, alright. Ye fancy a drink?'

'We're grand, thanks.'

'Suit yoursels,' he said, downing the remainder of his pint and motioning to the bartender for another. 'If ye don't want a drink, what are ye after?'

He said it with a smile, but the words seemed barbed.

'Well, it's a bit of a sensitive subject, actually. Do you mind if we have a chat somewhere a bit more private?'

Sean nodded and pointed towards a booth at the far side of the room. He waited for his pint while Adam and Colin got settled on the bench seats. They watched as Sean stumbled towards them, taking care not to lose a single millilitre of his stout.

'Right ye are,' he said, gulping down a third of his pint, before jutting his chin in their direction. 'Hit me.'

'Right,' Colin said. 'Remember the first night where we all had dinner?'

'Aye.'

'Do you remember the old woman?'

'I do. Bit mad, wasn't she?'

'A bit,' Colin conceded. 'Well, she's had her painting stolen, and we're looking to get it back. We're asking all the people from the dinner table if they know anything.'

'First I'm hearing of it, if I'm honest. I feel bad for the lady, but what do you expect is gonna happen if you parade a priceless painting about? Bit of a mad move if you ask me.'

'You haven't heard anything or seen anything suspicious?'

'Like I said, first I'm hearing about it.'

Colin looked disappointed.

'How are you affording being in first class?' Adam asked, suddenly.

'What did you say to me?' Sean said, all affability gone. His teeth were bared and the stink of stout clouded the space between them.

'It's just…'

'I know what you're about to say. You've read that bloody article that my dad did, slagging me off to high heaven about my spending. Let's not get things twisted here—he's right. I'm pap with money. Always have been, always will be. As soon as I get paid, I'm straight to the nearest bar or shop or what have you, and it's gone before I know it. I'm too generous for me own good.'

'So…'

'So how am I here? In a turn up for the book, old Daddy O'Connell paid for it. And it's not his way of saying sorry, neither. Don't you go thinking he's soft. I'm here for work. On a "networking mission" apparently.' He made air quotes with grubby fingers and necked the rest of his pint. 'Daddy told me to get to know people, look for investment opportunities or, more to the point, someone that would take me off his hands.'

'What do you mean?'

'He wants me involved in his company as much as I want this latest batch of crabs.' He pointed to his belt. 'I'm here to further his business interests, and if I can sweet talk someone into taking me on, then all the better.'

'So you and your dad aren't the best of friends? What happens if he does cut you off?' Adam asked.

'Then I'm out on me ear.'

Adam and Colin shared a glance.

'No, no, no,' Sean shouted. 'I'm not having you two wee pricks thinking that my possible lack of income means that I was desperate enough to steal that wee woman's painting. Money might burn a hole in my pocket when I have it, but I'm no thief. I'd rather live on the streets than take something that isn't mine, especially from an old lady.'

To Adam's ears, it seemed convincing.

'And if you're pointing fingers at anyone, I'd have a look at that Isiah fella. I've only known the guy a few days, and he's already tried to get me involved in some of his get-rich-quick schemes. I imagine he couldn't believe his eyes and ears when that dotty old lady brought her priceless art to dinner!'

10

THE PROPHET

AS IF THE day hadn't yielded enough excitement, there was another black-tie dinner affair to attend.

With knowledge of what the evening would hold, Adam and Colin headed off to the KFC on board and loaded up on chicken wings and chips. They discussed the type of person who would slather their meal in the Colonel's special gravy, and came to the conclusion that it was the work of a psychopath.

Then, talk turned to more serious matters.

Tonight's dinner would give them the chance to be in the room with all of the suspects once more, presuming that they were planning to attend. It was assumed that table arrangements would not be the same as the opening evening, and so they divvied the persons of interest up.

Colin would keep an eye on Sean and Vaughn. Easy to remember because it rhymed.

Adam would shadow Tex, Hazza and Isiah, the only person they had not yet spoken to about the missing painting.

Bellies full, they headed back up the stairs to their room, stopping off at Maggie's on the way. When she answered the door, they barely recognised her. It was as if her skin was shrinking, pulling it tight to her skeleton, exposing each and every bone.

'Hi, boys,' she said, her voice sounding like she'd smoked a thousand cigarettes since she'd last seen them.

'Hi, Maggie,' Colin said. 'We just wanted to check if you wanted a couple of handsome, muscular men to accompany you to dinner tonight?'

'We thought we'd call early enough that if you say yes, we've got time to go and find them,' Adam joked.

A small, brittle smile formed on her face, but only for a second. The sadness that she was feeling was plain to see.

'That's very kind of you, but I'm not going. The thought of being in the same room as the thief and scoundrel who took my beloved painting is too much to bear.'

'Perfectly understandable,' Colin nodded. 'We just wanted to let you know that we're still asking around. We promised that we'd find it, and we're not giving up.'

'You are good boys,' Maggie said, patting them on their arms. 'Your mummies must be so proud.'

With that, she bade them a soft goodbye and closed the door.

'Poor Maggie,' Adam said, as they headed to their own room.

Inside Colin, the fire to get the painting back grew even stronger.

COLIN AND ADAM appeared in the plush dining room wearing the same clothes as the first night. The same people looked at them with the same disgust. Adam was even sure that the pianist was playing the same song as he had been the first night—though, of course, one piece of classical music sounded the same as the next one in his mind. It was a bit like Groundhog Day.

Keen to keep a clear head, they grabbed a couple of soft drinks from the bar and chose a seat near the door, figuring everyone who came or went would have to walk past them.

Over the course of the next half an hour, nearly all of the players arrived. Hazza and Vaughn arrived a few minutes apart, both in very expensive suits. A short while later, Isiah entered the room with a very drunk looking Sean on his arm. There was no sign of Tex.

Adam was unsure if he was being paranoid, but he thought that Isiah had given them a dirty look as he'd entered.

Had Sean given him a heads-up that Adam and Colin would be looking to have a word with him?

Surely not, Adam thought. If Sean was so close to Isiah, he probably wouldn't have blabbed about his get-rich-quick ideas to them earlier in the day. He watched as Isiah led Sean to the bar, and heard them squabbling as the former tried to order the latter a soft drink. After much consternation, the Irishman stumbled off clutching a pint of lager, leaving Isiah to pay the bill.

The evening passed much as the last had. Edd, the captain, gave another speech, welcoming the first-class guests, as well as those from other parts of the ship who had splashed out on a ticket to the black-tie event. Adam was surprised that he left out his "going overboard" joke for the new faces in the room.

The assembled were asked to find a seat, and Adam was sure that their suspects made a point of scampering quickly to tables in the far reaches of the room-as far away from he and Colin as possible.

Small talk and introductions were made, the food came (squid ink soup for starters, duck heart with an assortment of odd vegetables for main) of which Adam once again ate absolutely nothing, grateful for the lasting fullness courtesy of Colonel Sanders. The others at the table were aghast when Adam returned his plate, practically untouched. He heard the mother and daughter, sitting opposite, muttering about how money changes people, and that there were poor folk on the street who would do disgraceful things for a morsel of that food that had been so unthoughtfully discarded.

Adam was about to answer them back, to tell them that he was as far from rich as it was possible to be, when something out of the corner of his eye caught his attention.

Isiah was weaving his way through the tables, headed for the door while typing a message on his phone.

'Make sure no one takes my dessert while I'm away,' Adam said, pushing himself out of his seat. 'It's the only part of the meal I have any hope for.'

'No worries,' Colin shouted after him.

As Adam crossed the floor, Isiah turned his head and cast a look around. Adam tried to act naturally and pretended that, instead of following him, he was on the way to the bar. He didn't acknowledge Isiah's nod.

When the door had closed behind his quarry, Adam gave it ten seconds and then followed suit. For a second, Adam couldn't see Isiah and thought he had blown his chance, but then he caught sight of his distinctive hairdo a little way down the deck and proceeded to tail him carefully.

Not that care was needed. Isiah was seemingly on a mission.

From Adam's point of view, it looked like he was trying to recreate the video of The Verve's seminal Bittersweet Symphony video. If someone was in Isiah's way, he simply shouldered into them, creating a path and never deviating from it. He got some dirty looks on the way, but was oblivious to them. As Adam passed the disgruntled victims, he heard Isiah called a few choice names. None of which Adam could disagree with.

He watched Isiah turn into a bar called Ricardo's. Adam sidled up to the window and peered in. It looked like a classy enough joint. Leather upholstered booths lined three of the walls, with the fourth taken up by a long, marbled bar with an array of drinks behind it. A barman in a tight shirt and waistcoat threw a thousand-watt smile in Isiah's direction as he took his drink order, probably in the hope of a hefty tip.

Adam watched Isiah lift his glass and walk to a booth currently inhabited by a woman with long, dark hair and a Mediterranean complexion. She smiled as he edged into the seat opposite her, his back to Adam, and leaned across the table to kiss her cheek.

Adam took his chance and ran to the booth that backed on to Isiah's. Thankfully, there was a wooden divide between the booths that afforded Adam some secrecy. He listened to Isiah and the girl make small talk for a while and watched in horror as a barman walked across the room, zeroed in on his table. Quickly, he grabbed a menu and pointed to a cocktail, hoping that the employee might mistake him for a mute. The barman nodded his head, noted down his order and walked away without a word.

Adam let out a sigh of relief, before going back to his covert surveillance.

And just in time, it would seem. The girl, who was called Marianne, was speaking.

'Can I come back with you?'

'There's no point,' Isiah said. 'The party is nearly over, and I'd have to buy you a ticket.'

'Oh.'

'It's not that I don't want to take you,' he placated. 'I just mean it would be better if you came to the next one, so that you can taste the food and hear the captain speak and stuff. It's an experience.'

'Is it expensive?'

'Yeah, but don't worry about that. I'll get you a ticket.'

'Last night you said that you didn't have a lot of money, though. I'm happy to pay.'

'Honestly, don't worry about it. I have a good thing going when we land in Barcelona.'

'A good thing?'

'Not for you to worry about.'

'Money?'

Silence. Adam supposed Isiah must've nodded, because Marianne's question sounded like a follow up.

'Enough to get me a ticket for the next party?'

Isiah laughed. 'If all goes to plan, enough to buy a yacht of our own.'

11

BARCELONA, SPAIN

COLIN'S TWO EXPERIENCES of Barcelona were as disparate as they came.

Firstly, like many men his age, he'd grown up mesmerised by its football team. Year after year, Messi and co had torn through the Champions League, thrashing minnow and monolith alike, while playing some of the most beautiful football the world had ever seen.

His second involvement with the Catalan city was second-hand through his grandad. It was a story that was brought out every Christmas day when sat around the table, much to the delight of everyone (aside from his grandad—Derek—who would busy himself with the gravy).

Fifteen years or so ago, when Colin was still in primary school, Grandad McLaughlin had travelled to the Spanish city for a weekend away. Usually softly-spoken and agreeable, he had spent a whimsical weekend away with his wife of thirty-seven years. They'd seen the sights, eaten local delicacies and perused the world-famous art that was housed in the city's many galleries.

They'd had a whale of a time.

On the final morning, they'd left their hotel looking for a spot of breakfast. Deciding on a picturesque café on La Rambla, they took a seat at one of its tables, sheltered from the morning sunshine by a large, lager-branded parasol. They ordered their food without looking at the menu, and waited.

And waited.

When a waiter walked past them, Derek engaged him politely, enquiring where their food was. The waiter marched off towards the kitchen and returned to tell them their huevos rancheros would be along shortly, and strode off again without apology.

Derek detested rudeness, but let it slide. He'd heard some nasty stories about finding all sorts in the food of those who complained, and was keen to have a completely sanitary meal.

Fifteen minutes later, the food was plonked down in front of them on plastic plates. The experience thus far was not living up to his vision, but he kindly put it down to a rumbling tummy and low blood pressure. He was sure that once the food touched his tastebuds, the lateness of the food and the insolence of the staff would soon be forgotten.

He was wrong.

The food was cold and inedible.

He summoned the same waiter again and complained. The waiter sighed and offered to get him another plate, though Derek refused. He reasoned things would not get better at this café, and got up to leave. The waiter held up a finger, and walked off. Mr McLaughlin imagined he'd gone to get the manager to come and apologise for such a nightmare scenario, and decided he'd accept with good grace, not wanting to end the holiday on a sour note.

The waiter returned alone, and sat the bill down on the table in a small metal platter. Mr McLaughlin laughed, thinking it a joke, and gathered his things. The waiter blocked his way and pointed at *la cuenta*, insisting he hand over the required amount of euros.

Things almost came to blows, when a passing police officer came to the rescue. He listened to both of their arguments, and though he sided with the Northern Irishman, insisted that the café be paid. They *had* made the food, after all.

Despite their flight not leaving until six in the evening, Grandad McLaughlin dragged his wife to the airport at 11:30am, insisting that he did not want to spend one more minute in a city filled with bent coppers and filthy, thieving scoundrels. He saw out the rest of the day with a Jack Reacher book, scowling at anyone who dared look slightly Spanish.

The experience had scarred him so, he'd never returned to mainland Europe.

Still, despite the cautionary tale, Colin was excited about visiting Spain's second city.

Or, he had been. He'd been looking forward to squeezing as much in as he could. A visit to the hallowed turf of the Nou Camp; climbing the many steps inside the Sagrada Familia, and seeing the artwork of Barcelona's most famed architect—Antoni Gaudí.

Instead, he was now planning on tailing Isiah Lookman to an art gallery, where hopefully he would try and flog the stolen painting, meaning Colin and Adam would have their evidence, and the whole debacle would be sewn up by the time they left port that evening.

He sighed, picked up his backpack and made his way out of the breakfast room as the city grew nearer, the ship slowing to begin its crawl to the quayside. Colin marvelled at the steady hand it took to guide a 100,000 tonnes of cruise liner into what was essentially a parking space!

Colin and Adam stationed themselves near the ship's exit, hoping to catch sight of Isiah so that they could tail him. As the ship came to a halt with the smallest of bumps, the crew launched into action and in no time at all, the gangplank was set and a crowd armed with DSLR cameras and Lonely Planet guide books disembarked in an orderly fashion.

Eventually, they spotted Isiah. He was dressed smartly: pressed shirt and tie, suit trousers, with a pair of Ray-Ban style shades perched atop his nose. On his back was one of those bags people take when they go hiking.

Adam nudged Colin, 'That bag is plenty big enough to be hiding the painting.'

'Agreed,' Colin said.

They watched him cast glances left and right, before smiling at the employee who was standing at the top of the steps and making his way down them. Colin and Adam gave him a head start and then followed.

They trailed him through the bustling streets, trying to keep their eye on him, while ignoring the beautiful sights the city had to offer. They tailed him to a swanky bar that was just opening its doors. He took a seat at an outside table, while Adam and Colin entered a bookshop across the street. From here, they watched him through the shop window, while pretending to peruse the books, which were mostly written in Spanish.

Isiah looked nervous.

Adam remembered the confidence and swagger with which he'd spoken to the girl from last night; how, after today's deal, he'd be rich enough to take her wherever she wanted in the world.

That self-assurance seemed to have deserted him. He looked around like a lost child and checked his phone every ten seconds or so. He nearly fell out of his chair when the waiter approached with his drink.

'What do we do?' Adam asked.

'We wait, I guess,' Colin replied.

'You don't think we should go and get the policia?'

'I think we let him sell the painting, then make our move. That way, we have concrete evidence that he has done something illegal. If we go now, he could say something like he was getting it valued for her as a surprise, or something.'

So, they waited.

The shopkeeper approached them in a friendly manner, and they told him they were just looking, while pretending to read the blurb of a book called 'Suburbio.'. After fifteen minutes of "just looking", the shopkeeper took exception, motioning to the door and muttering 'no es un biblioteca.'

Thankfully, Isiah was wrapped up enough in his own thoughts to notice a shifty looking Adam and Colin scrambling out of the bookshop and spilling into the perfume shop next door.

The conflicting aromas and overpowering scents made Adam's head hurt the moment they were through the door, though mercifully, across the plaza, Isiah jumped as his phone vibrated on the table. He read whatever the text said, downed the rest of his beer, and stood.

Adam and Colin followed him, taking care to avoid one of Isiah's many paranoid glances. At the end of the street was a small art gallery. Adam took out his phone, ready to snap a picture of the rogue dealer entering the shop. Isiah stopped by the window, and spent a minute or two looking at the canvases on display, before taking a step forward and disappearing down the alley at the side of the shop.

'What's he doing?' Adam asked.

'Not sure,' Colin said, already making his way over. 'Maybe there's a back door?'

They strode across the street, and hooked their heads around the entrance to the alley. There, at the far end, was Isiah. He was talking to a shifty looking man, who was peering into the gaping opening of the backpack. The man nodded, and Isiah looked relieved. The man reached into his pocket, shuffling his hand around like he was trying to take hold of something.

Suddenly, he produced a little silver whistle and blew it. All of a sudden, the alleyway was teeming with police officers. They rushed from both sides of the narrow lane, almost knocking Colin and Adam into the gutter. Two grabbed Isiah and slammed him against the wall, slapping handcuffs around his wrists. One opened the bag and lifted out a huge block of cocaine, wrapped in cling film and held together with duct tape, and showed another officer.

Adam and Colin watched as the rest of the bag was emptied, and left when it was clear that there was no painting.

Their suspect pool had just dropped by one.

12

A MULTITUDE OF UNEXPECTED EVENTS

THE NEWS OF Isiah's arrest passed around the ship like wildfire, and Colin noticed at dinner that night that most of their suspects were keener than usual to keep their distance from he and Adam.

They were only two days out from Venice, and if they didn't find the painting soon, Colin knew that it would be gone for good. They had to step up their game.

At a table in the corner of the room, they discussed what their next step was. Perhaps it was time to go nuclear—ask the captain to search rooms or implore him to make an unscheduled stop into the nearest port so that the police could intervene.

That was perhaps the most sensible plan, but Colin had a burning desire to be the one who took down the thief. Images of poor Maggie, unconscious on her cabin floor kept surfacing in his memory, and he knew he couldn't hand the reins over to someone else. Not yet. Not while there was still the chance to catch the bastard themselves.

As frustration pooled, they once more went over the suspects.

Vaughn had a film he really wanted to make, and the producer had backed out. Could he have stolen the picture to cover the lost money? Adam's counter-argument was that he probably had enough money in his wallet right now to fund his passion project, without having to steal. Hell, he'd been paid almost ten million for his last film. He was hardly in need.

However, Sean *was* in need. Cut off from the family business and here on the boat in the hope of gaining employment. It was a highly embarrassing situation to be in, especially after being publicly mocked by his own flesh and blood. Surely, the lure of an easy four million (at least) was reason enough to steal the painting.

Hazza was in a similar position. On the first night, he had hinted that his family thought him an idiot, frittering away his grandfather's inheritance by leading a playboy lifestyle. The chance to show them that he wasn't such a plonker must be tempting, and returning home from a lavish holiday with the news that he was no longer dependent on their cash was a pretty nice incentive.

'I still can't see past Tex,' Adam said. 'He has the most skin in the game. Art is his thing.'

'Yeah, but imagine selling the painting and not being able to tell anyone. From his website, it seems that the prestige is half the reason he's in the game at all.'

'Aye, but I can think of at least four million reasons why he might keep his mouth shut. You heard him. Ebbs and flows, and this painting is probably enough to say goodbye to rainy days for a good old while.'

'So what do you suggest?' Colin asked.

Adam's suggestion would have to wait, as Vaughn McClusky had appeared at their table. He beamed at them, holding a tray with three glasses of amber liquid.

'Gentlemen,' he said, 'I hope I'm not interrupting anything, but I felt like I should both apologise and thank you for the other night.'

He passed a glass to Adam.

'Firstly, an apology to you. I was in a foul mood when we spoke last. I'm in a very fortunate position where I can act for a living, and I wouldn't be in this position with support from wonderful people like you. Secondly,' he passed Colin his drink, 'a thank you. After your pep talk, I got off the pity train and mobilised. Like I said, I'm in a fortunate position, and I have total confidence that this film will be a success, so thanks to your advice, I've decided to put up the money myself. When we get to Venice, I'm meeting the producer on his yacht to iron out the details, but without your wise words, that probably wouldn't have happened.'

He held his glass aloft and they all clinked together, before sipping at the whisky. Colin knew that Adam had never been into that particular drink, as he felt the burn in the throat was more akin to torture, but today he was acting like he bloody loved it.

'Now,' Vaughn said. 'Ask me anything.'

For the next half an hour, drinks flowed and so did conversation. Adam was in his element, ohh-ing and ahh-ing as he found out juicy details from behind the scenes, Vaughn's future plans and a unique insight into the actor's much publicised battle with a life-threatening illness almost a decade ago.

'Let me ask you a question,' the actor said. 'How is Maggie? I've not seen her about.'

'I don't think anyone will until we hit port. She's taken it very hard.'

'Makes my blood boil,' Vaughn replied. 'Are you still looking into it? Any theories?'

Adam told him about his hunch—that Tex was behind it. They scanned the room, to discover that, once again, he hadn't shown his face at dinner. To Adam, this was further evidence of his wrongdoing. He was keeping away in the hope that he could make it off the ship without being questioned again.

'Why don't we get the captain to open up his room?' Vaughn said. 'Surely, a quick search would clear this whole thing up.'

'We could, I suppose,' Colin shrugged.

'And no time like the present,' Vaughn said, rising to his feet and throwing the rest of the expensive whisky down his throat.

THE CAPTAIN WAS shocked and appalled that a theft had taken place on his ship, and that he was only finding out about it now. He told them in no uncertain terms that had he known about it from the moment it had happened, Maggie would have been reunited with her artwork a long time ago. He snatched a skeleton key card from his office and marched with them through the ship towards Tex's room.

The captain strode in front, a man on a mission, with Vaughn on his heels. Adam and Colin struggled to keep up.

'Should we tell Maggie, first?' Adam asked.

'I don't think so,' Vaughn replied, looking back over his shoulder without breaking pace. 'If things get violent, we want her out of harm's way.'

Colin almost laughed at the way Vaughn had delivered the line. Adam, on the other hand, loved it. He knew that the situation was terribly serious, but the fact that he was part of something that resembled a Vaughn McClusky movie was not lost on him.

They descended staircases and brushed past people who looked on agog.

When they got to Tex's cabin, they stopped in a line, pressed against the wall. Captain Edd knocked briskly on the door and shouted the occupant's name.

There was no answer.

He held his ear against the door and narrowed his eyes, straining to hear movement from inside.

'Mr Rivera, I'm coming in,' he shouted, and pressed the key card against the shiny sensor to the side of the door, causing the little light to turn from red to green. The door clicked open and swung inwards ever so slightly.

Edd pushed lightly, and stepped over the threshold. Vaughn went next, and before Colin or Adam could follow, they heard the captain shout a few choice words.

The reason for his expletives quickly became apparent.

13

THE CONTENTS OF TEX'S CABIN

COLIN FOLLOWED VAUGHN into the room, so close behind him it felt like a parachute jumper leaving a plane in a war movie. Perhaps he was getting carried away, what with being in such close proximity to the actor.

Adam was less keen to enter the room. The captain's oaths had shaken him, and he hoped that the cause of the shouts was simply the discovery of the painting, though something within him knew different.

He rounded the corner, shoulders scraping against the doorframe, eyes partially covered by shaking hands, to be confronted with…

Nothing.

Slowly, he removed his fingers from in front of his eyes and glanced around. There was nothing out of place. As when he had come on his little covert operation, there was no painting, no easel, no hint that anything was wrong.

And then he looked over to where Edd, Vaughn and Colin were standing. They were peering into the bedroom with ashen faces. Adam took a step towards them.

'Mate,' Colin said, 'I don't think you'll be able to handle it.'

'Shut up,' Adam replied, not wanting to lose face in front of Vaughn. 'Whatever it is, I'm sure I'll be grand.'

Colin shrugged and moved out of the way, letting Adam take his place.

One glance at the scene was enough to send Adam running for the open door, where he hurled his guts over the ledge and into the frothing sea below. He knew that what he had just seen would be etched into his brain until his dying day.

The open en-suite door.

Tex's body in the bath.

The blood.

Adam heaved again, his stomach cramping and his throat burning with the bile that came in torrents.

He felt a soft pat on his back, and took a moment to regain his composure. Using his sleeve, he wiped gunk from his chin and turned to find Vaughn looking at him with sympathy.

'I feel the same, mate. Bloody horrific,' he said. 'Edd's going to stay with the body. He's asked me to go and tell his second-in-command, so that they can phone ahead to Venice and have the police on standby. You want to come with me?'

Adam considered it, and then shook his head.

'No worries,' Vaughn said, tapping him twice on the chest before rushing off.

Colin appeared a few minutes later, his face white; his expression a far-off stare. He leaned on the railing beside Adam, and neither of them said anything for a very long time.

Finally, Adam spoke.

'Do you know what happened?'

'There's a note.'

'A note? What, like he did that to himself?' Adam repeated. 'Jesus. What did it say?'

Colin pulled out his phone, navigated to the photo album and passed it to Adam, whose eyes flitted wildly about the screen, trying to take in all the details at once, but finding it hard to concentrate.

He closed his eyes for a few seconds, and when he opened them, it seemed they were ready to follow his orders. He read from the start of the letter.

> *I couldn't live with the guilt. That poor old woman. It was a moment of madness, and I couldn't live with myself any more. Cracthen is at the bottom of the sea. I couldn't bear to give it back—couldn't bear to see Maggie's disgust, so I tossed it overboard in the middle of the night. I've robbed the world of a masterpiece, but I've robbed a family of something worse. Tell her I'm sorry. I'm so, so sorry.*
>
> *Tex*

Adam re-read the letter a few times before passing the phone back to his friend, just as Vaughn reappeared with a couple of the crew.

'Boys, we're no use here anymore. Let me buy you a drink.'

They nodded and followed the actor to the nearest bar, where he bought a round of beers. They toasted the painting, and they toasted Maggie, who would be heartbroken when she found out about her masterpiece's fate.

They had one more after that, though Adam could see that Colin wanted to be elsewhere. When Vaughn offered another round, they declined and parted company.

'You okay?' Adam asked Colin as they walked back to their cabin.

'Not really,' he said, and Adam knew he was thinking about poor Maggie.

The rest of the journey was spent in silence. Tex's door had red tape across it, and a crew member standing to the side, presumably to keep an eye on it until they reached Venice, and so that an unsuspecting maid wouldn't have to encounter what was behind the door, should she stumble into the room mistakenly.

As soon as they got back to their room, Colin collapsed onto the sofa and put a cushion over his face. Adam sat opposite, quietly, letting his friend have his moment.

'So it was him all along,' Adam said, finally. 'And the prick has thrown the painting away. What are we going to tell Maggie?' Adam asked.

Colin simply shook his head.

THE REST OF the day was spent in a cycle, with Colin relaying what he'd seen inside the room, and then extended periods of silence.

As well as Tex's body in the bath, there was the hand-written note and an iPad on the bed, left open on a webpage about an art auction on the day they arrived in Venice.

Adam's assumption had been that the guilt of planning to sell the painting at said auction is what had tipped Tex over the edge. The fact the webpage was open as he'd done the deed surely lent credence to that idea.

But, something wasn't sitting right with Colin.

It all felt too… set-up?

That wasn't quite the right sentiment to sum it up, but Colin was finding words hard to come by. In his mind, the open door to the bedroom, the note and the perfectly positioned iPad was all just a bit too convenient.

Though, they had been going there to accuse him of stealing the painting and there were no signs of a struggle, so who was to know?

The police would soon establish if it was a crime scene or not, though the inclusion of the note would surely lead them down a very opportune path. The guy was a suspected thief and the death had happened in international waters. He couldn't imagine the Venetian police force tripping over themselves to open up an investigation.

He also imagined that Captain Edd would push for that, too. A felo-de-se on his boat was bad enough, but even fouler play was worse. The phrase 'there's no such thing as bad publicity' didn't quite work here, and he imagined the cruise company owners would quite like the story of the dead art dealer to vanish as quickly as possible, and who could blame them?

Day turned to night, and slept crept up on Colin, who called it a night with his thoughts on the scrawled note.

14

REASONABLE DOUBT

SLEEP, THOUGH, HADN'T managed to keep a firm hold on Colin.

Every time he'd drifted off, images of Maggie floated into his mind. Maggie lying on the floor. Maggie's tears as she realised her beloved painting had been stolen. Future Maggie disembarking the ship, facing a life without her priceless heirloom.

It broke his heart, and short of dredging the ocean, he wasn't sure what he could do. And so, he'd spent most of the night staring at the ceiling, hoping inspiration would strike.

He kept thinking back, too, to Tex and the guilt that had driven him to take his own life. It was a horrible thing to say, but Colin was finding it hard to feel any sympathy for him. He'd stolen from an old lady, he'd lied about his involvement to Adam and him, and all for what? A quick buck, as the Americans would say.

Colin wondered if the art gallery in Venice would be annoyed that he'd gotten their hopes up by telling them that he was in possession of... whatever the painting was called. Colin couldn't quite remember, but knew it was similar to that character from Mean Girls, like Isiah had pointed out on the first night. Gretchen, was it?

And then something hit Colin like a lightning bolt. He grabbed his phone from the floor and pulled up the pictures, swiping until he got to the photo of the note Tex had left behind.

He skimmed the photo until he found the vital piece of information that blew this whole case wide open again. Without even looking at the time, he hollered Adam's name.

THE SHIP WAS sinking. Adam was sure of it. There couldn't be any other reason for such a volatile awakening.

Within a few seconds of hearing his name, he was bolt upright, his dressing gown already tightly wrapped around his body as he fled for the door.

His senses returned in incremental stages upon entering the suite's living space. Colin sat on the sofa, curled up under a duvet staring at his phone. That meant that the ship couldn't be in an emergency situation, and Adam's temper started to bubble.

'Did you call me?' Adam asked, his voice thick with sleep.

'Obviously, yeah,' Colin said. 'Who else is going to be shouting for you?'

'Do you know what bloody time it is?'

'No. Do you?'

'No, but I know it's early. Too early.' He rubbed his eyes. 'What's the matter?'

'Tex was killed.'

'Shut up.'

'I'm serious,' Colin said, tapping the sofa for Adam to sit down beside him. Obediently, Adam shuffled across and took his place, as requested.

'I can tell you now, this is going to be a hard sell,' Adam said.

'Allow me to make a believer from a disbeliever, Doubting Thomas.'

'Thomas?'

'The Disciple. Goodness me, your general knowledge is appalling.'

'I didn't get out of bed to be insulted,' Adam tutted. 'Tell me what you've found.'

'Right,' Colin began. 'Well, I know he was our main suspect for a while, but now it strikes me as odd that Tex would steal it in the first place. I mean, he's a fan of art, and he must come into contact with world famous pieces all the time.'

'Yeah, in galleries,' Adam said. 'Not just sitting at a dinner table with a dotty old woman and no security.'

'Fine, I take your point. But, don't call Maggie dotty again. If you do, I'll slap you.'

'Apologies.'

'Accepted,' Colin nodded. 'Now, even if Tex *had* stolen the painting, why would he throw it overboard. It doesn't make sense. You could tell he was absolutely blown away by seeing it in real life. Why would an art lover deprive the world of a true masterpiece?'

'Guilt?'

'Nah, I'm not buying that.'

'Your argument so far is what the police would call circumstantial, at best,' Adam said. 'Consider me unconvinced.'

'Okay,' Colin allowed. 'Allow me to present the coup de grâce.'

He passed Adam his phone and showed him the Google page for the stolen painting.

'Remember the name.'

'Grachten,' Adam mouthed.

'And now look at Tex's note.'

Adam navigated to the photos and pulled up the note.

'Cracthen' Adam said, puzzled.

'You're telling me that an art dealer is going to get the name of a famous painting wrong?'

'Jesus,' Adam said, stunned. 'So, what does this mean?'

'It means,' said Colin. 'That someone on this ship killed Tex and tried to pass it off as suicide by guilty conscience. And I think I know who.'

THEY MARCHED ALONG the deck, Colin on a mission and Adam urging him to see reason.

After finally being convinced of Tex's innocence, Colin had proceeded to tell Adam his theory.

Colin was convinced that Vaughn McClusky was behind the stolen painting and Tex's untimely demise. Adam had laughed at first, and when he saw that Colin was deadly serious, began to list the reasons why it couldn't be him.

1. He was rich enough to buy the painting if he wanted
2. He got paid double the painting's valuation on his last film alone
3. He was in the public eye. He was never going to put his career at risk for the sake of a quick buck
4. He'd been with them when Tex's body had been discovered

'Don't you think it's a coincidence that he started helping us, that he came with us to Tex's room, just as we discovered his body?' Colin asked.

'He *was* helping us. Helping being the key word here. Did you see his reaction when the body was found? He was white as a sheet. He ran off to get help.'

'He's an actor!' Colin said. 'Of course he's going to know how to react.'

'Dude, you're wrong on this one. Trust me.'

'Nope. I'm going to see him.'

'Then you're on your own.'

Adam stopped trying to talk sense into Colin and doubled back, hoping for a few more hours sleep. He felt bad arguing with his best friend, but he was starting to stress about the wedding, and was running low on energy and patience. What should have been a lovely, relaxing pre-wedding holiday had been the exact opposite, and he was very close to giving up.

Colin was wrong, and he could find that out alone.

COLIN WAS CONVINCED that the painting would be waiting behind Vaughn's door, and that taking the actor by surprise would be the best way of finding it.

He marched up to the door and knocked on it sharply three times, then pulled to the side so that he could not be seen through the spyhole. He could hear movement inside the room, but the door remained unopened.

After a minute, Colin knocked again, and a half-dressed Vaughn finally answered. Colin couldn't help but admire his chiselled abs and those cheekbones, though cursed himself for it.

'Colin, how are you? You feeling okay after yesterday?' he asked, stifling a yawn.

'Uh-huh,' Colin said. 'I was wondering if I could come in for a quick chat.'

'How about you give me a couple of minutes to get dressed,' Vaughn said, motioning to his pyjama bottoms and bare chest, 'and then I'll treat you to some breakfast?'

'Nah, it's cool,' Colin said, who took a step forward. 'It won't take long.'

'Seriously, mate, if you want to chat, let's chat, but not here, just give me…' Vaughn turned to look behind him, and Colin seized his chance. He ducked under the actor's arm and took a few steps into the room.

'What the bloody hell do you think you're doing?' Vaughn thundered.

'I think you're hiding something,' Colin said. 'I think you have the painting.'

'The painting is at the bottom of the ocean.'

'That's what the phoney suicide note said,' Colin answered.

'Phoney?'

'Yeah, phoney. As in someone else wrote it for Tex after he was killed.'

'Killed?' Vaughn repeated. 'Nonsense. Look, it's a traumatic thing seeing a body…'

'I've seen plenty,' Colin interrupted. 'Now, if you don't have it, you won't mind me looking around.'

'I don't have it, but I absolutely do mind you looking around. It's my bloody suite.'

Colin took a look around the room from where he stood, though there was no sign of the painting. He glanced sideways at the bedroom door, took a step towards it, when Vaughn growled.

'Don't you dare.'

As quick as a flash, Colin darted towards the door, and heard Vaughn's footsteps behind him. He made it through the door before Vaughn tackled him heavily to the floor.

'I told you not to…' Vaughn said, raising his fist.

Colin was spared a punch thanks to a well-timed intervention from the bed. A beautiful woman, wearing very little, pleaded with the actor not to get violent.

Vaughn nodded, and let his arm fall to his side, before letting Colin to his feet.

'Colin, meet Samantha.'

The woman covered herself with the duvet, and extended a hand in Colin's direction, which he shook.

'The reason I didn't want you barging in here is that Sam works on the ship, and employee-guest relations are strictly prohibited. We wouldn't want my companion here getting into any trouble now, would we?' Vaughn said.

'Sorry,' Colin said, sheepishly. 'I didn't mean to intrude.'

'Well, intrude you did. Can you keep this under your hat?'

'I don't care who you are sleeping with. I only care about the painting.'

'I appreciate that. I want poor Maggie to get the painting back as much as you do. Tell me about the faked note.'

'Nah, don't worry about it. I'm probably reading too much into it. I'll let you get back to… it.'

Colin bolted out of the bedroom and out of the front door, grateful for the fresh sea air that filled his lungs and cooled his cheeks, which were burning like a furnace. He felt like he was losing his marbles.

He had convinced himself that Vaughn was behind it all, when really, like Adam said, he *had* only been helpful the entire time. In desperation, Colin was simply lashing out at anyone he could think of.

He resolved to make things right with Vaughn before they reached Italy. He thought about going back to see him now, but decided to let him cool off for a while. He didn't fancy being on the receiving end of a fist, should Vaughn change his mind. As he started to walk towards his own cabin, he thought he caught sight of someone peering at him from around the corner.

When he looked again, they were gone. Colin ran to the end of the passageway, and hurtled around the corner.

There was no one there. The corridor was completely empty.

He stood for a while, in the hope that whoever had been there (if they had been at all) would be forced out of their hiding place. After a few minutes, and no movement, Colin gave up.

Perhaps it had been a trick of the light, he thought, as he turned and made his way back to his own cabin.

WITH HIS TAIL tucked firmly between his legs, Colin grovelled apologies to Adam, who accepted graciously, even after Colin had told him about stumbling into Vaughn's bedroom to find a mostly-nude woman in his bed.

'I doubt he's going to be buying us any more whisky,' Adam laughed. 'But, who cares? We're getting off the boat tomorrow, and not a moment too soon.'

'Should we get drunk and forget about the painting?' Colin asked.

In reply, Adam opened the door to their cabin and ushered Colin out of it.

They chose a bar as far away from first class as they could, and set about draining the place of every drop of alcohol available.

The evening quickly became a blur, and involved karaoke. Adam brought out his version of Livin' On A Prayer, though struggled to hit the high notes and messed up the key change. He was applauded for his efforts by the friendly crowd who had gathered, though Colin did note some people with their fingers plugging their ears long after he'd left the stage.

Colin refused to bow to peer pressure and resisted the stage, instead ordering another round of drinks.

Mid-way through that drink, Adam's phone rang and he held up the screen to show that it was Helena.

'Probably time to be going, anyway,' Colin said. 'You head on and chat to your good lady, and I'll finish my drink.'

Adam gave him a slobbery kiss on the cheek and left the bar, professing his love to Helena as soon as he'd answered the call.

Colin sat back and savoured his pint. The woman on stage was storming through a version of 'Waterloo', much to the delight of a middle-aged couple who had taken residence on the dancefloor. When he was done with his drink, he got up from his seat and left the bar.

The ship was skirting the Italian coast now, the twinkling lights of the cities a welcome sign to Colin. He would be glad to set foot on land again, see Anna, and hopefully forget the whole debacle, though the shame of not being able to get Maggie's painting back would surely haunt him.

He made it to his room, and stood by the balcony outside, appreciating the view. He heard the footsteps too late.

Before he could react, someone had kicked his knees and he'd toppled to the floor. Punches and kicks rained down on him, and, somewhat ridiculously, Colin's only thought was to protect his face for the wedding photographs. He crawled into the foetal position and curled his arms around his head, as a pair of boots and knobbly knuckles took aim at his ribs and legs.

Despite the beating, Colin's main thoughts were on the strangely out of place sound. It sounded like whoever was attacking him was shaking a maraca. A quiet chk-chk-chk noise punctuated the spaces between Colin's grunts and shouts.

As soon as it had started, it was over, thanks to an approaching drunken couple. Colin breathed a sigh of relief, and lay listening as the offending footsteps retreated, and the couple rushed to his aid.

15

GOTCHA

'IT'S A GOOD thing,' Colin said, over breakfast, which they'd ordered to their room.

'A good thing? Are you off your head?' Adam spat.

'It means there is someone on the ship who wants us out of the way.'

'Ah, you're right! That *is* a good thing,' Adam said, sarcastically.

'Don't be hysterical,' Colin said, wincing in pain as he adjusted his position on the sofa.

'Me? Hysterical? Why would I be hysterical? I mean, I'm getting married in two days and my best man, my best friend in the world, has just taken a kicking from an unknown assailant.'

'Look,' Colin said. 'It means that whoever took the painting obviously doesn't like us looking into it, especially as Venice draws nearer. They thought they were home and dry, that we'd give up after their failed Tex set-up. Not only are they a thief, they're a murderer, too.'

'It has to be Vaughn!' Adam said, jumping up.

'What do you mean?'

'You went to see him, barged into his room and then took a beating. He's the only person we've spoken to since you realised the whole Tex thing was a red herring.'

'He's the only person we've spoken to, but I forgot to tell you about something. When I left his room, I was sure I saw someone watching me. When I ran towards them, they were gone.'

'What? They disappeared into thin air?' Adam looked sceptical.

'It made me think that there wasn't really anyone there at the time, but maybe whoever it was saw that we were still investigating and tried to take me out.'

'That would leave Henry and Sean.'

'Hazza,' Colin corrected.

'Nah, Hazza is what his friends call him, and we are no friends of his.'

The rest of the morning was spent plotting. Venice was only a few hours away, and they wanted to speak to each of their suspects. They reasoned that whoever attacked Colin last night would not feel as confident in handing out a beating in the daylight hours, or with so many people around, so it was safe to split up to cover both bases.

Colin would try and find Sean, and Adam would track down Hazza.

COLIN WINCED WITH each step, pain flaring in every joint and nerve, or so it seemed.

For once, the size of the ship was against him, and he spent an unhappy half hour toddling around, unable to summon up the reserves of strength to make much of a go of it.

Frustrated, he stopped at a coffee shop and found a table in the back corner, where he sat clutching a bottle of water with his head down on the cool surface of the table, hoping Adam wouldn't come this way and see him at such a low ebb.

He'd put on a decent show for Adam earlier, trying to play down the incident, but the truth was he was scared. It was unbelievable that there was someone on the boat who would attack, steal and kill, and that they were still roaming free.

With that awful idea in his head, he took a deep breath, steadied himself and then carefully hoisted himself up from his seat. He hoped and prayed that if he did come across Sean, that he didn't have to put up too much of a fight.

ON THE OTHER side of the ship, Adam was hunting for Hazza like a man possessed.

Sweat pooled on his back and in his armpits, such was the ferocity of his search, but he didn't let that bother him. Instead, he picked up the pace.

He poked his head into every bar, café and shop he came to. He barged into the spa and scared the receptionist half to death with the ferocity with which he barked Hazza's name. The poor woman shook her head and ran into the back room.

Adam felt bad, but only momentarily. He was sure the spa's guarantee to relax and rejuvenate worked on the employees, too. She'd be kicking back, stress-free in no time.

Unlike him.

He could feel the muscles in his shoulders tighten, as they often did when he was feeling stressed out.

After another fruitless half-an-hour, he was ready to give up, when he realised he'd not checked the most obvious place. They'd stumbled across Hazza in the casino when they went looking the first time (which felt like months ago). Perhaps he was there again?

Adam travelled up an escalator and made his way down the corridor, where the sounds of jubilation and despair began to fill the air. He turned into the casino, where gamblers were hunched slot machines, cashing in chips and refilling drinks at the well-stocked bar.

He studied each table, spotting Hazza at the far side of the room, staring intently at the playing cards in his left hand. After ten seconds, he set his cards down and pushed some more coloured chips into the middle.

Adam stood for a while, watching him, wondering if he was their man. Eventually, he decided there was nothing to be found out from being on the other side of the room, so started to make his way over.

And then he saw it.

He realised that while he'd been watching, Hazza had been using his left hand for everything. Checking his cards. Pushing the chips. Pouring the fruity cocktail into his mouth.

Now, he raised his right hand to scratch his nose, and Adam was surprised to see that it was bandaged. Hazza grimaced like the action was causing him pain, and Adam knew why.

Hazza was the one who had beat up Colin.

In a flash of rage, Adam marched across the floor, picking up speed as he went. When he neared his target, he was almost running. All the stress of the past few weeks seemed to melt away as he rugby tackled Hazza onto the card table, causing chips to scatter like broken glass, and a series of audible gasps arose from those who had been enjoying their game just seconds before.

'Get the captain,' Adam shouted to the dealer. 'This man is trouble.'

16

THE ROGUE

EDD HAD TAKEN the accusations against Hazza extremely seriously, and had come to the casino to find Hazza struggling under Adam's weight, who in turn was straddling him in an imitation of a citizen's arrest he'd seen Mark perform on *Peep Show* once.

Hazza continued to protest his innocence, but complied with the captain's orders to go with him until the police arrived. Adam had passed Edd his mobile number, as he was keen to hear what decision the Venetian police came to.

He returned to the cabin to find Colin slumped on the sofa, and relayed what had just happened.

'You tackled him onto the table?' Colin repeated.

'Yeah. Maybe I went a bit far, but when I saw that bandage, I thought of him beating you up, and I lost it.'

'I'd hug you if I could,' Colin said. 'But I think it might hurt my ribs.'

The ship was slowing now, on its final approach into Venice. The boys watched from the balcony, and were blown away by the beauty of the place. Their train north to Lake Garda wasn't until later that evening, and Adam was looking forward to spending a few care-free hours wandering the streets of Italy's watery wonderland.

They had packed earlier that morning, though having mostly lived out of a suitcase, it hadn't taken long. Now, they scooped up the last items and shoved them in their cases, before checking under the bed and in nooks and crannies for odd socks and the likes.

Then, they said goodbye to their room and made their way towards the first floor for the final disembarkation, with one detour en route.

When Maggie opened her door, she was dressed in a flowing, colourful dress.

'We thought we'd come and say bye,' Colin said. 'We're so sorry we couldn't be more help.'

She pulled him into a tight hug, and told him to stop being silly. It was time to forget about the painting, she said, and move on.

Adam filled her in with the latest developments, and she smiled. A little bit of hope twinkled in her eye. She held up a finger, and disappeared into her room, reappearing a few minutes later with an envelope, which she handed to Adam.

He tried to resist, though she insisted.

'Treat yourself and your good lady wife to a wee treat on honeymoon,' she said, and gave him a hug too.

They said their goodbyes, and Adam and Colin made their way to the exit.

Looking around, Adam was sad that they hadn't utilised the ship to its full potential. There were so many parts of The Elysian that they hadn't even been to, so focused were they on trying to retrieve the painting.

Still, it had been for a noble cause, and hopefully the police would be able to interrogate Hazza and find out where he'd hidden the painting.

A huge crowd had gathered in the vast expanse of space, eager to get off and explore a new city. There was a buzz in the air; an infectious one. It was time to forget about what had happened over the past week, and focus on what was to come.

The wedding!

His thoughts of "I Dos" by the lakeside were shattered by a commotion on the other side of the waiting area. There was some jostling, and Adam assumed it was the normal bustle that came with being part of a crowd, and went back to his daydream. Then, he saw a flash of unruly ginger hair.

It was Sean, shoving his way through the assembled passengers, trying to get as close to the door as possible. Adam watched as his rucksack collided with a little girl's head. Her father shouted after Sean, but he was almost at the door, which had just opened.

'Someone's in a hurry,' Colin said, having also noticed the hubbub.

'I wonder did he make any inroads with a new job,' Adam replied.

'Who knows?' Colin said. 'I'm looking forward to never thinking about any of these people again. Especially Vaughn, who I never got the chance to apologise to. Hopefully we don't see him before we leave!'

The crowd was pouring through the door now, making their way towards the city.

Colin and Adam's plan was simple. Walk to the nearby train station, stow their cases in a locker so that they didn't have to cart them around all day, and then enjoy their day. Adam couldn't wait to visit Ciao Gelato. He'd researched the best ice-cream shop in Venice long before they'd arrived, and discovered they did a honeycomb and white chocolate mix. He was eager to get moving!

The train station wasn't far, but it took longer than anticipated, on account of Colin's bruised and battered body. When they arrived, they stuffed their cases in a yellow locker, deposited a couple of Euros in the slot and collected the key.

Just then, Adam's phone rang. It was a number he didn't recognise.

'Hello.'

'Is this Adam?'

'Yes.'

'It's Edd, here. I just wanted to let you know that Henry's story checked out. He claimed he cut his hand helping a barmaid pick up a smashed glass. We spoke to the barmaid in question and she confirmed the story. The police have also searched his room and didn't find the painting. They are letting him go, though they are going to investigate Mr Rivera's death. You might need to give a statement, as you were there when the body was discovered, though they might be happy with my version of events. Am I okay to pass your number on?'

'Yeah, no problem,' Adam said. 'Thanks for letting me know.'

Adam communicated the content of the phone call to Colin, who closed his eyes and sighed.

'It's Sean, isn't it?' he said

'That might explain why he looked so eager to get off the boat this morning,' Adam nodded.

'At least we know where he'll be.'

Colin pulled out his phone and swiped through the photos. He stopped on the picture of the iPad on Tex's bed, that was open on a website of an art auction due to take place today in Venice, today. Colin mouthed the address a few times, and then typed it into Google Maps. The little blue line showed them that the auction house wasn't too far away.

'I say we go catch our thief red-handed!' Adam said.

ESPOSITO'S AUCTIONEERS WAS housed in a stunning little building. Near the Bridge of Sighs, it was tucked away in a little back street. The stonework may have been ageing, but it was doing so gracefully. Ivy crept across the façade, trimmed away near the narrow windows, and a small, gold sign beside the door was in keeping with the tasteful décor. A well-dressed man welcomed them in Italian, handing them a brochure which they accepted.

Inside was a flurry of activity.

At the front of the room, an auctioneer with an ornate wooden gavel in his hand was speaking at the speed of light, motioning to a canvas on an easel next to him and trying (Adam assumed) to enthuse the bidders into upping the price. At the side, a row of smartly dressed employees had phones to their ears and fingers whirling over computer keyboards, presumably communicating with would-be bidders who couldn't make it to the Venetian auction house.

There were three auction-goers locked in a bidding war, one raising his numbered paddle covertly, the others not bothering to mask their passion for the prize on offer.

Eventually, paddle man backed out, leaving a two-horse race.

The man with the round glasses and clean-shaven face was not to be outdone, and finally triumphed. He looked delighted at the win, and shook hands with his adversary, who congratulated him passionately.

Adam was wondering if an auction in the UK would end so cordially, when he spotted a tense looking Sean on the far side of the room, twirling a strand of his long, ginger hair around one of his fingers, and staring at the auctioneer like the man might give him the secrets to everlasting life.

Adam and Colin didn't want to make a scene, so they took a seat and bided their time. Adam concluded that it would have been an enjoyable way to spend an hour, except for the fact they were about to try and apprehend a killer.

On the penultimate lot, Sean suddenly became animated. The painting was quite bleak; a row of houses separated by a glowing river of fire. There were three suns in the sky, though they provided no light for the land. Adam found the whole scene very unsettling.

Sean, though, seemed to like it very much as he was using his paddle to great effect. There was only one other person in the room who seemed to be interested, and even they dropped out reasonably quickly.

Following a fist pump, Sean got to his feet and walked to the payment desk. Colin kept an eye on him while the final painting was wheeled out. They had both assumed that the famous stolen painting would be kept until last, perhaps as a surprise, as it wasn't listed in the auction catalogue.

When it was unveiled, they were dismayed to see that it was not Maggie's painting.

'Maybe it sold before we got here?' Adam suggested.

'Maybe,' Colin shrugged. 'But why would he hang about? Surely if you'd stolen a painting and sold it illegally for millions, you'd want to get out as soon as possible.'

'Agreed. Maybe he's waiting for the payment to go through?'

They watched Sean finish at the finance desk, shake hands with the employee who had dealt with him, and make his way towards the door. Adam and Colin followed him outside, into the small courtyard at the front of the building, where they called his name.

Sean spun on the spot; confusion plastered across his face.

'Lads, ye alright?'

'Grand,' Colin nodded. 'You must be buzzing.'

'I am, aye. What are you doing here?'

'Well, we thought Hazza was behind the painting theft. As a matter of fact, we left him for the police to deal with on the ship, but it seems his story checked out, and they've let him go. And then, we see you hotfooting it off the ship and, lo and behold, you end up at the very auction Tex had been planning to attend. Bit odd, no?'

'Not really, pal. I had nothing to do with the old lady's painting, like I already told you.'

'Why are you buzzing then?' Adam asked.

'Because Tex gave me a tip off about an up-and-coming artist who he believed is going to make it big. One of his pieces was going up for sale today, and Tex had told me he reckoned it was a good investment opportunity, so I was eager to get here. And, I won it at well below what he thought it was worth.'

'But…' Adam started.

'Look, lads, short of putting my hand on my heart and swearing I wasn't involved, I don't know what I have to do to convince you.' He turned to go, and then spoke again. 'Oh, by the way, what did you do to the actor?'

'Vaughn?' Colin said. 'Why?'

'Well, I was near his room when I saw you come out of it, but I hid round the corner.'

'Why?'

'Because I couldn't be arsed with the hassle of talking to you. All you've done the whole holiday is ask questions and throw accusations around, and I didn't have time for that. Anyway, not long after you'd left, I crept out of my hiding place and Vaughn was outside his room, downing some of those pills he always carried around with him. He looked furious. He saw me and asked had I seen you, but I lied and said no. He looked like he wanted to kill you.'

Adam and Colin shared a look.

'Well, anyway boys,' Sean said. 'I'd be lying if I said it was good to see you again. See ye!'

And with that he sauntered out of the courtyard, and out of their lives.

17

ALAN SUGAR WOULD BE TERRIFIED OF THIS BOARDROOM

VAUGHN MCCLUSKY PULLED out a little handheld mirror from his pocket and checked himself out.

Though a crack ran the length of the glass, it didn't stop him admiring how suave he looked, even if he did say so himself. The suit he'd just bought at the most exclusive tailor in the city hugged his muscular figure; the facial and haircut he'd had that afternoon had got him right in the mood for business.

He was ready to close this deal; the one that would take his career into the next level.

A little flutter of nervousness reminded him that a meeting with Mr Palmer was not something to be trifled with. The man was shrewd, and needed to know that there was serious investment and intent behind a project before he'd even consider putting his name to it.

Hell, owning a yacht that was moored in Venice was not something that happened by being a pushover, and Mr Palmer was certainly no pushover.

Still, Vaughn liked to think that his little gift would sweeten the deal before they even got to talking about the numbers. He was confident that come the end of the night (or the next morning, depending on how the party panned out), he'd be leaving the yacht with what he needed.

That nervousness was still there, though, so he shouted through the partition of the limo, telling the driver to take care while he made a drink. He felt the car slow by a few miles per hour, and reached towards the well-stocked drinks tray, grabbing the bottle of his favourite brandy and a lowball tumbler. He added a few ice cubes, and swirled the contents, his eyes drifting to the window and the passing Venetians who had no idea a genuine movie star was in their midst.

Ten minutes, and another drink, later, the limo pulled to a smooth stop in one of the private parking spaces reserved for guests Mr Palmer's. The driver, a little man with a bulging belly wearing an ill-fitting suit, opened the door for Vaughn, who got out and waited while the chauffeur pulled his bags out of the boot.

Vaughn tipped him and made his way towards the superyacht. It really was a thing of beauty, all sleek lines and sophisticated details. Even the gangplank, which he took his time on, looked like it had been sculpted by a master of his craft.

He was greeted at the top of the steps by Mr Palmer's personal assistant, Doris Braine, who always seemed immune to his flirtatious charms. He often thought that maybe it was part of her job description. After all, not many women of the world could remain resistant to his magnetism once he really turned it on. Doris had remained a tough nut to crack, but he wasn't one to shy away from a challenge.

She led him through a series of passageways, past walnut doors and gleaming white walls, into the bowels of the ship. They were underwater now; he could hear the water slapping against the side of the yacht.

'Is Mr Palmer in a good mood?' Vaughn asked.

'When is he not?' Doris said, without looking back.

Vaughn shook his head at her aloofness.

They turned one last corner and there in front of them, behind a door of frosted glass, was the fabled board room. Vaughn could only imagine the deals that had been struck in this room. Palmer had produced some of the greatest films of this century, and Vaughn felt his palms grow slightly damp at the prospect of being part of his canon.

Doris held the door open, and Vaughn brushed past, slightly closer than was necessary, but what was a bit of harmless fun between friends?

'Who do I have to hump around here to get a scotch on the rocks?' he said to her, before striding towards one of the comfy chairs dotted around the huge oak slab of a table.

His mind was still on Doris's rump when he sat down, so much so that it was only as he looked up that he noticed Adam and Colin sitting across the boardroom table from him, next to Mr Palmer.

'What the…' he started.

COLIN WATCHED HIM harass the PA and stride into the room like he owned the place, and wondered why he hadn't seen that Vaughn was behind all of this sooner. He'd had a hunch, which he'd followed, but the film star's charisma, as well as Adam's doubts, had thrown him off the scent.

It was almost funny to watch the instantaneous change in Vaughn's demeanour, from king of the world to dumbstruck pauper. It was even funnier when his eyes settled on Grachten, which was hanging on the wall above Mr Palmer's head.

'I imagine you'd like to know why we're gate crashing your million-pound meeting,' Adam said, once Vaughn had sat down.

Vaughn opened and closed his mouth like a beached guppy, his eyes flitting between Adam, Colin and Mr Palmer, who was watching him with not an iota of expression on his face.

'Cat got your tongue?' Adam continued. 'No worries. We've got you bang to rights anyway, so you can sit back, shut up, and enjoy our little presentation. Colin?'

'Thank you, Adam,' Colin said. 'I'd like to start by saying you fight like a bitch. I mean, what type of man attacks someone from behind?'

'The kind of man who would steal from an old lady,' Adam interjected. 'An absolute scumbag.'

'Ah, yes. You see, Vaughn, we finally got there. Might have taken us a little longer than usual, but you were a worthy adversary. Shall I talk you through our little journey of discovery?'

Vaughn simply stared, so Colin went on.

'Firstly, your little box of pills. You didn't mind flaunting them while regaling everyone with your little backstory. Good for sympathy, that well-known battle with illness that ended with you losing an organ. No spleen means a poor immune system, which means a couple of phenoxymethalpennicillin every day to keep you right. Although, that's not all you're taking, is it? We did a bit of research, found out about your sleeping pill addiction. That little box you carry with you rattles like a musical instrument, what with you taking four pills each day, and when you were kicking and punching me while I was on the floor, I thought I heard a maraca. I thought I was losing my mind at the time, but that's what made me finally realise it was you.'

He left out the fact that he'd needed a further clue from Sean to put the two facts together.

'The second clue was Poor Tex's bedroom,' Adam took over. 'The room looked too set up, so we figured it must've been staged. Granted, we only came to that conclusion in the past hour or so, but who better to stage someone taking their own life than someone who spends their own life on a set? I imagine when they open Tex up, they'll find some of your sleeping pills in his blood. It didn't look like he put up too much of a fight.'

'And the third, and possibly the most irrefutable fact, is that you sent the painting from Lisbon to Mr Palmer, here, via courier. You could've chosen any name in the world as an alias, but you had to choose Len Fist, the name of your character in Jawbone. The arrogance is mind-blowing.'

Colin laughed out loud, which seemed to stir Vaughn into action. He jumped up from his chair, and started to march towards the door.

'Sit yourself down,' Mr Palmer said, producing a gun from a holster that had been hidden below his jacket.

Vaughn stopped in his tracks. He turned to face the table again. 'You're not going to shoot me.'

'Try me,' Palmer replied. The calmness in his voice was unnerving.

Vaughn hesitated, and looked like he was about to call Palmer's bluff, just as the board room door flew open and several Venetian police officers barrelled through at the same time, knocking Vaughn to the ground where they wrenched his arms behind his back and tightened handcuffs around his wrists. He tried to put up a fight, but a few sly kicks to the ribs did the trick of quietening him.

Unbelievably, as he was led out of the yacht by the unimpressed Venetian police, he was screaming about how much the suit cost.

'How long until our train?' Colin asked.

'Enough time to reunite Grachten and Maggie,' Adam said.

Mr Palmer rose from his seat, took the painting off the hook on the wall and passed it to Colin. Before coming to his yacht, they'd worried that he wouldn't believe them, or insist on keeping the painting, but he'd been very keen to see justice done. It had been his idea to lure Vaughn into the boardroom for the showdown.

'You could make a movie from Vaughn's little escapade,' Colin joked as Palmer waved them off the yacht.

'You know what?' he said. 'I just might.'

18

I DO, I DO, I DO, I DO, I DO

IT WAS A perfect day for a perfect wedding. The sun was shining, and a light breeze ruffled Adam's hair. His nearest and dearest were assembled on one of the elevated terraces of the medieval Scaligero Castle, with views overlooking the endless lake and jagged mountains. It was picture perfect.

He and Colin had already been here for a few hours, sorting the chairs, blowing up balloons, and helping the old caretaker erect the cream canopy, under which Adam and Helena would be saying their vows.

He'd had a couple of wobbles. It was all feeling very real now, and he started to panic about forgetting the vows, or falling over, or farting loudly during a key part of the ceremony. He'd already asked Colin if he had the rings three times.

Once the guests had started to arrive, Adam had relaxed a bit, safe in the knowledge that everyone in attendance was rooting for them, though he had shed a few tears as he'd greeted his mum.

Now, Adam's heart started to beat overtime as the string quartet plucked the first notes of Canon In D, signalling Helena's arrival at the end of the aisle. He heard gasps from the congregation as she made her way towards him, and only turned to look at her when she was by his side.

Adam spent a few moments taking her in. The stunning ivory dress (that fitted perfectly, thank God), the subtle make-up that accentuated those spectacular eyes, the delicate kink in her dark hair.

'You look beautiful,' he whispered. 'I love your dress.'

'Thanks,' she replied. 'It has pockets.'

She hammered home the point by shoving her hands in them, which Adam nodded at.

'You don't look so bad yourself,' she smiled.

With that, the vicar began the ceremony, which passed in a blur of song and repeated vows and applause. When it was time to kiss the bride, Adam caught his mum's eye, grimaced, mouthed an apology to her and gave Helena a peck on the lips.

They walked hand in hand down the aisle as a married couple to "You Make My Dreams" by Hall and Oates, receiving pats on the back and hugs, while multicoloured confetti was thrown over them. Helena shot a confused look at an old woman in a snazzy dress who was sitting at the end of one of the rows, clutching a framed painting.

ON THE SECLUDED beach, accessible by a secret door in the bowels of the old castle, they finally had a moment to themselves.

Well, almost.

A very passionate Italian photographer was directing them, making them hug and kiss and cuddle against the magnificent backdrop of the lake. He'd make them repeat a pose, or hold it for a ridiculous amount of time until the light was just right, or a wave crested at just the right time behind them.

Adam was finding the whole thing very awkward, and was sure he looked like some sort of uncomfortable stick insect in most of the snaps the photographer had taken so far.

Next, he made them attempt to skim some of the shale that littered the beach on the glassy surface of the lake.

'I wish he'd hurry up and finish,' Adam whispered to Helena, as he tossed a stone towards the water. The sunlight reflected off his ring, and he rotated it on his finger, wondering how long it would take it feel normal.

'I know. It's a bit of a nightmare,' Helena replied. 'Oh, I never got a chance to ask. How was the cruise in the end?'

'Aye, it was good,' Adam nodded.

'And you managed to stay out of trouble?' she asked.

'Mostly, yeah,' he said. 'Colin didn't manage to stop me having a go at the karaoke.'

She laughed, and Adam heard the click of the photographer's camera. At least there'll be one natural looking photo, he thought.

Adam had deliberated on how much to tell his new bride, and reckoned honesty was the best policy, especially on his wedding day. Best to start the rest of their lives with no secrets between them.

'Oh, and you know Vaughn McClusky?'

'The movie star you like?' she said.

'Yeah. Well, we managed to get him arrested for stealing a painting from an old lady, so he's going to be going to jail.'

'What?!' she gasped.

As if God was smiling down on him, the photographer decided he had what he needed from this particular scene, and proceeded to tell them what he wanted them to do next.

Adam was suddenly very interested in what he had to say.

AUTHOR'S NOTE

Here we are, at the end of book six!

When Sean at Red Dog Press offered me a six book deal for the Stonebridge series, I snapped his hand off, thinking myself very lucky. I have loved writing each book, and it has been absolutely humbling to have found a readership that cares for the characters as much as I do.

Adam and Colin have changed so much over the course of the series. Listening to The Curious Dispatch of Daniel Costello made me realise how green behind the gills they were, purposefully so, and it's lovely to see them mature and find their place in the world.

I'm very lucky that, thanks to YOU, the series can continue, and the boys will still be a fixture in my life. This is down to you wonderful readers, who continue to support me with your kindness. With thousands of authors and millions of books on offer, it still blows me away that you are choosing to spend your hard-earned cash on words that I've written.

I'm also hugely thankful to Isis Audio and Stephen Armstrong for bringing this particular little corner of Northern Ireland to life through the audiobooks. I don't think I've ever felt as proud of anything in my life as when I listened to that opening chapter of Danny Costello.

I hope you continue to enjoy your trips to Stonebridge.

Love,

Chris

ABOUT THE AUTHOR

Originally hailing from the north coast of Northern Ireland and now residing in South Manchester, Chris McDonald has always been a reader. At primary school, The Hardy Boys inspired his love of adventure, before his reading world was opened up by Chuck Palahniuk and the gritty world of crime.

He's a fan of 5-a-side football, has an eclectic taste in music ranging from Damien Rice to Slayer and loves dogs.

Printed in the USA
CPSIA information can be obtained
at www.ICGtesting.com
CBHW061238081224
18659CB00010B/461

9 781914 480409